THE HENCHA QUEEN

THE THARASSAS CYCLE
BOOK THREE

J. SCOTT COATSWORTH

ALSO BY J. SCOTT COATSWORTH

Liminal Sky: Ariadne Cycle
The Stark Divide • The Rising Tide • The Shoreless Sea

Liminal Sky: Redemption Cycle
Dropnauts

Liminal Sky: Oberon Cycle
Skythane • Lander • Ithani

Liminal Sky: Tharassas Cycle
Tales from Tharasses • The Dragon Eater • The Gauntlet Runner
The Hencha Queen (March 2024) • The Death Bringer (September 2024)

Other Sci Fi/Fantasy
The Autumn Lands • Cailleadhama • Firedrake • The Great North
Homecoming • The Last Run • Wonderland

Short Story Collections:
Androids & Aliens • Spells & Stardust Collection • Tangents & Tachyons

Contemporary/Magical Realism
Between the Lines • I Only Want to Be With You • Flames
The River City Chronicles • Slow Thaw

Audiobooks
Cailleadhama • The Autumn Lands • The River City Chronicles • Skythane

I want to thank everyone who took the time to join me on this grand adventure, and my husband Mark, who doesn't really understand this crazy thing I do, but nevertheless supports it wholeheartedly.

ACKNOWLEDGMENTS

I WANT TO ACKNOWLEDGE the fabulous Kelley York at Sleepy Fox studios for the great cover, and the beta readers who made it through the first three books: Jamie Lee Moyer, Kristin Masters, Lee Hunt, Timothy Bult, and Sue Philips.

And finally, I want to acknowledge Steven Radecki at Water Dragon Publishing, who took a chance on publishing this series after meeting me at BayCon. I am thrilled to be working with Steven and his team!

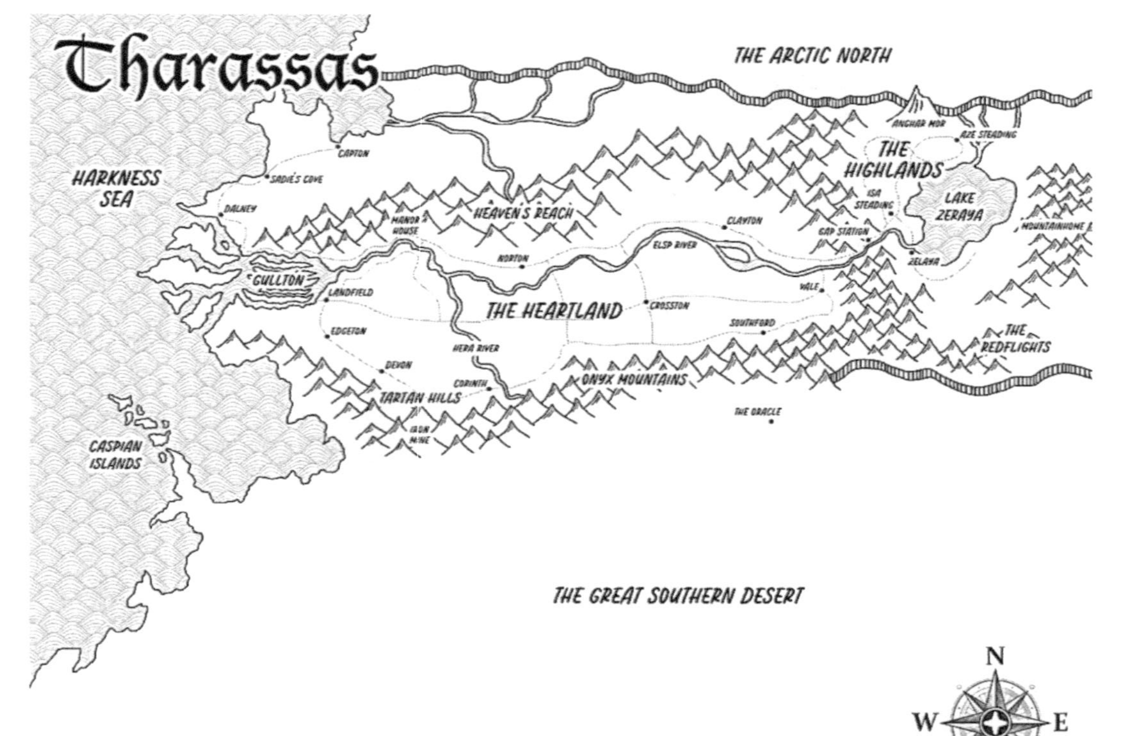

Tharassas
THE ARCTIC NORTH
HARKNESS SEA
ANGHAR MOR
AZE STEADING
THE HIGHLANDS
CAPTON
SADIE'S COVE
ISA STEADING
LAKE ZERAYA
DALNEY
HEAVEN'S REACH
CLAYTON
GAP STATION
MOUNTAINHOME
MANOR HOUSE
NORTON
ELSP RIVER
JELAYA
GULLTON
WALE
LANDFIELD
THE HEARTLAND
CROSSTON
EDGETON
SOUTHFORD
THE REDFLIGHTS
DEVON
HERA RIVER
CORINTH
ONYX MOUNTAINS
TARTAN HILLS
THE ORACLE
IRON MINE
CASPIAN ISLANDS
THE GREAT SOUTHERN DESERT
N
W
E
S

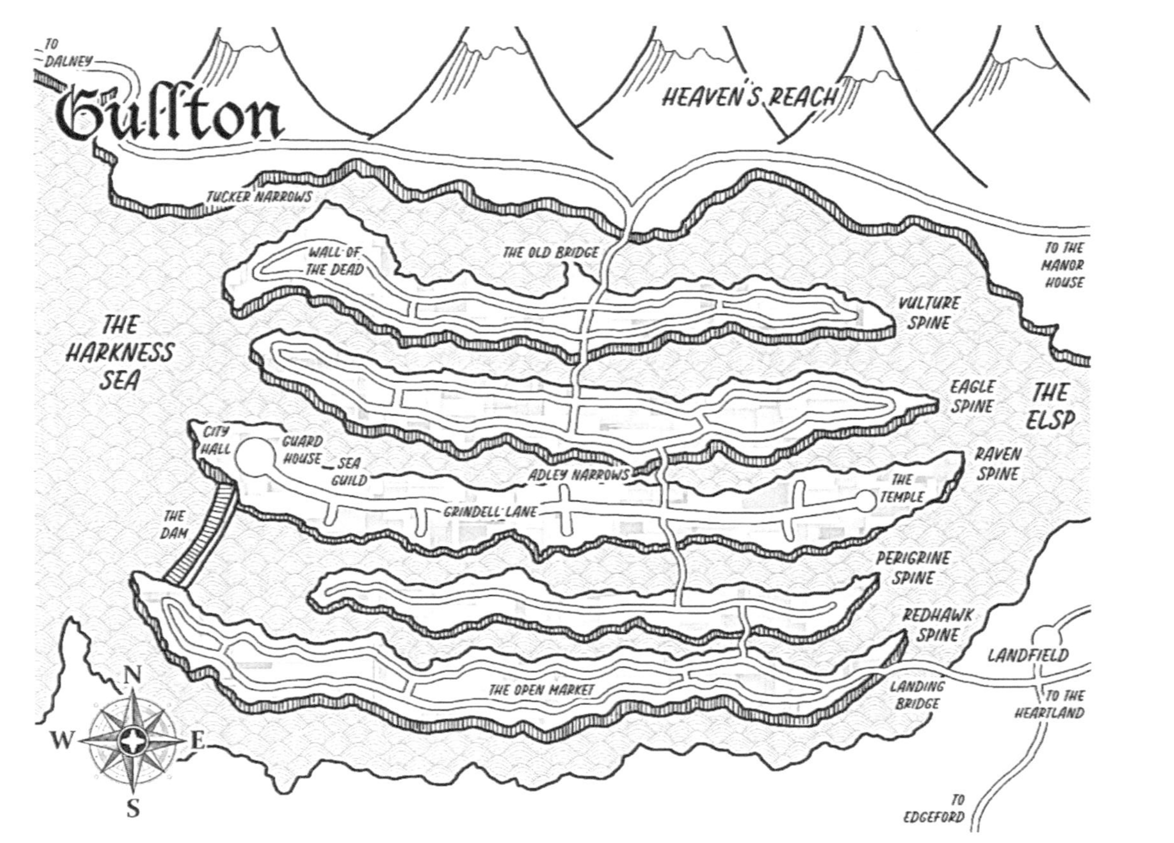

TO DALNEY
Gullton
HEAVEN'S REACH
TUCKER NARROWS
THE OLD BRIDGE
TO THE MANOR HOUSE
WALL OF THE DEAD
VULTURE SPINE
THE HARKNESS SEA
EAGLE SPINE
THE ELSP
CITY HALL
GUARD HOUSE
SEA GUILD
ADLEY NARROWS
RAVEN SPINE
THE TEMPLE
THE DAM
GRINDELL LANE
PERIGRINE SPINE
REDHAWK SPINE
LANDFIELD
THE OPEN MARKET
LANDING BRIDGE
TO THE HEARTLAND
N
W
E
S
TO EDGEFORD

PROLOGUE

S PIN'S QUANTUM BRAIN was in flux, trying to process everything. Aik was under the spell of some strange entity. Another artificial construct like himself?

Raven had been at Anghar Mor. His first friend in almost a hundred years, lost.

And what about me? He'd been human once. A husband with a daughter named Sera. The same Sera who had flown with him on the *Spin Diver*, much later. He was certain — facial structure and voice matching didn't lie. And her laugh had been the same, thirty years after he'd lost her on Earth.

His human memories were patchy. They'd tried to eliminate them when he'd volunteered to become a ship mind. Or maybe they'd sequestered them, and that part of him had been damaged in the crash.

Whatever the reason, all he had left were tantalizing clues.

He'd always felt a special affinity for Sera, and now he knew why. She was his, or she had been. Her death, a hundred years prior, felt as fresh to him as the present moment.

Did she know? What had they told her that day when he'd left her — and her mother — to begin his transition?

More pieces fell into place. Her mother's name was Genevieve. His Gen. They'd been deep in debt for infertility treatments and an unexpected relocation after a fire destroyed their entire neighborhood in Upstate New York.

My sacrifice saved them. Pain sparked through him like a static charge. *Why did I have to find out?*

He'd been perfectly happy as *Spin the ship mind.* But now he knew what he'd lost, and it was as vast and deep as the Grand Canyon.

He would have wept, if he'd still had human eyes

•　　　•　　　•

News of the world flowed into the spore mother through her children, the forerunners. It was cold, bitterly cold outside, and only marginally better in the dark place under the mountain where she lived, like her two foremothers before her. She'd released some of her children into the cavern, and they'd improved her dwelling considerably, making it hot and damp like back home.

Home. Her memory was fragmented, incomplete. She could feel the broken edges, the gaps in the knowledge of her foremothers that should guide her. She had more questions than answers.

Where am I from? Certainly not here. This world was unsuited to her kind, though that could be changed. It was far too cold and dry to sustain her progeny outside the mountain walls.

Where is here? There was no answer for that one, either. It was *not home.*

She was the third of her kind here. Of that she was certain. The previous two must have failed. She would not make the same mistakes. If only she knew what they were.

Every day she understood a little more about her strange home. Every day she grew stronger. Still, she couldn't do this alone.

A few days earlier, she'd felt *him.* One of the progenitors from an earlier cycle. He was... strange. *Broken maybe, like me. Lost.*

He was far to the west, his presence faint against her mind. So she'd sent the forerunners to find him. There'd been mishaps. She wasn't ready to reveal her presence yet, but something had gone wrong, and they attacked a herd of native animals.

Ruthlessly she'd recalled those ones and destroyed them, ignoring their cries as they extinguished themselves in the glacial snow.

She'd birthed another batch, and these did their job properly, contacting the progenitor and planting a seed.

Now she understood. He had bonded with one of the local creatures, and that bond was an uneasy one.

No matter. He was on his way to her. She would take him in, heal his broken pieces, and maybe he would heal some of hers. Then they would know what to do.

In the meantime, she would begin to prepare the way for him and his kind.

She *thrummed* happily as her form shifted and grew. Soon she would release her seeds. Soon the world would begin to change, and it would be time for their return.

1

RISE

A SHARP CRACK FILLED the wine cellar. Kerrick swung the heavy mallet back and then assailed the flopwood boards that blocked the tunnel entrance again. The ancient wood splintered under the blow, sending shards clattering across the stone-paved floor.

It felt good to work out his frustrations. Still, the stubborn wood held out against his assault.

He rested the mallet on the black-tiled stone floor, wiping the sweat off his forehead with the back of his hand. Even after a hundred years, the barrier was strong. He'd tried to pry the boards out of the solid stone, but they'd been fastened in too tightly. *Brute force it is.*

"You're doing great!" Cor'Lea's voice was artificially bright, and she was as tall as he was, maybe a little taller, peering over his shoulder at the sealed tunnel entrance.

Silya had tasked her with bringing him down here to check out these hidden caverns under the Temple, in preparation for the coming war. Important, sure, but also clearly an excuse to get him out from underfoot while she prepared for her official Raising.

He grunted. "Thanks. These boards are hard as iron." *And hard as Silya's will.*

One day things would be different between them, once this crisis was over. *I just have to be patient.*

Coral laughed. "I'm sure a big, strong man like you can break through them easily." She squeezed his bicep appreciatively.

He shrugged her off. He wasn't sure if the gawky initiate was flirting with him or just trying to encourage him to get on with it, but either way, he wasn't interested. "Stand back." He hefted the hammer again, and she scurried out of his way.

He suppressed a smile, swinging the mallet around for another heavy blow.

Craack.

This time the board buckled inward visibly. *Another few hits should do it.*

He pulled back the heavy iron hammer again and hit the same spot with blow after blow. *Craack. Craack. Craack.*

The mallet broke through and a board fell away into splinters, clattering across the stone floor. *One down, three more to go.* "Why did they seal this cavern up?"

Cor'Lea gestured at the natural chamber. "There was a winery here before the Temple. Sister Dor said they used to use it for extra wine storage." She looked around the natural chamber, which was now filled with wooden shelving holding a variety of bottled food stores. "When Jas ordered the Temple to be constructed, they kept this wide cavern and blocked off the rest of the tunnels."

"Just in case the gully rats got in?" That thief Raven had apparently made his home in one of the underground tunnels. Who knew who else — or what else — lived down there?

Cor'Lea snorted. "Maybe."

Are tunnels all connected, somehow? That was one of Silya's most urgent projects, to map out the network of caverns beneath the city. *Another reason she sent me down here — to get me out from under her robes.*

A few more whacks at the next board served to both break it and let out his frustrations at the situation preventing him from doing his sworn job and keeping them apart. And at what she said was coming.

Craack. Craack. Craack.

The board snapped in half, and he judged that he'd cleared enough space to step through into the blocked-off tunnel. "Hand me that lantern?

Cor'Lea complied, taking the opportunity to brush his hand.

He rolled his eyes. *I should be flattered.* But his heart was already taken.

It was times like these he wished his brother Enrick were still alive. He'd know what to do. He'd been absurdly confident about everything, even though he'd been younger than Kerrick.

Kerrick wasn't great with women.

He took the lantern and stepped over the bottom board, holding it in front of him. The bright light temporarily blinded him as he sought to get his bearings.

"What do you see?" Cor'Lea peered through the hole behind him.

His sight adjusted, and the tunnel's walls came into focus.

He whistled. Stacked along the side of the tunnel were hundreds of crates, all strapped together in groups and sealed. "It's ... I don't know what it is. But I'll bet Silya will be surprised." They'd have to find a place to put all this stuff — whatever it was, it was likely rotten after all this time. Silya needed somewhere to store people, not ancient goods.

Cor'Lea stepped carefully over the splintered boards to join him. "What do you think's inside them?"

The long row of crates disappeared into the darkness. Who knew what the ancients had considered valuable enough to stash down here. Coin? Lost treasure? "One way to find out. Does the Temple have a crowbar?"

•　　•　　•

Silya shifted uncomfortably on the hard seat of the throne. Her golden robes made her itch, and her muscles ached from the hour she'd spent on the training field with Hes'Enn. The Temple sword master had pushed her as hard as when she'd been an initiate, and she had the bruises to show it.

And why shouldn't I? Even the queen needed to stay in fighting form. Still, her aches and pains argued for a little relief.

The fact that her connection to the hencha had strengthened only made things more complicated. They were curious as children sometimes, poking at her and asking what this meant or what that sensation was. *Quiet!*

Cor'Lea had helped her sort out her gully bird's nest of hair into some semblance of order before taking Kerrick to the cellar. But that was as far as she'd been willing to go in a nod to regal decorum.

Sister Dor had shaken her head, but hadn't said a word out loud.

"… solemn responsibility to the hencha gatherings and to the people of the Heartland …," Dor droned on, reading from the official Raising text.

Silya wished she could hurry things along. She couldn't wait to see what Kerrick found, and she had a million other things that needed doing. Besides, the sooner she could get off this uncomfortable chair, the better.

Patience, little one. Her mother's voice from childhood came to mind unbidden, making her want to squirm all the more.

She lifted her thumb, making a small blue flame appear and disappear there. *I'm a human flint.*

"Mim'Aya!" Dor stared pointedly at her thumb. "Please show a little respect for the ceremony."

She hung her head. "Sorry, mim." And just like that, she was an initiate again, despite being raised to the highest post in the land.

The other sisters present, Tela, Aster, and Sallia, shook their heads and whispered softly amongst themselves.

Silya blushed. *I am acting abominably.* She sat up and squared her shoulders, ashamed of the bad example she set. *Surely I can sit still and not fidget for all of five minutes.*

Dor nodded and continued. "By the power vested in me as first aide, I hereby name you the Hencha Queen, Seventh in the Royal Line. Sister Tela, the staff, please?"

Is it finally over? She barely remembered the staff. She'd last seen it from a distance in Yen'Ela's hands, when she was a little girl.

Sister Tela lifted up a black-cloth-wrapped bundle as if it weighed fifty kilos and handed it to Dor, who balanced it awkwardly and slipped off the covering to reveal the staff.

Silya whistled. It was beautiful. Entwined ebony branches twisted around one another, capped with carved hencha leaves. She reached out to touch it, and a thrill of blue fire ran up her arm. It looked ancient and new. "May I?"

Dor nodded, a slight smile quirking the edge of her lips. "It's yours now."

She stood, took the black staff, and lifted it into the air, her various aches and bruises vanishing in an instant. It was lighter than she expected, yet filled with the weight of years. It felt alien to her touch, setting up a strange buzzing in her arm, and yet it felt comfortable, as if it had always been a part of her. The strange dissonance intrigued her.

Sister Tela's eyes widened. "It's true. 'She will carry its weight as if it is nothing.'"

Foolish human. That thought was not her own.

Silya repressed the urge to chuckle. Even the hencha were bored.

Instead, she closed her eyes and slammed the butt of the staff into the ground, making her audience gasp.

She felt the weight of it now, and the gathered power of the hencha. They were right — this ceremony was a farce, a human foolishness. What need was there for all this pomp and circumstance? One either did things or one didn't, and whether one had an official Raising didn't make a lick of difference.

Still, she knew the ceremony's rituals weren't for her. They were for the sisters.

Someone gasped.

She opened her eyes. She had grown, or the room had shrunk.

The sisters drew back in fright, their faces washed in blue by the light that emanated from her. She held out her arms — they were as black as the staff, gnarled like wood.

A flight of wisps appeared from the doorway, dancing toward her like embers from a fire. They encircled her, spinning around her like bright blue sparks. She felt alive, electric, bursting with energy as the hencha poured themselves into her.

The sisters dropped to their knees and put their heads to the ground. "All hail the Hencha Queen!" they intoned together. "May she live a hundred years."

The voices held more than a little fear.

She tried to speak, to tell them to get up off the ground. *Surely that can't be good for old joints?* But all that came out was a raspy sound, like wind through the branches.

Just beyond her sight, she could *feel* the world. Beneath her feet, thousands of living things thrived and scurried through the darkness of the caverns that riddled the spines. The Elsp teemed with little flashes of life, fish swimming in its channels and avoiding fishermen's lures.

Further afield were hencha gatherings ... vast fields cultivated by humans. Or were they the ones doing the cultivation? There were stands and forests of trees — flop trees and violet pines and ring trees, and even a few she didn't recognize. Trees with huge heart-shaped leaves, and spindly dry things in the deserts to the south.

Erphin and verent and eircat and ix, and even tiny rainbow-winged orinths. All a part of the vast tapestry of the world.

All connected to one another ... and to her — so different from humans' independent universes, where people touched only flesh to flesh.

The hencha had been speaking to her more regularly since Sister Daya's end-of-life ceremony in the gathering the night before, but this was different. Deeper. *She* was different, and it scared her. She wanted to feel more, to be more. *What if I lose myself in this vastness?*

She gasped and let go of the staff.

It fell heavily to the ground with a clatter.

She blinked and looked around. She was back to normal size, her skin pink and firm once more. The sisters were slowly getting up to stand before her, and the wisps were gone.

She staggered, feeling suddenly light-headed.

Dor caught her and eased her onto the throne.

For once she was grateful for its solid weight. "Is that normal?" She used the sleeve of her robe to wipe sweat off her forehead.

"No, Mim. Not that I'm aware." Sister Tela stared at her as if she was one of the woman's precious leather-bound books. "You are *unique*, my dear." She patted Silya's hand gently.

She gripped the arms of the throne, feeling every bit of the fancy carved swirls beneath her palms. *Why did I choose this?* She swallowed hard. Now that she'd finally achieved her dream, a part of her just wanted to be *normal, boring old Silya* again.

She let the hencha go, and the world slipped back toward something she recognized. She took a deep breath and gathered her wits about her. "Get up, the lot of you. I may be the Hencha Queen officially now, but enough with the genuflecting. I'll not have you poor sisters scraping around on your old knees every time I lift this damned staff."

Tela pulled herself up off the ground, her grateful smile quickly hidden. "Yes, Mim. Congratulations. You are now officially the Hencha Queen."

Well, I'm the vessel for the Hencha Queen. But she knew what Tela meant. "Thank you, Sister." She nodded, trying to maintain the solemn dignity of the moment, only slightly ruining it by scratching her nose, which suddenly itched like crazy.

Dor picked up the staff with some difficulty. "I can put that away for safekeeping —"

"Thank you, but I think I'll keep it." She accepted it gratefully, admiring its beautiful craftsmanship. She was well and truly the Hencha Queen now. Tri'Aya would be proud of her, and that both annoyed her *and* made her happy.

"Yen'Ela only used it for formal occasions —"

She met Dor's gaze. "I'm not Yen'Ela." She meant to be a new kind of Hencha Queen. What that meant, exactly, she wasn't sure, but she felt it to her bones.

Dor held her gaze for a moment, searching her eyes. A ghost of a smile crossed her lips, and then she looked away. "Of course."

Silya ran her hand along the intricately carved wood of the staff. If it helped her connect more easily to the hencha, it would be worth it. And it would signal to the people that she was more than just Sil'Aya — she was the Hencha Queen. That would be important in the days to come, annoying or not.

Besides, she longed to feel that interconnectedness again.

She touched Dor's shoulder. "I trust you. But you need to trust me in this." She closed her eyes for a second, feeling the greater world around her.

Her aide nodded. "I do, Mim."

Her eyes widened. "So we're back to that again?"

Dor chuckled. "Yes, *Silya*."

"That's better." She stood, running a hand through her hair to put it back in order. "Thank you, sisters, for attending this —" She chose her words carefully. "— necessary ceremony."

Even Tela snorted at that one, though she covered her mouth quickly and had the grace to blush.

The sisters had been greatly disappointed to have such a small Raising, but it felt right to Silya, given the circumstances. Now was not the time for pomp and circumstance, unless it advanced the cause. *End of the world and all.* "So, what's on today's agenda?"

All four sisters started speaking at once.

"I've drafted a list of tasks the Temple needs to deal with most urgently ..." Dor held out a piece of hencha parchment, shaking it wildly.

Sal'Moya cleared her throat. "The initiates are frightened. We must do something to settle them ..."

"I've been searching the archives ..." Sister Tela tried to get a word in edgewise.

She was elbowed out of the way by Sister Ast'Una, who had her own ledger that she shoved forward into Silya's face. "We can't possibly store up enough grain to feed the whole city for a day, let alone weeks. Look here —"

"Enough!" She drew herself up to her full-yet-unimpressive height and slammed the staff into the paved flooring with a satisfying *thwack*, taking advantage of the dais and her newly vested power to silence the bedlam. "We'll address *all* of those issues, but you need to share them with Sister Dor, who will prioritize them for me."

"Thank you, Mim." Dor practically glowed with satisfaction.

"Please get things in order. I'll meet you upstairs shortly." She caught sight of Kerrick hovering in the doorway at the back of the room. "Meanwhile, I have other pressing things that need attending to."

For one thing, her communication from her mother was overdue, and that worried her. *What's afoot in the highlands?*

Dor curtseyed. "Come with me to my new office, Mims, and we'll get all of this sorted out." She seemed inordinately proud of that.

The woman was a godssend, and richly deserved the new quarters Silya had found for her next to her own. Sister Sallia had been less sanguine about being relocated, until Silya had pointed out her new room's proximity to the dining hall. Sal'Moya did enjoy a good foldover at mealtimes. Or six.

"Ser Kek needs me," she said softly, gesturing to him. "I'll be back up to my rooms as soon as I can."

Dor looked over the other sisters as if they were mere initiates, a scowl on her face. "Yes, Mim. Don't worry. I'll corral this lot and have an organized agenda prepared for you."

She squeezed Dor's shoulder gratefully. "Thank you." She retreated to the vestibule behind the throne, set down the staff to slip out of her fancy robe, and hung it on a hook there to be retrieved later.

Kerrick popped his head into the small chamber. "May I come in?"

She nodded. "Of course. I'm just getting changed." She slipped on a much smaller robe — still golden but made out of a more suitable fabric. Dor had impressed on her quite firmly that she could no longer wear the initiate's robe in public, comfortable as it might be, now that she'd been officially Raised.

She turned her attention to Kerrick. "What did you find? I'd imagine at least an inch of dust."

He grinned. "Yes. Lots and lots of dust."

Her eyes narrowed. "So why are you grinning like a gully bird who just caught an inthym?" He was in an uncharacteristically good mood, after sulking around for days.

"Because we found something else. Are you free to come take a look?"

Now he'd piqued her curiosity. "Of course. What is it? Some hundred-year-old bottles of wine?"

He shook his head. "You're not getting it out of me that easily. You have to come see for yourself." He took her hand, barely leaving her time to grab the staff, and practically dragged her out of the vestibule and back through the throne room, which was thankfully now empty. It wouldn't do to have someone see her being hauled along like a child, no matter how enthusiastic he was about his mystery find.

She pulled her hand away. "I can get there on my own."

He smirked. "Of course, Your Highness." He sketched an elaborate bow.

She sighed. Sometimes she missed being *just Silya*.

She followed him out into the hallway, debating whether to simply carry the staff or to tap it on the ground every other step, which made her feel a like an old woman. She settled for something in between, carrying it aloft but tapping it on the ground when she nodded at the other sisters and initiates they passed.

Their course took them down four short flights of stairs, by a number of surprised sisters who genuflected when they saw her and the staff. Silya smiled gamely at them, trying to keep her poise, wondering what the rush was about.

At last, they descended below ground level, a long stairway that led down to the storage caverns. The staff came in handy for counterbalancing on the steep stairs.

She hadn't been to the cellars in almost a year and hadn't known about the tunnel entrance, which had been all but forgotten until Dor had mentioned it during dinner at the Mansion House.

The final stairway had been cut into the rock and led down almost a hundred steps. Their footsteps echoed as they followed it down, but otherwise it was quiet. Too quiet. "I never did like this place."

He glanced at her over his shoulder. "It is a bit stifling."

At last, they reached the end, where a wide, metal-banded flopwood door stood ajar.

She stepped into open space of the cellar, relieved to be free of the narrow stairway. The high-ceilinged natural cavern was thirty meters long and about half as wide, lit by electric lights like the rest of the Temple. Its stalactites and stalagmites formed a beautiful backdrop to the shelves and shelves of preserves and grape and hencha wine and other stored foods and goods. Its floor had been filled in and paved with flat stones at some point in the distant past.

He led her past the wine racks. Each bottle was neatly labeled with date and vintage. The small vineyard adjoining the hencha field didn't produce nearly enough grapes to fill the cellar, but the hencha wine more than made up for the difference, providing income that helped support the Temple and its work.

She was slowly learning all about products and income streams that provided the Temple its revenue, but she had grown tired of crop reports and bank accounts and the like. She had enough on her plate already. *We need to hire a good accountant.*

She was surprised the quakes hadn't caused more damage down here, but most of the casks, bottles, and assorted chests and crates were strapped down tightly.

Cor'Lea emerged from the newly exposed tunnel entrance as they approached. Seeing Silya approaching with the staff, the gangly initiate bowed halfway to the ground.

Silya pulled at her collar. "Enough of that. Get up, girl." *Even though we're just a year apart.* She tried to keep the irritation from her voice. She was starting to understand why her mother's voice always sounded so clipped. Responsibility for the work and behavior of others was *annoying.*

Cor'Lea got up and brushed off her robes. "Yes, Mim'Aya. It's ... this cavern is amazing." Her eyes were as big as saucers.

"What is?" The broken boards that had sealed up the tunnel were piled neatly in the corner, so much firewood now.

She peered into the dim light of the tunnel. Something was stacked up against the wall, visible in the flickering light of a single lantern hung from a protruding hook in the ceiling. "We'll need to string some more permanent lights in here."

Cor'Lea nodded. "Working on it, Your Highness."

She growled again. "So what did you find?"

"Crates, mim," Kerrick said, picking up a wooden panel that had apparently been pried off one of them.

Silya stepped into the narrower space and her eyes adjusted to the dim light. The staff began to glow, shedding a blue light in the tunnel. Her eyes narrowed as she assessed its black wood, now shot through with blue lines the same color as the wisps. *What other secrets do you hold?*

He whistled. "That's handy."

She shushed him. He was right about the tunnel though. There was dust aplenty, enough to make her sneeze.

"Hencha bless," Cor'Lea whispered.

"Thank you." And there were crates. Lots and lots of crates. "What's in them?"

Cor'Lea shook her head. "We don't really know. We've only opened a couple. Glass bottles in the first one, and some strange black boxes in the second."

She rubbed her nose to ward off another sneeze. "All right. I want to get Sister Tela down here to catalog what's stored here to see if any of it might be of use." So they'd used this tunnel as an old storeroom. "And for godssakes, let's get this dust cleaned up." She sneezed again despite her best efforts.

"Yes, Mim. I'll get right on it." Still, she lingered.

Why was Coral hovering about? Once the initiates had emptied the tunnel, they could start preparing it for the siege to come. Her blood ran cold at the thought.

She turned to Kerrick. "We'll need to get this cleared out anyhow, if we're going to house people here when the time comes."

"Of course." He grinned. "But that's not all. When did they seal up this tunnel?"

She frowned, thinking back to the notations on the old tunnel map Sister Tela had brought her from the archives. "Maybe a hundred years ago. Why?"

He held up the panel, under the lantern light. "Look closely."

It was covered with dust like the rest, but someone — probably Kerrick — had wiped off the worst of it.

She squinted at the writing there, in neat block script, but it was hard to make out in the blue light. "I can't see what it says. Bring it out into the cellar." She stepped back into the larger, better-lit cavern.

He followed, carrying the lid.

She peered at the letters again and gasped, almost dropping her staff. The writing stood out clearly in the bright electric light.

Attn: Silya Aya.

2

TRAINING DAY

CHALA SLID DOWN the mountainside, spear in hand, stalking one of the mountain ix that lived on the steep slopes of Mountainhome. She could feel the herbivore's presence through the emp. It held onto the steep mountainside with white claws not unlike those of her verent, grazing on a patch of dried grass, unconcerned. One of its three sharp horns had been broken off almost to the stump.

She closed her eyes. The ix fur would be soft, luxurious, and warm against her skin on a chilly winter night, and the sparse meat from the skinny beast delicious in the Kitchen cookpot.

Getting out of the caverns did her good. The others often looked at her in pity because she hadn't bonded a verent. She was an outsider here, different from all the rest, even Jai — he was reifaine, native to these mountains, while she was suifaine, born in the dry heat of the Suarenn — the Great Southern Desert, as the wetlanders called it.

Only Raven had really made an attempt to get past her walls.

Chala spat. *No different than back home.* She was an expert at making the best of things, even when life gave her sour hencha berries.

Though she hated to admit it, she hoped little things like the ix fur and meat would make them treat her less like a failure, and more like an essential part of the team.

Especially Astrid. She was enchanted by the highlander, though she tried her best not to show it. Astrid reminded her of Elrys, though they looked nothing alike — one short, pale and soft, the other lithe and strong as a cayah. *The same force of will, maybe?*

Time for the hunt. She cleared her mind of useless thoughts. She crouched behind a granite boulder, peering through the green-purple branches of a hembra bush at her quarry.

The ix perched on a rocky outcrop ten meters away, its head cocked and looking around nervously. She could *feel* its concern. It must have sensed her presence. Its beard of tangled white fur flicked about comically as it searched for its pursuer.

Blast it. Better make this quick. Chala raised her arm, quiet as an inthym, ready to leap up and launch her spear into the animal's neck.

The ix bleated twice and took off up the mountainside, its spindly legs finding purchase where any other creature would have slipped and fallen to its death.

Cursed sands. Something had spooked it, and she was fairly certain that it wasn't her. She considered going after it, but it was far too quick for her on these steep, rugged slopes.

A crack behind her froze her in her tracks, and her gut rumbled with a ravenous hunger not her own. *I'm not the only predator on these slopes.*

Chala spun around, bringing her spear up as the eircat leapt, the sharp white claws of its forepaws extended toward her, all screeching and jagged teeth.

She slipped sideways and thrust the spear upward, catching the beast's shoulder and knocking it sideways. It landed hard with a fearsome high-pitched growl, jolting the spear out of her hands and breaking it in half.

Chala stumbled backward, heart racing, grasping for something else to use as a weapon. She slipped her hunting knife out of its sheath with practiced ease and fell into a crouch.

The creature pulled the spearhead from its shoulder with its teeth and spat it out. She could *feel* the heat of its angry gaze.

A strong blow, but not fatal. It would have been handy just then to have a verent at her beck and call.

The eircat turned its attention back to her and snarled. It was gaunt, ribs sticking out.

This close, she could see it was a mangy, if large, example of its kind. Its white fur was dirty and falling out in clumps in several places. And its eyes were red.

What happened to you? She almost felt sorry for it. *But not enough to become your meal.*

She slipped around the boulder, putting solid rock between them. From its size and the gray tinge of its pelt, it was old. It probably thought she'd be easy prey, but she had an advantage. She could *feel* it through the emp, and she could block her own emotions so it would be blind to them.

Chala kissed the blade. It was a gift from her mother, sharp as a razor. *Forgive me for the life I am about to take.*

The eircat leapt on top of the boulder, searching for her, breathing in labored huffs, but found nothing but air.

Ten paces away, she leaned against another outcrop, keeping her breathing smooth and shallow. Running would be fatal. Even weakened by the wound, the beast was faster than her, especially on these uneven mountain slopes. She had to wear it out. *Sooner or later, it will tire.*

Its lungs were probably already filling with ichor from the wound.

Chala scrambled up another boulder, worming her way between two of the hembra bushes and getting her arms scratched up for her troubles. *No matter. Cuts heal faster than hearts.* She turned back to watch her stalker.

The eircat paced in front of the boulder, looking for a way to get at her.

Thank the shifting sands they don't hunt in packs like desert cats. Chala was no fool, but she knew when to take a risk. She could wait until the beast's loss of ichor — already an indigo stain across its chest — weakened it enough to slow it down. Or she could flip things and bring this to an end before *she* grew tired and became eircat food.

She picked up a loose rock about the size of her fist and threw it past the eircat. It clattered down the hillside.

The beast turned to look at the commotion.

Chala gathered herself and leapt over the hembra bushes, coming down hard on the eircat's back.

The impact knocked it to the ground. Confusion and fear mingled with anger, radiating from it like heat, as they tumbled half a dozen meters down the slope together. The eircat snarled, trying to rip at her with its claws, but she was out of its reach.

She held tightly to its back as it flailed about, keeping away from its reach. The fall battered her arms and back, but she didn't let go.

When they rolled to a halt, it lay there for a second, stunned.

She shook her own head to clear it, and then raised her arm and slammed the knife into the eircat's soft neck.

The animal howled, then gasped piteously as its indigo ichor flowed out onto bare rock. Its eyes glazed over as it looked up at her one last time.

A wave of its pain assaulted her, blinding her for a moment as the beast shuddered in its death throes. The claws of its forepaw *clacked* on the stone. Then it went still.

Chala gasped, trying to catch the breath that had been knocked out of her during the fall. She struggled to inhale, her vision turning red, but at last sweet, cool air filled her lungs.

She got to her feet uneasily, swaying as she surveyed her kill. *Feeling your victim's pain makes killing harder.*

Still, she had no regrets. It would have killed her too. Strange how demented it had seemed. *Probably just starving.*

The eircat stank, and now her clothing and skin did too from such close contact.

She checked herself over. No breaks, just a few cuts and bruises. She had the luck of the Jor'Oss today.

She glanced reluctantly up the hillside to where she'd last seen the ix. *I'll get you another day.*

She put away her knife and prepared to drag the cat's carcass back to the Kitchen for dressing.

• • •

Raven/Breeze held their breath as they plunged toward the valley below at breakneck speed. Breeze had given him control — a supreme exercise of trust — and if he'd been in his human form, he would have broken out in a cold sweat. *Now?*

Wait. More a concept than human words, but clear nevertheless. Breeze's excitement bled through the link, feeding Raven's anxiety.

The waters of Mountainhome's lake flew up at them with alarming speed as the wind whistled past Breeze's flattened ears.

Beside them, Jai's verent Angel dove too.

Too close. They were going to splatter themselves across half the valley, at this rate. *Now? Please let it be now.*

Wait. Breeze sounded a lot steadier than Raven felt.

Sweet Helja, we're going to die! He tried to keep that last thought from Breeze. He fought against every life-saving instinct as the turquoise pool expanded in his vision. The lake wasn't deep enough. *Now?*

Now!

Raven spread their wings. They caught the air, catching it like sails and pulling them up hard just before impact. They shoot across the lake together, skimming the surface close enough to create their own wake. Almost perfect, though their left wing dipped into the cool water and kicked up a spume of mist that splashed across Angel's face.

Raven's anxiety turned to glee, heightened by Breeze's own satisfaction. *Woo hoo!* If he'd been riding on Breeze's back, he would have thrown his hands up in the air.

Hey, watch it!

Raven/Breeze blinked at the strange voice in his head. *Sorry!*

A weird pause followed. Surprise? *You can hear us?*

They caught an updraft and circled back up into the green sky. *Of course we can. Breeze can, so I can. Can't you?*

Jai/Angel rode the same updraft, just a heartbeat behind them. *Only with you. Apparently.*

Guess I'm special. Their mouth formed a wide, toothy verent grin. *This talking for both of us thing is weird.*

He wondered briefly how he could make use of his newfound abilities in his old line of work. Having a verent following him everywhere would make stealing things ... difficult. Still, it would have helped to have a verent at his beck and call when he got into a tight spot.

And there could be advantages to silent communication.

That made him think of Spin. *Where are you, little guy?*

And of course, *that* led his mind back to Aik, who he'd been trying not to think about all morning. Raven sighed.

They leveled out, flying high enough above the lake that they could see over the lower peaks to the south.

Come on. We'll figure this out later. Could be handy, but I'm starving and so is Angel. Jai/Angel sounded annoyed, but Raven could feel their satisfaction at how the training was going.

By mutual consent, human and verent didn't hunt together, or eat. Tearing at a just-killed hunk of animal with his own teeth while its ichor — or blood — sprayed everywhere would be ... disturbing.

Scaredy cat.

Surely that's not how Breeze would say it. Was his own mind translating what the verent thought?

They passed back over dry land and caught another updraft, spiraling up after Angel toward Mountainhome. The sky was bright green and free of clouds — such a *normal* day. Hard to tell the end of the world was approaching.

Jai had been sketchy on the details about the Rise, but that had to change. If he was going to help save the world, he needed to know what they were fighting.

Below, he spied Chala hauling something up the mountainside. Breeze's nostrils identified it as an eircat. She felt ... *determined.*

Raven shuddered. The woman was fierce. *Don't ever let me go up against her in a fight!*

Breeze snorted his amusement. *You'd lose.*

I bet she'd kick your verent haunches too.

She's intense. They landed hard, exhausted from the morning's exercises, their diamond-sharp talons unleashing a spray of rock shards from the Kitchen ledge that rattled down the mountainside. Raven was in awe of the great beast who let him fly with it. With *him.* Getting used to the three verent sexes would take some time. *Thank you.*

A blast of warmth filled him, Breeze's equivalent of a *you're welcome.*

As soon as Breeze settled, Raven emerged from the verent back, flowing through that strange gray moment of lapsed consciousness. It was much less disconcerting than it had been the first few times — he'd come to think of it as a cleansing, almost a moment of meditation as he came back to himself.

He slipped off of Breeze's back, not with the practiced ease Jai displayed, but in a way that he felt wasn't entirely embarrassing. At least he didn't fall on his face. *That's got to count for something.*

He unlatched the leather sack he'd strapped to Breeze's back and pulled out his clothing.

Jai was already getting dressed.

He felt the heat rush to his face. *Not sure I'll ever get used to this whole naked-in-the-open thing.* The price of merging with the verent. Still, he did get an appreciative look at Jai's backside.

A simple look never hurt anyone. Twin red tattoos ran down the man's back, parallel to his spine, wings spread in flight.

"Like what you see?"

He could feel Jai's amusement through the emp link. He turned away, opened the bag, and took out his own clothes. He pulled on his underclothes quickly and turned to see Jai looking him up and down.

Jai buckled his belt. "No need to be embarrassed. You're beautiful too. Not bad for a Gull —"

"Hey! I don't call you a *cheff*." The whole *gully rat* thing was getting old.

"I was going to say 'Gullton man.'" Jai sat to pull on his boots. "Are all Gullton folks so self-conscious about their bodies?"

He blushed at his mistake, and more. "Not everyone." *Just me, it seems.* He wasn't sure how he felt about being looked at *like that* by Jai. He had Aik, after all. *If we ever find each other again.*

He'd never been exclusive with someone, but Aik made him want to be.

Still, he had been the first one to look.

Jai winked at him. "No need to be embarrassed about your feelings, either. We all have them."

"Doesn't it get old, being an open book all the time?" He put on his pants and shirt, and sat on a wide, flat rock to put on his socks.

"You can learn to block it, you know. You just teach your emp when you want to broadcast your emotions and when you don't."

"Now you tell me." He looked up at Jai. "You really can't hear the other verent?"

Jai shook his head. "They can all talk to one another. That's how we communicate with each other. But *this* is new." He stared at Raven. "There's something special about you, Heartlander."

For a second, he wanted to retreat to his lair. All this being in touch with his feelings — and everyone else's — was wearing him out. His leg chose that exact moment to cramp. "Ouch."

"Muscle aches?"

He nodded. "How'd you know?"

"We all had them the first few times. Chala has some fellin root to help with the pain."

He knelt and rubbed his calf. "It's passing." He retrieved his boots and pulled one of them on, lacing it tightly. "I saw her hauling something up the mountainside."

"An eircat, I think." Jai extended a hand to help him up.

He took it, feeling unsteady. "Breeze thought so too. No way she killed it single-handedly, right?" He'd never seen one, but stories of their fierceness were legendary. You were lucky to come away from an eircat encounter with all of your limbs intact.

"And yet …" Jai turned to greet her. "Can we give you a hand with that?"

Chala crested the edge of the rock shelf, hauling her prize behind her. Scratches covered her neck and arms, the blood already drying. "Yes."

Raven and Jai exchanged a glance. *That* was unlike her. He tried to read her, but got nothing. She must be good at blocking.

They hurried to help her lift the carcass. It stank to Heaven's Reach, like carrion and sewage. Raven wrinkled his nose.

"On that rock over there. I'll bleed it out, and then cut off the hide."

He looked at the razor-sharp teeth and blanched. Much bigger than a house cat, with an elongated face, eyes frozen in a rictus of death. Shaggy, white hair framed the face and light pink nose. It was rank, unlike anything he'd had ever smelled before outside of a barn stall.

He imagined it waking in his arms and shivered. "Scratched you up good."

They set it down on the designated rock. "Didn't touch me. Got those on some hembra bushes."

Raven's eyes widened. "You ... killed an eircat, and it didn't leave a mark on you?"

Chala pulled the beast's head back and sliced its neck. Ichor spilled out, darkening the rock below. "Yes. He scared away my ix." As if that were explanation enough.

I wouldn't want to be your enemy.

She flashed him a wicked grin. She felt through the mange of grayish white fir around its neck. "This is odd."

"What?"

She pulled her knife from its sheath and cut away some of the fur, exposing a small wound. "This."

She squeezed the edges of the cut, expelling ichor and a hunk of something.

He looked away, his stomach churning. *I didn't need to see that.*

"What is it?" Jai sounded far less disturbed than he was.

He risked a glance.

The wet *thing* in Chala's hand shuddered and began to glow, a bright red light emanating from it.

She dropped it on the ground and crushed it with her heel.

"What in Jorja's name was that?" Raven stared at the red and purple smear.

"That was what we're fighting." Jai's jaw was tight, and he and Chala exchanged a freighted glance.

"I'll check it over as I skin it, in case there are more."

Jai nodded curtly. "Come on, Raven. Let's leave Chala here to her work." He pulled on Raven's sleeve and practically dragged him into the Kitchen.

What in Heaven's Reach was all that about? "Shouldn't we help her ..." *What? Cut off the skin?* He hadn't a clue how to do that.

"Dress the kill? You'd probably find yourself at the wrong end of her knife. Chala's very particular. She's only ever lets Astrid help."

He glanced over his shoulder at the bright terrace. Chala was already peeling back the hide. The sight of the creature's naked flesh and bones made him feel sick. "You're probably right. What was that thing?"

"I'll tell you later." Jai flashed him that bright grin and waved him on. "Let's grab a bite. We still have a long day of training ahead of us. Then tomorrow we'll take a little trip."

"To where?" It would be good to get out of the valley.

Jai nodded. "Where the verent come from." His enthusiasm was infectious, though Raven was half convinced it was fabricated to distract him from whatever it was that Chala had pulled out of the eircat's neck.

Still, he let himself be distracted. He enjoyed spending time with Jai, and more importantly, he trusted the ce'faine. "That I'd like to see." Flying a verent thrilled him, unlike anything he'd experienced before in his young life.

Even better than thieving. *Maybe.*

•　　　•　　　•

Kalix folded his wings and waddled into his home, happy to be back in the wide, welcoming stone walls.

He was proud of his otherling. He didn't even mind so much being called Breeze. He'd picked up from Raven's mind that the word meant the gentle wind that blew across the world, something he enjoyed immensely on a warm summer afternoon in front of the family cavern.

None of the other otherlings — humans, he supposed he should call them — spoke to everyone the way his could. And when they were together, he felt complete.

Still, he was disturbed by what he'd seen, the little alien creature that had glowed like a red star. It awoke so many of his ancestors' memories.

Dark days were coming, the like of which his kind hadn't experienced in hundreds of generations — so long that the shared recollections had worn thin. Defeat the last time had been costly, but the skirryn — and the collective — had survived.

If such drastic steps were needed again, the otherlings would all likely perish along with the invaders. There had to be a better way.

Raven and his kind were a light in the world, even if they were also capable of wanton destruction. They would learn, in time.

You're fond of him. Sorix's tone hung somewhere between wonder and disapproval.

You're still unsure?

She nuzzled up next to him. *You know me. I hate change.*

Kalix rubbed her with his snout. *What kind of skirryn are you?*

One who loves you. And Velix too. They're changing, you know. Soon we'll all change again. Are you ready to be the egg layer in the family?

I thought you hated change. His amusement bled through their link.

Well, maybe not all change.

A flurry of wings announced Velix's return with the two kits. A wave of sadness passed over him, quickly extinguished.

Ah, you miss our third. He's part of the otherling ... the human, you know. He longed for the child-who-never-was too.

I know. But it's not the same.

Flyx clambered up his back, nipping at his neck. *Velix took us to the lake. It was cold!* He shook his little body, splashing water over Kalix and Sorix.

Aryx glared at him. *You're such an idiot.* She climbed more gently onto Sorix's back, settling into the flat space there and purring.

Velix bobbed their head. *It is warmer than usual. The ice is melting, and the red stars are coming. It won't be long now.* They settled in next to their bonded pair.

Kalix felt safe and protected. *For now.*

3

CORYX

S PIN TREMBLED inside his metal shell.

Aik had done as he'd asked, and had left him on. The urse plodded on — the sky was still green, and a cool breeze blew at their backs, rushing through the trine grass along the edge of the road with a sound like a river — but the real world had suddenly become strange, unreal, and grotesque.

It had been his, once. He'd given it up for his family. His wife and his beautiful little girl, Sera. The pain of those memories threatened to crack him open like an egg.

How had she become captain of the very ship he'd been placed in? Had his unconscious memories somehow worked to bring them together?

His recovered recollections of her childhood were fragmented, incomplete. Yet he could still *see* her. If he shut out his outside stimuli, he could still remember how it *felt* to hold her in his arms. The arms he no longer had.

He'd left them to save his family from the debt collectors, who had threatened to imprison him and his wife, Genevieve.

That name still sounded so sweet to his ears. Her touch, her scent, like lavender in the early morning ...

Time had ground them both to dust.

And yet, he'd had that precious interlude with Sera on the *Spin Diver,* and here on Tharassas while she made a life for herself with Jas. A blessing beyond measure. Bitter was the loss, but he wouldn't let that taint the sweetness she left with him, every time he immersed himself in her memories.

So he savored each and every one he had of her, and the few he still retained of her mother. And he cursed the men who had done this to him, and those who had forced his hand. *Even if I did agree. I should have found another way.*

"Spin, you okay, buddy?" Aik's voice was tight, as if he were mulling over his own worries.

"Yeah, Chief. Fine." Surely *Spin* wasn't his real name. Spin was the name of the ship mind who'd run the *Spin Diver*, but something had come before.

He searched through his newly acquired memories, running through a hundred, a thousand, a hundred times that in an instant.

There it was.

Tyson Jackson. Ty to his friends.

I had a name.

●   ●   ●

That damned fool boy. Triya was about ready to spit blood.

Aik had gone off on his own with that initiate from the Temple — Desla? — and he'd taken her last two urses too.

Mes had brought her news of the missing mounts just before dawn. She'd watched the caravan the whole gods-cursed night, but they'd not thought to mount a watch on the stables. Though how he'd managed to sneak by such a seasoned Guard ...

Triya shook her head. *Doesn't matter now.*

The urse tracks in the snow led up the road toward the Highlands. *What are you up to, Aik Erio?*

She knew what this was. Young love. The idiot had gotten tired of waiting for the caravan to reach the Highlands. She'd let her own heart lead her once, too. She still missed Willem on cold winter nights in the Manor. *Never again.* If you didn't open your heart, you couldn't get hurt.

A pair of eneet chased each other through the tree branches of the violet pines above, stopping to chitter angrily at her for barging into their home.

"Right there with you." She was angry at herself for not seeing this coming. Usually she could read people better. *You're slipping, Triya.*

They could manage without the urses — it just meant the two remaining guards would have to ride with the rest of them on the wagons. Still, it rankled her. *Isn't Raven supposed to be the thief of the three?*

And what if those fireflies returned? Somehow, he'd been able to protect them all, even though she still didn't understand it.

I'll catch up to you soon enough, boy. And then we're going to have a little reckoning. This time she did spit.

"Do you want us to go after them, mim?" Mes looked nearly as angry as she was, her brow knitted and teeth clenched. If Aik had been in front of her, she would have broken him in two. "I can trade with Merriwither for one of their urses and —"

Triya frowned. Sure, they could see about buying an extra urse from the trader or renting one from the Station. She should probably do that, in any case. It would be best if someone was mobile. But sending her two guards off would mean stripping the caravan of its remaining protection, and also more work for those left behind. "No, I need you here. We'll find them eventually, but right now we have goods to move."

Mes held her gaze for a moment, pursing her lips, then looked away. "Yes, mim."

Triya patted her on the back. "Cut the boy a little slack. He's in love."

Mes was looking at her as if she'd lost her mind. "Mim, no disrespect, but he stole two urses from you. I've seen you run men to ground for less."

She laughed ruefully. "True. But Aiken Erio's no normal man. He has a role to play in what's to come, mark my words." And with that she put it behind her and turned back toward the station. There were trades to be made, breakfast to be had, and a caravan to get on the road. She was always at her best when there were things to be accomplished. "Come on, Mes. I need you to pick up the slack."

She turned to go, and Mes followed her, grumbling forcefully under her breath about that "stupid gully rat."

•   •   •

Aik's urse clomped along at a steady pace. He was stocky, more so than poor Elly, who'd been sent back to the Manor House days earlier. Still, he was docile enough. Mes had him well trained.

It was still dark out, but the sky was turning a deep emerald green in the east.

At his side, Desla was dressed like a warrior, in white hencha-fiber pants and a matching looser top, with leather chaps and a tight leather vest. Her short sword hung at her side. So different from how the sisters normally dressed in the city, in their flowing robes.

By Desla's reckoning, they were at the far edge of the pass. The steep rock walls had drawn back, letting them out into a high elevation forest filled with violet pines. Patches of purple and orange flowers dotted the shadows under the trees, and blue wisps spun in and out of the darkness, making a fairyland of the little forest.

After pushing hard the first couple hours, he decided they were far enough away from Triya and her minions to give the beasts a short break. By now, she was bound to be aware of his thievery, and he wanted to be nowhere close to her when she exploded. He kept looking over his shoulder as the sky in the East went from black to gray to light green, expecting some kind of pursuit, but so far there was nothing.

In the clear, but starving. He'd been stupid to leave without stealing some food for himself. For the two of them. *Aik Erio, you're an idiot.*

Spin was strapped in at the top of his pack. The little familiar had been very quiet — thankfully so, since Desla didn't know about him yet. Sooner or later, he'd have to tell her, but they'd cross that bridge when they came to it.

His stomach rumbled, and he looked over at her, wondering if she was hungry too. "I don't suppose you brought anything to eat in that pack of yours, did you?"

She shifted her shoulders. "I might have gone back to the station's kitchen to grab a few things before we left." She glanced at him, her eyes narrowing. "Not sure I want to share them, though. Are you telling me you set off on this, what, week-long expedition, and didn't think to bring any food?"

"No. I mean, yes." He sighed. He probably deserved that look. His inner voice had gone quiet — probably satisfied now that he was on his way, but he could beat himself up just fine without it. "It was a spur of the moment thing. Are you regretting coming with?"

"Only a lot." She snorted. "Lucky for you, I'm a sister. We're trained to always be ready." The sun was rising in the east ahead of them, its rays touching the tips of the trees that lined the road.

"A sister?" Despite his foul mood, he couldn't resist needling her. Just a little. "I thought you were only an *initiate*."

She sniffed. "One more crack like that and I won't tell you what I know that might help us both." She turned away, staring at the road ahead of them. "Did no one train you to live off the land in the Academy?"

It was his turn to snort. "What land? There were pubs and the Market and the Guardhouse cantina to feed us." He scratched his right arm absentmindedly, waiting for her biting response.

Desla was stubbornly silent. Women were like that ... hit you with something unexpected and then go all quiet on you. He loved them, but men were easier, somehow. Like with Raven. It was simpler ... *and* more complicated.

Somewhere out there — hopefully at Anghar Mor — Raven waited for him. He was sure of it. *I'm coming, Rave.*

They started down the long slope in silence, descending from the patchy forest and into the open sweep of the purple grasslands. They'd left the last of the snow an hour earlier. The cold had reached right into his bones, but the sunlight was a balm on his naked face.

He rubbed the back of his neck, uncomfortable in the expansive quiet, broken only by the whisper of a breeze through the trees. Still, he vowed not to be the first to speak.

In the distance, the waters of Lake Zeraya sparkled under the rising sun. The world around them was calm and peaceful, as if they were the only living creatures in it.

The pressure built inside him to say something, *anything* to fill the gap, but he resisted.

The trine grass shifted in mesmerizing patterns in the wind that blew down from the gap, and something fluttered briefly above the purple blades to their left before settling back into the grasses.

"All right, I'm sorry. You may not be a full sister yet, but you're more of one than I am." Aik blushed, ashamed he'd been the first to break.

She burst out laughing. "That has to be the most half-assed apology I have ever heard."

He shrugged. "Sorry. Not feeling so great about myself this morning." He'd gone rogue, a thief like Raven. Only worse, because he did it in spite of his own moral compass. Being a Guard was all about duty and protection, something they'd drilled into him at the Academy, and he'd just neglected both. *For what? Love? Fear? Compulsion? I should be stronger.*

She nodded. "I thought it might be something like that. You don't usually break the rules, do you?'

He shook his head vigorously. "I'm a Guard." As if that explained everything. Growing up in his mother's armory shop, it had been all he'd ever wanted. He'd sat behind her shop counter, staring at the tall, brave, handsome Guards who frequented the place. Wanting to be like them. To *be* them.

Sometimes wanting to be *with* them, man or woman.

"I'd guess you were like that long before you first put on the uniform."

He looked away, stung. Yes, he'd been a good boy his whole life, taking care of his mother since his father had left when Aik was only four. She'd instilled a strong sense of right and wrong in him, and it had always guided him.

Until now. There was a certain illicit thrill to taking what he wanted — no, what he *needed* — everyone else be damned. It scared him.

You like it.

The voice was back. He shuddered, shoving it away. *What's happening to me?*

He needed a distraction. "So what's this *privileged information* you have?"

She studied him for a minute, as if deciding if he was worthy, and then nodded, turning to look back at the dirt road. "I know where the Temple safe houses are." She sounded angry. Or maybe disappointed?

Raven was right. These sisters — Desla included — were more trouble than they were worth, with their secrets and wiles. "What's a safe house?"

She shifted in the saddle, rubbing her urse's neck. "It's less grand than it sounds. They're small shelters along the way that provide temporary cover for traveling sisters. Each one is stocked with hardtack. Not as good as cave cheese and foldovers, but it will keep you alive."

"Ah." That would make things easier, though he worried about becoming even more indebted to the Temple. "And how do you know where these safe houses are?"

"Sister Tela gave me a map, just before we left."

"That's ... fortunate." It would also give them a place to camp out of sight, in case Triya caught up to them. "Where's the next one?"

She frowned. "We passed one just coming out of the pass. There's another a half day's ride, down in the valley near the lake." She shifted her shoulders again.

"Perfect." Poor thing was probably not used to carrying all her belongings on her back. He had trained for this ... well, not *this* in particular. But he'd done endurance training in the Guard with a pack much heavier than this one. "Why don't we stop for a moment? Stretch our legs?"

She nodded gratefully. "That would be nice. It's already getting warm."

Aik wiped a thin layer of sweat from his brow. It was warm. *Isn't it supposed to be cooler in the Highlands?*

The mountains were retreating behind them. As they mounted a rise in the road, the Highlands spread out below. "This looks like as good a spot as any."

He dismounted and set down his pack, giving his shoulders a break. Desla followed suit, stretching her arms. Together they turned to take in the view.

A sea of purple grasses filled the wide valley, broken up here and there by human settlements, visible mostly as dark patches of cultivated fields and stately lines of orchards amidst the purple sea. The wind flowed through the wild trine grass, carving patterns of peaks and valleys as if it were water. The air was thick and heavy, carrying a sweet, sharp scent that must have been coming from the grasses themselves.

In the distance, the waters of Lake Zeraya were a deep green, mirroring the sky above.

"It's … beautiful." Except for the steadings, it was much less tamed than the fertile valley of the Heartland.

"It is." She took a deep breath. "I've never been here before. I always wondered what it would be like to wander."

"Me too." He eyed her pack. "I have extra room — I could take some of that weight off of your shoulders. If you want." The urses had no saddlebags, as Triya carried everything they needed in the wagons.

She pursed her lips, staring straight ahead. "I can handle it just fine, thank you."

He felt a sudden arctic chill. "I'm sure you can. I'm just saying, it's not fair that you should carry all the food you brought. Not if we're going to share it."

She shrugged. "That's still very much in question." Her eyes met his, and a smile played at the edges of her lips.

She knows I'm giving her an out. Women were just smarter. *At least, smarter than me.* "Besides, your urse is smaller than mine. Ursey here can carry quite a load."

She looked him up and down. "I guess she'd have to."

"Hey, cheap shot!" Still, even her veiled insult made him feel better. *At least she's not mad at me anymore.*

"And seriously? Ursey? That's the best you could come up with?"

"Kerrick, then. I'll ride him hard." He scratched the urse's flat nose, and she purred like a kitten.

She barked a laugh. "No, I think Ursey is better." She smirked. "I'm so telling him you said that when we get back to Gullton."

He shivered. "*If* we get back."

Silence fell between them once again. *That killed the mood.*

They stood together watching the wind-blown grasses.

This time, it was Desla who broke the silence. "All right, we can redistribute things, as long as it's for the common good." She dredged up a weak grin.

"That's the spirit." He unlaced his pack. Sunlight glinted off Spin's shiny shell.

"What's that?"

"Oh, this? Nothing." He frowned. Now he was lying, too. *So much for good Aik.*

She reached past him and plucked out the silver sphere. "Doesn't look like nothing to me." She whistled. "It's beautiful."

"Please give that back. It's … it was Raven's."

Ours.

He growled. *Shut up.*

Her mouth made a little moue of surprise, and she handed it back sheepishly. "I'm sorry. I didn't know." She squeezed his shoulder. "We'll find him, somehow." She unlaced her own pack as he tucked Spin back into his.

"No, *I'm* sorry. I'll … tell you what it is. Later." She'd taken a big risk coming with him. It was only fair.

You don't need her. The voice sounded like it was sneering.

Stop talking to me. It had been a good morning, but now he had to contend with the godsdamned gauntlet again.

She touched his shoulder lightly. "Whenever you're ready." She handed him some hencha-leaf wrapped packets. "Keep these on top so they don't get squished. We should eat most of it today and tomorrow, as it won't last much longer."

"Noted." He hoped he didn't sound like too much of a jerk. He tucked each packet carefully into his pack, and then hefted the whole thing into the air to test its weight. *Not bad.*

"What do we tell them?" She laced her own pack back up.

"Who?"

"Anyone we run into on the road? We should have a story."

He pulled his pack back up onto his shoulders. It was heavier, but he could manage it. "We tell them we're Triya's advance scouts. It's not too far from the truth."

She shook her head. "Well look at you. Lying again. I thought the Guard frowned on that sort of thing?"

"Hey, you're the one who wanted to have a story." He sighed. She was right. It was becoming far too easy to ignore his better angels.

She had the grace to blush. "Sorry. I'm just … I'm a little out of my depth here. I am still just an initiate."

Of course you are. He'd totally missed the fact that she was probably feeling as lost as he was. "We'll figure it out. And Des?"

"What?" Her eyes met his.

"I'm glad you're here."

She flushed again, but she nodded. "Someone has to keep you out of trouble. You're like an eneet in an eircat's den."

"Let's get going. I want to make this *safe house* of yours before dark." The faster they went, the sooner he'd find Raven. And maybe between them, they could figure things out.

Raven had always been the smart one.

She climbed back up onto her urse and scratched the beast's neck affectionately. "I think I'll call mine Ursia. More feminine." It warbled happily under her touch.

"Sounds good." In truth, he *was* glad she'd come, the gauntlet's snarky comments notwithstanding. He held the reins back and extended her arm. "After you."

Morning bled into afternoon as they pressed on into the valley. The violet grasses were so tall they were sometimes hard to see over, even on urseback. The whole world had narrowed to just the two of them, and Aik was grateful for the distraction.

That strange, almost magnetic tug pulled him forward, toward Anghar Mor. It was unsettling. He could feel the weight of the gauntlet on his arm, even though the thrice-damned thing had vanished once again. And when he closed his eyes, the strange skull they'd unearthed in Triya's storeroom haunted him, filling him with sadness.

Sometimes he thought he caught sight of a red spark in the air over the grasses.

It was a beautiful fall day, even so, if a bit warmer than normal.

He pushed it all to the back of his head, instead engaging Desla on what her life had been like in Devon.

"Devon's not what most people expect."

He glanced at her, his eyes narrowing. "A backwater country village, full of farmers?"

She stuck her tongue out at him. "There are farmers, certainly. But it's a proper town now, with its own culture and traditions." She looked up at the green sky as a breeze from the lake ruffled her blond hair. "We have a business district and a weekly Market Day, and the meer is always going on about us being better than Corinth, even if Queen Jas did come from there."

He nodded, frowning slightly. "I've never been down South." He'd never gone much of anywhere except for Heaven's Reach, and that had been a training exercise.

"Most gully rats haven't. You're all a bit snobbish about the whole thing." She smiled to take the sting out of her words. "I can't tell you how many times I heard someone in the Temple say 'Devon? How exotic. I've never even been over the bridge to Landfield.' People are so insular." She shook her head, adjusting the pack on her shoulders.

"Maybe so." There were a lot of things he'd taken for granted about the wide world around him, assumptions that were coming back to haunt him now. He scratched the back of his neck, wishing the tugging sensation would go away. *Maybe it's pulling me toward Raven.*

What would happen once they found each other again? Would Raven run to him, overjoyed to have him back? Or would he have found comfort with someone else? *Like I did ...* The guilt for that act ran deep.

What if he can't forgive me? His heart skipped a beat. *Or ... what if he's dead?*

He refused to believe it. *I would know. Somehow.* "So why did you leave?"

She was quiet for a long time. They rode on together in silence, broken only by strange noises he assumed were bird calls, and the comical *keeyip* of a flight of orinths when some of the thumb-sized green and orange insects flew by, checking out the visitors.

I shouldn't have asked. "You don't have to answer."

She shook her head. "It's all right. It's just ... it's all tangled up inside." She brushed a strand of blond hair back behind her ear. "There was a boy."

He laughed. It felt good, lightening his gloomy mood. "There usually is. What did he do?" The pained look on her face made him regret it immediately.

"Nothing. Arvy was ... beautiful, inside and out. We would have married ..."

I'm a farking idiot. "Oh for hencha's sake, I've stepped in it, haven't I? He died, didn't he?"

She shot him a startled look. "No, he's fine. Living in Devon still, married to one of my cousins now. They're starting a family." Again, that flash of pain crossed her face.

"What, then?" *Back off, Aik. She'll tell you if you want to.* "I'm sorry. I'm prying."

"No, I don't mind. It's good to have someone to talk with about it." She snapped off a blade of the long grass that trailed out over the roadway, twisting it between her thumb and forefinger and staring at it as if it might have some secret meaning. "I was pregnant with Arvy's child. My child." She let go of the blade, allowing the breeze to catch it, and her hand slipped to her stomach. The wind caught the bit of grass and carried it away toward the lake. "She … didn't make it."

"I'm so sorry, Des. That must have been awful." Thank the Gods that had never happened with Silya. They'd been careful, but still … "And he left you? Heartless bastard."

"No. He wanted to stay. I just … couldn't." The flighty Desla he'd first met was gone, and for the first time the deep sadness she kept hidden came to the surface. "Every time I looked at him …"

He bit his lip. "I'm so sorry, Des —"

"What's that?" She cut him off, standing up in her stirrups to gaze into the distance.

He followed her gaze. A few hundred meters down the road, a rider was kicking up dust as its mount gallomped up the hillside.

He had no idea how busy this road was normally, but it had seemed awfully quiet up until then. He squinted at the approaching urse. "Someone's in a hurry."

Whoever it was slowed to a canter as they came into view. The rider wore a heavy home-weave top and aur-leather chaps, along with a wide-brimmed hat tied under their chin, hiding their face in shadow. Long blond hair was tied back behind their neck.

Aik lifted a hand in salute. "Afternoon." The sun climbed toward its apex.

The rider looked up. *Just a girl.* Young … maybe seventeen? "Hello." She came to a halt, staring anxiously at the road behind them. She cast a quick look back over her shoulder.

"Are you all right?" Her voice was calm, soothing, all the sadness washed away.

"I … no. No I'm not. I have to get to Gap Station." Her eyes were red, her cheeks puffy as if she'd been crying.

He frowned. "What happened?"

"They … something attacked our steading." Her face was dirty, except where a tear had washed a thin trail clean down her cheek.

"What attacked you?"

She cast a worried glance in his direction, raising an eyebrow.

His frown deepened. *I should* be concerned. Instead, a barely concealed contempt for the woman filled him — disgust at her filthy state.

"They were … bugs."

"Glowing red bugs?"

The girl's mouth fell open. "Yes. They just appeared in the night. I was out watering the aur. I heard the screams and ran to the barn door …" She looked down at her urse, rubbing its gray neck. "They were everywhere. I hid inside the barn, then took Cheel here and we ran." She was shaking.

"What's your name?"

She shifted on her saddle. "Maur'Isa. Maura to my friends. From Isa Steading —" A catch in her voice interrupted the last bit.

"Where's the steading?"

Maura looked over her shoulder and shuddered. "A half hour back that way. There's a sign." She wiped her cheek with the back of her hand, smearing the dirt on her cheek.

Des turned to him. "We should help her —"

"The station's just a few hours' ride back that way." He pointed the way they had come. His patience with the young woman had just about run out. "Come on. We need to keep going if we're going to make the safe house by nightfall."

Her gaze bored into him. "We can't just leave this poor girl." Her glare said *What in the green holy hell is wrong with you?*

Maur'Isa sniffed. "It's all right. I can take care of myself." With one more frightened look over her shoulder, she shook the reins and pushed past them, urging her urse to a gallop again and heading up the road toward the pass.

"What was that?" Desla's eyes narrowed to slits. "We should have helped her."

He shook his head. "There's no time. We need to get to the safe house. It will be dark soon enough. And besides, you heard her. It's dangerous out here."

Part of him knew he should have at least *tried* to help. Somehow he couldn't bring himself to care.

She glared at him. "You're not the Aiken Erio I know." She shook her reins and her urse lurched away from his, down the road.

That hurt. "Desla —"

"I don't want to talk to you right now." Her voice was frostier than the snowy Gap.

He sighed. *Maybe she's right. I should feel ... something.* But even now, thinking about it only brought up a sense of disgust.

You don't need her. Was it his imagination, or did it sound satisfied?

He didn't bother to shush the gauntlet this time. He shook Ursey's reins, urging his urse on after her.

He *did* need her. *Best to try to keep her happy.*

•   •   •

"I'm sorry." It was maybe the tenth time Aik had said it. Not because he actually *felt* sorry, but because he knew he was supposed to. Because Desla expected him to. "I don't know what else you want me to say."

They rode side-by-side along the widening roadway. The grass along the edges blocked the view in all directions, but now and then they would crest a hill and catch another glimpse of Lake Zeraya in the distance. Several times, he'd thought he'd seen something hazy and white amongst the grasses, but it was too far away to make it out.

"I heard you the last nine times." Her voice hadn't warmed up. Not one bit. But at least she was finally talking to him again.

Relief flashed through him. "I really am."

"Why did you treat Maur'Isa like that? She just went through something horrible and traumatic." Her eyes finally met his. "It's not like you."

He shook his head. "I'm ... ever since the attack in Clayton, I'm not myself."

Her eyes stayed locked on his. She clearly wanted more from him.

He sighed. "I have these dreams."

"Dreams?" She bit her lip, looking back down at Ursia's neck. "What kind of dreams?"

"About the attack," he lied. He didn't want to tell her what he'd really seen. The forerunners, attacking his friends, and blood on the snow. So much blood. *Forerunners? Where did that come from?*

She looked away. "I thought it might be something like that. We all respond to trauma differently. When she told you about the attack on her own steading …"

"That's it exactly. It brought everything back." *Let her believe it.* It was a small lie, but it was worth it if it made things easier. "I just want to get to Anghar Mor. To find Raven."

She held his gaze for a moment, then gave him a sharp nod. "Fine. But we have to make a quick stop first."

He scratched his chin. "Where?"

Her warning look silenced him. "We're here." She pointed at a wooden sign, hand-painted with the letters "Isa Steading."

He wanted to object, to urge her to keep going to the safe house. The compulsion tugged at him more forcefully now.

But she was the only one who knew how to find it.

If he could, he would have kept riding, all the way to Anghar Mor. The gauntlet urged him on, but he'd likely kill his urse, and then he'd have to walk the rest of the way. A quick stop was a small price to pay, if he could ignore the tug for just a few minutes. "All right. Let's go have a look."

They turned up the dirt lane. It was lined by a short fence, posts and planks painted purple. The native grasses faded away, quickly replaced with neat rows of corn. As they proceeded up the lane, they passed a hencha gathering, the purple leaves rustling even though the air was still. Aik had the feeling they were watching him, a group hostility that made his skin crawl, even though the plants had no eyes. He wouldn't trust any berries from *those* plants.

Farther up the road, there were fields of cotton, wheat, and even a small orchard of strange trees with red trunks and broad, heart-shaped purple leaves.

"Bandies!" She practically squealed in delight. "We used to have a bandy tree in our yard in Devon. They're so good."

He shook his head. He'd never heard of such a thing. "What are they like?"

"They're about the size of my hand. Red with purple spikes. Really sweet and juicy inside, once you get past the seeds …" Her voice trailed off as they rounded the orchard and came into sight of the steading house.

A pristine white dome had shattered the building, cutting it in two. It looked as if it had grown out of the middle of the single-story home, pushing the walls apart as like they had exploded from within. Around the central dome, a few smaller ones had sprouted. They reminded him of —

"Coryx. Like in Norton." Her eyes were wide.

He nodded. The strange houses. They were *exactly* like that, but without the cut-out windows and doors. Still, they triggered something else in him. A strange feeling of déjà vu.

A hum filled the air, something so low he wasn't aware of it at first.

"Aik?" Fear cracked her voice.

He turned to find her and her urse surrounded by a swarm of the glowing red fireflies.

Forerunners. The word came to him again, unbidden.

The bright crimson lights slipped around her in a growing swarm, more of them appearing from the orchard and what was left of the barn.

"Aik, getting a little worried here." She sat ramrod straight, still as a statue, her eyes darting back and forth to watch the slow-moving red cyclone that engulfed her.

His right hand tingled.

He looked down to see the gauntlet shimmer back into existence. He raised his arm and stared at it.

She cleared her throat. "Aik ..."

Without thinking, he raised his hand and flicked his suddenly gauntleted wrist at them, like they were cherry flies he was shooing away. *Not her.*

The forerunners buzzed angrily in unison, then rose as one and dissipated as rapidly as they had appeared.

He blinked. *How did I do that?*

"Um, thank you?" She looked at him the same way she had at the whirlwind. "How did you ...?"

"I don't know. I just did." *What am I becoming?*

She shuddered, turning away as if she were afraid to meet his gaze, then slipped off Ursia to approach the nearest dome with caution. The urse pranced back a few steps, watching the domes warily. "They've got to be connected. Those bugs —"

"Forerunners."

That earned him another frown. "Those *forerunners* and these coryx. I think it's growing from something." She knelt beside the smaller one, and her face blanched. She got up and ran to the fence, retching into the grass.

He barely noticed. He was staring at the other domes.

They were beautiful — white, clean, and pristine, and they called to him. They *belonged* here in a way that the squat, ugly farmhouse didn't. He could feel it in his bones.

He slipped down off Ursey and approached the one that had so disturbed her.

It was growing. He could feel it reaching for the green sky.

A human arm stuck out from under the edge, hand clenched as if in pain.

It was discordant, at odds with the symmetrical beauty of the coryx. He tried to make sense of it.

All at once, it snapped into place.

It was feeding on a *child*.

The strange malaise fled, and his gut twisted in horror. "Oh gods." He sank to the ground to touch the little hand, wondering who it had belonged to. Maura's daughter? Brother? Cousin?

He looked up at the dome, consuming the person inside. "Farking green hell." A wave of nausea flooded him.

He turned away and fell to his knees, throwing up, his guts finally expressing what his heart couldn't. He knelt on the hard-packed earth as his stomach emptied itself, heaving its contents onto the ground and leaving the foul taste of acid on his tongue.

The ground shook beneath him, as if the world itself was revolted by what he had seen.

Another wave of nausea seized him, and he dry-heaved until there was no more to come out. He was left staring at the puddle of his own vomit.

A warm hand touched his back, rubbing him gently. "I know, Aik. I know." Des knelt next to him, putting her arms around him until the shaking — inside and out — subsided.

He looked up at her, feeling as miserable and wretched as the woman they'd met on the road. "What in Heaven's Reach happened here?"

She was as pale as death. "I don't know. But we need to go. Before it happens to us too."

He nodded. He stood unsteadily and managed to shuffle back toward Ursey. *Such a stupid name.* The urse had retreated a few steps back down the lane, but she stood her ground as he approached her.

Every instinct urged him to run.

Still, he knew they should gather some food. It would be good to supplement the hardtack with something fresh. "Let's grab what we can — some ears of corn and a bit of that bandy fruit. Quickly, though. I don't want to stick around here any longer than necessary."

"That makes sense." She glanced back at the domes.

He followed her gaze. They seemed bigger than before. He wondered what would happen when they reached maturity.

He decided he didn't want to be around to find out.

They picked what fruit they could close to the fences, stuffing it into their packs, and then mounted up.

"Let's get away from this place." He spurred Ursey back down the lane, and Desla followed him gladly.

The shock of seeing that poor child's hand had shaken off the numbness that had settled on him, and he didn't want it to overtake him again.

He cursed himself for the hundredth time for putting on that stupid gauntlet. It had led him down a long, dark road, and he knew he hadn't seen the end of it yet.

He decided he'd tell her everything when they reached the safe house.

Maybe she can help me figure out what's happening to me. And how to stop it.

4

A Little Company

KERRICK HEFTED the slender device in his hand, not entirely convinced it would do as Silya claimed. It was yet another unexpected, unexplained thing in a bewildering series of events. They were living in a time of great change — the imposing verent, an unknown threat from the North, and even the heavy staff that she carried around effortlessly.

And here he was, standing in the middle of the Temple's hencha gathering, getting ready to talk into a little black box. Feeling like an idiot.

He touched the strange material the gadget was made of. It was firm, but not as hard as metal, and not as cold either.

Every one of the things they'd found that morning in the secret stores — Silya had dubbed them "long talkers" — was identical, down to the last line and curve. *How is such craftsmanship possible?*

He'd have called them magic, but Silya had another name for them. "*Technology.*"

Of course he knew the word. "Technology" was for things like new wagon axles and electric lights, which were wonder enough. This was something else altogether. *Magic.*

"Are you there?"

The voice coming from the box startled him so badly he almost dropped it. Gripping it more tightly, he looked up to see Silya emerging from her rooms onto the wide balcony, a good fifty meters distant, her face lit by the rays of the midday sun.

He pushed the button on the side, like she'd shown him. "Yes. I hear you clearly." He waved back, and his heart skipped a beat. Somewhere on the long trek back to Gullton, she'd gotten past his defenses, and now his whole body tingled whenever she was near.

It was most unbefitting of a man of his age — almost twenty-six — and a sergeant to boot. He shoved his feelings down ruthlessly. "This is amazing."

She waved at him. "It really is. I wonder how much range these have?"

Being able to talk at long distances like this would revolutionize things — even if the range was only a few hundred meters. There were twenty of them, making them more precious than iron. *Maybe she'll give me some for the Guard.*

"I don't know. It's —" Her voice cut out.

He frowned and pulled the device away to look at it. Had it just … died? Broken? Lost its magic? He had no idea how these things worked.

The earth rumbled, then began to shake.

He crouched, bracing himself against the ground with his free hand as the earth trembled and the noise grew. It was a bad one, at least as strong as the quake that had tumbled the Old Bridge into the Elsp. The noise grew, the violence shaking the hencha plants and the very soil in which they grew. He looked up at the Temple in alarm. *If it collapses …*

The great round structure stood firm, as the noise reached a crescendo. The shaking seemed to go on and on.

Ay'Oss let it end. If the earth goddess heard him, she gave no sign.

One of the initiate dorms shuddered. As he watched, horrified, two of its stone columns collapsed with a resounding *crash*. Somehow its heavy roof held, balanced on the remaining two supports.

Oh gods. It was just past lunchtime. There were probably initiates still inside.

Kerrick latched the long talker on his belt and sprang into a run, making his way back toward the Temple as best he could over the shuddering pathway. "Get everyone out! It's coming down!"

The ground still shook underfoot, and it was like running across a sizzling frying pan. *It's too far …*

One of the last two columns holding up the roof slipped, and the whole thing came down on its side with a thundering roar, kicking up a cloud of dust.

Just as quickly as it had begun, the quake was over, and the world went silent. He stopped, staring wide-eyed at the destruction.

Then the screaming started.

"… Jas protect us. Are you all right?" Silya's words came out clearly from the black box on his belt.

He waved at her and gestured to the fallen dormitory.

Silya edged over to the railing and peered down, and her mouth opened in an "O" of surprise. "Farking hell." She took in the collapsed dorm, then looked at him. "I'll meet you there. Freja grant that no one was hurt." Her voice crackled through the long talker.

He came up short at the scene of the collapse and called up to Silya using old-fashioned technology — his own voice. "Better bring the Temple medic, and as many strong arms as you can gather."

She nodded, and then vanished back into her suite.

From underneath the rubble, a white arm extended in bloody surrender.

•　　•　　•

"Oh gods above." Silya covered her mouth with her hand, stifling a cry as Kerrick and Pes'Osa lifted Fess'Ima's limp body out of the rubble. She was the only death, although there'd been multiple injuries when the roof of the dorm had collapsed. *Thank Jor'Oss the rest are mostly scrapes and bruises.*

They'd been lucky, but she'd have to see what she could do to shore up the other dorms. One more thing to add to her already overwhelming to-do list.

Looking at the initiate's pale, lifeless form, Silya didn't feel so lucky.

They laid the poor girl on a stretcher. Pes'Osa knelt to arrange her, placing her arms by her sides and tucking a wisp of golden hair behind her ear.

Sister Sal'Moya stood at her side, shaking. "She was so excited to become a part of the Temple." She sniffed and wiped a tear from her puffy cheek. "Her mother sent her down from Sadie's Cove — the youngest of seven daughters. She was so proud to be here representing her town and her family."

That got Silya's attention. Her father had been from Sadie's Cove, a small village along the cold northern coast. Had Fessryn's mother known her father?

She hugged herself tightly, reminded of Daya's death just a few days earlier. "I'll send them a letter myself." It was Temple tradition, but she'd never had to pass on this kind of heartrending news before.

"Yes, Mim." Sal'Moya squeezed her hand.

Kerrick and Pes'Osa were about to lift the stretcher to carry the poor girl's body inside. Too much death, and her time as the Hencha Queen had barely begun.

"Wait." *I should at least say goodbye.* They hadn't been close, but they'd been initiates together before Silya's sudden Raising.

He met her gaze and nodded. He stepped back from the body, and Pes'Osa followed his example.

She wasn't sure why, but she knelt next to the girl's body and lay down her staff. Fessryn was lovely even in death, the beauty of youth, of promise yet unfulfilled.

Silya touched her cheek. It was still warm — it was unnatural for someone dead to still feel so alive. *I need to be sure.*

She closed her eyes, and the essence of the hencha filled her, a balm to her fragile soul. She'd been training with Dor on her concentration just before testing out the long talkers with Kerrick, and the hencha mind was close to her.

It reached through her hand and into Fess'Ima.

Fire flooded her and gasps filled the air all around her, but she was lost in the communion with the hencha. She searched for Fess'Ima's soul, for the essence of her being.

She is alive.

She blinked. *Surely they couldn't mean …* The girl was pale as death herself.

But through the hencha, she could feel it too, the merest spark of life still burned inside Fess'Ima like a candle buffeted by the wind.

We can save her.

Her heart leapt, color returning to her gray vision. "We can save her?" she whispered, so softly that no one else heard her. No one besides the hencha.

There's a cost. The hencha said it matter-of-factly, with no judgment.

What cost? It mattered not. She knew she would do it.

A piece of yourself. It will take you time to recover.

A bit of herself seemed a small price to pay for the girl's life, in the balance. *I'll pay it. We have to help her.*

The hencha mind's assent encouraged her. *We will help you. Put one hand on the girl and one on your staff.*

She obeyed, closing her other hand around the black wood.

She tensed as something new flowed into her. *Fire? Water?*

Power. It had no name, and no human description seemed quite right. Wide and vast, it poured through her, and her arms began to shake with it as it passed through her hands and into Fess'Ima.

Blood of the world. The hencha expressed it with such reverence that she shuddered.

Silya gasped as it surged through her, eating away at her insides like acid. The staff lit up with a brilliant blue light, and the gathered crowd gasped, taking a step back. it burned, but she held on.

Her entire being focused on the girl's prone form.

Inside the initiate's mind, they found the spark. *I've got it …*

The little light slipped away.

She frowned. *Where did it go?*

The sadness from the hencha was palpable. *We are too late.*

No! She drew more from the staff, pressing ahead. Fess'Ima was still alive. She knew it, and she would not give up so easily. Not when it meant she'd have to write that horrid letter to the girl's parents. *I will not let her die.*

It's too dangerous. You'll burn yourself out.

I have to try. How would Triya feel if she lost me?

She drew on the blood of the world, taking in as much as she dared until it burned her skin from the inside like lava with each beat of her heart. She clenched her teeth against the pain and expanded her awareness. *It has to still be there. Somewhere.*

She found the spark again. It was now just a glowing ember, the tiniest bit of fire.

This time she poured everything she had into it, the blood of the world surging through her own and into Fess'Ima.

Her body shuddered like a tree in a hurricane as the spark inside the girl guttered and almost went out. She held her breath.

Suddenly it flared into a full-blown fire of its own. Color returned to Fess'Ima's face, and Silya held on for dear life, riding the wave like a runaway urse. Spittle leaked from the corner of her mouth, and pain lanced through her mind, but she didn't let go.

Fess'Ima's body bucked, and the girl took a loud, ragged breath before collapsing back to the stretcher.

Silya let go of the girl's cheek and the staff as the hencha left her, her insides going suddenly cold.

She swayed back and forth, the world blurring around her, before she started to fall.

Warm arms caught her, laying her down gently, and something soft was placed under her head.

Her stomach churned in protest and every muscle in her body seemed to cramp all at once. She was tired beyond words, wanting only to crawl into bed.

Still, none of that mattered. *Did I do it?*

She will live.

The hencha were still there, at the edge of her awareness. Like a parent after they put you to bed and blew out the lantern.

And so will you. You pushed yourself too far.

Thank the gods. The hencha's disapproval burned like acid, but she didn't care. Fess'Ima would live. That was all that mattered.

Kerrick's concerned gaze was the last thing she saw before she blacked out.

●   ●   ●

Blisters covered the world.

Silya blinked, unable to process what she saw. The wide bowl of the Highlands should have been filled with purple grasses that moved like water in the breeze. Instead, white pustules infected the earth, horrid things of varied sizes that piled on top of one another like tumors and seemed to have swallowed up all the other life.

Yet they were alive, too. She could feel it, a malevolent force that flowed through all of them, connecting them to … something else.

One of the larger ones burst, belching out a cloud of glittering dust that turned black as it touched the air.

Not dust. Spores. That cloud would carry the wretched blisters even farther across the Highlands, if there was still any of it left untouched.

She shuddered. What had happened to the Steaders? To the ce'faine?

•   •   •

Silya awoke in a pool of cold sweat. Pain arced through her head, and she felt as weak as a newborn kitten. *What happened to me?*

Her mouth was dry, and her arms might as well have been hundred kilo weights, they were so hard to lift.

There's a cost.

It all came flooding back to her. The long talkers, the quake, and the terrifying collapse of the dorm. And what had happened next, the terrible risk she'd taken. *Poor Fess'Ima.*

She moaned, and Kerrick was there in an instant, hovering over her. His brow was knitted in concern, filled with lines she didn't remember. "You're awake!"

Had he aged overnight? "Fessryn …?" She tried to lift her hand to touch his cheek, but failed.

He nodded. "She'll live. What you did, bringing her back from the dead …"

She shook her head, the movement barely perceivable. "Not … dead …"

"Well, whatever you did, it was reckless. It drained you." He sat on the bed and put a warm hand on her forehead. "You're still cold."

She nodded, about all the movement she was capable of. "Staff?"

"It's right here, beside the bed."

"Hand it … to me."

He lifted it, grunting with the weight. "How do you carry this thing around so easily? It must weigh a ton." He lay it next to her.

"Don't know. Not that heavy." She reached out, slowly, her hand moving centimeter by agonizing centimeter toward the polished black wood. At last her fingers touched it, and flames sprung up along its length, flooding her with warmth. She was still bone-tired, but time was short. "I have. To get. Up." The Highlands were in danger, and there was so much to do.

Kerrick crossed his arms. "Oh no. Hencha Queen or not, you're not shrugging this one off."

Another face swam into view. Dor.

"Ser Kek is right, Mim. You just about used yourself up. Silly thing to do for one girl, when you have a whole city to care for." Still, she didn't sound *too* disapproving. Together, they made an implacable wall next to her bed.

There was no way she was getting by them, and the far side of the bed seemed a hundred meters away.

"Saved that poor thing's life, you did." Dor managed a slight grin. "The whole Temple's abuzz about it."

An immense sense of relief washed over her. Still, she had to get up. *I can't let myself laze around in bed while others might be dying.* Tri'Aya wouldn't let herself be bedridden like this. She tried to sit up once more, but her body wouldn't obey her. "I need —"

"You *need* your sleep, Mim. We have things well in hand. The maps we found in one of those chests included a survey of the caverns under Gullton. We're matching it to what we already have. Did you know they used to call it Gully Town?" She chuckled. "It will save us hours of work. The hencha have been extremely helpful collecting all the information."

"That's good." *I had a dream …* It had seemed important, but the details eluded her.

Kerrick leaned over and kissed her cheek. "Sleep, my love," he whispered in her ear. He took the staff from her and set it back by the bedside. "It will be here when you awaken."

My love. Her eyes went wide, but Dor either hadn't heard or wasn't concerned. She had to satisfy herself with the fact that they were in private. No one else would know. She squeezed his hand, not trusting herself to say it aloud.

The warmth of the hencha enveloped her, and she sank back down into the covers. She'd have to do something about the sweaty sheets later, but it could wait.

One more thing flitted across her consciousness. "Triya ...?"

Dor shook her head. "Nothing yet."

She nodded. Her mother was headed to the Highlands, the place Silya had seen in her dream. There had to be a way to warn her.

The flitter. When she woke, she would see that it was finally fixed. And then she'd carry the warning herself. She needed to see the Highlands with her own eyes.

Satisfied with her plan, she fell back into a deep, undisturbed sleep.

•   •   •

Silya awoke again, this time to the sound of subdued voices and quiet laughter.

At first she thought her ears were deceiving her. Who would be merrymaking in her rooms? Surely she was dreaming.

But there it was again, Coral's cheerful laugh.

A tantalizing aroma filled the room. Something meaty, intertwined with something fresh-baked and sweet. Golden light filtered in from her receiving room.

Her stomach gurgled loudly.

What time is it? She sat up in the semi-darkness, glancing at the window. The sun had set. *Holy green hell, I slept the whole day away.*

Her body still ached, but the weakness had fled. *I can live with it.*

She hoisted herself out of bed, grateful to get out of the soaking sheets. She released them from the mattress and placed them in a pile in the center of the bed. She'd have to wash them later.

Or let Dor arrange it.

It still irked her to let others do things for her, but she had more important things demanding her time. She had to let go of the initiate she'd once been.

She pulled on her soft mur silk nightgown — there were some perks to being the queen — and put on the slippers someone had thoughtfully left beside the bed.

She sniffed herself. A bath was certainly in order, as soon as she could manage it.

I need some fresh air. She picked up the staff and quietly padded over to the doors that led out to her terrace. She opened one of them, letting in a cool breeze that played across her damp skin, salty like the sea.

The world outside was calm, deceptively so, as if nothing at all were amiss. Below, the hencha gathering sang, their melancholy melody suiting her mood. They felt the pain of the Highlands.

From above, Pellin's pink light shone on the tranquil scene, mixed with the golden glow of Tarsis.

She looked up at the heart-shaped sea on the larger moon for a few minutes, content to just let the breeze soothe her.

"It's a beautiful night." Dor's voice startled her.

She nodded, unwilling to leave the peaceful scene just yet. If she turned around, the responsibilities of her office would find her once again, embroiling her in a struggle she barely understood. One she had no choice but to try to win. "I was staring at the moons. I wonder if Queen Jas ever stood here and did the same?"

Dor snorted. "Well, since they completed the Temple after her death —"

"I don't mean *right* here." Still, she laughed too, and it lightened her mood a little. She leaned on the staff and closed her eyes, enjoying the stolen moment. Imagining she shared it with the queens who had come before her made it just a little more bearable. "Who's in the front room?"

"Ser Kek and Cor'Lea. The former because we can't get him to leave, and the latter in case you should awaken and have need of something."

"And you." She permitted herself the ghost of a smile. Dor never strayed far from her side, however much she might decry the same trait in the Guard. Somehow, she inspired loyalty in those around her, just as her mother did. *The berry doesn't fall far from the hencha.*

"Yes, *and me.*" Dor touched her shoulder. "I brought them up something to eat from the kitchen. Verla asked after you."

"She would." The woman was ever thoughtful of others, though she hid it well under her gruff exterior.

"Come eat something. You must be starving." Dor patted her shoulder and turned to go.

"I am." Her stomach gurgled again.

She was grateful that it was just Kerrick and Coral. She turned, searching for Dor in the darkness. "What's that wonderful smell that woke me up?"

"Ah, Verla has prepared a few steaks with a dried grayleaf rub. Absolutely scrumptious. And there might still be a foldover or two left ..."

"Sounds wonderful. Lead the way." With one last glimpse of the twin moons, she closed the door and followed Dor out to the receiving room, leaning on the staff for support.

Kerrick and Coral looked up as she entered the receiving room, going quiet. It was lit by a single flickering lantern, lending the place a warm, comforting glow. *So much better than the harsh electric light.*

Silya urged them to continue with her hand. "Don't stop the conversation on my account."

Kerrick jumped up and crossed the room in three bounding steps, sweeping her up in his arms and hugging her tightly. "Are you all right? You looked so small, after... So pale." He held her out at arm's length, searching her face. "I was worried about you."

He let her go and led her across the room. He pulled out a chair for her like a true gentleman.

She sank down onto the soft cushion, grateful for the respite. She leaned the staff against the table and pulled up an empty plate. The steaks were cold, but they still smelled delicious. "I'm ... better. I think I slept the worst of it off."

And starving. She speared two of the remaining steaks, along with some bacca root medallions that Verla had somehow cooked soft enough to eat. The glass flagon on the table was empty. "Is there more wine?"

Coral beamed. "You *are* better." She blushed. "Mim."

"None of that. We are all friends here tonight." For just a moment, she was content to let her worries and fears slip away, to be present in this moment among people whom she cared for.

Kerrick took up his place again across the table, and his eyes met hers as she sawed off a piece of meat and put it in her mouth.

It practically melted in her mouth, they savory taste of the grayleaf tickling her tongue. *Heaven.* "No need to stare at me like that. I'm *fine.*" Well, *fine* might be stretching it a bit, but certainly in the general vicinity of fine. "A full night's rest, and I'll be good as new."

"Coral, can you bring some more wine? The red 399 if you can find it. It pairs well with aur." Dor sent the girl off.

Silya nodded gratefully. "I *am* rather thirsty."

"Not that you'll have any steak left by the time she gets back." Dor raised an eyebrow as she wolfed the meal down. "It's like you haven't eaten in weeks."

Maybe that's part of the cost? "How is Fessryn?"

"Fess'Ima's recovering. I looked in on her a couple hours ago." Dor sat next to her and took one of the remaining foldovers from its platter. "You took quite a chance to save her. Yen'Ella —"

"Didn't have my abilities," she snapped, but she was sorry as soon as she said it. "Dor … I'm sorry. I know you two were close." *Guess I'm still a little cranky.*

Kerrick raised an eyebrow.

Dor nodded. "No, you're right. She never did master her abilities. But she was a good woman, and exactly what the Temple needed at the time." Dor set down her half-eaten foldover. "I was going to say she would have been proud of you."

"You think so?" Warmth spread through her at the compliment.

"I know it."

Silya squeezed Dor's hand lightly. "I'm sorry. I'm just worn out. I shouldn't have snapped at you."

Mollified, Dor flashed her a weak smile and picked up her foldover again.

Her mind was racing as all the things that needed doing came back to her in a flash. "We need to get the flitter up and running. There's something afoot in the Highlands, and I —"

"It'll be ready tomorrow. I checked with the Machinists' Guild. They've fabricated the part we needed, and Mas Olin says it will be installed in the morning. But Mim —"

"I'm going, Dor. I have to see it for myself." Of course she'd already taken care of it.

Kerrick grunted. "Are you sure that's wise? You almost burned yourself out today, from what Dor told me."

She slammed down her knife and fork. "I'm not an invalid. Please stop treating me like one."

Coral chose that moment to pop in with the bottle of wine. "They didn't have any more of the 399, but I found a 398 that Verla said was just as good … what?"

All three of them were staring at the poor girl.

"It's nothing. Dor and Kerrick here are just overly concerned about me. And I appreciate it. I do. I'm just tired."

Kerrick touched her hand. "You did a good thing. We just want you to take care of yourself. We need you."

"It's mutual." She squeezed his hand between both of hers, and then let go and turned to Coral. "The 398 will be just fine."

The initiate handed the bottle to her and stepped away, as if she was afraid Silya might bite her hand off.

Silya retrieved the corkscrew from the table and opened it in short order. "Sit, and we'll share this together."

Kerrick and Dor shared another of their conspiratorial looks, and then Dor handed her a glass.

She stared at them through slitted eyes. She didn't like this new alliance between the sergeant and her aide. Not one whit. "Seriously, I'm fine. After dinner, we'll plan tomorrow's outing. I want to leave as soon as the flitter's ready."

"But you have the Council meeting tomorrow night."

"I'll be back in time." They were treating her like a child.

She grumbled. She was the Hencha Queen, not a spoiled five-year-old. She poured herself a glass and reached to fill Kerrick's, but her fingers weren't working quite right, and it slipped out of her grasp.

He caught it deftly and set it down on the table. "After dinner, you're going back to bed. You'll do no one any good in this shape."

"I'm fine. I just …" Her hand shook. She pulled it away, hiding it under the table. "I'm fine."

Even Coral wasn't buying it. "You need your rest, mim."

She sighed. She *hated* not being right. "I'll go to bed after we finish this bottle. It'll help settle my nerves." She took a sip. It was good — sweet and full-bodied — but Dor was right. The 399 was better.

He filled the others' glasses, and Silya finished her meal in the company of friends, their companionship helping to soothe her jangled nerves as much as the food and wine.

When they'd finished the last drop, she got up unsteadily and reached for the staff for support. Kerrick appeared at her side instantly. "I'll help you back to bed."

I am tired. The alcohol suffused her with warmth, and the gnawing hunger was gone. "Good night, Coral. Good night, Dor."

The women nodded, and Dor kissed her on the cheek before slipping out the door.

"Come on." Kerrick's arm slipped around her waist as he led her back to bed.

The burst of energy that had sustained her through the meal as gone, and she was exhausted. She leaned the staff against the stone wall and let him pull back the covers, remove her slippers, and get her into bed.

He tucked her in and kissed her forehead, like her mother used to do when she was five. "Sleep well, my Queen." He turned to go.

"Kerrick?" She was fading fast. "Stay with me."

"Of course." He pulled up a chair.

"Not there. Here." She patted the bed next to her. "I need a warm body next to me tonight." *And maybe more.*

He frowned at that, but she couldn't quite figure out why. "Of course, mim." He untucked his shirt and pulled it off, revealing the beautifully tanned chest she'd seen once before, on their journey down the Elsp. He lay the shirt on the chair and started to pull off his boots and pants too.

She stopped him.

"What?" He searched her eyes.

"I ... I need to know this thing between us is something real." Her whole world was falling apart. There had to be one thing solid she could hold on to in the coming storm.

His eyes widened. "Are you saying ...?" The way he looked at her, the hunger in his eyes ... it was intoxicating. No one had looked at her like that since Aik.

"Yes." Such a simple word, but so much behind it.

He nodded. "You're not ... this isn't ..." His gaze strayed to her waist.

She laughed, breaking the tension. "No. Not my first time."

He sat on the bed next to her, tantalizing inches away.

She was afraid he'd lost his nerve. Men were so fragile. "What?"

"I'm just taking all of you in. Silya, you're beautiful." He leaned forward and kissed her, and her face burned like the hencha were with her. And yet, she was all alone, as if they'd sensed her need for privacy.

She pulled him down onto the bed and kissed him back, hard, thrilled by the taste, the touch, the smell of him. For the first time in what seemed like forever, she let someone in, letting her walls fall away and becoming a part of him in a ritual older than humankind.

For a few glorious moments, she let go of herself, of the world and all of its problems, and thrilled at her lover's touch.

When it was over, when his warm chest settled in against her back, she sighed with deep contentment and nestled in next to him, abandoning the world for a sweet, dreamless sleep.

5

ELLECK

CHALA WAS LOST IN THOUGHT. The sun had just crested the mountains to the east, lighting up the valley. She was sweeping the accumulated debris out of the wide cavern they called the Kitchen and onto the ledge outside, when a voice interrupted her.

"Back in a few minutes. I'm taking Sleeker down to get a bath." Astrid climbed onto her verent, not bothering to merge for the short flight down to the lake. The beautiful beast launched itself into the air, and they floated down into the valley together on the morning breeze. Had Jai and Raven left yet?

Chala wondered what it was like to *become* part of a verent. She'd ridden one, once, when it had brought her back to Mountainhome from her suifaine clan. But she'd been so scared she barely remembered the ride.

Not that she'd ever admit to fear.

"You could try again."

She jumped in her skin. "Off to the lake too?" She must have been deep in thought to allow Olly to sneak up on her. She clamped down on her spike of jealousy.

"Not yet." Olly saw right through her. "You know, the verent are willing, if you are."

"Not interested."

"Are you sure? Because you don't seem happy —"

"I'm fine," she lied. She pushed past him back into the Kitchen. Her mother had killed a charging cephlant with just a spear. *What are my problems in comparison to that?*

Olly followed her inside like a puppy.

She liked him. Not like *that* — her heart belonged to another, and he had all the wrong parts, besides. But still, she liked him.

She wasn't sure why. He talked too much. He was weak ... at least by ce'faine standards. And a white-bellied lowlander too.

Still, he treated her as an equal, not like some pitiful failure. "It's not something I can explain. I just don't *want* to. It was too hard, losing the first one."

Like losing a child. though she never said so to anyone but herself.

She'd been angry when she'd been chosen, when the verent had dragged her back here. She would have been the head of her village one day, with Elrys at her side.

At Mountainhome, she was an extra pair of hands that no one really needed. She grabbed the axe to chop some wood, anything to work out the frustration coursing through her, without killing Olly or one of the other verent riders.

We need you.

The voice vibrated through her like a note plucked on a theolin string, stopping her dead in her tracks. The voice sounded familiar. A woman. "What did you say?" She turned to find Olly staring at her.

"I ... nothing." His eyes narrowed. "Are you all right?"

Great, now I'm hearing things. "Nothing." She stormed past him again, out onto the ledge, where one of the verent had helpfully dropped a pile of wood. She pulled out a trunk and began to systematically reduce it to logs to feed the Kitchen fire.

Chop. Chop. Chop.

It had to be the verent. But why would they talk to her now? And how?

She wasn't bonded to any of them. *Just wishful thinking.*

A low growl filled the air, and a second later the world shook. Chala dropped the ax and grabbed hold of the edge of the cavern mouth, steadying herself as the quake tumbled the neat woodpile over, scattering the fruits of her labor across the terrace.

A loud crash came from the direction of the pantry. *That doesn't sound good.*

After what seemed like an eternity, the earth settled down again, leaving only a fine dust hanging in the air to indicate it had happened.

Olly met her gaze. "They're getting worse."

She nodded. "Want to check the pantry? I'll take care of this mess after I feed the fire."

He stood with her for a moment more, as if to reassure her that things would be all right.

"I'm fine. Go."

"Of course you are." He winked, and then disappeared back into the relative darkness of the Kitchen.

Chala sighed. *I really am fine.* She went back to work, putting the verent out of her mind.

Chop, chop, chop.

•   •   •

Jai woke Raven before dawn.

Laying in the bed Olly had built for him, halfway between sleeping and waking, Raven could sense Jai's excitement like a light coming into his room. He luxuriated under the warm hencha fiber blanket and the comfortable bed — an actual bed! — and he didn't want to get up just yet. It was cold outside, the cavern still dark save for the little bit of light that leaked in from outside via the main cavern, where the verent slept.

Company. Breeze's voice rumbled through his head, wiping out the last of the dream.

He'd been on a far-ranging adventure with Jel'Faya, his favorite author, exploring distant lands. He kept his eyes closed. Maybe if he pretended to be asleep, Jai would leave him alone.

Jai sat on the edge of his bed, holding a couple steaming-hot earthenware mugs full of akka. "Morning, starshine."

No such luck. "Go away. I'm asleep." He tried to ignore both the smell and Jai's glowing presence.

"People who are sleeping generally don't talk back."

He rolled his eyes. "Maybe I'm sleep talking."

"And you're remarkably coherent." He nudged Raven's shoulder. "Come on. It's time to get up if we're going to make it there when it starts." Jai waved the mug under his nose, then pulled it away when Raven tried to grasp it.

"Not fair." It came out as more of an indecipherable mumble. He really had been enjoying his dream.

"Come on. Get up. Or I'll call in the verentlings."

He groaned. Having Cat and Grey bounding on top of him was the last thing he needed. "All right. I'm up. I'm up!" He flipped the warm covers back, shivering in the cold in just his small clothes. "A little privacy, please?"

"You lowlanders and your prudish ways." Snickering, Jai left one of the mugs of akka on his small table and slipped out into the verent cavern.

Ten minutes later, feeling slightly more human with a mugful of hot akka in his stomach, he padded out of his room, still in his underwear, carrying an armful of clothing. He shivered in the early morning chill.

Jai raised an eyebrow.

"I'll just have to take them off again."

Jai chuckled. "Fair enough."

Angel arrived on the ledge in a flurry of wings, touching noses with Breeze.

The cool air didn't bother him as much as it used to, but cold was still cold. The sun hadn't yet mounted the edge of the valley.

He tucked his clothes away in a small leather sack he strapped to Breeze's neck. No saddles meant no saddlebags. Keeping his back to Jai, he added his underwear — they weren't that dirty yet, after all — ignoring Breeze's interested sniffing of his private parts. "I bet you don't smell all that great down there, either."

Breeze snorted. He emanated excitement, felt keenly through the emp, which only made him more nervous. What was Jai taking him to see?

"Ready?" Jai had stripped down too.

He tried not to notice. "I would have been *more* ready with a couple extra hours of sleep."

"Then you would have missed it." Jai climbed onto his verent and merged.

The sight of Jai basically melting away still kind of freaked Raven out.

He clambered on top of Breeze, letting himself sink into the verent, slipping through the gray haze that accompanied the change. Somehow the transition stripped away his fear, and soon he and Breeze were one. It was like being in a warm bath, bathed with Breeze's love — a feeling he could get used to. He was never really *alone* anymore. *Morning, my verent friend.*

He got a general assent that yes, it was indeed morning. Then Raven/Breeze rumbled across the terrace, and they were off.

There were a number of other verent out, even this early, but none of them were with Raven's human companions. He wondered how many there were — more than before? The skies already seemed crowded.

Why weren't verent ever seen in Gullton? Or over the Highlands? Queen Jas seemed to have known about them, but before Sister Tela had read them the prophecy, he'd never heard of the magnificent beasts. *Did the ce'faine know?*

They flew up out of Mountainhome and headed west, over the row of peaks like sharp teeth that separated the lush valley from the Highlands. As they crested the first one, the sun rose behind them, filling the world with light.

The snow lay thick on the mountains below, like frosting on a fresh-baked foldover. Raven was glad that he and Jai were encased in verent flesh.

It was all worth it — swallowing the verentling, the nausea, the fear he'd gone through — for these glorious flights. Up here, the world belonged to him. He could go wherever he wanted, soaring above the rest of humanity like an angel. Or a god. *Will I still feel that way when it comes time to fight?*

You'll be good. We will be good together.

They blinked their giant verent eyes. Breeze was getting better at speaking *human*. Or was he just getting more used to the verent's strange form of communication?

I'm getting better talking to you. There was a clear note of pride attached to that thought.

Raven/Breeze grinned a toothy grin. This whole being-two-things-at-once was supremely weird, but he was starting to enjoy it.

He glanced over at Jai/Angel. The other verent's eyes twinkled. *Tell Jai this is amazing!*

I can hear you, remember? They felt jealous. *Follow us to the shore.*

With a start, he saw they'd reached edge of the mountains. It seemed much closer than it had on the day he'd first arrived in Mountainhome. Maybe because he'd been daydreaming like a five-year-old.

Angel spiraled down toward the eastern edge of Lake Zeraya, heading for a narrow valley between two rocky ridges that descended almost to the waterline. Wide stands of violet pines filled the valley, some ancient and tall enough to poke above the top of the ridgeline, their branches shivering even though the air was still so early in the morning. This side of the lake looked empty of human habitation, but there was something happening down there, a great tumult of movement near the shore.

In the lake itself, white shapes bobbed, some of them leaping into the air in apparent excitement. And on the shore ...

What is this?

Hundreds of creatures, large and small, milled about on the shoreline. They were various shades of white, like the verent and other Tharassan wildlife, with short horns and long-clawed feet.

The joining. Breeze's voice came weighted with a series of images and feelings that made no sense to him, but an underlying sense of anticipation filled the air, shared by the verent.

Joining. As if that explained *anything*. Raven was about to complain to Breeze about that when he noticed something else.

They weren't alone on the skies. As they dropped toward the ground, a flock of large white birds circled them, checking out the newcomers, and one of them flew right past them and cursed at him with an indignant *squawk*.

In the distance to the northwest, Anghar Mor loomed, a dark presence against the bright green sky.

A memory tickled his mind. *Verent swarm in the icy north, when the twin moons are rising. Cayah in the harsh Southern Deserts lift their dappled heads from the sand. The erphin swim upstream, and the jexyn in their sky aeries hear the call to come to Anghar Mor.*

These birds ... are they jexyn? Breeze dropped toward the ground a short distance from the milling beasts.

Jai/Angel sounded surprised. *That's what the ce'faine call them, yes.*

And erphin and cayah too. Queen Jas had been right. But why were they all here?

Breeze alighted near the edge of a wide meadow near the lake shore, and the cayah parted to allow them room. The verent raised his head so they could see better. His vision was better than Raven's alone — sharper, and wider through his compound eyes. He could see almost all the way around.

Up close, the cayah were not so different from aur — big shaggy gray and white beasts with blunt faces and four legs — which were quite a lot fatter and more muscular than an aur's, and shorter too. Their horns were spirals, which *was* different, and their hides were dappled with gray spots. He could feel their collective anticipation too — at least from the ones closest to them.

One of the cayah let loose a deep warbling sound and waded into the lake, dipping its shaggy muzzle and spraying the air with shiny droplets of water that seemed to hang in the sunlight for an instant like sparkling gems before dropping back to the surface.

Some of the droplets continued to rise, flickering in the air like little stars.

Wisps.

He rubbed his eyes, making sure he wasn't imagining it, but there they were, flaring into life and spinning around the waterlogged beast.

An erphin broke from its pod to approach the huge beast, slicing through the water, its white dorsal fin leaning back. Unlike the cayah, the erphin was sleek, made for water. Its narrow, rounded nose touched the cayah's, and the erphin let out a delighted squeal, as if it were greeting an old friend.

He snorted. *Strange friends. As different from one another as me and Chala.*

The cayah ducked its head as if in in submission and lowered itself into the water.

Is it going to drown? His apprehension grew. *We should save it.*

Just watch. Jai/Angel radiated calm. Like they had seen this before, and there was nothing to be worried about.

They probably have. Raven crossed his mental arms and settled in to watch, impatient.

The erphin slipped around the submerged beast and climbed up onto its back, wiggling its way into place.

The water boiled. In the midst of it, the cayah and the erphin ... changed. The edges of the erphin seemed to melt, and oozed around — no, *into* the cayah.

I've seen this before. When Jai had first merged with his verent.

And earlier, when the mass of inthym had become one in the tunnel near his lair.

That seemed like a lifetime ago now.

He watched, transfixed.

One of the jexyn swooped down from the sky, circling the pair as they merged. As the frothing of the water settled, it landed on the back of the ... new creature. It spread its wings, and soon it too began to change.

The joining. It made sense now. All three were becoming one.

It was one of the weirdest things he had ever seen, but also strangely beautiful.

Mist rose from the turbulent water, obscuring the view. It was shot through with blue light — the wisps, surely — which shimmered in the hazy air.

All of the cayah around them had turned to face the water, bearing witness to the event. The water boiled, steam completely covering whatever was going on down there.

They leaned forward to see better.

Then white wings broke free of the mist, flapping and lifting a new verent into the air. It rose above the mist, a magnificent beast sparkling and wet in the early morning sunshine.

The cayah along the shore began to hoot and holler.

The verent. That's where they came from. And why they'd never been seen before. *Though sometimes they have eggs too?*

Yes. In our families. Breeze said it as if it were the most sensible thing in the world.

Queen Jas had known. *The hencha must have told her.*

Raven was ignorant about his world, and there'd been so many things that he'd had no desire to learn. *Like anything outside of Gullton. That will have to change.*

Yes, it will. Angel/Jai caught his eye and blinked in agreement.

He hadn't realized he was being so transparent.

The new verent swooped down onto one of the other cayah. The others shifted back, going silent, but that one didn't move a hair as the verent fell on it, seizing it in its claws and placing its jaws around the cayah's neck, snapping it with one impressive bite.

He was shocked at the violence against one of its former herd mates. *Why didn't it run?* The sight of the feasting verent made his stomach twist as indigo ichor from the cayah splattered the ground.

It gives its life for its cousin. Life is different, for them.

He would have snorted if he'd been in his own form. *That's for sure.*

More of the cayah edged past the feeding verent and into the water, and the erphin swam up to meet them. *How many verent will be — born? Made? — today?*

Jai/Angel looked around. *Maybe ten more? Not enough —*

Something *snapped* behind him.

Breeze spun around and set off toward the sound, nimbler than his hulking form might suggest, moving on instinct. He carried the two of them through the meadow and into the violet pine forest, radiating a fierce intensity. *What is it?*

Someone. Watching. They threaded their way through the pines, over dead logs and under low-hanging branches, nimble as an eircat for all of their great size. Dappled sunshine flashed past them, and their keen senses took in the smell of the rich sap of the trees, sweet and heavy like ripe hacka berries.

Ahead, something flashed through the woods, a bit of purple against the dim forest trunks. Whoever it was, they were fast, faster than Breeze among the trees. They radiated *fear.*

Jai/Angel dropped into the forest ahead of them, landing on an open knoll and roaring at the newcomer, a rough, guttural sound that made his blood turn cold.

The fugitive skidded to a halt, staring back at Breeze as the verent closed the remaining distance between them. Raven finally got a good look at them.

The ce'faine wore a purple shirt pulled tight around his chest — her chest? — with matching breeches ... hencha cloth, no doubt. Golden leather arm and shin guards protected their limbs, the leather intricately carved in swirling patterns and burnished to a shine, though it held various nicks and scars, especially on the arms. A thick ix-fur vest was dyed brown and wrapped around the torso.

Long, blond hair was pulled back into a braid and tied off at the end. There was a lump on their neck, and a heavy bow was slung over their shoulder.

They raised their arms in the universal symbol for surrender. "All right, you've got me." They smelled nervous, and their hand edged down toward a dagger's scabbard at their waist.

That wouldn't do much against verent skin. *I'll deal with this.*

He let go of his connection with Breeze, his body emerging from the verent's back as things went gray and fuzzy. When he was Raven again, the morning air felt cool against his naked skin.

The ce'faine's hand dropped to one side, eyes wide open in shock.

He slipped off Breeze's back and pulled his pants out of the sack strapped to his verent.

"What in the seven peaks?" Their expression changed. "You have an emp."

"So do you." He could feel it now, and could tell more about the stranger through his human filter. *Her, not his.*

Somehow the emp made the ce'faine woman seem less threatening, even if she were masking their emotions. Her smell gave her away.

Fear.

He forgot for a moment that he was naked in front of a stranger.

Her gaze shifted to the scales that covered Raven's arms, and then back to Angel, where Jai had also emerged. "What *are* you?"

"I'm Raven. Mas Rav'Orn, if you want to be formal about it. And this is Jai. And I'm a *who*, not a what." He took out his clothing and pulled on his small clothes and pants. "Who are you?" His shirt's homeweave settled comfortably across his shoulders.

She stood straighter. "I'm Elleck. Of the East Valley Clan." Her voice was higher than Raven expected.

"Elleck?" Jai's jaw dropped open. "It *is* you!" He raced forward and threw his arms around the other ce'faine. He looked over his shoulder at Raven. "We met at the Summer Meet, two years back."

"Jai?" Elleck laughed. "So we did. Though you weren't with one of these ..."

"Verent."

"These verent then." Elleck let go of him. "And you weren't so naked."

"Sorry. When we merge with the verent, our clothes don't." Jai returned to Angel's side and pulled out his own clothes.

Raven relaxed, kneeling to pull on his boots. If Jai trusted her … "You know each other?" The ce'faine looked familiar, but he was sure they'd never met.

Jai nodded. "It's a long story. Elleck … is on a journey of her own. We had a lot to talk about when we first met."

"That's an understatement." Elleck grinned. "I have a camp nearby. Care to join me for a meal? I want to hear about these beasties of yours."

"Verent." He spat the word out. Something about Elleck bothered him, even though she seemed to have Jai's approval. *I can't be jealous. Not of Jai. Right? Oh Gods, I'm radiating it, aren't I?*

If Jai or Elleck felt it, they didn't say a thing. "Sure. Lead the way." Jai's eyes met Angel's. "The verent are going to return to the joining. We have a couple hours to kill. Is that all right, Rave?"

He stiffened at the use of his old nickname. Only Aik called him that. "Sure … why not?" *Clearly I need to learn how to hide my feelings better.*

"Perfect." Jai leaned in to whisper in Raven's ear. "I don't think Elleck noticed." Out loud, he said "Come on, then, let's see this camp of yours." He clapped Elleck on the back, and they set off, chatting like long lost friends.

He turned three shades of red. Chastened, he followed Elleck and Jai up the slope, feeling like a third leg.

The sun warmed the narrow valley, and strange chirps filled the air, going silent as he passed them. He spotted a white creature no bigger than his hand skittering up one of the violet pines and ducking out of sight, sort of like an eneet, but bigger and with one big, tufted ear on the top of its head.

The wisps from the lake were here too, floating through the air and dancing on the light inland breeze, lighting the darkness under the violet pines. He grabbed one. It warmed in his palm, like a snowflake melting, and then its light went out. Something shifted in his head.

The erphin pressed against his back, and then they were forging a new life together. He raised his thick head and bellowed as they became one ...

He blinked. *What in the holy green hell was that?*

He stared at the darkened wisp. *I hope I didn't kill it.* He opened his palm, and the little thing rolled around it, pushed by the wind. Then it took flight again, and its light flared anew. It floated away, up into the sky.

They carry memories. What did it mean?

It was like the strange indigo river beneath Mountainhome where he'd found Chala.

"You coming?" Jai called from higher up the slope.

"Sorry. Got distracted." He hurried after the other two, his mind spinning furiously. There were so many things he still didn't understand.

He reached the top of the incline, but Jai and Elleck were gone.

The trees were thinner there, and the edge of the valley was bounded by a natural rock wall, covered with patches of blue lichen. "Jai? Elleck?"

"Over here." Jai's head popped out from behind the rock. "Come see this. It's amazing!"

He followed Jai's voice, the verent rider's excitement bleeding into his mind.

From the far side, the rock wasn't as solid as it had appeared. A narrow cleft in the wall led into darkness. *Underground, again.*

A strange reluctance came over him. He'd spent so much of his last few years in caves, first in Gullton and now in Mountainhome. Outside, at least, the sun warmed on his face, and he could see anything that might come at him. Maybe he'd just wait for them here —

Jai's hand snaked out of the darkness and dragged him inside.

"Hey —" Raven's voice dropped off as his eyes adjusted. He could feel Jai's excitement through the emp link, could smell it in his sweat.

They stood in the middle of a fairyland.

The small cavern was full of blue light, like his old lair back in Gullton. Homesickness surged in his heart as his fingers traced the blue lines on the walls. But the entry was only the start of it.

He followed Jay and Elleck through it into a larger space, almost twice as big as his lair. It was filled with little wisps that floated around as if on missions of their own. Their blue glows flicked back and forth across the room around thick natural columns that held up the ceiling, leaving trails in his vision. Then they cleared away, leaving space for them to walk through the wide cavern.

"What is this place?" His eyes were drawn to the waterfall that tumbled down the far wall. Not water, exactly. The same indigo liquid he'd seen in the caverns below Mountainhome. Lights flickered in the water too.

Elleck grinned. "One of the sacred caverns. Places where the blood of the world comes close to the surface." She knelt next to the waterfall, reaching for the strange liquid.

"Don't touch that!" The memories the wisp had set off still reverberated through his head.

"Why? It's harmless." Elleck cupped her hands and caught a handful. "See? They say drinking the water here lengthens your life." She met his eyes, and her own danced merrily. "That's aurshit, of course. But it does taste cool and wonderful on a hot day." She swallowed it, and didn't immediately keel over and die.

Well, that's something. He reached out cautiously, letting the liquid wash away the dirt from his hands. Something whispered in his mind, like a breeze in an ancient forest.

One of the sparks in the water slipped into his palm, circling almost curiously before slipping over the edge and down into the little underground stream that carried the water away to the gods knew where. *If I could bottle that, I'd make a fortune.*

Jai side-eyed him.

He blushed. Some of the thought must have slipped through. "Sorry." *Once a thief, always a thief.*

He looked up at a ceiling festooned with stalactites, visible in flashes as the wisps moved past them and lit them briefly with their blue glow. "Have you ever seen anything like this?"

Jai nodded, his eyes almost as wide as Raven's. "Once. It wasn't nearly as beautiful as this one, though."

He wasn't sure if he should tell Jai about Chala's private place beneath Mountainhome. Would that be a violation of her trust? Not that she had actually shown him — he'd snuck in after her like the thief he was. *I'll have to ask her later.*

Elleck knelt beside a pack made of tanned hide that had gone unnoticed in a corner of the cavern. Two of the wisps circled lazily down to spin around her. "Are you hungry? I brought enough hardtack for a week. I can spare a little."

"Sure, I could eat something." He followed the track of the wisps as they circled back up into the air to join the others. "I've never seen so many of them in one place."

Elleck shrugged. "They're drawn here, I think. All the sacred caves have them." She lay out a rough cloth with something that looked like overcooked flatbread. "I'm afraid we'll have to share the one canteen. At least we won't lack for water."

He barely heard her. He pulled one of the wisps from the air. His vision shifted as it tickled his palm, and suddenly his mind was floating above the three of them.

He let the wisp go, and his vision reverted to normal. "They're watching us."

Jai's eyes widened again, but Elleck nodded. "You can feel it, can't you? At the back of your neck?" She gestured for them to sit, broke off a piece of hardtack, and held it out to him.

"Yeah." He'd been feeling it since they'd landed in the narrow valley. It should have bothered him more, but like the verent egg, he was numb to it. *Which is weird, right?.*

He sniffed at the hardtack — it smelled nutty. He took a small bite, crunching the brittle piece between his teeth. It was surprisingly good, hearty and full of flavor, if dry.

Jai took a bite. "This is delicious, El."

Elleck beamed. "Made it myself. My own mother's recipe." Her eyes fixed on his. "So tell me about those beasts of yours. I've seen them in the sky once or twice, but never up close like that."

"The verent? They're ..." Raven looked at Jai for help. "They're a bit like dragons."

"Dragons?" Elleck raised an eyebrow.

Nobody knows what dragons are. He sighed and tried again. "They're ... protectors. Surely you've noticed things are ... a bit strange lately?"

Elleck laughed, a warm and pleasant sound. "Yes, starting with that whole ... melty thing you did back there. What was that?"

He decided he liked the ce'faine woman. He felt Jai's approval to go on. *Can Elleck feel it too?* "I ... we swallowed one of them. I mean, one each. It's complicated."

"A whole verent?" Elleck looked at him, and then at Jai, biting her lip. "You mean … like for dinner?"

Jai burst out laughing. "No, not like that at all. And yes, a whole one, but it was a baby, about this long." He held out his arms. "There was an egg, and it hatched, and the little verentling decided it would be more comfortable inside of us then out."

"That sounds awful." Elleck shuddered.

Raven grimaced. "That's an understatement." He could still remember the horrid choking sensation as it forced its way down his throat. "Anyhow, we're each now part of a verent family." He held out his hands for her to inspect the tracery of white scales.

Elleck ran her fingers over them. "They're beautiful."

It tickled. He pulled his arms away, and tried to pick up what she was feeling, waiting for a twinge of disgust or fear. But either she was extraordinarily good at hiding her emotions via her emp, or she had blocked him.

Elleck looked down at her own hands. Large hands, callused from hard work. "I'll bet you're very strong."

Well that's not what I expected. "Stronger, sure." He met her gaze, searching her eyes for a clue to how she was feeling. "I wasn't sure you'd believe us."

"After what I just saw?" Elleck shook her head, eyes twinkling. "It's not every day you happen across a couple of shape-shifting men."

"And yet you were expecting us, weren't you?" He wasn't sure why he thought so. Maybe some things were slipping through from her emp after all.

Elleck grinned. "You're perceptive, lowlander. I'll give you that." She pulled out a folded piece of hencha pulp paper from her pack and laid it carefully out on the ground between them. "My *eshem* gave this to me three days ago."

He and Jai peered at it. It was a map, neatly sketched out in black ink. The edge of the lake was clearly marked with a red X.

One of the wisps circled lazily down to hover over the map, as if scrutinizing it.

"She told me to come here, to this narrow valley near Lake Zeraya." She indicated it on the map. "She stressed that it was very important that I arrive before today, and then wait for some *new arrivals."* Elleck looked up at Raven and Jai with an appraising gaze. "I think you're right. I was waiting for you."

That strange sensation filled him again, like things were moving just beyond the corners of his eyes that he couldn't quite glimpse. "How did she know?"

Elleck shook her head. "I'm not sure. She sees many things the rest of us don't."

He clenched his jaw. *That* was singularly unsatisfying. "What's an eshem?"

"Each of the clans has one." Jai rocked back and forth, his eyes going unfocused as if he were falling back into memory. "Ours was called Mirah, and the previous one chose her." Jai *was* blocking his emotions. He could tell that now by their sudden absence. But a whisper of homesickness bled through.

He took Jai's hand and squeezed it.

Jai shot him a grateful look.

Elleck folded up the map and put it away, her hands shaking. "Ours is Alibeh. My mother. She had a woman in training to replace her — Cindra — who died in a cavern collapse two weeks ago, during one of the shakes."

Raven didn't need his emp to read Elleck's pain. "You were close?" There was something about the highlander, the way she spoke, the lines of her face …

Elleck nodded. "She was like a little sister to me, since the raid —"

Realization slammed into him like a lightning bolt. "You're Kerrick's brother … sister!" It had come to him in a rush, why Elleck looked so familiar.

Jai's eyes widened, a look comically repeated on Elleck's face.

"How do you know that name?" Elleck's voice dropped dangerously low, and her hand creeped toward the dagger that hung in the scabbard on her waist.

He gulped at the unexpected flash of anger. "Ser Kek … Kerrick's a Guard in Gullton." He'd almost said *a friend.* "He told us about you."

Elleck spat. "My brother is dead." She made it a simple statement of fact, though he could feel the doubt that gnawed around the edges. "They killed him when they took me." Her face was bright red.

He was shocked at the sudden change in demeanor. He could feel Elleck's emotion now, burning hot as a volcano, but he couldn't stop himself. "He's not dead. I've seen him. Talked to him. He's —"

"Liar!"

Raw emotion burst through their emp connection — grief, love, anger, loss — all mashed together like trine grass flattened by a heavy boot. It knocked him over and sent him sprawling on the rough, hard cavern floor.

Elleck's emotions were like a searing hot wind that flayed his skin from the inside.

Raven tried to push back, but he was unprepared for this kind of fight.

Elleck's rage burned through him, tinged with pain.

"Jai, help me!" He closed his eyes, willing the pain to stop.

"Elleck, stop it." Jai's calm, deliberate voice cut through the assault.

As quickly as it had begun, Elleck's burning rage vanished, leaving the taste of ashes in his mouth. He lay on the dusty cavern floor, his head pounding, staring up at the glowing blue wisps that circled him.

One of them dipped down toward his face as if worried about him.

Then Jai's face swam into view. "You all right?" He offered him a hand.

"I didn't know the emps could attack someone like that." He let Jai help him up and then dusted himself off. "You pack quite a punch."

"We're not *supposed* to use them that way. And the emp didn't do it — that was all her." Jai shot Elleck a stern look. "Elleck is sorry for what she did, *aren't you?*"

Elleck looked down at him over Jai's shoulder. "Sorry, Raven." She didn't look sorry, but her emotions were walled off again, so he couldn't really tell. She searched his face. "Kerrick's alive? Truly?"

He nodded. "He should be back in Gullton by now." *Maybe Aik's there too.*

"Ah." Elleck took a deep breath and let it out in a sigh. "That explains it."

"Explains what?" He exchanged a look with Jai.

"Why she chose me." She bit her lip, and a little of her old pain slipped through the link, soft and smooth with age. "I'm to ask whomever I find here to take me to Gullton."

6

REFUGEES

THE SPORE MOTHER tasted the air outside her den through one of her surrogates. It was warmer, thick with moisture. Her children were thriving in the world just outside of the mountain, and with them a change was coming.

Sometimes bits and pieces of those who came before floated through her mind — memories of bitter cold and ice. That was in the past. Now, glorious heat and a dampness in the air helped her children grow and spread.

The progenitor approached, though his progress was slow and fitful. She could sense him in the back of her mind. He was different from the other beasts she had captured and studied. Sharper. He didn't match any of the local flora and fauna from her previous, damaged memories.

Still, he would do. When he finally arrived, she would teach him, shape him. Forge him into a cultivator to tame the rest of this recalcitrant planet.

She pushed him a little bit. *Come, little one. I am waiting for you. Our time is coming.*

She was lucky his *aueel* had survived the last winter — when he finally arrived, she would have to determine how.

•   •   •

Triya soaked in the morning sun, hands guiding the reins of one of the aur.

The wagons rolled down the slope into the Highlands, the wheels rumbling on the hard-packed earth of the Gap Road. Lake Zeraya sparkled in the distance, sunlight glinting off her waves, and a few orinths slipped by in search of flowers, their green and orange carapaces flitting by in a flurry of lacy wings. *Must be a mud nest nearby.*

Everything *seemed* normal.

Still, something was off, but she couldn't quite put her finger on it.

Em slipped back between the edge of the wagon and the wall of trine grass that bounded the road. "There's someone coming on urseback, fast."

That wasn't unusual, though the general lack of the traffic on the road was strange. Triya signaled the other two wagons and slowed hers to a halt. "Caravan?"

Em shook her head. "No. Single rider."

In the silence, they could soon hear the clopping of the urse's shoes, and see the cloud of dust they kicked up. It only slowed at the last minute when the rider looked up at them wide-eyed.

The girl — she couldn't have been more than seventeen or eighteen — was a mess, her blond hair tangled, her dusty face tracked with tears. Her urse wasn't in much better shape, its purple tongue hanging out of the side of its mouth.

Triya climbed down from the wagon, driven by motherly instinct. "Morning. Well met."

The girl stared at her as if she were a phantom that had arisen out of thin air. "Who are you?" The girl's eyes narrowed, and she glanced over her shoulder. As if she were being chased.

"I'm Triya. Tri'Aya. From Gullton." Triya looked down the road, but there nothing else approached. *Nothing I can see, anyhow.* "Who are you? You look a fright."

"Maur'Isa. Of Isa Steading ..." Her voice caught, and then she burst into tears.

More like fourteen, maybe. Triya reached the girl and helped her down from her urse.

"I have to keep going." She shot another look over her shoulder at the valley behind her. "It's not safe back there —"

"You're in no shape to go anywhere." Triya looked around. She knew this area like the back of her hand. "Mes, Es, there's a turnout just ahead. Let's strike out for that."

The strange feeling returned, the sense of wrongness filling the air. Triya shuddered. She had long before learned to trust her gut.

"I can't. I can't go back!" Maur'Isa struggled in her arms.

Triya took the girl's chin in her hands. "Listen to me. We're not taking you back. We're just going a little ways ahead to a spot where we can pull the wagons off the road. We can't sit here and block traffic." Not that there was any traffic to block, but still. There were turn-outs every few kilometers along the roadway for caravans to use to pass one another. "You're safe with us."

"No, I'm not." Nevertheless, the girl allowed herself to be led back to Triya's wagon.

"Mes, can you see to Maur'Isa's urse?"

"Maura," the girl said softly.

Triya flashed her what she hoped was a kindly smile. "To Maura's urse?"

Mes nodded curtly, making room for the girl to sit as she slipped down to the ground, graceful as an eircat. "Yes Mim." She took the urse's reins, rubbing the scruff between its long ears. "We'll get you some water soon."

The wind pushed a couple blue wisps past them. Triya frowned. There were so many this year — did that mean something? She shook her head. *Silly to concern yourself about something so trivial.*

"All right, let's get moving," she called to the other wagons. "We'll take a break at the turn-out, while we sort this out."

Henner and Tomas nodded, and the caravan lurched forward, and Mes led Maura's urse alongside.

Triya's anger at Aik and Desla had slipped right over into anxiety. *What did you two get yourselves into? Get me into?*

She put her arm around the girl, who clung to her side. It made driving her aur harder, but the beast was well-trained, and Maura obviously needed comforting.

In a few minutes they reached the place where the road widened, carving out a space from the surrounding trine grass, and the wagons rumbled off the road into the clearing.

"Come on then." Triya helped the girl down from the wagon bench and led her to the edge of the turn-out, where a couple of wooden hitching posts stood like lonely sentinels. She leaned against one of the cross beams.

Em arrived with a canteen of water and some leftovers from the night before.

Maura took the water and drank it gratefully, almost as quickly as her urse lapped up its share a couple meters away.

"Careful, girl. Not so fast."

Maura nodded and put the canteen down, licking her lips and glancing at the road ahead. "It's too dangerous. I have to keep going." She handed the canteen back and pushed off toward her urse, only making it a couple stumbling steps before she almost tripped and fell.

"You're in no shape to go anywhere." Triya steered her gently back to the hitching posts. "Here, eat something. You must be starving."

The girl's fear warred with her hunger, her gaze shifting nervously from the road to the food being offered, but it took just a moment for hunger to win out. She took a chunk of bread and some of the cave cheese and put them in her mouth. "Thank you."

"You're hungry. You've pushed yourself and your urse too hard." She handed Maura the canteen, and the girl drank more water gratefully.

"Now can I go?" She started to get up again, but Triya pushed her gently back down onto the low fence.

"Not yet." Triya wondered what had her so frightened. She didn't want to proceed blind. "I need you tell us what happened. Don't leave anything out."

Maura swallowed hard, and nodded. "I will."

•   •   •

Aik tossed and turned in his sleep sack, feeling bloated and sick.

Images from the steading flashed through his mind. The forerunners and the way they'd obeyed his will. The strange white domes that looked like coryx. The dead child's hand. Even the bandy fruit trees, their heart-shaped leaves waving in the breeze.

Come. I am waiting for you.

He woke in a cold sweat. Had he imagined the voice? Or was it the godsdamned gauntlet again?

He eased himself up, staring wildly around the strange room. Orange moonlight slipped through the cracks in the squat logs that made up the walls of the safe house. *Safe from what?*

Desla lay next to him, snoring loudly, lost to the world.

What is wrong with me? His stomach rumbled menacingly, and he knew he was going to be sick.

Dressed only in his small clothes, he got up and opened the low door as quietly as he could. He stumbled out of the small shelter, determined not to sick-up in the confined space. From the hitching post nearby, the two urses turned to watch him.

He pushed a little way into the tall stands of trine grass surrounding the safe house and fell to the ground, his stomach seizing painfully. He emptied the half-digested hardtack and dried fruit onto the flattened grass, feeling wretched as the stomach acid burned his mouth.

When the worst of it was out, he dry-retched for a moment more. And then just as quickly as it had begun, it was over. It was awful, the bitter taste of bile in his mouth, but at least his stomach felt better.

He sat back in the dirt and took in a deep breath of the cool night air, then another, trying to calm himself.

In the distance, he could hear the waves of the lake lapping its shores, and the sound of the wind through the trine grass as each stem's three purple blades rubbed together, creating a sound like the flow of a river.

The two moons were chasing one another across the sky overhead, lighting the Highlands in an orange glow.

Other than the waves and the grass, the world was eerily silent.

The calm before the storm?

But there was something else too, a spark in the darkness, too close to be a star.

At first, he thought it was one of the fireflies, come to haunt him. They had a connection with him, even if he hadn't figured out yet what it was.

But no, it was bluish-white, a bright light that bobbed along in the breeze overhead. It sailed past his sight, over the waving fields of purple grass painted black by the moonlight.

A wisp. They were few and far between in this blasted land. He wondered idly where it was going before his own personal circumstances reasserted themselves.

I need water. Something to wash away the vile taste.

He stood and brushed himself off before re-entering the shelter, more of a wooden lean-to than a *house*. He had to bend to fit inside. *At least the voice is leaving me alone.*

Desla was sitting up, her canteen in hand. They'd refilled them in a small brook near the safe house, thank the gods.

"Sorry if I woke you." *I'm lucky to have you.* Without her guidance, he'd have been lost here in this strange place.

"I wasn't sleeping much anyhow." She held the canteen out to him, along with a slice of the bandy fruit they'd harvested earlier. "This will wash down the taste."

He took the canteen and the fruit gratefully. "Thank you." He was surprised she was being so nice to him, after the cold shoulder she'd given him earlier. *Not that I didn't deserve it.*

You all right?" Her eyes glinted in the dimly lit space.

"Yeah. Just a bit of a stomachache." He sipped the water but glared at the fruit in his other hand.

"Eat it. It will help calm your stomach."

"All right." He nibbled at it. It did taste good and helped to wash the acidic taste from his mouth.

"Those supplies have been here for a while, I'd imagine." She rubbed her own midsection. "Bit gurgly myself." As if in response, her stomach rumbled.

He laughed, spitting out a splattering of water. "Yeah, that's probably it." Better than the alternative. He tried not to remember his dreams.

She watched him in the darkness. "You seem more ... you than before." The silence stretched between them as she studied his face. At last, she nodded, as if she'd decided something. "The way you treated that poor woman on the road —"

"I wasn't myself." That was a bit of an understatement.

"Want to talk about it?"

Aik yawned. He was exhausted, and ironically, hungry again. But he didn't dare eat anything else. "Not yet." He handed her back her canteen.

She met his gaze, her eyes narrowing. "You need to let me in. You're carrying too much around on your own."

He grunted. *Women. Always knowing what's good for you.*

"Aik, you promised to tell me." There was more than a little exasperation in her voice. "Let it out. You were acting like an aur's ass, and I want to know why."

He clenched his jaw. "Can you be a little more blunt?"

That got a smile out of her. "No, I think that was just blunt enough."

He chuckled. "Yeah, I guess that's fair." He *did* owe her an explanation, even if he didn't truly understand it himself. *Now's as good a time as any.* "It's the gauntlet. Ever since I put it on ..." He hesitated. This was going to sound crazy.

"Go on." Her voice was steady, encouraging.

He bit his lip. "Sometimes, there's this voice in my head, telling me what it wants me to do."

"Fine, if you don't want to tell me —"

"I'm serious. It — makes me do these things sometimes. It scares the hell out of me."

Her mouth worked as if she were about to say something, and her eyes went wide. At last she managed to get it out. "Holy henchaballs, you're serious."

"As a thunderclap."

There was more than a little fear in her eyes now, and she edged back away from him. "Aik, That's ... not good."

He laughed harshly "That's all you have to say?" Though he wasn't sure what he'd been hoping for.

"You just told me you hear voices in your head." Her knuckles were clenched on the cloth of her sleep sack. "Are you going to hurt me?"

He snorted. "No. I've got it under control. Mostly." It hadn't made him do anything bad. Not really. And he'd snapped out of it on his own the afternoon before, hadn't he? "I'd never hurt you. Besides, I'll bet you could kick my ass all the way to Solsday if I tried."

Some of the color returned to her face. "Solsday? More like Martasday."

A faint smile crossed his face. "Martasday, then. But seriously, I would never hurt you."

She hugged her chest. "I believe you. But this it scares the hencha berries out of me." She let go of the sleep sack. "I trust you, Aik. But what if you're not *you*?"

He shuddered. "I don't know. I've been wrestling with this for days. How do I know what's me, and what's the gauntlet?"

She put a warm hand on his knee. "Are *you* scared?"

He met her worried gaze. "Every moment of every day."

She took his hands. "That must be horrible."

The courage she displayed, overcoming her own fear to comfort *him*, almost knocked him over. "What if it takes me over? What if ... I can't stop it?" It felt good to finally tell someone, to have someone to talk it over with.

Now he knew what Raven was going through. He just wished they were together so he could tell *him*.

She squeezed his hand. "We'll figure it out. Just ... tell me if something changes."

"All right." He owed her that much. "Guard's honor."

"And I'll do the same." She glanced at his pack. "Show me that shiny thing now."

He blinked. "Shiny thing?"

"That little silver ball you keep in your pack."

"Ah, Spin." She was trying to distract him. But she was probably curious too, just as he'd been. "I can do that."

It was good to change the subject. He retrieved the little sphere from his pack. "Spin, say hello to Desla here."

She shot him an *are you crazy?* look.

Spin was silent.

Aik frowned. "Spin?" He shook the little sphere. "Come on, buddy, don't make me look like an idiot here."

"Look, you're tired. We both are. Maybe we should get some sleep."

"I'm not crazy —"

Spin lit up, bathing the room in golden light. "I heard you the first time, Chief." He sounded surly, like he'd just been awakened from a good dream.

He raised an eyebrow. *Do you sleep at night?*

Her frown turned to something else. "What in the seven hells?" Her fear returned, painting her face white as she pushed away from him again, her back against the thick wooden logs of the shelter.

"It's all right. He won't hurt you." He remembered the first time Spin had talked to him. It had scared him half out of his shell too. "Raven ... gave him to me." It was close enough to the truth.

"There's a 'he' in there?" She peered at the sphere, her face still, pale. "What is it ... he?"

"Raven says it's the mind of the last ship that came to Tharassas from Earth. Right, Spin?"

"Sure, Chief. Whatever you say."

He frowned. Spin *was* in a foul mood. He hadn't even known Spin could *have* moods, other than his general snarkiness.

"Is it ... he dangerous?" She swallowed hard. She looked at Spin, then back at him.

He laughed in spite of himself. "Only to your self-esteem. Go ahead, touch him."

"Oh yeah, touch the cute little ball. What am I, a house cat?"

Her hand hovered above his silver skin. "Do you mind if I touch you, Spin?"

Golden light played over her face. "No, I don't mind." The whole tone of his voice changed, softened.

He likes her. That was new, too.

"Thank you, Spin." She reached out to touch the silver sphere, then pulled back as if she were afraid of being burned. "It's ... like magic."

"Not magic, friend of the chief. 'Any sufficiently advanced technology is indistinguishable from magic.' One of the great authors of the twentieth century said that." Spin's voice was different when he talked to Desla. Almost as if he wanted to impress her.

It caused ... feelings in Aik's chest. He frowned. *Why should I be jealous of a silver sphere? And for Desla?* "Sure."

She took the familiar from him gingerly. "I'll take your word for it." She peered closely at Spin's metal shell, poking at one of his lights.

"At least buy me dinner before you go prodding at my privates."

She snickered. "Sorry, um, Spin." Her eyes met his. "This was Raven's? How did he get it?"

"*Him.* How did he get *him.*" Spin sounded seriously annoyed.

Aik frowned. "He said he found Spin out at Landfield, where the ship crashed. But *he* has memories of Jas and Sera too, after. So I'm not sure that's true."

"Sera." Spin's voice sounded deflated. "I miss Sera."

The poor thing was lonely. He had stuffed Spin into his pack without giving him a second thought, as if he was just a thing, a possession to be carried around with his shirts, pants and underwear. "I'm sorry, Spin. I'm afraid I've neglected you."

Spin flashed brightly. "Thank you, Chief. That means a lot." Spin paused, and the lights flickered around his middle. "Are you my friend?"

Desla looked up at him, eyes narrowing. "Well, are you? Answer the poor thing."

Was it just his imagination, or had Spin's voice hitched a little when he asked? "Um … sure. We're friends." Admitting it was strange, but he'd grown fond of the little imp since Raven had left them alone together.

She turned her attention back to Spin. "You must know so many things." She was staring at him the way Triya had, hunger in her eyes. "Imagine what he could teach us."

It made him a little uncomfortable. "For now, he's going to teach us how to get back to sleep." He plucked the sphere adroitly from her grasp.

"Hey!" Both Desla and Spin said it simultaneously.

"Spin, we're all tired. I don't care if you sleep … or even know if you can. But Desla and I need to get back to bed."

"Yes, Chief." Spin's lights flickered off.

It was her turn to yawn. "This isn't over. I want to know all about it."

"About *him.*" Spin practically grumbled it.

She laughed. "About you." She stared at the little sphere in wonder for a moment, then shook her head. "But you're right. We both need to get some sleep if we're going to be awake for this quest of yours tomorrow."

Aik dipped his head. "Yes, mim." He set Spin on a folded shirt next to his bedside — it didn't feel right to just put him on the dirt floor — and stripped off his dirty underwear to slip back into the sleep sack. "In the morning, then."

"And Aik?"

"Yeah?" She'd taken it all much better than he'd expected.

"No more secrets."

"Promise."

She settled back into her own sleep sack, and in moments was snoring softly.

"Chief?" Spin's voice was pitched just for him.

He opened his eyes. "What, Spin?"

"Did you … ever lose someone?"

He wondered what was going on inside the little sphere. How the world looked from such an alien perspective. Wondering if he ever wanted more. "I lost Raven."

Spin was silent for a moment. His golden lights spun around, lighting up the safe house walls. "I hope you find him again." The little familiar's voice was filled with melancholy.

"You all right, Spin?"

"I'm fine. Just fine." The lights went out, leaving him in darkness, feeling more alone than ever.

•　　　•　　　•

"What does it want you to do?" Desla's question broke him out of his reverie. She was staring at his right arm with that speculative look he'd learned meant trouble.

They'd been on the road for a few hours now, heading north toward the mysterious mountain. The white domes appeared near the road sporadically, but the trine grass still mostly held sway.

Aik pulled out a piece of bacca root and chewed on it, thinking it through. "To go North. To Anghar Mor."

Her eyes widened. "Why? Because Raven is there?"

He shook his head. "I *hope* Raven's there. But no. I don't *know* why. Just that it has to do with what we saw at Isa Steading yesterday." He took a deep breath and then sighed heavily. "It was seeing that … child … that snapped me out of it." He shuddered. The poor kid … and the rest of their family too. He knew now why Maur'Isa had been in such a hurry to flee. "I can still feel it … the tug. All the time. But it doesn't control me." *Not right now, anyhow.* Who knew how long his semi-freedom would last?

"What does Spin say?" She glanced at his pocket. "You did ask him, right?" Her tone said she doubted he had the smarts to have come to such an obvious conclusion.

Ouch. "Yes, I asked him. He shared a memory with me. Of Sera. Queen Jas told her about a creature who wore it into battle."

"Ah." She looked away, staring at the clouds to the north that darkened the sky there to a forest green.

"It doesn't scare you?" He'd half expected her to turn tail and gallomp back to Gap Station.

Her gaze flicked back to him, and she took a moment before answering. "Like I said last night, it scares the holy green hell out of me. But what good does fear do?" He could feel her staring at him. "Could you turn around and come back to Gullton with me, if you wanted to?"

He thought about it. Sure, he could ignore the pull, for a while. But the mere thought of turning around made his skin feel like it had been set on fire. "No, I don't think so."

He sighed. This thing had its claws in him, deep, and he'd have to see it through to the end. Even if it killed him. It was a relief to finally admit it. There was power in surrendering to the inevitable.

"Then we'll just have to see it through and make the best of it." She didn't seem happy about it, exactly, but she said it with a steely resolution that he admired.

Coming over a rise, the sight that confronted them made him pull his urse to a halt.

A seemingly never-ending line of people filled the road — young and old and everything in-between. They were on urseback, riding aur, packed into wagons, or on foot. The refugees carried little — a few bulging sacks were piled onto the carts between and under the people — and they had the resigned look of those who have seen their own mortality firsthand.

He knew that look.

As the first of the hollow-eyed Steaders trudged past, Aik shared a startled glance with Desla.

"We should help them." Her demeanor brooked no argument.

He shook his head, defying her anyway, and this time it had nothing to do with the gauntlet. "We can't. What can we do? Share our food? There are too many of them." He backed Ursey off the road, into the grasses, to let the strange procession pass.

She did the same and slipped down from the saddle. She handed her urse's reins to him. "Still, we must." She opened her carry sack and took out some of the hardtack she'd packed up in the safe house. "There will be more for us tonight at our next stop."

"And if there's not?"

Her angry gaze told him he'd failed a test. "You can survive a day or two without eating. These poor folks ... they've lost everything."

The gauntlet's tug was insistent, pulling him northward, but he could resist it, for a time. Besides, they wouldn't get far until the refugees passed.

She was right. He knew she was.

With a grunt, he slipped down to the ground and pulled out his own meager supply of food, including the aur jerky he'd been saving for lunch.

She handed some hardtack to a woman of indeterminate age, covered in dust and grime. "What happened? Where are you going?"

"They came last night. Horrible things." She looked over her shoulder and shivered as if the Death Bringer himself were after her. "They attacked the aur first, and then they took my daughter." The woman held back a sob, squeezing a little blond boy's hand tightly. He couldn't have been more than five. "Jasper here was sleeping in the loft, thank the hencha. We got out and ran." She pushed a stray lock of hair behind her ear, then kissed the boy's forehead.

Desla knelt to talk to him. "Jasper, would you like some fruit?" She held up a few dried hencha berries.

Jasper looked up at his mother, who nodded. "Yes please." He held out his little hand, and she placed three of the red ones there.

"These are sweet, but you'll want to save them. Chew on one for a bit. You'll see what I mean."

Aik squeezed her shoulder. She had a way with kids, and it was clear how much the poor boy needed a little kindness.

I should want *to help.* The old Aik would have jumped at the chance, no matter how little he had. No matter what it cost him. But the delay ate at him, stuck here with the refugees when he should be moving forward.

Why help these people? They're all dead anyhow.

He cringed. The voice had been silent for a while, and he'd had the foolish, hopeful notion that it was gone for good. *Why? What's coming?*

But the voice in his head went silent again.

Bit by bit, it was stealing away his humanity, his loyalty, all the things that made him *Aik.*

Angry, he pushed back in the only way he knew how. He could make it wait. "Here, take this." He handed some of his own precious jerky to a man with no shoes, only socks that were wearing down to nothing on his feet. "Wait for a sec," he told the Steader, and went back to his carry sack. He pulled out his spare set of boots and handed it to the man. "We're about the same size."

The man looked at the footwear for a moment, as if he couldn't quite comprehend them. Then he took them, marveling at the leather as if they were the finest new thing from one of the caravans, although they were worn and old. "Bless the hencha. And bless you." The man threw his arms around Aik, hugging him tightly.

When the refugee finally let him go, he sank to the ground and pulled on the boots, grimacing as he tied them.

Poor guy probably has blisters. Des was right. There wasn't much they could do, but they could do something. *How did I forget that?*

For the umpteenth time, he cursed himself for trying on the gauntlet. It was changing him, slowly but surely, into someone else. He could feel it, poking at him as if testing his armor. As they witnessed the passing caravan and helped where they could, the pressure to move on grew, prodding him to wrap up this useless act.

Still, he resisted it, handing out almost every bit of his food and supplies, keeping only the things he absolutely had to have. *Where will you all go?*

The Highlands were no longer safe, and if they fell ... *Scratch that. They've already fallen.* He wondered how the ce'faine were faring to the east and south.

They ran out of useful supplies to give, and still the procession continued. He counted at least five hundred Steaders, every one of them with a hollow look of half fear and half hardened resignation. As the rest of the refugees passed, he and Desla stood by as mute witnesses, a duty that felt as important as the assistance they'd offered earlier.

Spin was quiet too, though every now and then he stuck a feeler out of his pocket to see what was happening.

If any of the refugees noticed, they gave no sign. Most were lost in their own misery.

When the last of the stragglers had passed, Aik turned to find Desla in tears. She'd kept up a brave face during the whole affair, but now her emotions were plain on her face.

"It's too much."

He nodded, though he couldn't *feel* it like she did. Instead, there was only the dogged determination to get on with it.

Maybe the voice was right. *The only way to finish this thing — whatever it is — is to get to the mountain.* And maybe Raven really would be there, waiting — stranger things had happened. At least it would be an end to the relentless *pull*.

Still, he could spare some of his dwindling humanity for Desla. He pulled her in for a hug. "I know," he whispered. "I know."

His own transformation was far worse than Raven's, which had been in body only.

He was losing his soul.

Raven, will you still love me when I find you? And a darker thought. *Will I still deserve it?*

"You're a good man, Aik. Remember that." She squeezed him tightly.

He shuddered. *Maybe so. But for how much longer?*

•   •   •

Spin brooded.

He'd been programmed to help humans. He'd always *known* that. Believed, even. And it had never bothered him. He was grateful that someone had decided to make him, to bring him into existence. And he loved his charges.

But now …

All of it was a lie.

He wasn't Spin the AI. He was Tyson, or at least the ruined shell of Tyson, a man who had once walked on two legs and lived and breathed, who had loved and fathered a beautiful child.

And this place … He knew the whole long, sordid history of the Tharassan Colony now — founded by white supremacists who abhorred people like him. Where most of the people were blond and blue-eyed. There were those like Raven who were different — inevitable contamination of the "pure" gene pool by the exotic visitors on the long runs out from Earth with supplies.

I don't belong here.

And yet Australia, back on Earth, had started out as a penal colony, but most Australians were not criminals.

How many generations did the stains of your ancestors last?

Aik and Desla — both blond and blue-eyed — were fast asleep, each full of their own turmoil and troubles, but looking peaceful in the golden glow of his light. *Do I hold you accountable for what happened more than four hundred years ago?* At least two hundred years before his own birth.

It's all just useless anger. The objects of it were long dead — the original colonists, the loan sharks who had brought him to ruin, and the company who had saved his family by taking away everything he had ever cared for. All gone to dust now, except for himself.

Nevertheless, it raged in him like molten lava, coloring his processes, making him moody and brittle. He wasn't operating at full potential, and yet he couldn't help himself.

I am what I am.

But what was that? Human? Machine? A little of each? *And what will I become, now that I know?*

He'd freed himself from one cage only to fall into another.

Is this enough? Being trapped inside a silver shell without even a ship to fly? Grounded and subject to the whims of his self-styled owners?

They meant well. He knew that, and yet it didn't help.

Desla reminded him so much of Sera, though they looked nothing alike. Both had the same gentle kindness, the same concern for others that often overrode their own good sense.

And Aik and Raven were good people, even if Raven stole for a living and Aik was shadowed by something dark.

He had no answers. But regardless of his own personal feelings, he had a responsibility to these two humans, and to Raven, if they ever met again. To his friends.

Reluctantly he shelved his anger, removing it from his day-to-day programming. He didn't excise it entirely, instead tucking it away carefully, like a precious possession, where he could bring it out again one day when he needed it. He'd earned it, and he needed to explore it more.

Just not right now.

Feeling more at peace, he shut down all but his autonomous features and dreamed of his own little girl.

Her laughter brought him a little peace.

7

VERENT IN THE STREETS

S ILYA TOUCHED THE BLACK WOOD of her staff for reassurance. It glowed where her fingers brushed it, leaving behind a lingering blue light.

Kerrick had left first thing, but not before leaning over to give her a lingering, regretful kiss. Something had changed between them for the better. It was time to let go of Aik, of the past that had hemmed her in.

Kerrick was her future.

Enough daydreaming. She closed her eyes, practicing one of the focusing exercises Dor had taught her, drawing on the strength of the hencha to keep going.

She was knee-deep in notes and orders and reports, all blending into a snowstorm of hencha-fiber paper that flew in and out of her office as if of its own accord. She had so much to do. Supplies to order, stores to inventory and relocate to the caverns, rosters to draw, as hush-hush as possible.

And all for naught. Word had gotten out from the disastrous meeting with the Council a few days before that something was amiss, and the people were starting to panic. Dor brought her reports of shortages as people began panic-buying, and a full-scale riot had nearly broken out at the Open Market on Redhawk Spine over a loaf of bread, of all things.

"Dor, I need the population figures for Vulture Spine!"

"Just a moment, Mim!" Dor's voice drifted over from her own office, one door down the hall.

Moving Dor up to a space next to the Hencha Queen's rooms had been one of her best ideas. Not that the ideas were coming so easily these days. She was blinded by a lack of news about real world events.

And yet she was buried in information. She needed to be an army, not just one woman.

Sister Tela had told her about how the original colonists — and their ancestors — had stored and organized things. Something called a *computer. I need a computer.*

Not that she'd even recognize one if she saw it or know how to use it. There hadn't been one in the boxes that Kerrick had unearthed beneath the Temple. Sister Tela had finished her inventory of the mysterious stash the night before, with some initiate help.

She fished the inventory out, sliding her finger down the neatly lettered list. Glass bottles — they could use those in the caverns for storage — water, maybe? Long talkers — she'd already used those. Small explosive devices with instructions. That had shocked her.

Still, they might come in handy —

"Here you go, Mim." Dor bustled into her office, reaching over a teetering pile of agriculture reports Silya had been meaning to go through.

"Thank you, Dor. There's a cavern under the spine with an entrance near the Wall of the Dead that might be big enough to hold most from Vulture Spine ..." But for how long? They couldn't hole-up underground forever. Food would run out first, and then water.

Fresh air was a concern too — so many people breathing the same air — she'd heard reports of miners trapped underground who had perished before they could be dug out.

And if any of those fireflies get in ... She shuddered.

Time was rushing by, heedless of her own wants and needs.

Dor had promised her the flitter would be ready by noon. She wanted to take a run out over the Heartland later in the day, and maybe a longer one the next day to the Highlands. *I need more time. And resources, and energy and ...*

"Mim!"

Her attention snapped back to the present. "Sorry. It's just … overwhelming."

Dor cleared a chair, setting the pile of papers there on the ground.

"Careful, Dor. Those are —"

"Important." Dor snorted. "I know, I know. It's *all* important." She settled into the heavy flopwood chair with a *humph* and glared at Silya. "Mim, you need a break. You're still recovering from what you did yesterday for Fess'Ima. That was truly a miracle."

She shook her head. "It was the hencha. Not me." Sometimes she despaired that she was just a vessel. And what if she burned herself out? *Will the hencha just choose someone else?*

"You don't give yourself enough credit. Everyone else left that poor girl for dead, but you gave her almost everything you had, and brought her back."

She barely heard Dor. Her mind was racing on to other things. "There has to be a better way." Her mother was like a Guard drill sergeant — she would have had this all organized by now. *Triya, I wish you were here.*

We can help.

The touch of the hencha was unexpected, but along with it, a welcome warmth spread through her, like immersing herself in bath water. Silya took a deep breath and closed her eyes. "How?"

"Excuse me, Mim?"

Her eyes opened. "Sorry, it's the hencha. A moment, please, Dor?" Her stomach rumbled. "And maybe a fresh cup of hot akka?" She held out her empty ceramic mug.

Dor frowned, but she nodded and stood, taking the mug and backing out of the room with a worried look on her face. "I'll request something for you for breakfast too."

"Bless you. I could eat half an aur." Dor always looked out for her, even when she didn't know she needed it.

"Of course, mim." She vanished down the corridor, whistling the Noninalya.

She pushed her chair back from the desk and lifted the staff, embracing it with both hands. The full presence of the hencha settled within her, and she closed her eyes again. *How can you help?*

We can remember for you.

She sat back in her chair, startled. *What do you mean?*

These hencha leaves — we can remember all the human scribblings on them.

Hencha leaves ... Silya looked around, confused, and then it hit her. They meant all the papers on her desk.

She stared at the stacks, trying to wrap her mind around what they were offering her. Somehow, they could absorb all the information. *Like a computer?*

Though she was pretty sure computers hadn't been plant-based — they'd been machines — more like the long talkers, probably. Kerrick had taken one apart, gently, and they'd looked at its mysterious innards, mystified at what they were or how the thing worked. *How much can you remember?*

All of it. The hencha opened themselves to her, and she could feel them — no, see them — in all their glory.

There were thousands ... hundreds of thousands of them, little points of light, all connected to one another and to her.

You are a computer.

Computer? The hencha were confused. Then they plucked the definition from her mind, and shifted to a heavy amusement. *In a sense, yes.*

But how will I read all of this, in time? She looked at the reports on her desk. There were too many. She was still only one woman. *I can't ...*

There are others who can hear us.

Her eyes flew open. That was new. *There are more?* She staggered at the implications. Were there a bunch of other potential Hencha Queens out there? *How many?*

Enough. We will call them to you.

She frowned. *Call them to me?* This was crazy.

She'd finally half convinced herself that she was special, or at least that she was uniquely suited to the post, however unsuited she sometimes felt. *But if there are others, why am I the Hencha Queen?*

Because we chose you.

She bit her lip. It was a singularly unsatisfying answer. *All right. Send me the initiates —*

They're not all initiates.

Well then. The hencha had been keeping their own secrets, apparently.

Still, why should it be such a surprise? No one knew why some people could talk to the hencha while others couldn't, so they were probably scattered throughout the general population — bakers, sailors, Guards … even thieves. She wasn't going to solve that mystery today. *Send them. What do they need to do?*

Absorb the information. Then we will know it, and you will too.

Absorb the information. They must mean "read the reports." *Why did you never tell me this before?*

You never asked. Was that sense of amusement back in the hencha's tone?

I didn't ask now. Or did I? How many other things hadn't she known to ask?

A sharp knock shattered her reflection and the hencha withdrew, leaving her feeling brittle and alone. She set the staff back against the wall. "Come in, Dor. I hope you brought three cups of akka on that tray." She could use the burst of energy.

The door eased open. "Sorry, Mim, it's Coral. Not Dor." The initiate slipped inside, looking around at all the paper, her eyes wide.

"Yes, Cor'Lea? What can I help you with?" The girl — young woman, she corrected herself — was usually more direct.

"I don't know, Mim. I just … I needed to come here." She blinked in confusion. "I heard a voice in my head."

"Ah." The hencha were good as their word, though she hadn't expected the new arrivals to begin so quickly. Still, Coral would be the perfect one to organize things. "I think you were sent to help me —"

Dor pushed open the door with her back, carrying a tray with a mug of steaming akka and some foldovers and cave cheese, looking around for a place to set them. "Mim, there's a Guard at the Temple door saying he needs to see you."

"Kerrick? Send him up."

Dor shook her head. "It's not Kerrick."

The hencha did say that they're not all initiates. "Ah. Take that breakfast into my rooms, and ask Verla to prepare enough for … twenty? We're going to need more tables and chairs too."

"Mim?" Dor frowned, her eyebrow raising.

"We're about to get some assistance." She got up and crossed the small room to open the door to her own quarters, taking her staff with her — she felt naked without it. "I'll explain as we go." She sighed with relief.

Help was on the way.

•   •   •

"Are you sure this is a good idea? I could stay here at the Temple, supervise the readers." Dor was staring at the flitter and wringing her hands.

The gangly mechanical contraption sat on the training field, above the rushing of the river past the edge of Raven Spine. It was a beautiful day, the green sky flecked with little clouds that pushed their way east like wingless birds.

"Coral already has things well in hand." The girl was an organizational marvel, ordering up additional tables and chairs and getting everyone set up in the throne room — Guards, sisters, bakers, and bricklayers. "I need you with me."

"Yes, mim." Dor didn't sound convinced.

Her own heart pounded, but she took a deep breath and tried to keep herself calm. Her firm grasp on her staff helped too. She could draw on its solidity and peace, easing her nerves. "Besides, it's perfectly safe. And we're just taking a test run today out over the Heartland." She'd wanted to see the Highlands today, but she couldn't spare the time. Tomorrow would have to be soon enough.

"That ... contraption looks like a deathtrap." Sister Dor side-eyed the flitter. She tugged at Silya's golden robes. "Just ... promise me we'll be careful. No unnecessary risks."

Silya rolled her eyes. *It's not like I'm going to be flying the thing.* "Of course, Mim'Ala." She made a mock curtsey, like she used to do as an initiate. "You need to relax, Dor. We'll be just fine. Didn't Yen'Ela ride in it?"

Dor shook her head emphatically. "She was scared to death of the thing. She —"

The sound of the little craft's iridescent rotors spinning up cut off whatever else she was about to say. The craft had been repaired and patched repeatedly. Jas had described the flitter as a giant orinth, but to her critical eye, it looked more like a decrepit cherry fly, sagging on the landing pad. It had to be two hundred years old if it was a day.

Only two were still in existence that she knew of. The city owned the other one, but rarely flew it anymore.

What was I thinking? "Maybe you're right —"

"Mim Aya!" A man maybe five years older than her, descended from the "cockpit" of the small craft, a broad grin on his handsome face.

At least she knew what to call it. Sister Tela had given her a crash course on the operation of the flying machine. She winced. *Bad choice of words.* "Mas …"

"Ost. Fen'Ost." He put out his hand. The air from the flitter blades ruffled his blond hair.

"Sil'Aya." She shook it, and her cheeks flushed.

"Yes, I know who you are, Mim." He winked at Dor. "And you, mistress of the Temple."

Of course he does. She felt like an idiot. Who didn't know the Hencha Queen?

Even Dor seemed taken by the flitter pilot, fanning herself. Or was that just nerves?

"Come with me." She squeezed Dor's shoulders. "You know the valley better than I do. You can tell me what's what. It will only take an hour or two."

"I'd *love* to tell you what's what …" she grumbled, and glanced up at the whirling blades, then over her shoulder at the Temple in the distance. "I really should keep an eye on your readers. Coral's so young …"

Dor had been alarmed at letting "perfect strangers" read the Temple's reports, even under the guidance of Coral and the hencha mind.

Silya closed her eyes. She could almost *feel* the hencha absorbing all that information. *Scratch that. I can feel it.* It was taking in all the alien — to it — concepts, assembling into a vast … database? *Is that the word Tela used?* For her to *access.* The archivist had been fascinated by the concept, which she'd read about in an old book in the archives.

So many new ideas. They would drown her if she let them. She needed to get away, if only for a little while. "Coral has it well in hand. Come on. I insist." She took Dor's hand, pulled her along, and climbed into the craft after Fen'Ost.

She settled into the seat next to the pilot, closed the flitter door behind them, and laid her staff in the space between them.

Dor took her place behind them, muttering under her breath.

Silya glanced back at her. "What was that?"

"I was saying, remind me to pick a different Hencha Queen when we get back."

She laughed. "I might take you up on it. It would be nice to be just an initiate again." It was a burden she would be happy to pass on to someone more qualified.

"Strap in." Fen'Ost demonstrated, snapping his belt into place. "You just press here to release it."

She helped Dor figure out her belt, then buckled her own. "You're sure this thing is safe?" It was meticulously clean, but it showed its age on the inside too, its once-smooth panels warped and discolored by time.

"Yes, Mim." The pilot ran his hand across the console, as proud as a newborn's father. "My family has run these for generations. One of my great, great grandfathers flew Jas from Corinth to Gullton in one of them. Gully Town, it was then." Fen'Ost ran a check of the flitter's systems.

"Please call me Silya. Not 'Sil'Aya' or 'Mim.' No need for formality here." If she was going to put her life in the flitter pilot's hands, he would damned well treat her like a *normal* person.

He flashed her a big grin. "Silya it is. You can call me Fentin, then." He leaned back and flashed Dor a reassuring smile. "I checked the craft out myself after I installed the replacement part from the Machinists' Guild. You two have nothing to worry about."

Dor said nothing.

"Hold tight. Here we go."

She wasn't sure what to expect as he eased the "joystick" — she was especially proud of knowing that one — forward.

Her stomach lurched at the motion as the craft lifted up smoothly. It was as if the ground left them, not the other way around. She held onto the armrest for dear life as they shot straight upward. Still, she couldn't help but peek at the world below.

She gasped. The view was quite literally breathtaking.

The spines shrank below them, their edges coming into focus as the flitter ascended. First Raven Spine, the white circle of the Temple standing out on this end. The rest of the spine trailed away into the distance between two branches of the Elsp, her muddy red waters churning on either side. Then Eagle Spine to the north and Peregrine Spine to the south came into view, followed by the last two — Vulture and Redhawk, whose mansions looked like toy houses from so high.

After a moment she forgot to be afraid and let go of the armrest, leaning forward to take it all in.

Fentin glanced in her direction. "Want to take a spin over the city?"

"Yes, please." It was glorious. All of the city, spread out below her in its magnificent, complicated, messy detail. "Dor, are you seeing this?"

"Not looking, Mim." Her voice was tense.

"Really, Dor, *this* scares you? The woman who faced down two hungry verent?" It wasn't *strictly true*, but she had been in the room, and Silya couldn't resist teasing her.

She looked over her shoulder, and Dor's eyes opened, just a crack.

"Seriously, you have to see this."

Dor growled, but she opened her eyes and leaned over to look out the window. She gazed out at the city below, then crossed her arms and snapped her eyes shut again. "All right, I looked. Satisfied?"

Silya hid a smile. "I suppose it's good enough. For now."

Fentin took them west toward the sea, above the central spine. Below, work crews were reconstructing some of the buildings that had burned after the first shake, and people were milling back and forth along Grindell Lane. Some stopped to stare at the craft, pointing up at them.

Flitters were a rare sight these days.

She tried to imagine what it had been like for the first settlers, when they'd landed out at what was now Landfield, Gullton's suburban district. Crossing the stark divide that separated stars, coming down onto a new world after decades of travel. Such a beautiful, lush world.

Up ahead, the black, imposing bulk of the Council Hall came into view, and to its left, the ancient hydroelectric dam that had powered the city in its early days. That had been one of Yen'Ela's projects, getting the old generators working again, and the reason they had electric lights in the Temple.

The flitter slipped past the edge of the city, and Fentin brought the craft around toward Heaven's Reach, just to the north. The mid-air swing did funny things to her stomach, and she closed her eyes, willing it to calm down.

They passed over the imposing Wall of the Dead, and she said a prayer to her father's soul. How far she'd come since that sad, lonely day two years past, when she'd interred his ashes in the wall under leaden skies.

Soon they were passing over the remnants of the Old Bridge. Its destruction, just a week earlier, had been in another lifetime. She made a mental note to look into recovering the iron from the wreckage, if they survived the current crisis.

She glanced back at Dor, who was looking out the other window at the tall peaks of Heaven's Reach, gaping.

She looked away, not wanting to make Dor close her eyes again. "Can we go out over the Valley?"

"Of course, Mim. Impressive, isn't it?"

Silya nodded. "It's breathtaking." *This is what gully birds must feel like.* Soaring above the city as if they owned it.

The hencha mind surged inside her own, soaking it up with her, seeming to enjoy her own giddy glee at the sight.

They slipped past the edge of the city and out over Landfield and the Elsp, where the river tumbled down a long waterfall. The homes on this side of the river were smaller than the mansions along the spine, clustered along the roads like campers huddled around a fire. The roof shingles were made of white stone mined in Heaven's Reach by the Miners' Guild and carted down to the city.

So many pieces that all had to work together to make the city — and society — function.

Which brought her back to the night's Council meeting. She had to find a way to convince them once and for all of the danger. Time was running out, and there was only so much the Temple could do on its own to prepare for what was coming.

For now, she just wanted to forget it all and enjoy the experience, a rare moment of peace amongst the onrushing madness.

Gullton receded behind them, and they soared over the broad valley between Heaven's Reach in the north and the distant peaks of the Onyx Mountains to the south. Somewhere down there lay Corinth, Jas's home, now a bustling town in its own right. And beyond those mountains? A vast, uncharted desert. *Does anyone live there?*

Still, it was the Heartland itself that called to her. The Valley was filled with hencha gatherings, thousands upon thousands of plants, all swaying to their own internal music. If she closed her eyes she could hear it, a strange alien melody that rose and fell like waves against the cliffs.

The blades above them sputtered, and the craft dropped half a meter before recovering. She gripped the armrest again, shooting a worried glance at Fentin. Behind her, Dor had gone white as a sheet.

"Nothing to worry about. Just a hiccup." He tapped the console. "She likes to keep us on our toes."

She gave him a stern look.

"I'll give her a thorough going-over before tomorrow's trip."

"Better." Though he'd already done that for this outing, hadn't he?

Fentin flashed her a grin. "She's an old lass, a bit temperamental, but we work well together."

"Tomorrow's trip?" Dor's voice sounded strangled.

"Yes. I'm going up to the Highlands to take a look for myself at what's going on."

"Silya … you can't …"

"You don't have to come." Why couldn't Dor understand how necessary this was? *I have to see for myself.*

"That's not my point. We *need* you. If something happens to you and you don't come back …"

She closed her eyes, determined not to say something hurtful. Dor was just worried about her. *I don't have to be like my mother.* Not in everything.

She turned to look at her aide again. Her friend.

The poor woman white-knuckled the armrests of her chair as if her life depended on it.

Silya squeezed her hand. "I'll be careful. I promise."

"It's not just you I'm worried about." Dor closed her own eyes, her fear plain on her face.

Silya took pity on her. "That's enough for today, Fentin. Take us home." After all, she'd done what she wanted to do. No need to prolong Dor's torture.

She didn't miss the grateful sigh that slipped Dor's lips.

On the way back, they followed the course of the Elsp — from up here, the passage that had taken her and Kerrick a day passed by in the course of a few minutes. *Such a marvelous machine. I wish we had more of them.*

Up in the foothills of Heaven's Reach, she thought she caught a glimpse of the Manor, its sandstone walls blending into the rock behind it. So much had transpired in such a short time since she'd been there.

I hope Triya writes again soon. She wasn't used to worrying about her mother. Tri'Aya could take care of herself in normal times. She was one of the most capable people Silya knew. But these times were anything but normal.

A shadow fell over the flitter.

She frowned. There were no clouds in the sky.

She peered up through the slightly cloudy "windshield" — another term she'd picked up in her quick study. Something long and sleek passed by far above, headed for Gullton by the look of things.

Two somethings.

Verent. What were they doing here? As far as she knew, they never ventured into the Heartland, especially in broad daylight. Not since they took Raven. "Did you see that?"

Fentin nodded. "Yes, Mim. I'd guess it's those verent things everyone's talking about?"

"Everyone's talking about them? But how ...?" *Ah. The Council.* She'd told them all about the giant beasts. Word must have leaked. "What are they saying?"

Fentin shuddered. "That they're huge beasties with teeth as long as my leg. That they steal children in the middle of the night for snacks. That —"

She bit her lip. "That's quite enough." There were some bits of truth in there. They *did* have big teeth. Not as long as a leg maybe, but long enough. And they *had* stolen someone away in the night, though he wasn't a child.

She snorted. *Well, maybe they* do *have that part right.* But she sincerely hoped they hadn't eaten the thief. "Can we go any faster?"

Dor groaned from the back seat.

"There's a heaving pouch back there under the seat, if you need it, Mim," Fentin said over his shoulder, and turned back to Silya. "I can goose her on a little, but this craft wasn't built for speed."

Or defense. She felt suddenly vulnerable and exposed up here. "Just get us back to Gullton as quickly as you can, and follow those verent." She reached back to pat Dor's leg.

Dor groaned again and grabbed the pouch.

Silya turned away before she could see the results.

A scant ten minutes later, the flying craft alighted a block away from City Hall. The location of the action was evident by the large crowd that had gathered in Founder's Square. The arrival of the flitter, which usually would have been an occasion of some note, merited barely a glance from the crowd.

"Thanks, Fentin." She squeezed the man's shoulder, wondering if Jas had felt like this when she'd returned to solid ground. "Please do run another check on everything. It will make Dor here feel better about our flight tomorrow." *And me too.*

"Of course, Mim. And I'll … take care of cleaning that pouch."

"So sorry, Mas Ost." A little color crept back into Dor's face.

"Don't worry about it. It happens to most of us, the first time."

Good man. There were so few of them who worked for the Temple. She'd have to rethink that little bit of policy too. "Come on, Dor. Let's go see the verent." She climbed down to the ground and helped Dor out of the craft.

Dor's face was pale, but she'd recovered her composure admirably.

Silya flashed her a reassuring smile. "Ready?"

"Tight as a theolin string, Mim." She said it with more conviction than she looked like she felt.

The mood of the crowd was more curious than frightful, which she judged to be a good thing. "Excuse me."

People at the edge of the assembly turned to scowl at her, but then backed away when they saw who she was.

"It's the Queen."

"Look, it's her!"

"She'll see to those beasts!"

The crowd parted, allowing her and Dor passage through to the square. *Which is round, not square at all …* Silya dismissed her silly thoughts. There were more important things to worry about. She was anxious to find out what the verent were up to. And to see if, somehow, she could get news out of them about Raven.

How do you talk to a verent? Maybe the hencha could help.

They slipped out of the crowd into the open heart of the square. The fountain's heart was shaped like a rocket, spouting water out of its tail. But her eyes were drawn to the two verent in front of it, and the three men who were staring wide-eyed at the crowd.

So the verent have riders?

They were all surrounded by a phalanx of Guards, holding out swords that looked like toothpicks next to the great beasts.

The verent seemed wholly unconcerned by the spectacle, lapping up cool water from the fountain.

Interesting. Two of the newcomers were *ce'faine*. Were they the ones behind the attack on the Manor?

One of them was tall, tanned, handsome enough, with scaled arms like Raven. The second … he? She? *They* were tall, and drawn taut as a bowstring, wearing forest greens and browns, with leather bands around their wrists. A bow hung over their shoulder.

Both had strange lumps on their necks.

The third was harder to classify. He wore homespun clothing, clean but very plain, his white shirt cinched at the waist with a belt. He had white scales on his arms too, and one of those bumps on his neck, behind his ear. His cocky attitude reminded her of …

Raven. "Oh my gods, it's him." *He's alive.* The news warmed her heart.

Dor turned to her. "Who, Mim?"

"Raven."

Dor's mouth dropped open.

"Are they verent too?" A little girl next to her pointed at Raven. The white scales on the thief's arms glittered in the sun.

"No, they're people, just like you and me." She tousled the girl's hair. "Come on, Dor. Let's greet the newcomers." She pushed past the Guards, her gaze intent on Raven. "Let me by. These people mean us no harm."

"Are you sure, Mim?" The apparent leader of the Guards, a tall woman with a square face whose blond hair was tied behind her neck with a broad leather strap, took a step forward, as if to block her way. "Those beasts —"

"Are my responsibility now." She dismissed them with a wave of her hand, her gaze focused on her friend.

Raven's eyes met hers, and his face lit up. "Silya!" He raced across the intervening space, throwing his arms around her to hug her tightly. "I am so glad to see you!"

She squeezed him back, surprised at the relief that flooded her at his safe return. "You're alive!"

He held her out at arm's length, and his eyebrows narrowed. "Don't sound so surprised." He wore the same clothes as the second visitor, made of rough but neatly sewn hencha cloth. She recognized the boots, though.

She touched his cheeks. "No, honestly I'm thrilled you're alive. And that you're here!"

"In the flesh." He laughed, a hearty sound. "Oh gods, it's good to be back. I never knew I'd miss Gullton so." He seemed lighter, more at home with himself.

"I know what you mean." She was grateful to be back on solid ground too, and surprisingly happy to see him. Despite her best hopes, she'd feared he was dead.

He let her go and glanced at her staff. "That's new."

She lifted the staff. "I'm *official* now."

"I see that." His eyes narrowed. "Do you still have my things? You didn't let the sisters give them away, did you?"

"Of course I do. I had them put in storage because they were taking up too much of my closet."

The relief on his face was palpable. "Thank Loja."

She looked over his shoulder. "Such company you brought with you. Are the verent … dangerous?" They'd seemed so at the Manor, but they hadn't hurt anyone. *Did you tame them somehow? And what's that lump on your neck?*

Raven shook his head. "I have so much to tell you, and Aik too, but not here." He looked around, and that frown returned. "Where is he?"

He was a different man. *No, scratch that.* He was a *man.* That was the bulk of it. Somehow, since he'd been taken from them —

was that really less than a week before? — he'd grown up. "He went after you."

"He did?" The brief smile was gone as quickly as it came. "But where is he *now*?"

"That's a long story, one not suited for airing in public." She took his arm and guided him toward City Hall. "Bring your friends. You're right. We do have a lot to talk about."

"Fair enough." Raven signaled for his new friends to follow, allowing himself to be led away. "Oh, and you should send for Ser Kek. He's going to want to be there."

It was the last thing she expected him to say. *You're just full of surprises, aren't you?*

8

HOMECOMING

RAVEN CLOSED HIS EYES, soaking in the sunshine as Breeze carried them back to his childhood home. Riding a verent was an entirely different prospect than being part of one, but still thrilling. And better to show up fully clothed, when dropping unexpectedly into the middle of a crowd in Gullton.

Elleck's arms were around his waist. Her excitement bled through her emp, although she shielded herself well. "This is amazing … how did you tame her?"

He laughed. "More like *he* tamed me. His name is Breeze, and his egg chose me. It's a long story."

"I'll bet it is." Her voice was full of wistful longing.

"Maybe one of them will tame you, someday." Though Elleck seemed as likely to allow herself to be tamed as an eircat.

Breeze flew far above the Highlands, so high he must have resembled a bird to anyone who might have looked up from below. Still, he could see all wasn't well on the ground. There were strange white splotches here and there among the fields and purple grasses, and more than a few plumes of smoke where fire had consumed acres of land. *Time is running short.*

"You really know my brother?"

He tensed, ready for another assault like Elleck's prior outburst, but none was forthcoming. "I ... yes. He wants to arrest me."

Elleck snorted. "What did you do?"

"Just a little minor thieving." It was more than he'd admitted to the other verent riders — except Chala, who'd figured it out herself. "You thought he was dead, all these years?" He knew more than his fair share about living with such soul-searing grief.

Elleck opened herself up to him through the emp, and the long and bitter sense of loss that had fueled her outburst earlier flowed into Raven like soured aur milk. "My mother ... my adoptive mother, Alibeh, explained it to me. One of the Steaders raped a ce'faine woman. It had happened before, but this time it was particularly brutal. Her clan tracked him back to my steading, and killed everyone there, except me." Her silence spoke volumes about her pain, and he felt it keenly through their link. "Or so I thought."

"And you?" He remembered his own mother's death. The scars it had left on him were still there, as clear as the burn mark across his right cheek.

"They spared me. I was younger than Kerrick, so I don't remember much. But they took me with them, back to the East Valley Clan."

"You had a different name back then. Elwick? Elrick?"

"Enrick. I changed it when I realized my true nature. Elleck suits me better." She was quiet for a moment, and he felt sadness battle with curiosity. "How did Kerrick ...?"

"He said he hid in the barn, under the hay. He ... heard the whole thing."

"Ah." A complex series of emotions rippled across her mind, from anger to remorse to a deep sadness. "That must have been hard for him."

He nodded. "I suppose it was." He hadn't given it much thought, but it did paint Kerrick, the man who had hunted him, in a different light.

They fell into a mutual silence, and the wind slipping past the verent's wings was the only sound.

Raven closed his eyes and tried projecting warmth, calm, even love. It was like what Elleck had done in the cavern, but the reverse, intended to heal, not harm.

Elleck's wall went back up, locking him out and bouncing his emotional parry back into his own head. "Thank you, but I don't need your pity."

He blinked. That was almost as bad as an attack. "He thought you were dead too, you know."

Elleck's control slipped again, and just for a moment he felt her deep longing. And something else. *Fear.* "I didn't."

He squeezed the saddle's handles a little tighter. "What are you afraid of?"

The wall came back up. "You *are* perceptive."

He pressed on. "Are you scared he won't accept this new you?"

"No. I am who I am. Whether he accepts it or not is up to him." She paused. "It doesn't matter to me."

He wasn't sure he believed that, but he could tell that she needed to. "Then what?"

Elleck sighed. "Enough about me. Let's talk about you. Are you worried Kerrick will arrest you when you get home?"

Raven thought about it. "I guess he can try. But I didn't have a verent before." He chuckled, imagining Ser Kek trying to get past Breeze's sharp teeth.

Elleck laughed too — sweet and warm.

Kerrick would like her — he was sure of it.

She leaned over to look at something below. "What's that?"

He followed her gaze. There was a long, dark line through the valley, running north to south. *Breeze, can we get a closer look? But not too close.*

What are you doing? Jai's voice came through clearly. He sounded annoyed. *The sooner we get to Gullton and then back home, the better. The others will be worried.*

Poor guy must be feeling left out. *There's something going on down there. I want to take a look-see.*

He could *feel* Jai's sigh. *All right. But let's make it quick.*

They spiraled down toward the ground. Soon the line resolved itself. Urses, wagons, and dots that must be people. All headed south, toward the Heartland. "That must be half the Steaders!"

Elleck leaned sideways to look. "We always hoped they would leave, but not like this."

He glanced over his shoulder. "You really are ce'faine now, aren't you?"

"It's how I was raised. I barely remember my previous life."

He flinched. "I know how that goes." He let just a little of his own pain bleed through the link for Elleck to feel.

"I'm sorry. Who ...?"

"My mother. I lost her in a fire when I was a kid."

Elleck squeezed him a little more tightly.

Breeze, take us back up. Don't want to frighten the Steaders. It was those strange white blotches, Raven was sure of it.

Something was stealing the Highlands away from them, a theft far worse than any he'd ever committed. All the more reason to haul themselves to Gullton and warn Silya.

The Rise is coming. He'd caught glimpses of it from Breeze and the others, but until now, it had been distant, a dark storm cloud on the horizon. Now it was here. *We're not ready.*

Ready or not, they'd have to find a way to face it.

Soon the verent passed over the point where Heaven's Reach came down from the north to meet the upthrust of the Onyx Mountains to the south, along the western edge of the Highlands. They crossed the Gap in mere moments to arrive at the Heartland. He hoped to avoid being seen by anyone on the ground — better not to scare the hencha berries out of anyone down there before they had to.

He wondered how many times before verent had patrolled these skies, too high to be seen as anything more than a distant speck from the ground. They passed the time in silence, each lost in thought.

Something glimmered far below, catching his attention.

He blinked. Probably a wagon crossing the Heartland. Maybe one of Tri'Aya's? He shuddered. That woman could burn the paint off a wall with a single look, and Silya had learned from the best.

"It's so ... beautiful." Elleck was staring at the patchwork of fields below, her voice wistful and sad. "Like one of the tapestries the weavers make for our homes."

Home. The emotion radiated through Raven, touching on his own homesickness. He'd never see his old lair again. He looked down past Breeze's wing, trying to distract himself.

Purple fields of hencha stretched for kilometers and kilometers, broken up here and there by pastures for aur and green squares of other food crops. The peaks of Heaven's Reach marched along in an unbroken line to their north, white tops glistening in the sun. And just ahead, the spines of Gullton came into view past the red tile roofs of Landfield.

The city appeared on the horizon, and then grew quickly, five irregular lines resolving themselves into the individual spines, outlined by the tumbling waters of the Elsp. As they approached, he could make out individual buildings — especially the grand round structure of the Temple, gleaming white in the midmorning sun. They flew past it, lower to the ground now, and out over Grindell Lane, his old haunt.

They descended into a hive of activity — people and urses and carts wandering the streets. The quakes had caused a lot of damage. It was going to take an army to repair the city once this was all over. *Assuming there are any of us left to rebuild.*

Even the Temple had lost a building, one of the smaller ones that sat east of the main structure.

Where? Breeze's thought slipped into his mind.

There's a wide place near City Hall. He pictured it in his mind, and Breeze's assent came through the link. "Hang on. We're going down."

Elleck's arms tightened around his waist.

Raven could feel her jitters through the emp link. "It's not so scary, really. At least if you're not an escaped thief who might be thrown in lock-up as soon as you land."

"Yeah, lucky, I suppose." She laughed nervously. "It's so big."

Breeze spiraled down toward a landing. From up here, the city really did look huge. It covered all five spines and extended over onto Landfield in the east like cereal spilled out of a bowl. Some of the older homes still sported their iconic red cone roofs, but the newer construction was much more rectangular.

A few of the burnt-out buildings were already being rebuilt along Grindell Lane. *That must be keeping the Builders' Guild busy.* He wasn't sure it was worth the effort, with more quakes likely on the way.

Some along the street had noticed the descending verent now. People pointed and screamed. Hopefully no one would think to shoot at them. Luckily the average citizen didn't carry spears or a bow and arrow.

He and Jai had discussed it. They'd decided that for both the comfort of their passenger and the already tense reaction they would provoke just by landing in the capital city, it would be best to arrive on verent backs, fully clothed.

The whole *getting naked* thing still bugged him, and he had no desire to do it in front of all of Gullton. Plus he felt really vulnerable without his clothes, and the Guard had those sharp, pointy swords and staffs.

Still, why not put on a show? He communicated what he wanted to Breeze.

Soon they were flying low over Grindell Lane, sending pedestrians and urse-drawn carts alike running for cover.

He grinned. *I think I like being a verent rider.*

Breeze alighted in Founder's Square, settling to the ground neat-as-you-please next to the rocket fountain. He tilted to one side to allow Raven and Elleck to slip off.

Jai's Angel landed next to them, and Jai descended on him, his face flushed. "What in the red hills was that?" His anger bled through their link.

He stumbled back a few steps, barely noticing the line of Guards that slipped out of the quickly gathering crowd to confront them. "I just … I wanted to make an entrance. Show these people what we could do."

Jai growled. "You probably alienated half the populace with that stunt. Seriously, Raven. You need to learn to think before you act. Be a mature adult," He turned to face the growing crowd, and an array of swords from the Guards quickly arriving on the scene from the adjacent Guardhouse.

Maybe landing in Founder's Square hadn't been such a good idea. "So what would a *mature adult* do about all of this?" He waved at the Guards.

Jai held out his hands. "We're not here to hurt anyone," he called out, loud enough to be heard over the din.

There were so many people here. Emotion filled the air — a heady mix of fear, excitement, and bewilderment that made his head spin. He did his best to block it out like the others had taught him. His emp helped, and the rage of emotions settled into a manageable background buzz.

Behind the crowd, something was settling to the ground.

He blinked. Spinning rotors slowed as it touched the street, glittering in the late afternoon sun. It looked like … a flitter? He'd seen one a couple times when he was younger. *Who still has a flitter?*

"Who are you?" One of the Guard, a woman Raven didn't recognize, took a hesitant step forward, her sword held out like a talisman against evil.

"Rav'Orn, at your service." He managed what he hoped was a charming bow. "I'm here to see the Hencha Queen and the Council."

"Rav'Orn? Mas Raven Orn?"

He blinked. *Here we go.* "Yes."

She nodded curtly, tossing her blond braid over her shoulders. "I have a warrant for your arrest, Mas Orn." Her gaze flicked to Breeze and then back to him, clearly unsure how to execute it, given the circumstances.

He'd never been more grateful for Breeze's presence. *I should have stayed in Mountainhome.*

Before he had a chance to respond, the crowd parted in the direction of the just-landed flitter.

Silya appeared in the gap, flanked by her aide Dor. She wore a golden tunic and tight-fitting pants and carried a black staff, but there was nothing else to mark her as the Hencha Queen. Still, it was unmistakable in the way she carried herself. She had changed too.

She held a hurried conversation with the lead Guard. The woman argued for a moment, then gave in, her shoulders slumping. The others backed away, swords still up. Then her eyes met his across the square.

Raven closed the intervening gap in a flash to hug her. "Silya!"

Silya hugged him back. "You're alive."

He held her at arm's length. "Don't sound so surprised." Typical Silya, always raining on his festival.

She touched his cheek, almost affectionately. "No, honestly I'm thrilled you're alive. And that you're here!"

"In the flesh." He grinned. "Oh gods it's good to see you. I never knew I'd miss Gullton so." He was … happy. It was a strange feeling, especially inasmuch as it involved Silya.

"I know what you mean." Her emotions were like the flickering of a candle, not as strong as from someone else with an emp, but clear nonetheless. She was actually glad to see him, joy threaded through with worry. He let her go.

Her staff looked heavy. It was compelling too — three strands of black wood braided together which glowed a soft blue through the cracks, barely visible in the bright afternoon light. It reminded him of his old home. "That's new!"

Silya held it up. "I'm *official* now."

"I see that." He narrowed his eyes. "Do you still have my things? You didn't let the sisters give them away, did you?"

She laughed. "Of course I do. I had them put in storage because they were taking up too much of my closet."

His shoulders sagged in relief. "Thank Loja."

She glanced past him at Jai, Elleck, Breeze, and Angel. "Such company you brought with you. Are the verent ... dangerous?" Then she looked at his neck, frowning.

Her confusion bled through, though it was muted compared to how Jai or Elleck *felt* to him. The whole *emp thing* would require some explaining.

He shook his head. "I have so much to tell you, and Aik too, but not here." He looked around for his other half, catching the eye of the lead Guard, who was glaring daggers at him. He looked away quickly. "Where is he?"

She paused, a pained look on her face, which shifted into something close to approval. "He went after you."

"He did?" The sunny glow in his chest vanished. He'd hoped to find Aik here waiting for him. "But where is he *now*?"

She took his arm and guided him toward City Hall. "Bring your friends. You're right. We do have a lot to talk about."

"Fair enough." He followed, almost not minding how she took the lead. "Oh and send for Ser Kek. He's going to want to be there."

This was not going at all the way he hoped. *Aik, where are you?*

Silya apparently recognized one of the Guards at the top of the steps in front of city hall, where a line of them had arrayed themselves to protect the building and the people inside.

"Das'Efrim?"

He grinned. "Yes, Mim. I'm honored that you remembered." He was about Raven's age, with short-trimmed blond hair and blue eyes, a bit like a shorter and skinnier version of Aik.

"Hard to forget such a good man as yourself." She seemed pleased to see him there. "Can you send someone to fetch Ser Kek for me?"

He bowed. "Of course, Mim. I'll go myself." He ran off, and Raven stared after him.

"You already have one of those," Silya said drolly, catching his gaze.

"A guy can still look." He flashed her his most charming smile, and just for a second, he felt like the old Raven. Then he remembered why he was here, and that Aik was not, and it vanished.

"Dor, can you check in with the Temple?" Silya put a hand on her shoulder, and he felt a burst of real affection there.

"Of course, Mim. I'll come find you." Dor headed off.

"Come on, then." Silya looked thoughtful.

He wondered if she was thinking about Aik too.

Another Guard led them inside, between the columns and through the tiled grand entry. They turned down a long corridor lined with electric lights.

The Guard turned to look at Raven and Jai every now and then, muttering something under his breath.

"What, never seen someone with scales on their arms before?" He'd had always been treated differently by the world, but as a thief, he'd been able to slip in and out without notice. But now ... *I'll have to start wearing gloves.* He missed the simple thief's life.

"No, Mas. It's just ... unusual to have a couple of cheff —"

Silya shot him a look.

"Sorry, *ce'faine* here in the city."

"Oh." Now he felt like an idiot. *Which means I really am home.* He smiled wryly. "Sorry."

They proceeded in silence, and finally arrived at a small meeting room with seating for twelve.

"Thank you, Mas. Please wait here. Ser Kek will be with you shortly." The Guard executed a shallow bow and ducked out of the room, pulling the door closed behind him.

Jai raised an eyebrow.

"Sorry. Some people are ignorant." *I sure was, before I met Jai and Chala.*

"They'll come around." Silya took a seat, looking as tired as he felt.

The room was stuffy. There were no windows, and the walls were filled with paintings of blond, white-skinned, blue-eyed men and women, few of which he recognized. Their names were engraved under each painting. He glanced at a few — meers all. None of them looked like him, or the *ce'faine*.

Elleck paced the small room like an eircat in a cage.

The door burst open, slamming against the wall with a loud *crash*. "What in the green holy hell are those things outside ...?" The newcomer's voice trailed off as he took in the visitors behind Silya. The man looked at the three of them, and then at their necks, finally dropping his gaze to Raven's arms. It was almost comical. *Must be someone important.*

He wore a neat white suit with gold piping down the seams, and his hair was an unusual shade — red. Maybe things were finally starting to change in the Heartland too.

"And who do we have here?" The man's smooth diplomatic side took over.

Raven hid a grin at the suddenness of the transition. Despite his slightly pretentious demeanor, he found himself warming to the newcomer.

Silya stood gracefully and gestured to Raven and the others. "These, Mas Axon, are Rav'Orn, and his ... traveling companions, Jai and Elleck." Turning smoothly to them, she continued, "And this is Mas Rex'Axon, head of the Gullton City Council."

Ah. The second most powerful person in Gullton. He glanced at Silya. *Or maybe the third.*

The councilor's eyebrow shot up at his name. "This is the thief?"

He rolled his eyes. "Is that all that anyone knows about me?" *Better than "godsdamned thief" or "that farking arsehole," I suppose.*

Silya shushed him with a wave of her hand.

The councilor met his gaze. "You do realize, young man, that there's a warrant out for your arrest?"

He paled. "Yes, Mas. But if I could just explain —"

Silya looked like she wanted to let him squirm, but her eyes met his, and she nodded. "Technically those charges were dropped. Weren't they, Councilor Axon?" She leaned into her power, flames lining her arms and down the staff.

"Ah yes, quite. I see, Mim Aya, that you've been fully vested by the Temple." Mas'Axon tore his gaze away from Silya's flickering staff and flashed her a knowing grin. The councilor seemed well-familiar with the use of power. "So, who are your … traveling companions?"

Thank the gods for friends in high places. Raven nodded, feeling the blood come back into his face, and shot Silya a grateful look. "Mas …"

"Rex'Axon."

"Mas Axon, these are Jai of the *reifaine*, and Elleck of the *haifaine*."

The councilor snorted. "First time we've ever had a couple of cheff in City Hall."

"Ce'faine," Silya offered in a stage whisper.

"Ah yes. We're being correct about these things now. My apologies." He turned his gaze to the newcomers. "I'd almost forgotten the border skirmishes were over. So why are a couple of … ce'faine here in Gullton? I assume those beasts outside are yours?"

"Actually, one of them's mine." He was proud of that fact, something he'd rarely felt before in his life.

Elleck stopped her measured pacing and looked at each of them in turn, her gaze coming to rest on Mas Axon. "Enough with the small talk. My *eshem* sent me here with a message." She set her pack down on the table and rummaged through it.

"Eshem?" Rex's eyebrow shot up.

"She's something like the Hencha Queen. Each clan has one." Jai absentmindedly rubbed the lump on his neck.

Silya was trying — unsuccessfully — not to stare at it. Then she blinked twice and looked at Jai's face instead. "The clans have Hencha Queens?" She caught Rex'Axon's speculative look, and a smile slid across her face. "Don't you even think about trying to replace me."

He laughed, putting his hands out, palms up. "Me? I was just thinking about the possibilities."

"Possibilities?" Though, from the look on her face, it was clear she was working through them too.

Mas Axon nodded. "Who knows what else is going on out in the wide world that we've failed to grasp, hiding in our little city by the sea?"

Silya nodded. "I'm starting to realize just how insular we've been, and how much we don't know."

Like what we saw in the Highlands. "About that —"

"Here it is." Elleck pulled out a flattened piece of hencha paper, and her eyes met Mas Axon's. "You're the leader of the Lowlanders?"

Silya nodded and mouthed "Close enough."

The councillor grinned. "Yes. Yes I am." He took the paper and carefully untied the purple ribbon.

The door slammed open again, and both Jai and Elleck settled into battle-ready stances, drawing their knives.

"Where is he?" Sea Master Zev'Nek stormed into the room. She'd managed to put on her traditional seafoam blue — this time a fine robe with a wide cowl edged in gold that lay across her shoulders. But her hair was a mess, as if she'd just been woken up. Her eyes lit upon Raven, and he could have sworn they burned with fire, bringing back the fears from his emp test.

He took an involuntary step backward.

"You!" Her finger extended toward him like an accusation.

He shrank back toward the corner of the room, that terrible dream flashing through his mind. *You eviscerated me, for the Gods' sakes.*

"Mim Nek!" Rex stepped between them and drew himself up, though he still didn't reach her height. "What in Heaven's Reach are you doing here? This is a private meeting."

"Mas Axon." She nodded at him, her face turning a bright red. "I didn't realize ... Someone brought me word of ... *this thief's* arrival." She filled those two words with a level of scorn he hadn't heard ... well, since Silya had used it to talk about him. "It changes nothing. The thief is back."

Silya cleared her throat, and flames ran down her arms and the staff again. "Against whom *all charges have been dropped.*"

Relief filled his heart, which slowed to something like a normal beat. He glared at the sea master, daring her to try to arrest him.

She swallowed hard and stepped back, seeming to realize for the first time that the Hencha Queen, too, was present. "Forgive me. I let my emotions get the better of me." Her gaze fell to Raven's arms, and one of her eyebrows raised.

He sighed. This whole *what's up with the arms* thing was getting old. "Of course, Mim. You have every right to be angry. But you should know, I had no choice, and I'm glad I did it."

Beside him, Silya gasped, and the sea master's eyebrow raised.

"You're … glad you stole something from a guild master?" She was as surprised as he was.

He nodded. He'd been running from this ever since that fateful day. Could it really have been just a week and a half earlier? It was time to stop. "I was meant to find that egg. I can't explain it. But it brought me to Breeze — my verent — and to the other verent riders. So I should really be thanking you."

The sea master was speechless for possibly the first time in her long and illustrious life. "It's … you … I mean …"

Mas Axon leaned in. "I think the words you are looking for are 'you're welcome.' Besides, the boy saved you from unleashing one of those beasts in the middle of Gullton."

Zev'Nek's face went three shades whiter than an inthym's hide. She swallowed hard, and then managed possibly the slightest bow Raven had ever seen. "You're … welcome." She choked a little on the last word.

Still, it was something. He turned to the councillor. "She can stay, if it's all right with the rest of you." He had no feud with her, not anymore, and she *was* an important part of the Gullton leadership.

Zev'Nek bowed again, this time to a more proper depth. "Thank you, Mas Orn." She was quick to adjust to the shift in power between them.

Like any good politician. He'd need to keep an eye on that one.

Rex'Axon looked from one to the other and smiled.

"Very good. Perhaps we can secure the room? We don't need any additional intruders while we figure this out." Silya glanced at Axon.

"Of course, mim." Rex'Axon leaned out into the hall and signaled to someone, with whom he had a brief conversation. Then he returned to his audience. "That should do it. We won't be disturbed again. Not without an army to knock down the door."

He and Jai exchanged a glance.

"What?" Silya's brow furrowed "Tell me."

"After he reads the letter." He met her gaze, and for once, he didn't squirm.

She frowned, but nodded. "What does it say?"

Mas Axon scanned the hand-written note. When he looked up, his brow was furrowed. "She wants an alliance. Between the cheff … ce'faine, and the Heartland."

The sea master hissed. "Not possible. The Steaders would never stand for it —"

"I think they might." Raven might be out of his depth in this room with these leaders of Gullton and the Heartland, but he'd seen what he'd seen. "The Steaders are evacuating the Highlands."

They all turned to look at him as if he'd gone mad, everyone except the *ce'faine*.

"It's true. We saw it ourselves."

Next to him, Jai nodded. The *reifaine* man had been quiet so far, seemingly cowed by the lowlanders. But now he found his voice. "There's a blight on the Highlands. All the steadings have been destroyed."

The sea master shot Jai a look that could strip the bark off a tree. "This is ridiculous. They want something. This is all some kind of grand trick." She looked to Mas Axon for support.

He raised an eyebrow. "I can't help but think that this is exactly what Sil'Aya here warned us about, not two days past." Mas'Axon looked at the paper thoughtfully.

"What *exactly* did you see?" She stared at him intently, but there was a note of encouragement in her voice.

She believes me! "There's some kind of ... infestation in the Highlands. From the air, they look like white blisters, sprouting out of the ground. The Steaders were all fleeing south."

Silya's hand flew to her mouth. "It's going to be a disaster. How will we feed them all? Let alone get them to safety?"

The sea master cleared her throat. She glanced at Mas Axon. "Surely you don't believe all of this? On the word of these ... verent riders?" It was clear she'd intended to call them all something else.

Silya nodded. "I believe every word. I trust Raven."

He blushed. He'd never thought he would hear those words from the woman who had once been his harshest critic. "You can see for yourself. Come with us. Or take your flitter —"

Someone knocked at the door.

Mas'Axon scowled. "I specifically told them to leave us be."

Silya opened the door just a crack. "Ah, these two are here at my request. Come in." She let Dor in, followed by a visibly upset Ser Kek.

The Guard's eyes met Raven's. "You're back. I heard it, but I didn't believe it." The man didn't sound all that happy about his return.

He backed up a step involuntarily, pinned by Ser Kek's gaze, and waited to be arrested, Silya's edict notwithstanding.

She looked up from her hushed conversation with Dor to shoot Ser Kek a warning glance.

He felt a flash of ... interest between them? Maybe more? *Wow. How long have I been gone?*

"Oh relax, Mas Orn. I'm not here to arrest you. All charges were dropped." Still, Raven could feel the unhappiness bordering on disgust that was coming from the sergeant. "No matter what the powers that be say —" and he shot a look at Silya and Mas Axon "— You're a thief and you always will be. You're no hero, Rav'Orn."

That stung. He took a deep breath, determined not to let himself be baited. "I'm sorry you feel that way, Ser Kek."

The sergeant met his gaze, and his lip twitched as something shifted in him. "Well, be that as it may, we have bigger concerns today. Like your huge friends out there."

He could sense Breeze through their link. The verent was splayed out on the warm pave stones, soaking up the sun. "They seem to be behaving themselves at the moment."

A look of surprise crossed the faces of everyone but the *ce'faine*.

"How do you know?" It was the sea master who voiced the question.

"I can talk to them, just like Silya talks to the hencha." Maybe he should have kept that quiet, but he was tired of secrets.

Silya nodded, looking thoughtful.

"Interesting." He could almost feel the gears in the councilor's mind turning.

Ser Kek's gaze moved past him, to Jai and then to Elleck. His eyes narrowed. "I know you. Somehow"

Elleck nodded. She was sweating.

He could *feel* her raw nerves, though she blocked the worst of it from him and Jai.

Her mouth moved without speech, but at last something slipped out, almost unintelligible.

"What?" Ser Kek radiated confusion.

Raven blinked. It was the first time he'd ever seen the stern man look lost. He tried not to enjoy it too much.

Elleck found her voice. "I said 'of course you do, you big aur.'"

Ser Kek's eyes went wide, and he staggered back a step. "It can't be … Enrick?"

Silya's gaze met his, her eyes wide, and he nodded.

Kerrick's sister bit her lip. "Elleck now. But yes. It's me."

"How is it possible?" He studied her, as if trying to make her *fit* what he remembered about her, and his eyes narrowed. "How do I know if it's really you?"

A sly grin crossed her face. "Remember Tucker's Rock?"

"Holy green hell, it is you." Ser Kek shoved the table out of his way, making the sea master jump backward to avoid it, and swept her up in his arms. "Oh sweet mother of Jas, it's you! But how … Where … What?"

Relief flooded him, coming mostly from Elleck. She'd been so afraid of how Ser Kek … Kerrick would react. It was hard to think of him as Ser Kek, seeing him so overcome. *So human.*

She cupped Kerrick's cheek. "It's a long story. Now's not the time to tell it." She pulled him out to arm's length. "You've grown into quite the man."

"I see I can't say the same about you." Confusion warred with happiness in his mind.

She frowned. "Like I said, long story. One I *promise* to tell you all about, later." She put her arms around him and squeezed him tightly. "For now, this is enough."

"I can't … I just … it's you." He was stiff in his sister's arms. "Thank Jor'Oss you've come back to me."

The sea master cleared her throat. "While I love a tender family reunion just as much as the next person, I'm afraid we have more pressing issues to deal with."

"Starting with this." Silya held out another piece of paper. "Dor just brought me a new report from my mother, Tri'Aya, who is in the Highlands as we speak."

"Is Aik all right?" She must have news. Raven hoped it was good.

"Aik left the caravan to go after you, apparently with Des'Rya." Her voice made it clear that she disapproved of the initiate's choice. "Tri'Aya confirms what Raven and his companions told us. The Highlands are lost, and the refugees are flooding into the Gap as we speak."

"How will we feed them all?" The sea master looked around, and he could feel her shock at the looks of disapproval her words elicited. "What? It's a fair question."

"We'll do what we have to." Silya's voice was steel, as she pointedly ignored the fact that Zev'Nek was asking exactly the same question she'd asked moments before, when the sea master had rebuffed her. "The Temple will send aid. We need to find places to secure not only the refugees, but also the rest of the citizens in the valley towns." She sighed. "We need an army to get all of this done."

Jai and Raven exchanged a glance. "We'll help where we can." Jai squeezed his shoulder. "We can ferry people back and forth as needed."

Silya nodded gratefully. "How many verent riders are there?"

He swallowed hard. "Four, mim."

"All right." He could feel disappointment off her like spume from the sea, but she nodded again. "That's four more than we had before."

"But there are hundreds of verent." Jai met her gaze.

Her face brightened. "Will they listen to you?"

"I believe so." He glanced at Jai, who nodded.

Relief surged through her, and he felt something in her shift from resignation to determination. The edge of his lips quirked up — when Silya decided upon something, she was a force to be reckoned with.

"Mas Axon, can we call the Council together *now*? Things have clearly changed." It was not a request, however carefully it might have been phrased as one.

The councillor glanced from Raven to Silya, his composure faltering slightly. "Of course, Mim." He went to the door to speak with one of the Guards, and the whole room exploded into motion.

As the others made plans, Raven only half listened. Poor Aik was out there alone with a chatty Temple initiate, searching for him. *In danger because of me.* He should have taken Aik with him when the verent had come for him. *I should have found a way.*

Jai's hand touched his shoulder. "You can't go after him. Not now." Their eyes met, and Jai opened up to him. He was scared. But he was resolute too.

"I have to. Aik —"

"Made his own choice. You told me he's a capable man, right? He can take care of himself." His brown eyes met Raven's, warm but filled with something like regret, too.

He shook his head. "This is all my fault. I should have brought him with me. If anything happens to him ..." He could still see Aik bleeding out on the table from his emp dream. *I can't lose you again.*

"We have a responsibility. We need to return to Mountainhome and tell the others what's happened. Then we must save as many as we can, however we can."

He tried to deny it. But then he thought of Olly and Astrid and Chala. They'd be worried, more so when he and Jai didn't return by nightfall. And Silya was counting on him.

Jai was right. Aik could take care of himself if anyone could. *Aik, forgive me.* He would do what he had to, and then go after his soulmate. *That's what he is.*

Raven?

The voice in his head caught him off guard. *Aik? Is that you?*

Surprise, then laughter shot through the link.

No. It's Olly. How ... where are you? Are you all right?

He opened his eyes. Jai was staring at him. "What is it? You ... went away for a second."

He grinned. "It's Olly!"

9

THE FOG OF WAR

SPIN HAD NO TEARS, but still he wept.

While his friend Aik and his companion Desla plodded through the warm fog of the Highlands, he was wrapped in his own cocoon of darkness.

His anger at what had been done to him had been swept aside, replaced by a soul-killing sadness that weighed him down. *Ennui*, the French would have called it.

My entire existence is a lie. A lie he himself had helped to craft, which somehow made it that much worse. He was complicit in his own downfall. *Am I even a little human anymore?*

It had seemed necessary at the time, a hard choice to relieve his family's crippling debt. His student loan was in the millions, and he'd recently taken on a private loan to help Sera, who'd been born with a congenital heart defect.

The loan sharks were circling, and he was scared to death they might hurt the ones he loved.

I did it for all the right reasons. He and Genevieve had discussed it for weeks, and she had begged him to find another way. In his pride, he'd refused, insisting that there was no other way.

In the end, with medical bills looming and enforcers pounding on their door, he'd let Amsplor take him, and transfer his self, his essence — *my soul?* — into one of the new hybrid ship minds. Knowing that his past would be wiped away. At least he would feel no pain.

I saved them.

Sera's childhood laughter echoed in his mind.

How much pain did you *feel?* How did it shape you? What did I do to you, my beautiful little one?

He replayed his recorded memory of her, the one he hadn't wanted Aik to see.

•   •   •

She held him, her hands warm on his metallic skin, staring at him in wonder. "I found you. I always knew I would." The green sky of her new world arced over them like a promise unfulfilled. Or a new awakening.

"Thank you, Sera. I was quiescent in that field for a long time. I thought everyone had forgotten about me."

A bittersweet smile flashed across her face, and she shook her head and repeated herself as if he hadn't understood her correctly. "I *found you.* You don't understand what that means right now. But maybe someday you will." Her eyes were moist. "I never forgot about you. I love you, Ty. Remember that."

She tucked him in a pouch to carry him back to her new home.

•   •   •

She called me Ty.

It had made no sense to him at the time. He'd chalked it up to one of her weird *humanisms*, of which there were many. Humor, lies, even the unexpected joy of laughter, all once mysteries to him, until he'd remembered being human once too.

Now it was clear. She hadn't just been talking about finding him in the landing field.

She knew who I was from the moment she set foot on my ship. If not sooner.

And he had failed her again, not recognizing his own flesh and blood. Now it was a hundred years too late.

I don't deserve a name.

Spin wept for all the lost time, the missed opportunities to talk with her about what really mattered. For the pain she must have felt, even if he didn't, losing not only her father and mother, but everything else she'd left behind. And then her wife Tavi, when she'd failed to come out of cold sleep alive during the last run to Tharassas.

He wept, last of all, for what his own wife Genevieve must have gone through when he'd left her to raise their daughter all alone.

At least now he *knew*. He was himself again, or as much himself as he could be, locked inside this quantum mind.

I love you, Ty.

She'd known who *he* was, and somehow that had to be enough.

I love you too, little princess.

•　　　•　　　•

Desla sweated in the warmth, blotting her forehead repeatedly with her last extra shirt, one of the few things she hadn't given away to the refugees.

The world smelled like death.

Everything was amplified by the suffocating heat that had settled in over the Highlands. The sky was gray, stuffed with flat clouds that hid the sun and the two moons.

She took another sip from her canteen. At least water was still plentiful along their route.

The safe house they'd planned to stay at the night before had been destroyed, displaced by one of those strange coryx things. So instead, they'd bedded down in a hollow not far from the lake, and she'd taken almost everything off to avoid the oppressive sultry air. It hadn't been nearly enough. She'd sweated through most of the night until a blessed breeze across the lake had brought them a little relief.

Aik had slept like a mudmole in the winter. He'd been dead to the world, seemingly unbothered by the heat, his right arm radiating its own like a furnace.

What am I doing here? She was a nobody, a simple girl from the provinces, so out of her depth it would be funny if it weren't so deeply tragic. She'd made a promise to Silya to look after him, but what was she supposed to do about whatever had possessed him? Gauntlets and alien creatures were far more than her mother had ever taught her to expect out of life. *Then again, it's the surprises that show you who you are.*

Above, a handful of wisps floated by on the warm breeze. She'd been seeing more and more of them, reminding her of springtime when she was a girl. They would burst from the bandy trees back home, the trunks splitting open to spill out a handful of the magical sprites.

These ones descended to dance around her, and cool air enveloped her. It was her imagination, surely. Simply her desire for little relief from the tedium and unending warmth of the ride. Still, they made her smile.

Then they floated away and were gone, and she was sweaty and sticky once again.

Now Aik rode ahead of her, slumped over his urse, following the now-empty roadway. They'd seen no one else since the refugees the day before. It was Terasday, by her best calculations, but everything melted together out here in the heat. She'd never been to the Highlands before, but she was sure it wasn't supposed to be like this.

He had shown her the gauntlet two nights earlier and had explained the strange circumstances that had led to his current state. Flashes of the old Aik still shone through here and there — sweet and charming — but he was slowly being subsumed by it. She stared at the pack on his back, soaked with his sweat. *How can I help you?*

She wished Silya was there. The Hencha Queen would know what to do. *Maybe I should ask Spin.* That wondrous creature had been mostly silent unless asked a direct question.

"We should stop to eat." His voice was as flat and dull as the clouds above. Still, he'd spoken a coherent sentence. It was something.

"Yes, that's a good idea." They'd kept a little from the stores at the first safe house, and she'd harvested a few bandy fruit and some hacka berries on the way. It wasn't much. She hoped the next shelter was intact, or they were going to go hungry soon. *If the heat doesn't kill us first.*

They found a huge, undamaged flopwood tree just off the roadway to sit under, and she tied the urses to one of its wide branches. It was a little cooler under its broad leaves, and she was grateful for the relief.

Ursia nibbled at one of the leaves, and then spit it out, extending her long neck to nibble at some of the trine grass that poked through the tree branches.

Aik slipped off his urse, moving like a sleepwalker, and settled down with his back against the tree.

She opened her carry sack and rummaged through for what was left of their stores. There was a carefully wrapped piece of cave cheese she'd been saving, the fruit, some jerky, and the last of the hardtack.

He looked blindly at the branches above, no help at all.

"Here, eat this. It will perk you up." She laid his portion of their meager meal on her soiled shirt next to him, folded with the clean side up, and settled down with her back against one of the tree's wide branches. She closed her eyes and nibbled on the cheese, letting it melt on her tongue and savoring the salty complex flavor. Camping made everything taste good, even things you didn't like at home.

Not that cave cheese fell into that category. She'd always loved it, part of the reason she'd saved this last bit.

She cracked her eyes open to peek at him.

He hadn't touched his food.

She poked him with a fallen branch. "Eat. You need to keep up your strength."

He blinked, turned to look at her, and nodded. He'd explained how he was supposed to find Raven at Anghar Mor, but they'd seen neither hide nor hair of any wildlife, including verent. *If we're getting close to where the verent lived, wouldn't we have seen some of them by now?*

He picked up one of the bandy fruit she'd cut open. He took a bite, frowned, spit it out, and dropped it back on the soft cloth. He picked up some of the hacka berries and a piece of their remaining hardtack instead and chewed absently, his gaze still lost in the tree branches.

"Well, you're absolutely delightful company today." She moved on to some of the hardtack herself, breaking it off and taking a gulp of water from her canteen to soften it in her mouth. Its rich, nutty taste rewarded her taste buds.

"What?" His eyes focused on her, and he frowned. "Sorry. I know, I'm not all here." He looked down at the berries in his hand as if surprised to be holding them.

"I'm worried about you." She searched his face for signs of the old Aik, the one she'd met with Raven in the Temple.

"If it makes you feel any better, I'm worried about me too. Where are we?" He took another bite, this time smiling as the juices spilled down his cheek. "These are good."

"Glad to see you eating something." She pulled out her map from her carry sack. "By my best guess, we're about a day away from the mountain." She'd caught glimpses of it in the distance, its broken cone smoking.

"Good." He nodded, finishing up his berries.

"We should be there sometime tomorrow." She was still far from convinced she wanted to go there. *I should turn around and head home.*

"Raven will be waiting for me there." His eyes unfocused, and she could see that she'd lost him again.

She sighed, but she knew he needed to believe it to keep going. Besides, she'd promised Silya to look after him, and she wouldn't make it more than a few kilometers on her own.

The red bugs — fireflies, he'd had called them — had appeared at random intervals to check them out. They'd kept their distance, swirling around the two of them and their urses — but she was sure that was because of Aik and his strange gauntlet. They were connected somehow, and she doubted that deference would be extended to her if she were alone.

So, north it is. "We could camp here, enjoy the cool." What she wouldn't give for a dip in the cold waters of the Harkness right about now.

He shook his head emphatically. "We have to go on. Raven needs me." His eyes took on that faraway look again, and he chewed at his hardtack without expression.

She sighed. He'd been like that all day, present for a moment and then lost again. Like poor old Sister Thora, who spent most of her time in her rocking chair, lost in childhood memories.

She was starting to fear what would happen once they arrived at the mountain. She very much doubted that Raven would be there, whatever Aik thought.

But what will be?

•   •   •

Aik moved in a fog, literally and figuratively. A heavy fog had dropped down to ground level an hour before, obscuring the way forward, but the clouds in his mind had plagued him all day.

Their world was still as a corpse, reduced to the road directly ahead and the tall purple grass that lined it.

He could feel *her*, somewhere ahead, pulling him toward her. Who she was, he wasn't sure, but she held him in her thrall. Her voice had replaced the gauntlet's, somehow warmer but just as compelling.

Come to me.

Ursey plodded steadily ahead. Somewhere behind him, Desla's mount clomped along, hoofbeats muffled by the damp air. Time had lost all meaning, becoming just one step after another in the hot gloom.

Sometimes Raven rode beside him on a verent, the creature's tail whipping back and forth in irritation. He wouldn't talk to Aik, his eyes focused on the road ahead, thin lines of worry creasing the corners of his eyes.

When he looked away, distracted by a sound in the mist, Raven and the verent would disappear.

He rubbed his eyes with one hand, holding Ursey's reins with the other. The fog was hot, making him sweat under his shirt and trousers. The gauntlet blazed like fire on his arm, even though he couldn't see it.

You're almost there.

Her voice whispered to him like an old friend, encouraging him to keep going.

Still, it would be dark soon, and Desla needed rest. He'd seen it in the way her shoulders sagged, how her eyes stared at him blankly even now as he pulled back on his urse's reins to wait for her.

We have to stop. That was his own thought, but the only reason he was sure of it was that it wasn't urging him to go on.

The final safe house was close, Desla had said ... half an hour ago? An hour? Time slipped from his mind like the sweat dripping down his face, but for her, he tried. "Are we almost there?"

She halted next to him, staring at him blearily. "I think so. Spin?" She had pulled up her top, wrapping it around her breasts like a halter, her stomach slick with sweat.

"Close."

Spin was unusually tight-lipped today. Still, Aik didn't have the strength to dig into what was bothering his little friend. "We should find it and stop for the night."

She wiped sweat off her forehead with a cloth he recognized as one of his old shirts. When had she taken that? "Thank the hencha."

So close. The gauntlet urged him to keep going.

Tomorrow, he promised it. He was tired too, though not as tired as he expected. Maybe the gauntlet was keeping him going.

The voice in his head went silent, which he took for acceptance. Or at least resignation.

"There should be a large rock by the roadside."

He scratched his chin. "A rock that marks the path to the safe house?"

"That *is* the safe house."

Aik blinked, making sense of the words. "Sounds easy enough. How far?"

"I don't know. Not too far, I hope?"

He nodded, then realized she probably couldn't see the gesture. "All right. Let's go. Do we have anything left to eat?"

She yawned. "Not much. A little hardtack. I'm hoping there will still be stores at the safe house."

"I hope so." He wasn't that hungry, but she must be starving.

Something about their interaction restored a small piece of himself, and he felt closer to human, at least for a moment. "Come on. Maybe it will be cooler inside."

"That would be nice." Her tone said she thought it was highly unlikely.

Ten minutes later, the rock, a huge chunk of black basalt that pierced the Highlands soil like a stout arrowhead, loomed ahead in the gloom. The sight brought a little cheer to his heart. "There it is!"

"Good." She sounded less excited, wiping her brow again. She must be exhausted. He'd been drilled in the Guard for endurance, but he had no idea what kind of training Temple initiates underwent.

When they reached the outcrop, he circled around the edge of it, urging his mount on. The urses were tired too. A good night's rest would do them all good.

A tiny part of him pushed him to keep going — that magnetic northward tug that had pulled at him for days. He resisted it, determined to have something to eat. And to let Desla, at least, get some sleep.

On the far side of the stone was a narrow cleft, as black as night against the gray world around them.

We need light. He cast about for something he could set aflame to create a makeshift torch. There was nothing. Only kilometers of trine grass, rustling in the chill wind. How else could he provide light?

Spin. The familiar hadn't spoken for a while — something he hadn't even thought about in the grey stretch between camps.

Aik slipped off Ursey's back, trusting the urse not to bolt. He pulled the silver AI out. Spin resumed his spherical form, golden lights flickering around his circumference, providing just enough light to see by. "Hey there Spin ..."

"Good morning, Aik." The familiar's voice sounded different. Less sarcastic. *And what happened to "Chief"?*

They exchanged a glance. "Spin ... it's evening. I think." Even Desla sounded unsure of that.

They'd been traveling through the gloom for so long that it was hard to tell night from day anymore.

Golden lights spun around the familiar again. "Yes, it is. I'm sorry. I'm not myself."

He grunted. "That makes two of us. Do you mind lighting things up for us?"

"Of course." Spin brightened considerably. "Is this a safe house?"

"Sure is. Last one before Anghar Mor." He looked to Desla for confirmation.

"Yes. After this we're on our own."

That didn't sound at all ominous. He held Spin aloft to illuminate the narrow entrance. He shuddered. *I hate tiny spaces.*

He judged they could fit the urses through the gap. Better that than to leave the poor things to the unpredictable weather and the fireflies. "Come on. Let's get inside. Maybe there's cave cheese in there."

She revived a bit, licking her lips. "Or fresh-baked foldovers!"

He grinned. "And a bottle of cold hencha wine!"

"What are you waiting for? A feast awaits us." She laughed, the first time he'd heard anything approaching happiness from her in days. It warmed his heart.

He took the reins and led Ursey into the narrow passage, holding back his anxiety, though his body trembled. *It's just a passageway, nothing more.*

The tight cleft extended only a couple of meters before opening into a wide hollow inside the rock. It was neat and clean, though something white scurried out of sight into a crevice as Aik entered. *An inthym.*

That reminded him of Raven.

They had to be getting close to Anghar Mor. Maybe they'd be reunited tomorrow. The thought thrilled him, and he felt better than he had in days.

One corner of the cavern was banked with rocks and filled with old ashes, and there was a stack of unused logs next to it. With the oppressive heat, that was the last thing they needed. Still, it did seem a little cooler inside than out.

"How does it look?" Her voice behind him was amplified by the narrow cleft.

He moved aside, pulling his urse to the far edge of the cavern, away from the fire pit. There were metal hooks in the wall to tie her to. "No chilled wine. But otherwise, it looks good."

She emerged into Spin's golden light and took a good look around. "Better than sleeping in the open. At least I can breathe in here." She tied Ursia next to Ursey and explored the rock hollow.

He set his pack down and found a secure place to put Spin, on a rock shelf just above eye height, where his light would illuminate most of the space.

He found an old aur hide tied up next to the entrance that could be lowered to block most of the outside air. *Cozy as a mud mole in a mud hole.*

She was halfway up the rock wall, reaching into a dark recess. "Found the cache. Looks like the gods-cursed inthyms have been at it, but most of it seems intact."

He nodded. "Good. I'm starving." His stomach rumbled. "I'm going to get some grass to feed the urses."

"Go ahead. I'll set up a meal."

He nodded, grateful for her presence. She reminded him who he was.

He slipped outside, and the oppressive heat hit him again like a sledgehammer. It had to be early evening, though the hot fog made it impossible to guess the exact hour.

He used his knife to gather some fresh trine grass for the urses. *If Raven really is up here somewhere, the verent must love heat.* He'd never heard of the Highlands being so warm, especially in the fall.

I can't let myself be too hopeful. With one last look into the fog, he re-entered the rock hollow, slipping past the leather barrier, arms full. He deposited the fresh-cut grasses between the urses, pausing to scratch Ursey's long nose.

She dipped her long neck to taste a sample, then warbled her approval and took a couple of long stalks in her mouth and chewed them to bits. Ursia soon followed suit.

He rubbed both urses down, wishing he had some sugar for them, or some fresh hacka berries. "What do we have?"

She was unpacking one of the homeweave-wrapped bundles she'd pulled out of the hollow's makeshift pantry. "Looks like some more hardtack and some dried vegetables."

"No fresh-baked foldovers?" Aik licked his lips. *Guess I'm hungry after all.*

"No, but there are some dried hencha berries too. If it wasn't too hot for a fire, we could make a hearty stew. Still, the hardtack with the berries will be kinda like foldovers."

He snorted. "I admire your optimism."

She froze, staring over his head. "Aik, look."

He turned to follow her gaze. A line of wisps threaded their way out of the cleft into the hollow, spinning around the room and taking up residence in the air above.

"There's no breeze in here. How …?"

Their blue light merged with Spin's to paint her face a pale green.

The air cooled noticeably, chilling the sweat on his skin. "What's happening?" He reached up toward the circle of wisps, but they danced away from his hand.

Her face lit up with wonder. "I think they're cooling down the cavern for us. Look." She held out her arms. They were covered in goosebumps.

"How is that possible?" He'd never known the wisps to act like this, let alone have the power to change the temperature.

"I don't know." She watched them raptly. "You know what this means? We can have a fire, if you still want that stew."

His stomach rumbled, but still he watched at the wisps. Something inside him was deeply uncomfortable at their presence. Which was silly — the cool air they brought felt wonderful. *How did they do it?*

For as long as he could remember, there'd been wisps, usually in the springtime. But they'd never acted like this. *One more strangeness in a world of strange.*

"Aik?" She was at his side, touching his shoulder.

He shook his head, clearing away the fog. "Yes, some stew would be nice."

He pulled out his fire kit and arranged some of the wood in a pyramid in the pit. A little of the drier trine grass fit underneath, and in a couple moments, cheery yellow-purple flames were licking at the air. "Spin, you can douse the light."

"Got it, Aik." The golden light vanished, and the cavern took on more of a purplish-blue hue.

Des joined him beside the fire. Her face was coated with grime.

"You're a mess." He was one to talk. His own hands were covered with dust, and there was grime under his nails from days without a bath.

She wrinkled her nose. "You don't smell so good yourself."

He sniffed his armpit. It was worse than an aur stall. "Fair enough. Let's get some supper going, and then we can talk with Spin about tomorrow?"

"Sounds good." She bit her lip, but turned away before he could ask her what was wrong. She pulled out their cook pot and filled it with water from one of the canteens.

He wondered briefly why the voice wasn't urging him on. *Maybe she gave up on me? I should be so lucky.*

Silya was always telling him what a stubborn lunkhead he was. Maybe he'd finally won their battle of wills.

Whatever the reason, he vowed to enjoy it while it lasted, and savor the simple pleasures of warmth, food, and a good place to sleep.

He glanced up once more at the wisps, wondering and grateful.

After he and Desla finished their small but hearty dinner, they sat side by side with their backs to the rock wall of the enclosure. Outside, the fog had given way to a heavy rain, creating a thundering backdrop, but inside all was cheery and almost comfortable. He said a small prayer of thanks to whomever had stocked the safe house.

His belly was full of stew — carrots and potatoes with a bit of heartroot for spice. She had even managed a suitable dessert, with reconstituted hencha berries wrapped in water-soaked hardtack, to make something akin to a foldover when it was cooked over the flames on a metal spit she found in the pantry. The warm juices had dripped down both of their faces, making them laugh, and they'd stuck their hands out into the warm rain to rinse off the stickiness and washed the dirt from their faces.

"Listen." Her head was cocked to one side.

"What? I don't hear anything."

"The rain. It's beautiful." The thrumming of the rainfall had increased, drowning out even the cracking of the fire.

"You organics get all excited by a little water falling from the sky." Spin sounded sarcastic, but there was a wistfulness there too that surprised him.

"Come on!" She got up and took Aik's arm, pulling him up. She drew him outside into the rain — warm, but cooler than the oppressive heat before.

The wisps followed, and together they danced in the downpour, bathed in blue light. He held up his arms and let the rain wash him clean, running down his face in rivulets. He was happy for the first time in days, caught up in the primal moment as the specter of the gauntlet retreated in the face of such joy.

She was beautiful in the rain, hair plastered to her face and all. She reminded him of Silya, strong, intelligent, and somehow still lovely in the face of all they had gone through.

Caught up in the moment, he swept her into his arms and kissed her.

She pushed him away. "What's wrong with you?"

He blinked. He caught just a glimpse of the confused, maybe angry look on her face before she rushed back into the shelter.

The wisps followed her, leaving him all alone in the rain. Suddenly he felt cold, despite the warmth of the rainy night.

Why did I do that? She was pretty enough, but he had Raven. He'd done that and more with Aer'Lis back at Gap Station. *What's wrong with me?*

He ducked past the hide cover and found Desla laying her clothes out on a rock by the fire to dry.

"Don't touch me." Her voice was steel.

He stood there, unsure what to say to try to make things right. "I'm sorry. I don't know what came over me." Even as he said it, he was still admiring her near-naked form. He forced himself to turn away from her.

"I know you're not yourself, but still... I think it's best if we sleep on opposite sides of the room tonight."

"All right." Aik sighed. "I'm really sorry, Des." He hardly recognized himself anymore.

"Leave her alone." Spin's voice sounded ... different. Somehow more human?

"Don't you start telling me what to do. You're just a piece of space junk Raven picked up in a field." He regretted the words as soon as they came out of his mouth.

Spin's little sphere went dark.

"I'm sorry, Spin. I didn't mean —"

Desla's glare cut him off.

Great, now neither one of them is speaking to me. He shouldn't be here. He should be out there looking for Raven. *My friend. My love. My soulmate.*

They hadn't had time to define what they were to one another, and now maybe they never would, but he knew they belonged to one another. He closed his eyes, trying to see Raven's face the way it had looked just before the verent arrived. The surprising vulnerability. The love in his eyes, even if he hadn't said it.

"Farking hell."

As if to cap off what was already a horrid night, the tug reasserted itself, pulling him north.

He had to find Raven and figure out a way to put an end to this. The gauntlet, the verent, the Hencha Queen — they were all connected, somehow. He could feel it.

"We should go."

She was settling into her sleep sack on the far side of the fire pit. She looked at him like he was crazy. "Go where? It's raining like mad out there, and we didn't bring rain gear. And anyhow, we both need some rest."

He bit his lip. The need to follow the urge was growing in him again.

But she was right. They should wait out the storm. It wouldn't be safe for her out there, though he suspected the gauntlet would protect him.

"Is it talking to you?" She was staring at his arm.

"Not right now." At least she didn't think he was crazy anymore. "But I feel … I need …"

She nodded. "I get it. Look, it's already late. Let's try to sleep, and we'll get up and leave just after dawn, when the sun has come up. We should make it to Anghar Mor before sunset, right, Spin?"

The sphere lit up again. "At your current speed, yes, by late afternoon."

What she said made sense. They would be there in less than a day. *I can wait.* "All right."

She sighed with relief. "Good. I can make us a quick, hot breakfast, and then we'll be out of here just after sunrise."

He swallowed hard. "Desla, I'm sorry. I really didn't mean to —"

"I know." She settled into her sleep sack, turning her back on him and pulling it close around her. "Go to bed. We can talk about it in the morning. Night, Spin."

"Good night, sweet girl." Spin's lights went out again.

Sweet girl? That was a strange thing to call her.

Only then did he realize that the wisps had vanished, leaving only the dying fire to light the room.

His skin was warm, and his clothes were almost dry.

He lay down on top of the sleep sack, crossing his arms behind his head and staring at the ceiling. His rational side agreed with her. They should wait and leave in the morning when the sun was up.

But his gut told him to leave now. *How can I trust you?*

You belong with me.

Her voice was warm and filled him with longing. Still, he resisted, afraid whatever he found at Anghar Mor would strip him of whatever humanity he still had.

He watched Des's slumbering form for a while, scared that he'd burned his only remaining bridge. Worried she wouldn't forgive him. And still drawn to her.

She's not safe with me around. It was a frightening realization.

At last, he fell into a troubled sleep.

10

ASCENSION

SILYA GATHERED HERSELF, ready to enter the dragon's lair again. That old metaphor suddenly made a lot more sense.

She squeezed the staff, drawing comfort from the warm wood as it came alive under her touch, blue veins lighting up the intervening spaces between the braided wood.

This time she was dressed much more practically, in tight-fitting black pants and a black shirt Keh'Sel had sewn for her when she'd asked for something she could wear during her training exercises. It suited her much better than the flowing golden robes. Her only nod to the office was a golden sash she'd donned for the evening's meeting.

Dor had frowned at Silya's proclamation, oft repeated, that she planned to be a new kind of Hencha Queen. Still, she'd kept quiet about it, for once.

That was a bit mean of me. Her temper was running short. Even with all the evidence — and two live verent showing up on the Council's doorstep! — some of the councilors were still reluctant to authorize a full-scale preparation for the troubles that were coming.

The hencha were restless. She could feel their anxiety through the link with the hencha mind.

She took a deep breath, trying to calm herself, and them.

"You all right?" Raven looked nervous too. Though why someone who flew a verent should be nervous about facing a bunch of stuffy humans was beyond her.

"I always get nervous before these things." Not that she had all that much experience yet with *these things.*

He nodded. "I know. I don't like people. Why do you think I lived in the lair?"

She laughed. "And you think people like *you?*"

He grinned. "Fair point." His eyes unfocused in that way they did when he was *talking to the verent. Do I look like that when I speak to the hencha?* And could the hencha help her talk to the ce'faine eshems? That was worth looking into. Later. Right now she had to keep her mind on the meeting.

Coral poked her head into the waiting room. "They're ready for you, Mim."

She nodded. "Tell them we'll be a minute."

Coral's eyes widened, but she nodded and slipped back out of the room.

Raven raised an eyebrow.

"Make them wait. It's a power thing." Dor's wiles were rubbing off on her.

He chuckled. "You really were made for this."

She couldn't decide if that was a dig or a compliment. She wondered where her disdain for the thief had gone. *Verent rider,* she corrected herself. This was a new Raven, a different man than the one who had stolen the egg. That seemed a lifetime ago. "Thank you."

He seemed as surprised as her by the lack of a biting response.

She'd sent Dor back to the Temple with Jai and Elleck, and the verent. Kerrick too — he had a lot of catching up to do with his sister, and having him here pacing the room would have been too distracting. "Are you ready for this?"

They'd hatched the plan with Mas Axon hours earlier, and she'd just gotten word that she had the support of enough of the other councilors.

He gulped. "I guess so. Are you sure this is a good idea?"

She shrugged. "Absolutely not. But it's our best play. The Council's evenly divided, and Mas'Axon wants a show of force if he's going to side with us."

"I hate politics. And politicians." He looked around the waiting room as if in search of something he could break.

Silya felt the same. She met his gaze. "That's why this is perfect. Let's shake things up a bit. Just tell them what you know, and I'll handle the rest." She took his hand. "Aik will be all right."

He shot her a surprised look. "You sure?"

She knew where his head was. Truth be told, she was worried about Aik too, and his strange gauntlet. "He knows how to take care of himself. Desla's with him, and my mother has gone after him too. If there's one thing I've learned, it's that Tri'Aya always gets what she wants."

"I think that's a family trait."

That was most definitely a dig. She smiled.

"I hope Desla is all right, too." The girl had an iron spine — they could have been sisters in a different life.

"The cheese stealer?"

She stared at him. "What?" Sometimes Raven made no sense at all.

"Never mind. That woman scares me, like someone else I know." He squeezed her hand to take away the sting of that last bit and let it drop.

"Desla or Tri'Aya?"

He grimaced. "Take your pick."

Fair enough. "All right, let's do this."

Coral popped her head into the room, sweating. "Mim —"

"We're ready." She'd kept them waiting long enough.

The initiate blushed. "Thank Jas. This way." She led them out of the room and down a narrow, darkened hall. Ahead, it opened up directly onto the stage where the Council awaited them impatiently.

She'd insisted on being at the table this time. *No more audience box.*

A low roar rose from the crowd. This was going to be a very different meeting than the last time.

She glanced back at Raven. "Ready?"

He nodded, his face pale in the dim light.

"Remember, you're a verent rider. These are just people."

"And you're the Hencha Queen." He squeezed her hand and let go.

Strange times call for strange allies. With that benediction, she called on the hencha, lighting her arms on fire. "Time to put on a show."

•   •   •

Kerrick took the stairs two at a time, eager to see his brother — his sister — again. The changes in her would take him a while to get used to, but next to finding her again, they didn't matter. Not one whit.

Silya had given them the use of her rooms, a kind gesture, but one he wasn't overly concerned with at the moment. The *where* didn't matter. It was the *who* that he worried about. *Where did you come from? Where have you been all these years? How did I not know you survived?*

His own survival that fateful night was down to dumb luck.

Someone from the neighboring steading had found him when they'd come to see what had happened.

The smoke from the burning of the Aze steading had been visible for miles. They'd found him hidden in the barn, and it had taken Mim Eydra's promise of some fresh hacka berry tarts to get him to come out.

They'd told him everyone else was dead, and then they'd taken him back to their own steading. He'd never seen his boyhood home again. Or Enrick.

And now his brother was back again.

Only Enrick was Elleck now, and she was one of the *ce'faine.*

It all made his head hurt.

He paused at the door. A red rage filled him, a deep simmering anger that boiled up from the depths, turning the purple flopwood door to crimson. *Why am I so angry?*

His hands balled into fists, and he almost turned away.

All of these years lost. While Enrick ... Elleck lived a whole new life, half a world away. All that pain for someone he'd thought was dead. *It's not fair.*

He growled, annoyed at his own indecision.

This is stupid. Standing here, while his only living kin was just on the other side of the door. Elleck didn't deserve his anger. He ... she was here now. She'd gone through the same trauma he had.

She. That was going to take some getting used to. He snorted, annoyed at himself again. Why should that be any more of a surprise than his lost sibling's reappearance?

He raised his hand again and knocked.

After a moment the door opened.

Elleck was there in front of him, staring at him, biting her lip, her eyes just like his. Seeming less like the *ce'faine* warrior and more like a frightened little girl.

She looked so much like him. But different too, and not just because she wasn't Enrick anymore. A whole different life lived. A different culture.

She stepped back to let him in, and they circled one another like eircats, each wary of making the first move.

She's as nervous as I am. Somehow that helped.

"I'll leave you two to it, then."

He started, surprised by the husky voice. He hadn't even noticed the initiate seated at the long table. A tray was covered with fruit and foldovers and bread and cheese, and two plates attested to the meal they'd been sharing.

"I'm sorry. I can come back ... Mim ... Ost?"

They shook their head. "Mir'Ust. And that's all right. I have duties to attend to. I was just keeping Elleck here company while we waited for you." They gathered some of the bread and cheese from the tray and slipped past, kissing his sister on the cheek. "It'll all work itself out." Then they were out the door, closing it behind them.

What will work out? Me? He stood in the middle of the room, unsure what to do.

Elleck returned his gaze with one of her own. "*What?*"

He laughed involuntarily. *There's the brother I remember. Sister. Farking hell.*

"I thought you were dead ..." They both said it at once, and this time it was her turn to laugh nervously.

"It's ... really strange to see you again. Like this." Her long braid, her warrior stance. Her cheff clothing. *Ce'faine.* He'd hated them for so long ...

She blushed. "I'm sorry, brother. I didn't mean to seem ... *strange.*" She turned away, sitting down heavily at the table, and began to tear a poor helpless hunk of bread into small pieces.

I've stepped in it again. "That's *not* what I meant." He sank down in the seat recently vacated by the initiate and reached across the table to take her hand. "Look, this is hard for both of us, but you're family. My only family." *Besides Silya.*

She met his gaze, her face as hard as his. Two stone gazes, like statues facing one another. "I never expected to see you again."

"Me neither." He bit his lip, still not sure what to make of this sudden, unexpected miracle. "I've spent most of my life hating the cheff—"

She flashed him a warning look.

"The ce'faine, for what they did to my family. What they did to *you.* Seeing you here, dressed like one of them ... it threw me."

Her features softened. "Ah. I thought —"

"That I had a problem with who you are, now?"

She nodded. "It's been a long road. Not everyone has been understanding."

It must have been so hard for you. He squeezed her hand. "I'm grateful to have you back. So you're different than you used to be, in more ways than one. So am I. I wasn't this handsome musclebound man you see before you when we last saw each other."

"Musclebound, yes. Handsome ...?"

He ignored the dig. "You're here. That's what matters." He squinted at Elleck's neck. "But what *is* that thing?" Raven and Jai had them too.

"Not now, brother. I'll tell you when the time is right, but it's nothing harmful." She touched his arm. "Right now, I just want to spend time catching up with you."

He glanced down at the pile of crumbs on the table. "If I let go, will you be nicer to that poor loaf of bread?"

She smirked. "It had it coming, sitting there looking so delicious and all."

He chuckled. "I agree. That hunk of cheese there is mocking me too." He released her and picked it up, crumbling it into its individual curds.

She smiled wickedly. "And the battle is joined." She looked at him *that way*, the way they'd challenged each other as kids, and he knew it was on.

He stared at her hand as she clutched a piece of the poor, tortured bread. "Don't even."

She threw the hunk of bread at him, her look daring him to return fire.

"Oh, we're doing it like that, are we?" He picked up a ripe bunch of hacka berries and threw one at her. She ducked.

A wide grin stretched her cheeks. "You're going to regret that, brother-mine."

In seconds their armistice devolved into a full-on food fight, whose only loser was Silya's apartment. Food flew back and forth across the table, which became a barricade as Kerrick slipped to his knees to hide behind the dubious protection of his chair.

An extra ripe blue hencha berry executed a beautiful arch over the chair's wooden back to drop on his forehead, exploding and sending juice trickling down his face.

He returned fire with a barrage of grapes.

Elleck ducked around the table, heading for the protection of a golden upholstered chair and firing a series of cheese curds at him as she crossed the intervening space.

He stuffed one in his mouth and continued his grape offensive.

When they ran out of ammunition at last, he laughed. "Oh gods that was fun. I haven't been that silly since ..." *Since I lost you.*

He swept up his sister up in his arms, squeezing her tight and squishing a red hencha berry into one of Silya's white ix pelt rugs. *She's going to kill me.*

He didn't care. His doubts about Elleck melted away, and while the anger remained, it wasn't directed at her anymore. "I'm so glad you're here."

She squeezed him back. "So am I, *older* brother. So am I."

"Do you play stones?" He tapped the drawstring sack at his waist.

This time she grinned. "Not wetlander stones. I've tried that at the Winter Meet with some of the traders. Real warriors play *ce'faine* stones." She emptied her own pouch onto the table, brushing aside the various foodstuffs that littered the battlefield. "You game?" Her eyes sparkled.

The stones were different from Gullton ones — round instead of oval, and there were ten instead of eight. Still, how hard could it be?

"Show me. I'll bet I kick your ass inside of three games."

A wide grin showed him the challenge was accepted. "Take a seat. While we're at it, I'll tell you all about the emp."

•   •   •

Silya wanted to scream.

Things were *not going well.*

Kem'Hoya had lined up a slew of rich "witnesses" from Peregrine Spine to angrily denounce the "foolishness" and "entitled nature" of the new Hencha Queen, who dared to think she could lecture the citizens of Gullton on what they ought to do.

Thankfully this fell flat, as the rest of the assembled citizenry had responded with hisses and boos as the parade of wealthy merchants had made their way up to the audience box to protest their sorry conditions.

Now the Council itself had devolved into a free-for-all.

Amused but also dismayed, she caught Rex'Axon's eye across the table. The head councilor nodded.

She summoned her flames for dramatic effect. The sound of the staff's impact with the hollow stage echoed through the hall, sending a shock through the room. All eyes turned to her.

"My dear Councilors, with your blessing, I'd like to call the testimony of one Rav'Orn, of Landfield." He hadn't lived there in years, but his childhood home had been on the other side of the river. So technically she was right.

The Council conferred among themselves, and after a moment of hurried whispers, Mas Axon nodded. "The Council will allow it."

Silya gestured to the verent rider.

Raven stepped out of the darkness at the edge of the stage. Only she saw his nervousness, and only because she knew him so well. "Mim, Councilors." He essayed a deep bow, acting properly respectful. For once.

She glanced at the row of guild masters seated along the back of the stage. All the official ones were there — Sea, Beast, Builder, Electrical, Lamplighter, Machinist.

The sea master met her gaze and nodded, keeping the peace.

Thank the gods for small favors. The woman had been a powerful enemy, and she hoped she would become just as strong of an ally. "Rav'Orn, please tell the Council why you're here."

Kem'Hoya snorted, but settled down at a glare from her nephew on the Council, Nes'Hoya. "Let's hear what the man has to say."

Thank you. "Raven?"

The room went silent as a tomb. Even the audience was quiet. The verent rider was the one many of them had come to see. Word of the strange events in Founder's Square had passed quickly from one spine to the next.

Raven looked around the huge auditorium, his face going white. He cleared his throat. "Ah ... yes. Mim, Mir, and Mas. Six days ago, I was abducted from Tri'Aya's home by a couple of verent."

There were gasps of surprise from the audience, but the councilors nodded. They'd been filled in on the basics before the meeting.

"They didn't harm me. On the contrary, they took me to their home, a hidden valley east of the Highlands. It's where I met Jai and the other verent riders."

Mir'Ossa cleared their throat. "How many are there?"

"Verent, or riders?"

"Ah ... both?" They stared at Raven intently.

"Four riders. Maybe three hundred verent?"

A ripple of surprise went through the audience.

"So you're here representing four people? Do I have that right?"

"Yes, Mir. And a crap-ton of verent."

The audience laughed at that, and Mir'Ossa's face reddened.

She frowned. They needed Ossa's vote. "What Raven means is that he has a substantial fighting force at his disposal, and he's here to offer its help."

"To fight what?" Kem'Hoya stood, resisting her nephew's attempts to pull her back down. "I'm sorry, but this is the second time you've come before us, asking for a sizable chunk of the city treasury ... to do what, exactly? Hide everyone in the dark?" She laughed, as if to show how ridiculous that sounded.

"Mim'Hoya —" Silya agreed with Raven. She hated politicians.

"No, I don't want any more excuses. No more 'this might happen' or 'we're facing a grave danger.' Where is it?" She turned to face the audience, her real target. "Aside from the quake, where's the proof that there's anything going on here besides a natural tragedy?"

There were grumbles of agreement from the crowd, and from at least one or two other councilors.

She grimaced. Things were getting away from her. "Mim'Hoya, if you'd just listen for a moment longer —"

"The Highlands are lost." The words silenced the whispers and muttering like water over a fire.

All eyes turned to Raven, and the whispers resumed.

"There was a line of refugees headed for the Gap as long as Raven Spine." He closed his eyes, lines of pain creasing his face. "If you want to see the destruction, I'll take you there on Breeze's back. The troubles aren't coming, Mim. They're already *here.*"

Silya frowned. They'd hoped to save that bit of information for private session, to keep the panic down in the citizenry, at least until the Council had a working plan. But maybe Raven's instincts were right. They were losing, after all, and something had to be done to turn the tide in their favor.

Kem'Hoya looked up at him as if he'd gone daft. "The Highlands ... what do you mean, they're *gone*?"

Dor had pointed out that much of Mim Hoya's wealth had come from Highlands trade. She was one of Tri'Aya's main contacts in Gullton.

"There's an ... infection. Or maybe infestation is a better term. The steadings have all been destroyed." Raven closed his eyes. "I saw it on the way here."

Kem'Hoya sat back down, clearly shaken. "That can't be true." She looked at him, and then at Silya, and finally at Rex'Axon, who nodded solemnly. She took a deep breath and regained her composure, fanning her face with her hand. "Still, we shouldn't overreact. Not until we know more —"

"What do you want? Another *study*?" Silya loaded the word with as much sarcasm as she could muster. "We're out of time, Mim Hoya. If we don't act now, it won't be grave danger we're facing, but extinction." She glanced at Rex'Axon. "I nominate Mas Rav'Orn to the city Council, to represent both Landfield and our new allies."

The hall exploded in confusion.

"Can she do that?"

"Landfield's never had a seat on the Council."

"He's not even a gully rat anymore. Besides, how do we know he's telling the truth?"

She sighed, but the grumbling in the audience told her Kem'Hoya had hit a nerve. "Adding Mas Orn to the Council will give us a valuable asset in the days to come ..."

A young man, dressed in the simple dark blue of a page, slipped out of the darkness to kneel at Kem'Hoya's side. He whispered something in her ear, and she went white as an inthym, which was impressive in a woman as pale-skinned as she was.

"Auntie, are you all right?" Nes'Hoya leaned in to hear her reply as the page vanished back into the darkness. Then she stood up abruptly and followed him.

Chaos broke out around the table.

"Where is she going? We have Council business to deal with!" The meer jumped to his feet, staring after the vanished Peregrine Spine councilor.

The other councilors were talking animatedly amongst themselves, while an air of confusion haunted the audience.

Silya whistled like a common street whore, drawing attention to herself. All speech silenced, leaving the whole room looking at her. "Councilor Hoya, what just happened?"

The younger Hoya met her gaze. He was not that much older than her. "I'm sorry. Mim'Hoya just received confirmation that one of the steadings she works with —" He paused, as if he couldn't quite believe what he was saying. "That it no longer exists."

A few citizens got up and made their way toward the exits.

She raised her voice. "It's important that we all remain calm. There's no immediate threat —"

Rex'Axon pounded his gavel on the table, and the room went quiet again. "I'd remind the audience that this is an official Council session. Please remain seated until we declare a recess."

There was a grumbling in the crowd, but no one else got up.

He nodded at Silya. "I'm sorry, Mim. Go on."

She glanced at Raven, who nodded. "All right. Can we take a vote on the ascension of Rav'Orn to the Council? Meer Alton?"

"Yes, my dear, the vote may proceed. We still have a quorum."

She relaxed for the first time in an hour. With Kem'Hoya gone, it would likely be near-unanimous.

Rex'Axon called the vote. "In the matter of the addition of a seat on the Council to represent Landfield, and the awarding of that seat on an interim basis to Rav'Orn, how do you vote? Mir Ossa?"

"Aye, for Vulture Spine."

"Mim Oyl?"

She held her breath.

The woman's eyes met hers through her thick glasses. "Aye for Red Hawk."

"Thank you," she mouthed.

"Mas Hoya?"

"Aye for myself and Eagle Spine, and aye by proxy vote for Kemmie ... Mim Hoya."

Rex'Axon waited expectantly.

"Oh. For Peregrine Spine."

She blinked. *That* was a surprise.

Axon nodded. "And aye for Raven Spine. Which seems appropriate." He winked at Raven. "Meer Alton?"

The meer nodded.

"Passed. Rav'Orn, please take Kem'Hoya's seat, for now. If she returns, we'll rustle up another chair."

"Thank you, Mas'Axon." Raven took his seat next to Nes'Hoya, looking flustered, but who wouldn't be? He'd just been thrust into the spotlight, and Raven famously didn't like attention.

She remembered her own hasty ascent to power. It hadn't been easy.

Rex'Axon stood to address to the audience. "This completes the public portion of this meeting. We will have news for you posted later this evening, after the Council has time to discuss our next steps. In the meantime, I'd advise you all to remain calm and —"

The wide double doors at the top of the center aisle burst open and a man entered, a merchant by the look of him. "Those verent are attacking Landfield —"

The hall erupted again in chaos. This time audience flooded to the exits, shouting and trampling one another in panic.

"Raven, what in the seven green hells —" Silya's voice was cut off as one of the Council Guards hurried her off-stage. She recognized him as the Guard who'd let her into the council hall the first time, what seemed like a lifetime ago, and whom she'd met again just that afternoon. "It's Das'Efrim, right?"

"Yes, Mim. Short for Dasin. This way. We have a safe room prepared for you and the Council." They passed down the dark hall and through the waiting room she'd occupied before, and the screams and shouts of the crowd faded behind them.

"Good. Is your family …?"

"Safe, Mim. Thank you. Now we have to make sure you're protected."

"Get word to the city Guard. They must block the bridge and the docks. No one can leave the city, and we have to keep the peace as best we can."

That brought him up short. "You said it was safest to leave —"

"That was last week. It's too late for that now." With what was coming, no place could be entirely safe. "We have to get everyone to the safety of the caverns below the city in the next few days."

She rubbed her temples. *How much time do we have?* There was no way to know for sure.

They arrived at the safe room, with a door barricaded by three more of the Council Guards. One of them swung the heavy flopwood door open and ushered her inside.

"Of course, Mim. I'll see to it."

She squeezed his shoulder. "Thank you, Das'Efrim. For everything."

"Yes, Mim." He bobbed his head and disappeared through the doorway.

She took a seat, waiting for the others to arrive, seething at the panic running rampant through her city, and her locked away with nothing to do about it.

Raven, what did you do?

11

Jimey

IT'S NOT MY FAULT. Sorix glared at Kalix, then turned to look at the ruins that had just a moment before been the perfect perch from which to observe this part of the human "city." Wooden beams were scattered across the stone opening between "buildings," and there was water *everywhere*.

Humans were running back and forth around them, so recklessly that she had to lift her wings up out of their way to avoid knocking any of them over. They emitted high-pitched noises that Kalix told her were a sign of extreme distress.

It's most certainly your fault. I told you not to land on it. She could feel his distress, radiating off of her mate like heat. His head swung back and forth, eyes moving from one human to another as the fragile little creatures ran for cover.

Raven is calling. His white skin took on a sickly blue tinge.

Tell him ... I'm sorry.

Kalix turned to look at her. *You're what?*

Sorry. She shook out her wings, almost knocking over another human who was running by her at exactly the wrong time. *You heard me.*

Will wonders never cease. Sorix, apologizing to a human.

Actually, you're doing it for me. She grinned, showing her long teeth.

He was silent for a moment, ignoring her, or talking to their human. Or both.

Our human. She supposed he was, now.

When did I start thinking of him that way?

•   •   •

What did you do? Raven could feel Breeze in the back of his mind.

The verent seemed strangely contrite. *We're just stretching our wings. We wanted to see your home.*

We?

Squint and I. Thunder is home with the kits.

He groaned, though he was secretly pleased at how well the verent were learning to communicate with more than just images. *You scared people half to death. They say you're attacking the city.*

He wished he still had Spin to talk to. He always knew the right thing to say, even if he was a smartass about it. Leaving him at the Manor had been a boneheaded mistake. He hoped Aik had retrieved the little familiar. *My friend.*

"This way please, Mas." One of the Guards ushered him down a long hall insistently.

"Of course. Thank you. Where are we going?" He wasn't used to being treated like someone *important.* Usually he was the one people were being herded *away* from.

"A safe place, Mas Orn."

He snorted. Safe from the verent?

We were just curious. Angel didn't mean to break the thing. In his mind's eye, a water tower came crashing down in the middle of one of Landfield's wide lanes. Thankfully no one was standing there. *Get back to the Temple. I'll deal with this.*

"In here, Mas." The Guard held open a door for him, surrounded by a couple others. Being so close to so many Guards gave him the willies, but he took a deep breath to calm himself. "Thanks, Mas ..."

"Mir Ema." The Guard nodded. They were curious about him, but not afraid. That was a good sign. "Just doing our duty." They nodded smartly, and turned smartly to retreat down the hallway.

"What in Heaven's Reach is going on out there?"

He turned to find Silya in his face, backed up by two of the other Councilors ... Nes'Hoya and ... Len'Oya? Oyl? He'd never paid much attention to politics before.

Their anger preceded them like a storm cloud, not that he needed the emp to feel it. Silya's face was red, and her fists were clenched. She reached up to tug on the cowl that wasn't there, and ended up tugging on her collar instead.

The room was small, bounded by white brick walls bereft of decoration, with a small table and six chairs at one end.

He slipped into his most disarming manner, one he'd used countless times when caught thieving or slipping out of someone's bedroom. "It was all a misunderstanding." He sank down into one of the chairs in the windowless room and put his head in his hands. "The verent just wanted to stretch their wings, and they knocked over a water tower."

"Which the city will now have to pay to replace." Len'Oyl ... yes, he was fairly sure it was Oyl ... was scowling at him.

The others arrived in a rush, and soon it was just the Council and the heads of the various guilds. All staring at him. The level of emotion in the room ratcheted up a notch.

Silya's hands were on her hips, always a bad sign. "You have to fix this, Raven. There's going to be panic in the streets."

"Going to be?" The sea master raised an eyebrow.

"Maybe raising him to the Council wasn't such a good idea." Mas Axon frowned.

I didn't even want to be on your silly Council in the first place. But done was done.

"Raven ..." Silya was scowling at him the way she used to. Which was strangely comforting.

He asked his emp to bring things down a notch, and the anger faded from his mind, giving him space to think. "Look, I'll take care of this. The verent didn't mean any harm, and the sooner I can show everyone that, the faster this will all blow over." *Breeze, change of plans. To me.*

Coming.

He turned away from all the accusing eyes. This was more like his old life. He sighed and pulled open the door, eager to leave the tangled nest of anger and fear behind.

One of the Council Guards blocked the way. "Sorry, Mas, but you need to stay inside for your own safety. The Guard is dealing with the situation."

That's a horrible idea. He looked up at all two meters of him. The man was imposing, his muscles thick as cordwood.

Someone was likely to get themselves killed. And if one of them hurt Breeze or Squint ...

He tried to push past him, but the man was solid as a mountain. "I need to go." He looked over his shoulder at Mas Axon. "You do all want me to make this better, right?"

The Councillor nodded. "Let him through."

The Guard moved aside. "Sorry, Mas." He bowed.

"Just doing your job." At least they weren't trying to arrest him this time. Some things *had* changed.

He slipped through the halls, admiring all the pretty furnishings he would have stolen in his thieving days — that carved onyx bust of the first meer would have been worth a fortune, though hard to offload. And that tapestry of the First Gather was still beautiful though its woven colors had faded with age. But how would you get something like that out the door without somebody noticing?

He frowned. It was hard to picture going back to that simple life after Breeze. *I'm not that person anymore.*

Then he was out the front doors and into the fresh air of Founder's Square, waiting for his verent. The smog that often hung over the city had been absent of late, maybe because of the strong ocean breeze, or maybe because everyone was hunkered down, waiting for whatever was to come. The streets were empty, the forlorn breeze off the Harkness his only company. Well, that and Silya, who had followed him out of City Hall.

She came to stand next to him, scanning the sky. "Are you all right?"

"Not really. I'm not cut out for this." From lowly thief to verent rider and Councilor in a week. *It's too much.*

She snorted, a sound most unbecoming a Hencha Queen. "Tell me about it. They made me queen and expected me to fix everything." She tugged on her collar, a gesture Raven didn't need the emp to interpret.

"What do you and I know about politics? About war?" He sighed. "I wish Aik was here."

"Me too." Her hand found his, her touch warm.

He squeezed hers tightly, then let go as Breeze appeared in the distance above Grindell Lane, with Sorix behind him. His new family.

His friend soared fifty meters above the highest building, the nearly completed three-story edifice that was going up where Lander's Pub had been.

"They're breathtaking in flight." Her eyes were wide. The wonder pouring off her made her more beautiful, almost childlike.

"They are pretty amazing when you're flying them, too." He grinned. "One day I'll take you up for a ride."

She gave him the side-eye. "Like I'd ride on your back. Dream on." Her look turned thoughtful. "Maybe Jai will take me, if I ask nicely."

She looked so serious that Raven was about to make a sharp retort. *Why Jai instead of me?*

Then a slow grin slid across her face. "I'd love to go up with you sometime."

"Kerrick might have a problem with that." He'd seen how close they'd become. Not that he disapproved. She seemed … mellower.

"It's not like you're competition."

Raven snorted. "It's a date, then."

Breeze landed on the cobblestones before them, his wings setting up a rush of wind and dust. He scrambled onto Breeze's back. *Let's go.*

Where?

Where you and Squint knocked over that water tower. They had some fences to mend.

Sorry, Raven. Squint slipped into his mind, sounding more contrite than he had ever heard her. He raised his eyebrows.

I know. I think she's warming up to you.

That was a welcome change. *I think you're right.*

Breeze leapt into the air, catching an updraft from the warm cobblestone street, and spiraling up into the sky. He waved at Silya as she grew smaller below him.

She's happy you are alive.

That surprised him. Not the happy part. He'd felt it clearly himself, with or without the emp. But that Breeze somehow knew? *How can you tell?*

The hencha talk. Breeze leveled out, his powerful wings pulling them on toward Landfield.

Raven rolled his eyes. It seemed like everyone was talking to everyone these days. *What are you all saying about me?*

Still, if Breeze could talk to the hencha ... that could be useful.

They passed over the Temple, its gleaming white dome shining like copper in the late afternoon sun. He thought he caught a glimpse of Angel in the training field at the southeastern edge of the complex, and that had to be Jai, in his riding leathers, storming out to meet her.

The sunlight sparkled off the waters of the Elsp, the headlands of Raven Spine casting a long shadow that almost reached Landfield on the far side of the estuary. Then they were across the narrow patch of water and over Gullton's newest suburb.

It hadn't changed much since he'd been a boy, growing up there on a small side street in his mother's cottage. Landfield was *all* small streets. It was where most of the working population of the city lived, and had grown organically over a hundred years, spreading out in curved cobblestone lanes and twists of cul-de-sacs like gray vines.

The heart of Landfield was Landing Square — a wide, stone-paved space surrounded by cafes and small shops, supposedly the site of the first ship's landing, four hundred years earlier.

He wasn't sure he believed it. How would they know exactly where the ship had come down? It had been a field of grass when they first built the square. Besides, it was far from where he'd first found Spin.

Now the square was a mess. The wooden tower had crashed into the plaza, smashing to pieces and filling it with water. Most of it had drained away, but the square was as quiet as Grindell Lane had been.

News travels quickly in Gullton. He sighed. He'd have to help clean up the mess. *Was anyone hurt?*

No. It was almost empty. Breeze sounded contrite. *Where should we land?*

Next to the wreckage. We're going to perform a little community service.

If Breeze was confused by the term, he said nothing.

They alighted next to the worst part of the mess. Raven could feel eyes upon him from the second floors above the shops that lined the square, and from the dark maw of the Green Skies pub on one corner. It was a little creepy.

Time to put on a show. Help me move this wood over there. He pointed to a spot next to the fountain in the middle of the square — a chunk of wreckage from the last run that an artist had crafted into a massive, twisting metal fire. Spin's ship. The stone basin was cracked and empty. *More quake damage?*

As if in response, the ground rumbled briefly. He grabbed the ridges of Breeze's neck to steady himself until the ground settled down.

After waiting a few seconds to make sure it was truly over, he got to work, picking up a two-meter-long span of wood. *Look at me, doing manual labor.* That had always been more Aik's thing.

He pushed that thought out of his mind.

Breeze took a large chunk of wood in his mouth and lifted it with ease, trotting over to the fountain to lay it next to the first.

They worked together, slowly moving the pile out of the way.

As they did, the doors around the square opened. A couple of people ventured out onto the cobblestones to watch, and then a few more.

Word spread as they worked, clearing part of the mess. Sweat soaked his brow, even with the salty breeze coming in off the Harkness as the sun settled toward the horizon.

Laughter interrupted his task. Raven stopped in his tracks, surprised, and looked around for the source.

"Mera!"

A little girl was running straight at Breeze, her mother chasing after her. The child looked all of two years old, dressed in plain brown homeweave, her long blond hair tied back in pigtails with red ribbons — the only fancy thing about her.

Breeze set down his load and extended his nose toward the girl, the tips of his sharp teeth gleaming at the edges of his mouth.

The whole world stopped, as everyone held their breath.

The girl laughed again and reached out to pet the verent's snout.

Breeze dropped his head lower and emitted a low purring sound.

"Get away from that ... that thing!" Her mother had stopped a meter from the intimidating verent, but now she ran forward to snatch her daughter away.

"He won't hurt her. He's as tame as a kitten." *A kitten with claws a third of a meter long.*

As if on cue, Breeze rolled over on his back, spreading out his wings.

Raven scratched the softer hide under his chin, and his purring increased in volume. "See?"

"Are you … sure?" The woman looked at him for the first time. "Who are you?"

"Rav'Orn. Verent rider, and the new Councilor for Landfield." He bowed. "And you?"

"Mehn'Enn, and this is my daughter, Mera." She blinked twice. "Wait … Landfield has a Councilor?"

Mera hid behind her mother's legs, seeming more afraid of Raven than his verent.

He grinned. "Yes, Mim Enn. As of about an hour ago. I thought I'd help clean up the mess that the verent made." He rubbed Breeze's stomach. "This is Breeze, and he's very sorry for what he did."

It was Angel's fault. Breeze's tone was surly.

They don't need to know that.

Mim Enn stared at him a moment longer, and then nodded. "That's very noble of him." She stepped forward, shaking like a leaf, but determined. "May I?"

He nodded. "Of course." *Hold still.*

She scratched Breeze's chin, and the beast rumbled happily. "Oooh." She stepped back again.

"He likes it. Go ahead."

She edged away from Breeze's long teeth. "That's quite enough for me, thank you."

He knelt next to the little girl, pulling the old verent tooth he'd found at Mountainhome out of his pocket. He'd been wondering what to do with it, and this seemed like the appropriate thing. "This is for you."

Mera looked up at her mother, who nodded. She took it in her hands, her eyes big as saucers. "What is it?"

"It's a verent tooth. Be careful — it's sharp. But it will bring you good luck."

Mera grinned. "I want to be a verent rider one day."

"Maybe you will. Or maybe, like your mother, you'll be a …" He looked up at Mim Enn.

"Baker." She smiled gratefully.

"A baker, then. You can be whatever you want." He glanced at Mehn'Enn.

The girl's mother nodded. "Of course you can, Mer'Ehn." She even felt like she believed it. She knelt to pick up a piece of wood. "We're happy to help clean up the mess."

Raven gave the two of them a thumbs-up. "The more hands, the faster the work."

It was as if a dam had broken. The other Landfielders surged forward, pitching in to dismantle the broken water tower and move the debris to the growing pile by the dry fountain.

In less than fifteen minutes, with the town's help, the tumbled, broken bits of wood had all been cleared away, neatly stacked in the center of the plaza.

He looked around, struck by the feeling of community that flowed from the crowd. With a grunt, he climbed the pile to address the by-now rather large crowd, while Breeze curled himself around the fountain. "Hello, Landfielders."

Everyone turned toward him, watching him expectantly.

He blushed. He wasn't used to speaking to crowds. *I suppose I'll have to learn.* "My name is Rav'Orn. Raven to my friends. I grew up here, in a small house over on Laurel Court. I know what life is like in Landfield."

A rumble went through the throng as they pressed closer to him. "You're a Landfielder?"

"Through and through." He thumped his chest with pride. "Look, I know things are scary, but if we stick together, we'll get through this. Just like we did today."

There was a satisfied rumbling in the crowd.

"I'll have water carts here in the square in the morning for anyone who needs it. And if you need anything else …" How could they reach him? "Send word to the Temple, and they will get it to me until I can set up a formal office somewhere."

"Here in Landfield? Or on the spines?"

He laughed. "Here in Landfield, of course." His smile vanished. "Look, there's a storm coming, but we'll weather it together. You have my promise."

A cheer went up from the crowd. "Landfield, Landfield, Landfield!"

Pride surged through him, from the citizens through his emp. To finally have someone like them to represent them, the lowest of the low, meant everything.

He stepped off the makeshift platform, feeling something strange and new. The admiration of others. All his life he'd been cursed and spat upon as a thief and a gully rat. But these people ... they liked him. They put their hopes on his shoulders. *I hope I can live up to it.*

Maybe he'd live here when it was all over. He'd miss the lair, but he really had grown up in Landfield, and he knew its people.

People were approaching Breeze now, cautiously. The verent settled in next to the fountain, soaking up the afternoon sun, and let them touch him. There were lots of *ooohs* and *aaahs.*

"Raven?" A man's voice, this time.

He looked around for the source of the voice. His gaze alighted on a tall, lanky blond man who was staring at him, mouth agape. He looked familiar ...

"Jimey?"

In two long bounds, his old friend closed the distance between them and took him up in a bear hug. "It's so good to see you, Rave."

Raven nodded, flooded with unexpected emotions. *Jimey. Jimey farking Aza. My first crush.* In a flash, he was a child again:

Jimey hugged him tight. "I'm so sorry, little guy. It's too late. Your mamma ... she's gone." Jimey's arms were warm, safe.

He blinked, coming back to himself. "You're ... taller."

The last time Raven had seen him, Jim'Aza had been about fifteen, lanky and awkward. The man before him was anything but. He was ... solid, was the best word he could come up with. And handsome, a neatly trimmed beard gracing his strong jaw.

"You're ... a verent rider? Is that what they call it?" Jimey seemed as nervous as he was.

Raven grinned. "Yeah, who even know there was such a thing?"

Jimey shrugged, his blue eyes twinkling. "You're not such a little guy anymore, either." He glanced over his shoulder. "Hey, do you have time for a quick cup of akka?"

He looked around. The people were dispersing, although a few were admiring a preening Breeze. Their fear seemed to have dissipated. "I really should get back to the Temple ..."

Jimey looked down, a heavy sigh escaping him. "Of course. You have more important things to do."

Actually, I do. But this was *Jimey*. Just looking at him made Raven's pulse race.

Breeze?

Go. I am performing some community service. A pack of children was crawling over his back, laughing and screaming.

That made him smile. "Sure. I can spare a few moments. Is there somewhere close by we could go?"

Jimey's face lit up. "In fact, there is. Follow me, Raven Verent Rider." He took Raven's hand with the enthusiasm of a ten-year-old and led him through the thinning crowd toward a two-story building at the edge of the square. It was a small pub with seats and tables spilling out onto the cobblestones. It was also basically empty. Not surprising this late in the afternoon.

"Looks good." In truth, he was hungry. It had been hours since Verla had cobbled together a snack for them before the meeting. He was starting to fall in love with the Temple cook.

Jimey gestured to a stout metal table. "Take a seat. I'll bring us out something."

He frowned. "You know the owner?"

For his reply, Jimey pointed to the sign above the corner of the building, a wide grin splitting his face.

Aza's Pub.

Raven blinked. "*You're* the owner?" Jimey really had come up in the world. When he'd had lived with the Aza family, Mim'Aza had made a meager living doing laundry and taking in clothes and other small items to repair.

"One of them."

"You and your mother?"

A shadow crossed Jimey's face. "No, she passed on two years ago."

That punched him in the gut. "I didn't know ..." *How did I not know?* She'd been a second mother to him.

"She loved you too, little guy."

He blushed. "She was a good person." She had always been kind to him. "So who's your partner?"

"You'll see." Jimey winked at him, and disappeared inside.

He took a seat, letting out a sigh of his own.

Just that morning, he'd woken up in his room in Mountainhome, as separated from his past and his old life as he'd ever been. Since then, he'd witnessed the creation of a verent, reunited Ser Kek with his long-lost sibling, calmed half the city, and now he was having akka with Jimey freaking Aza. *Life is weird.*

People nodded at him as they went past, a sign of respect Raven wasn't at all sure he would ever get used to.

In the center of Landing Square, Breeze had wrapped himself around the old fountain again, soaking up the last of the late-afternoon sun. *You all right over there?*

Breeze's only reply was a contented snort.

It was a surreal scene, especially if you knew the world was likely coming to an end. Still, he sensed the underlying tension in the air. People were scared.

My people. He'd turned his back on Landfield years before, but it was still where he'd felt most at home. It was a working-class neighborhood, full of regular folk, and they *needed* him. He should be with Silya, figuring out how to save all of them.

What am I doing here? Did Jimey think … did he expect …? They'd never actually done anything together when he'd lived under Mim Aza's roof, though he was pretty sure Jimey liked men too.

Jimey returned carrying a tray with three ceramic mugs and a plate piled high with foldovers.

Three mugs?

"Raven, this is Orel'Aze — Orely to his friends. My husband." Another man appeared from the darkness of the pub, shorter than Jimey and with sandy-blond hair and a crooked nose.

"Raven? I've heard so much about you." Orely leaned down to hug him, and Jimey winked at him over his husband's shoulder. The man had an infectious grin.

Jimey set down the tray.

The love between them came through clearly, making Raven feel like a third wheel. "I should probably go —"

"I know. But stay for just a moment and have a foldover. You *must* be hungry after all that work."

I am starving. Maybe he could stay for a bit.

There was something comforting about seeing Jimey and Orely together. Jimey had always been a loose end in his life, and to see the man so obviously smitten and happy … If he closed his eyes, he could almost pretend they were himself and Aik. "I guess I can spare ten minutes."

In his mind, Breeze warbled happily.

Raven took one of the foldovers. Though it was cold, it looked delicious — light and flaky, just like he liked them.

"Good." Orely took the seat to his right, and Jimey to his left. "Now tell us all about this whole verent rider thing."

He took a sip of the steaming-hot akka, letting it warm his stomach as they looked on expectantly. "Are you sure? It's not for the faint of heart."

Jimey chuckled. "Faint of heart? Who always stood up for you against the neighborhood bullies?"

He laughed. He'd forgotten that. "Fair enough. But remember, you asked for it." He took another sip, and then launched into storytelling mode. "It all started when I swallowed a dragon …"

12

ANGHAR MOR

"SPIN."

The familiar roused from his semi-quiescent state. He'd been dreaming about his little girl. "Chief? What's up?" His golden lights flashed. "It's the middle of the night. Why are *you* up?"

Aik was leaning over him, bathed in his glow. "I have to go. It's not safe for Desla to come with me. I don't know what's going to happen to me." He scratched his right arm. "Tell her to go home."

Spin would have frowned. Wished he *could* frown. "You should tell her yourself."

He shook his head. "Better this way. You can help her get home, right?"

A rising sense of alarm threatened his uneasy peace. "You're not leaving me, are you?"

"Keep it down. I don't want to wake her." Aik touched his metallic skin. "You've been a good friend, Spin. With luck we'll see each other again, but I have to do this alone."

Spin couldn't feel the warmth of Aik's touch. Not like he used to when he'd been human too. But he could sense it.

He remembered touching Sera's head like that, her own skin warm under his gentle fingers. That last time. "Please don't go."

He wished Genevieve had said those words to him, all those years ago. That she had made him stay.

Aik blinked. "I have to. I did something I shouldn't, and ... she's better off without me around." Aik's hand withdrew. "We'll see each other again. But this is something I have to do alone. Please, Spin, do this for me."

What did you do? Spin's lights blinked in distress. He'd already lost Genevieve and Sera and Raven. But the look in Aik's eyes compelled him to agree. "I will."

"Thanks." They stood there awkwardly for a moment, man and once-man, each lost in their thoughts.

Then Aik turned to gather a few things, glancing at Desla's sleeping form. He crept quietly past her, lifted the protective flap, and was gone just like that.

Spin monitored the narrow exit from the safe house for a long time, hoping Aik would relent and come back. When he didn't, Spin settled down to watch over her.

She was so much like Sera.

They looked nothing alike. Sera was black like him — or like he had been — did that change just because you no longer had a body? Des was as white as a daffodil. But they had the same drive, the same compassion, the same lust for life.

Spin would do what Aik asked and make sure Desla was safe. At least he had a purpose, something to cling to while he rode out the waves of emotion that wracked his soul. *Do machines even have souls?*

And once this was all over, what then?

He'd never been a religious man. But maybe, just maybe his wife and his little girl were out there somewhere in the cosmos, waiting for him. It was something to hope for. And if not, sweet oblivion would end his cares. Free of his original programming, he could end things, if he chose.

A strange calm settled over him at the thought.

He'd watched over Sera many a night, just like this. Only she and Jas had known about him, of all the people in this world.

He pulled up one of those memories, of his daughter gazing at him in the dark for a moment before closing her eyes and drifting off to sleep.

Sleep well, my sweet girl.

•　　　•　　　•

Desla turned over in her sleep sack. She was warm and comfortable, snuggled tightly inside the confines of the thick material, dreaming of home. The smell of fresh-baked foldovers filled her mother's kitchen ...

Her eyes flickered open, and for a moment she forgot where she was, staring at the dark rock walls in the dim sunlight that slipped through the hide flap.

Sunlight.

"Aik, we're late! We need to get up!" They'd planned to leave before sunrise.

She pushed off the sack. While it was far cooler in here than it likely was outside, it was warm — the wisps were gone. Still, she longed for a cup of hot akka. "Aik?"

Her voice echoed in the small space, but Aik didn't reply. Maybe he'd had gone out for a call of nature.

She pulled on her boots, catching a whiff of her feet in the process. She needed a good, long soaking in some hot, soapy water. *That's not going to happen anytime soon.*

With a sigh, she got up to pull back the hide to let more light into the hollow. She surveyed the small cavern in the dim light.

His pack was missing, but his urse was still there.

He's gone. "Damn fool boy." Not that she was any older than he was, but still. Everyone knew men matured later.

He must have gone ahead, where it would be hard to take an urse, especially under these conditions. How had he gotten his gear and left the safe house without waking her? *Did you put something in my akka?*

She discarded that thought almost immediately. He wasn't that clever or devious. He'd have needed to find some fellin root to slip into her drink, and she would have noticed its bitter taste. *Wouldn't I?*

More likely he'd quietly hauled things outside, where they'd make less noise, before packing them up.

"Damn you, Aik." He'd left her stranded in dangerous territory. She could head for home, she supposed, but her chances of making it back in one piece were slim. If those fireflies didn't get her — and without Aik around, that seemed likely — she might be waylaid by desperate Steaders, or eaten by whatever was turning the steadings into an out-of-control science project.

I could stay here. The idea had its appeal. It was a *safe* house, after all. But she'd run out of wood and food in short order, and water soon after, and then what?

"Good morning, Desla." Spin's voice sounded fake-cheery, like when her mother would sit her down as a child with a bit of particularly bad news.

"Spin! You're still here!" That was a stroke of luck. Aik must have left the strange little creature with her. "When did Aik leave? Did you see it?"

Golden lights spun around the familiar, brightening up the room. "He left at 1:53 this morning. He wants you to go home and take the urses with you. He asked me to watch over you."

What a strangely specific time. She snorted. "He can take his suggestions and shove them up his —"

"Suggestions aren't physical. Maybe he could use a stick instead?"

She laughed out loud. "Yes, I think a stick would work just fine." *Though Aik might disagree.*

She should go after him. She knew Aik's destination, and it was less than a day away. With any luck, she could catch up to him on the road.

Silya asked me to look after him. That decided her. She didn't make promises lightly, especially to the Hencha Queen. She really didn't want to disappoint Silya. Besides, she had the best chance of survival if she was with him. "Can you guide me to him?"

The lights whirred again. "I can try. Take me outside and I'll see if I can find him. I need a direct line of sight to the sky."

She blinked. *That's new.* "All right. Do I just pick you up?"

"Yes. I'm pretty tough."

She imagined he must be, to have survived a century or two and the crash landing of his ship. She picked him up gingerly, making sure to hold onto him tightly. "Hey, don't I get a nickname?"

Spin's lights flashed in what she guessed was surprise. "Do you *want* one?"

She slipped past the leather covering and felt her way through the narrow passage out of the cavern, the bright sunlight from outside partially blinding her. "Sure."

"What about Big Cheese?"

Big cheese? She shook her head. frowned, thinking about it. She did like cheese. Rather famously apparently. Still … "How about 'Friend'?"

Spin was quiet for a moment, and she wondered if he'd heard her. Then his golden lights flashed again. "I'd like that."

"Done." The air was already quite warm, a bad sign for the rest of the day. At least the clouds had lifted, but the air was already muggy.

"Though I still reserve the right to call you Cheese."

She smiled. *There you are.* "How will you find him?" Aik had said something about an Oracle, but that sounded like superstition.

"Just a moment. Scanning."

She frowned. Spin had a language all his own.

She looked around — the landscape outside the safe room continued to change.

The ground rumbled underfoot, as if the very world was unsettled by what was happening. The grasses were infiltrated by more of the coryx things, their white domes poking above the purple field like blisters.

A little red worm about the size of her index finger inched by, leaving a mucus-laden path. It wasn't from any species — Tharassan or human — that she recognized. *Strange.*

At least there were no fireflies, although a few stray blue wisps floated by overhead. A strange sense of relief filled her at the sight. *Shouldn't we have seen some verent by now, though?* "Almost done?"

"Just found one of the remaining satellites. Locking signals now."

What in Heaven's Reach does that mean? She was anxious to pack up and set off after Aik. He already had a long head start. She tried to make out the bulk of Anghar Mor to the north. They should be close enough to see it now, but it remained hidden behind a ridge of clouds.

"Download complete. If you're warm, we can go back inside, Friend."

"Yes, please." Desla wiped sweat off her brow. She slipped back into the cleft, the cooler air a balm. She set Spin down to pack up her things, starting with the sleep sack. "What's a satellite?"

Spin suddenly sounded more formal, like one of her teachers in the Temple. "In its broadest definition, a satellite is an object that orbits another object. Pellin and Tarsis are both satellites of Tharassas."

She laughed. "You were talking to the moon?"

"A satellite can also be an artificial construct. The original colony on Tharassas had a network of fifteen satellites that regularly monitored conditions on the ground — weather, seismic activity, seasonal shifts, and much more. Three of these satellites are still operational. I was able to uplink to one to download its latest data."

She tied off the sleep sack and poured a little of her remaining water on the coals, coaxing smoke and steam from the white ash. Not that there was anything in the cavern to burn, but old habits ... "What does that mean?"

"This." A map appeared above the device.

She gasped. It floated in the air, a design as intricate and colorful as any tapestry. That was magic, if she'd ever seen it. "What is it?"

"This is a satellite image of the Highlands, two weeks ago. It was stitched together from multiple passes by the three remaining satellites, so it is not a real-time image."

"It's ... beautiful." She peered at the vivid picture. Lake Zeraya was at its center, and mixed patches of wild purple and cultivated purple and green spread out from the lake's shores, mostly in a narrow band on the western side of the lake. In the north, Anghar Mor was perched at the edge of a glacier, its broken spire giving off a stream of smoke that trailed away to the east.

"Use your fingers, pinching or stretching them to make it smaller or bigger."

She reached out hesitantly, as if it might burn her, but she felt nothing more than a slight buzz when her fingers intersected the map.

She traced the lines of the few roads, getting her bearings, making parts bigger and then smaller. She could swoop in and see details as fine as a person riding urseback down Zeraya Road. *This is amazing. What other secrets are you hiding?*

"That's where we spent last night." She shivered and backed the view out. "And there's the first safe house. And this ..."

It was Isa Steading, where they'd first found the strange coryx. *That poor girl.* She wondered if Maur'Isa was safe. "What does this look like now?"

Spin's lights spun. "This is a new composite, from the last two days."

The map transformed. The healthy purple and green colors of the trine grass and human agriculture were mostly gone, replaced by blotches of sickly white that reached as far south as the Red Flight Mountains.

Her hand flew to her mouth. She'd seen it with her own eyes, but still …

"The invading flora are spreading rapidly through the valley. Based on imaging from the last two weeks, they originated from Anghar Mor."

Where Aik thought Raven was. "How long until there's nothing else living here?"

"Calculating."

She bit her lip. No way she'd make it home alive, through all those kilometers of enemy territory.

"Three days."

"And where's Aik?"

A flashing red marker appeared on the map, about two thirds of the way between the safe house and the slopes of Anghar Mor. "Here."

"Thank you, Spin." She was so out of her depth here. Machines in the sky overhead, magical maps, and a talking sphere … still, Spin had never steered them wrong. She had to trust him. Besides, she was better when she had something to do. "No time to waste, then."

"We're going back to Gullton, Cheese?"

She grinned. Apparently Spin wasn't as happy with her choice as he'd seemed. Or he just liked poking fun. "Not a chance."

"What, then?"

"We're going after Aik." She packed the pot and her few other things.

Spin's golden lights flashed. "Good. Sera would never have given up. I'm glad you won't either."

That Sera? Spin was full of surprises today.

Shaking her head, she made a quick, cold meal of some of the bandy fruit they'd found the day before, along with half of the hardtack and aur jerky left in the safe house stores. She packed the rest up to take with her. Unless they found something to else to eat, they would starve soon enough, but that was a worry for another day.

Mamma never said life would be easy. Then again, she'd also never said that Desla would be chasing a man half out of his mind across an alien hellscape, without as much as a hencha berry foldover to eat.

Shaking her head, she attached her sleep sack to the top of her pack.

She'd send the urses off. They were well-trained, and with any luck they'd make it back to Triya and the caravan. If not ... she had no grain left to feed them with, in any case, and there was nothing but desolation where she was going. Hopefully the fireflies would leave them alone.

She took them outside. She stopped to scratch each of them on their long, wide noses, and took a little extra time with Ursia. "You took good care of me. Now you be careful out there, you hear?" She slapped each of the urses on its haunches, watching as they took off back toward home, a lump in her throat.

When they had vanished out of sight, she took one last regretful look at the rock outcropping that had sheltered them for a night. It had been a safe place, and she was sad to have to leave it behind.

A few of the wisps dipped down from the sky to spin around her. The oppressive heat lessened, just a little.

"What are you, really?" She reached out to one of them, but it danced away before she could touch it.

There was no response. Still, she felt a little less alone. "Ready, Spin?"

"Ready, Cheese."

She laughed. "That's Big Cheese to you." She picked him up and slid him into a shirt pocket like she'd seen Aik do a couple of times, feeling him shift to fit his new home. A tentacle popped out, surveying the world around them.

She raised an eyebrow. *Magic indeed.* "Then off we go, after the gauntlet runner."

•　　　•　　　•

Aik stumbled across the empty, desiccated plain, holding up his hand to block the glare of the sun off the ice wall ahead. How there could still be ice in this infernal heat ... though the occasional sharp crack reverberated across the empty plain as a part of the glacier collapsed.

It was blasted hot out, the ground a mix of exposed rock and broken shale. Still, the heat didn't bother him, not nearly as much as the single-mindedness that drove him onward now that he was so close to Anghar Mor.

The fog from the rainfall the night before had lifted a couple of hours earlier, not long after sunrise, leaving the air thick and muggy enough to drink — if only! — even though the hard-packed earth was already dry.

The mountain loomed ahead of him, a forbidding, black cone of rock, its broken peak beckoning him on. Or mocking him. He couldn't decide. "Rave?"

"I'm here." Raven walked alongside him, looking brighter and more cheerful than he had felt in days. Weeks, maybe. "You're almost there. You can do it."

He blinked, and Raven was gone.

More delusions. Earlier he'd thought he'd seen a full meal pop up out of thin air just ahead of him — roast aur, a thick creamy potato-bacca soup, cave cheese, and of course, hencha berry foldovers fresh from the oven. It had vanished as soon as he reached for it.

I'm going to die out here.

He lifted his canteen to take a sip, but only a drop or two fell on his dry tongue.

Tri'Aya had been right about him. He'd barreled into this whole thing unprepared, and then left behind the one person who had offered to help him. *If I die, it's my own farking fault.*

He was dead tired. His soul was heavy, as if he dragged it behind him on a long chain that left its marks on the dry, dusty path. He stopped in his tracks, closing his eyes and resting for just a moment.

When he re-opened them, something sparkled in the sunlight ahead. *Water?*

He blinked, waiting for it to go away. But as he limped toward it, it stayed stubbornly in place — a puddle of rainwater in a cleft in the empty land. He fell to his knees in front of it, scooping up a handful and pouring it into his mouth.

It was hot and brackish, bitter, and full of minerals. But it was wet, and he swallowed it gratefully. He splashed some of it on his face, sighing in relief as it washed away the sweat and grime. Then he took a few more sips and filled his canteen. It was probably full of awful things, but he didn't care. It was wet.

Keep going. You're almost there.

He frowned. He'd long since forgotten who the annoying voice was, but it drove him onward, toward that jagged peak.

"You look like something an eircat dragged into its burrow." Raven was peering down at him, fists on his hips.

Aik tried to say his name, but all that came out was a croak.

"Come on. Get up. You'll die out here." Raven knelt and helped him to stand, his hand cool on his exposed arm.

"How did you get here?" He looked around, blinking. "I've been looking for you for days ..." Or had it been weeks?

Raven was gone, and the only footprints in the sand were his own. *Godsdammit. Another delusion.*

The ground shook, almost knocking him down again, and the mountain ahead belched a huge column of black smoke.

He sighed and shuffled forward again, eager to end his maddening journey. Eager to find the *real* Raven.

Ten minutes later he collapsed, unable to go on.

He held out a dusty hand toward the mountain, clutching at it one last time as if he could touch it, before his face hit the cracked, dry ground.

•   •   •

Desla found Aik's pack in a patch of dead trine grass next to one of the domes, a couple of kilometers north of the shelter. It was mid-morning in the Highlands, but she felt like she'd been transported to an alien world while she slept.

She was surrounded by coryx. So many of them that they piled on top of one another in places, making strange geometrical shapes. One of them had burst open as she passed it, sending a sparkling glitter into the air.

Spores. She knew how the spore mothers back in Clayton worked, but they were nothing like these ... things, other than in general shape. Both were white domes, but she'd never heard of someone's house going rogue and taking out an entire town.

They were clumped along her pathway, leaving barely enough room for Des to thread her way northward. *But will I be able to make my way back home, when this is over?*

The idea that it might never end chilled her to the bone.

The wisps had followed her, weaving around her as if guiding her way, and somehow keeping the world around her cooler than it should have been. She was grateful for the relief, almost as grateful as she was to Spin for tracking Aik's path.

She knelt next to his pack and pulled everything out with sweaty fingers. She sorted through the contents. Not much of use, except for a hunting knife. She stuck it in her own pack, which was half full.

He hadn't even taken any food with him from the shelter — proof the old Aik was still in there, somewhere. *Taking care of me.* She closed her eyes and said a quick prayer to Jor'Oss for luck.

"We'll find him, Cheese." Spin was peering into the empty pack.

"I hope so." She was grateful, too, for his simple presence.

She took a few of the less-dirty clothes and tucked them into her own pack and decided to leave the rest of his behind.

Soon she was headed north again, toward the broken peak that seemed always just on the edge of the horizon, when she could glimpse it at all through the sea of white domes. *Maybe I should have taken Aik's advice and gone home.*

"Spin, where is he now?" She'd rigged a cloth "necklace" for him that hung around her neck, and he'd obligingly changed shape into a teardrop-shaped pendant with a hole near the top to hang from.

Spin seemed to like being out in the open. He'd explained something about energy and sunlight. She could relate — having the sun warm your face was one of the pleasures of life. *Except when it's already so miserably hot.*

"Sorry. The satellites are out of range. His last known location was about ten kilometers north. Estimating current location at thirteen now."

"Thanks, Spin." Satellites and talking spheres. She lived in a world of miracles. Too bad not all of them were good.

She hadn't seen any of the glowing red bugs since the day before. Maybe it was too hot for them too? Or maybe the wisps were keeping them away.

She looked up at the pack of them — there had to be close to forty now — that paced her as she worked her way north. Every now and then, one would swing down past her as if checking to see if she was all right.

She took a deep breath and plunged ahead, hoping against hope to catch him before he got to the mountain. At least she still had her strength.

I need a distraction. "Spin, tell me a story." He had to know some good ones.

"About what?"

"Tell me about Sera." She squeezed her way between two of the coryx that were awkwardly close to one another.

"Are you sure? I could tell you an old Earth nursery rhyme about a boy and a girl who were eaten by a candy witch ..."

She laughed. "Um, no thanks. Sera, please." She'd always been fascinated by the woman, who'd come so far to live among them, and who had fought for her place amongst people who looked nothing like her.

Spin sighed. "Sera it is." His lights flashed, whether in resignation, or annoyance, she couldn't tell.

Why are you so reluctant to talk about her?

"Sera was a starship pilot, along with her wife Tavi, when I met them." He sounded strangely wistful. "They flew my ship, the *Spin Diver*, on its last run to Tharassas, a hundred and thirty-three Tharassan years ago, when Earth was collapsing ..."

•   •   •

Aik stumbled the last few steps across the empty plain, his feet aching and his breath ragged. He'd managed to crawl his way to another patch of brackish water, and that and the driving need had pulled him back to his feet to keep going.

Ahead of him, the black wall of Anghar Mor blocked his path, pock-marked with small holes, like cave cheese gone bad.

I miss cheese. He managed a bitter smile. He turned to tell Raven, but his soulmate was gone again. *Too bad. You would have liked that one.*

He glanced over his shoulder at the way he had come. The world was dead, everything cooked into oblivion, and there were dark splotches in his path.

He looked down at his feet. The edges of his boots were red, dripping blood. *Farking hell.*

"Raven. Raven, where are you?" He spun around unsteadily. He'd done it. He'd come to Anghar Mor. So where was he? "Raven!"

His voice echoed across the plains, but no one responded.

The world shimmered, from the heat or just from dehydration and sheer exhaustion. He couldn't be sure which. *I might be going a little mad.*

You're almost here.

The voice in his head, pushing him to go on, was the last straw.

He fell back against the rock, sliding down to the ground, and sobbed.

He was burnt out, a hollow husk of the man who had once been Aik.

He wanted Raven. Needed him. His friend. His soulmate. *My first real love.*

The sun didn't care, beating down on him like a hammer on an anvil.

Eventually he exhausted even his ability to cry. He just sat there, his back against the warm rock, staring at the empty green sky. Content to be still.

A bit of smoke trailed over it from the mountain peak above, a black stain across an otherwise perfect day.

This is where I die.

He closed his eyes, seeking comfort. His body ached all over, but especially his feet, which throbbed inside his boots. His throat was dry, the last of the canteen's dirty water long since gone.

He must have drifted off into a fitful sleep because the next thing he knew, someone was shaking him.

"Aik!"

"Rave?" Aik opened his eyes, looking up into Raven's eyes. "Is it really you?"

Raven smiled. "You made it."

"Oh gods, Raven ..." Something wasn't right. The voice. Too high to be Raven's.

His features shifted, becoming softer, the hair longer, and blond. "Aik, it's me, Desla."

He blinked. "Des?" Was it his imagination, or did she have a blue halo? He felt suddenly cooler too, as if she'd carried him away from this awful place to rest by the refreshing breezes of the sea.

She looked around. "Was Raven here?"

Disappointment threatened to crush him. "I ... don't know. Maybe. I thought he was?"

She knelt next to him. "You look parched. Here, have some water, but just a little." She held a canteen to his lips.

He sipped at it greedily, sighing in relief as the tepid water wet his mouth and trickled down his throat. When she pulled it away, he tried to grasp it, to drink more.

"You're dehydrated. A little at a time is better." She looked over her shoulder. "I don't think there was anyone else here. I only saw your footprints in the dirt. You did a number on your feet." She shook her head in apparent disapproval at the state of his boots. "Can you walk?"

"I think so. If you help ...?" He hated asking.

"Of course." She slipped her arm under his awkwardly, balancing the pack on her back as she helped him to his feet. "Come on. Let's find a place to shelter. It's too hot out here, and another storm is coming."

He sniffed the air. "How do you know?"

She managed a wan smile. "Spin told me. He's quite amazing, your little friend."

"Hello, Chief."

He laughed, but it quickly became a sob and then a wracking cough. He leaned against her for support.

Her brow knitted with concern. "Can you stand on your own?"

"I ... don't know. My feet are bleeding, I think." They protested his new upright position sharply. There was a sharp intake of breath; his or Desla's, he couldn't say.

"I see that. Come on. I saw some crags a little way along the mountainside. Maybe we can find a place, out of the wind."

"I'll try." He let go of her, putting a hand to the rock wall, and stood on his own, albeit shakily. His feet blazed with pain. "Des?"

"What?" She sounded curt.

Are you angry with me? "Thanks for coming after me." Raven had to be here somewhere. *He'll find us, and ...*

His mind wouldn't come up with anything after the *and*.

And we'll figure it out later. It would have to do.

The strange voice had gone silent in his head.

Aik allowed himself to be led, hobbling after Desla and Spin. Her cool, firm hand helped steady him as they went in search of shelter.

•   •   •

Triya watched their escort warily.

The firefly hovered a few meters above them, following their progress through the ruined grasslands.

When it had first found them the day before, she'd been sure they were about to die, but so far it seemed content to pace them, keeping track of their journey northward.

They were following that damned fool boy into hell, and not even the green-holy kind. No, this hell was a hot, muggy alien landscape filled with strange white domes that let off showers of sparkling dust every now and again.

She couldn't even say for certain if it was always the same one. Several times they'd spotted others zipping by, on their way to who-knew-where.

For now at least, they seemed to present no direct harm.

She'd sent Maur'Isa on with a full stomach, along with the other wagon filled with their remaining trade goods, in the hands of her two drivers. There was no one left to trade with, a hard fact she'd have to contend with once this was all over. *If we survive it.*

Only she, Mes and Em had continued on.

Not long after that, they'd encountered the rest of the refugees, a seemingly endless parade of human misery. She'd recognized a few of them — she'd spent decades cultivating relationships with hundreds of steadings. She gave them what she could.

Things were soon going to get very crowded at Gap Station.

In the end, they gave the wagon to one of the families near the end of the line, led by an older man called only Nimes who was struggling to keep the pace.

"Bless you, Tri'Aya." He'd bowed deeply at the gift, showing the bald top of his head in the middle of his wild white hair. "Whatever you have need of, when the time comes ..." His voice hitched.

"No thanks necessary. You're doing me a favor, taking it back to the Gap, Mas Nimes." She'd known him for ten years, a proud man who farmed a rocky patch of land on the north side of Lake Zeraya.

His eyes filled with tears, and he nodded, reaching out a shaking hand to squeeze her arm.

Then his family helped him up onto the wagon, along with a couple small children, and they set off after the others.

"That was nicely done, mim." Es's gaze followed the wagon as it headed off south.

Triya shrugged. "He needed it more." She eyed Es's rented urse. "You don't mind if I ride with you?" She didn't fancy walking the rest of the way, and they'd only hired two urses at the station.

"Of course not." Es grinned and helped her up to sit behind her.

They found a treasure trove on the way — a grove of bandy trees at the old Isa Steading. They were about the only thing left standing. Triya and the others had picked as many of the strange spiky fruit as they could manage and piled them in the back of the wagon. She'd kept a bunch of them, tied in sacks at the back of each of the urses.

At least they wouldn't lack for food, even if it became repetitive.

Mes and Em followed the road as it threaded its way through the coryx-gone-wild. Mes had her hand on her sword hilt, though what good a sword would do against any of this, Triya had no idea.

She couldn't help but feel they were being herded into a trap. She should have left well enough alone and headed back home. *Aik, what have you gotten us into?*

Throughout it all, it got warmer and warmer, until the heat became an oppressive presence that sometimes made it hard to breathe. It was unnatural. Triya shuddered.

They had plenty of water, though, and they drank it copiously.

The sky above was leaden gray, as oppressive as the bleak road that threaded its way through the strange growths. She'd sent her last umvit off to Gullton … there would be no return messages. If it made it safely, Silya would know what was happening here.

Two days before, Em had spotted something in the sky. A verent, she'd thought, maybe two. Triya had to take her word for it. Her eyesight wasn't as good as it used to be. And yesterday they'd traveled in miserable rain for half the day.

Still they hadn't found Aik or Desla. She had to admit, if only to herself, that the two of them might already be dead.

Now they trudged along under a clear sky, the broken tip of Anghar Mor visible on the horizon. If anything, it was worse than the day before. The rain that had brought some relief had evaporated, creating a muggy haze that got under her clothing, so that even sweating didn't cool her down.

"Do you hear that?" Mes pulled her long blond hair back from her ears.

"What is it?" Triya cocked her head, looking over Em's shoulder. A hot breeze blew over the forlorn landscape, ruffling her hair, but nothing else stood out. *I have old ears too.*

Who was she kidding? Everything about her was old. *When did that happen?*

"Hoofbeats, I think."

They hadn't met anyone else on the road since the horde of refugees. She hoped Silya would find a way to take care of them, though she didn't see how. "Maybe Mas'Erio has come to his senses?"

Mes snorted. "I'll show him his senses when I reach into him and pull them out of his head, through his mouth."

Triya chuckled in spite of herself. She might be inclined to help.

They stopped, waiting to see who approached them. They didn't have to wait long.

Two urses appeared at the top of the next rise, gallomping down the road and kicking up dust.

Mes's own urse wherried in excitement.

"I think those are ours, Mim." Mes stared at the approaching urses, hand over her eyes.

"You're right." The urses slowed to a canter, approaching the three of them with caution.

"That's Em's Erra for sure. And my Eska!" Mes slipped down from her borrowed urse's back and threw her arms around the newcomer. "Hello, gorgeous!"

Triya frowned. "So where are their riders?"

Mes looked northward. "If they're headed for Anghar Mor, I'd guess they cut the urses loose. The country gets a bit rough up there to go on urseback." She sounded grudgingly respectful.

Triya considered their changed circumstance. "I'd guess we're not far from having to leave the road ourselves?"

"Yes, Mim. Half an hour on urseback?"

Triya glanced at their escort. "I don't suppose we have the element of surprise on whatever's waiting, with that little firefly

watching us. Let's send the urses back and go on foot from here."
Hopefully they'd make it back to Gap Station together. Hers were
well trained – they'd follow the others home.

"Yes, Mim," her guards said in tandem, bringing the ghost of a
smile to Triya's lips.

Em looked back the way they'd come. "Do you think they'll be
safe?" She rubbed Erra's muzzle.

"Safer than where we're going."

Part of her relished the idea of walking for a bit. She was
saddle-sore from so much riding and missed her own bed and
dining hall. That surprised her. Normally she thrived on being out
in the open air. *These aren't normal times.*

With a heavy sigh, she slipped off Mes's urse, her old bones
protesting. She untied her pack and set it up against one of the white
domes.

Mes followed suit, then she got the beast turned around and
gave it a slap on the haunches.

It wherried and took off the way they had come, followed by
the other three.

Safe passage. Loja bless you. She traced the infinity sign in the
air across her chest and turned to look at the broken peak ahead.
"Let's go. The path isn't gonna walk itself."

She set off, and the two women she trusted most in the world
followed after her.

13

REFUGEES

SILYA LOOKED OUT of the flitter's battered windscreen hungrily, drinking in all of the valley below. Flying was such an amazing thing, to float high above the world and see it like only the birds and the gods could — no wonder Raven loved his verent so.

The hencha gatherings called to her, filled with *need* and *love* and *pain* as their brethren were consumed by the strange new threat in the Highlands. Each death rippled throughout the whole collective, and through the link to Silya herself.

At least she knew now what had them so riled up, if not what caused it. *Is this war?*

She wondered if the *eshem* felt it too. It was still strange to think that there were others like herself. She'd always thought the Hencha Queen was unique, the *chosen one*, and to find out there were others — both the eshem and those who had answered the hencha's call to help in the Temple — was a shock. *You never told me.*

You never asked. The hencha were a constant presence in her mind these days, providing her comfort and updates on their progress with the speakers in the throne room — what she'd taken to short-handing others who had the ability to talk to the hencha.

Long gone were her worries that they would forsake her.

In the sky her to left, Raven rode Breeze, having little trouble keeping up with the flitter. They'd decided it would cause less disruption if the verent rider arrived at the Station fully clothed, as he had in Gullton.

To her right, Kerrick and Elleck rode Jai and Angel.

They would part ways at the Gap, the four of them going on to meet with Elleck's clan and its eshem.

They'd barely had time for a goodbye in the morning, but the night they'd spent together — it would carry her through the coming dark days until he returned. She blushed at the thought, no longer concerned who knew about the two of them.

The world might be ending, and she was done hiding. *If not now, when?* "How long until we get to the gap?"

"Another half hour, Mim." Fen motioned at the back seat. "Will she be all right?"

She hated breaking her promise not to make the poor woman fly again, but she needed Dor. No one was as good as she was at organization, and they had a whole nation to sort out in a few days. Who knew when the threat from the Highlands would invade the Heartland too? There had already been incursions, reports of the fireflies stinging aur and other beasts. *Testing the waters?*

Dor had her hood pulled over her head and was staring pointedly at her toes in their leather sandals.

"You all right back there, Dor?"

"Yes, Mim."

She rolled her eyes. *So we're back to that, are we?* "You'll tell me if you're not?"

A longer pause, this time. "Yes, Mim."

Silya let her be. *I'm pushing you too hard.* She needed to find more help. Maybe Coral would step up. It was time for her to become a full sister.

Maybe it's time for all the initiates to be raised. She needed all the help she could get, even if it risked offending the other sisters.

She closed her eyes. *Show me the map.*

Of course. Her proxies had been hard at work, feeding the hencha everything they could read about Gullton and the cave systems beneath it. Now it appeared in her mind, sparkling below her as if she were a gully bird soaring high above the city.

It was exquisite, filled with such detail that the hencha must have used other sources beyond the dry reading she'd been feeding them. *Maybe actual gully birds, for aerial surveillance?*

The world was far more connected than she'd ever suspected. *And the caverns?*

The map lit up with blue light, the surface of Gullton disappearing to show five interconnected sets of lines, one for each spine. Like arteries. Again, the level of detail was such that some other source of information had to have been tapped by the hencha. And far below, even more caverns that connected to the mainland under the Elsp.

A mystery for another time. *Thank you.*

Time grows short. The distress in their collective voice was clear.

I know. All this thought and effort given to protecting the humans under her charge, and she hadn't done anything to help the hencha. *What can I do for you?*

The response was immediate. *Stop the death bringer.*

She frowned. The Death Bringer was a tale mothers frightened their children with — a beast with long, gnashing teeth and wicked claws that dropped with poison. Surely they couldn't mean the same. *What — or who — is the death bringer?*

He comes. Soon.

She bit her lip. They either wouldn't or couldn't tell her more. *Time will tell.*

She unrolled one of the paper maps Sister Tela had prepared for her of the Heartland and the Gap. Tela had a gift for drawing, even if she was no Sol'Eria.

There were several caverns noted from the initial survey that were close enough to Gap Station for her purposes. It would be a challenge, but if she could convince the Steader refugees to take shelter, she could arrange to provide them with enough food and water for a couple weeks. Beyond that … *If this isn't over by then, we're all dead anyway.*

She'd spent half the evening poring over old military texts. There were few enough of them. Tharassas had a relatively peaceful history since it had been settled. There'd been a few uprisings over supply shortages in the first hundred years, and of course the border tensions with the ce'faine.

Spin might have known more. She was dying to talk to the little creature, a throwback to a bygone time. What did he know? What could he share that might make the whole world better?

Or worse. Hadn't rampant, uncontrolled knowledge been what had destroyed Old Earth?

Still, he might hold some of Earth's old military texts, and that could be exceedingly useful.

Then again, the enemy here had no troops. They didn't even know what it was they were fighting. Not really. *How do you fight a war against a force of nature?*

The land was rising now toward them, the fields of the central valley falling behind and the peaks of Heaven's Reach marching south to meet the walls of the Gap ahead.

They passed over a strange group of white domes, and small stick figures poured out of them to look into the sky.

Her breath caught. For a moment she feared the enemy had taken its first steps into the Heartland. Then she remembered that some of the outlying towns used a strange, giant fungus for their homes. *Coryn? Coryx?* They looked much like what her mother had described in the Heartland.

Strange coincidence. Then again, she didn't believe in coincidence.

The flitter sputtered, dropping a few feet before recovering.

She grabbed the arm rests, shooting a worried glance at Fen. "Everything all right?"

Behind her, Dor groaned.

Fen nodded. "Likely just a hiccup in the fuel line. I'll check it out when we land."

She shuddered. The craft was old, *really* old. Maybe she should have gone on verentback. Raven had offered. But she didn't want the Temple to be beholden to creatures she didn't fully understand.

Of course, that could describe the hencha too. *Why did I think this was a good idea?*

"Everything all right in there?"

Kerrick's voice startled her. She turned to find Angel/Jai flying next to the manmade craft, with Kerrick and his sister on their back. He waved.

"We're fine!" She shouted over the noise of the flitter blades. "Don't get too close!"

"We won't. Your little mechanical craft spooks the verent." He raised his arm. "We're off to see the *ce'faine*. Back as soon as we can!"

She blew him a kiss, blushing like a silly initiate.

She wasn't sure from the distance, but she thought he winked.

Angel's powerful wings pumped the air, pulling the verent ahead and catching a current that lifted her and her riders up and out of her line of sight.

A few minutes later, they were over the Gap, a narrow, deep cut in the land between Heaven's Reach in the north and the Red Flight range to the south. She caught flashes of reflected light down there, where the Elsp wound its way along one canyon wall into the sunlight. Soon, the station came into sight, at a point about halfway in where the walls widened to create a broad clearing in the middle of the canyon.

She gasped.

There were hundreds of tents and other temporary shelters set up around the central building, extending all the way to the walls of the Gap itself. Smoke from numerous campfires filled the air, blowing up and away toward the Highlands on a stiff breeze. There was a clearing near the station too, where only a few people milled about.

A loud rumble filled the air, and the ground below her shook. There were collective shouts of alarm, loud enough for her to hear over the thump-thump-thump of flitter blades, and then everything settled down again. An apt reminder that time was growing short.

What if the caverns collapse? Or already have? She'd have scouts sent out to check them before the refugees were sent on. She sighed. *One challenge at a time.*

The flitter set down in the trampled grass of the clearing, with Raven and his verent not far behind.

She opened the flitter door to a world of deprivation, grief, and sorrow. The shelters, which viewed from above were somewhat organized, revealed the chaos beneath. Hundreds ... no, thousands of hollow-eyed Steaders, seated on the ground or on makeshift seats, huddled around the dancing flames of cook fires.

There was a palpable sense of rolling disaster, of the losses these people had suffered that had uprooted them from their homes and sent them here.

The vast scale of human misery around her was overwhelming. *Where do I even start?* What could the promise of Temple or City funds do for these people?

She took a deep breath and exhaled, and then grabbed her staff. *All we can do is try.*

"Jas save us." Raven appeared at her side, staring at the camp.

She squeezed his hand. "Let's hope she listens."

The refugees were coming out of their shelters now, staring at the newcomers and especially the verent. Their fear was palpable too, filling the air with its stench. Or was that just the vast unwashed populace?

No pretty speech would fix this.

"Mim?"

She turned to find a young man staring at her. He was well dressed ... probably from the Station itself. "And you are?"

"Aer'Lis, Mim. Son of the station master. You're *her*, aren't you?" His gaze strayed to the flitter and the verent curled up next to it, and then snapped back to her.

"The Hencha Queen? Yes." She drew strength from the staff, calming her frayed nerves.

Aer'Lis nodded. "Very good, Mim. We're so glad you are here. We've done what we can for these ... visitors. But we don't have enough to help them all. And our regular guests ..." He trailed off, seeing the look on her face.

"Mim." Dor was at her side, a cold hand on her arm. Poor thing looked pale as an inthym.

"What?"

"You don't need them."

She looked down to see the flames licking her arms and her staff. She closed her eyes. "You're right." She took a deep breath, consciously extinguishing them. It had become her go-to reflex, using the fire to intimidate anyone in her way. She turned back to Aer'Lis, determined to use only the power of her office and her own force of will. "*Regular guests?* Aer'Lis, look around. These people have lost their homes, their land, their livestock — everything that they couldn't carry away on their backs."

She had failed them. She'd known this was coming and she hadn't done enough to stop it, or to help those in its path. *I should have found a way.*

At least Mas Lis had the grace to blush at that. "Yes, Mim."

Her guilt gnawed at her. Never mind that she couldn't even convince her own people. "You have food? Water? Firewood?"

"Yes Mim. But ..."

"Get everyone in the Station — staff and guests alike — out here to help these people. Bring out whatever food you have. I will make sure the Temple provides more. And bring warm water and wash cloths — or better yet, let them inside to use whatever facilities you have. Let these people clean their wounds. Can't you see what they've been through, for Jas's sake?"

She realized was looming over him, feeling larger than normal, as sometimes happened with the hencha. *Well, maybe just a little magical intimidation wouldn't hurt.*

The poor boy was shaking, and even Raven looked pale.

"Yes, Mim. Right away." Aer'Lis turned tail and ran, and a low cheer went up among the refugees who had gathered around her.

She turned to face them, and her heart broke to see so much pain and loss. How many hadn't made it out of the Highlands?

"That was a bit harsh." Raven raised an eyebrow.

She shook her head. She wouldn't apologize for her anger. "He needed to hear it."

"Maybe so." Raven touched her shoulder. "But you have no need to feel guilty about this. You did what you could. We all did."

She closed her eyes and nodded, grateful. "Maybe." When she opened them, she caught a hint of unexpected compassion in his eyes. "You really have changed."

"Tell anyone and I'll deny it."

She looked into his eyes, wanting him to really hear her. "I *see* it. And I'm glad you came back."

He sighed. "I just wish things were normal again. I miss normal."

"So do I." There were worse things than living an everyday, boring life. Someday maybe they'd have that once again.

She turned back to the crowd to find a young woman at the forefront with long blond hair, staring at her. Silya flashed her what she hoped was a comforting smile. "I'm Sil'Aya. And you are?"

The girl blushed, barely apparent under all the grime on her face. "Maur'Isa. Maura."

"Well, Maura, it's good to meet you." Silya approached her and touched her cheek. Some of the hurt and pain flowed through to her from the girl, and there was a corresponding surge from the staff as it absorbed the emotions. She blinked. *I didn't know I could do that.*

"Thank you, mim." The change in Maur'Isa was immediate — her face glowed, and she threw her arms around Silya, surprising her with a fierce hug.

Silya hugged her back. "You're welcome. We have to stay hopeful. This too will pass."

"Yes, Mim. Norja's blessings on you." She did the sign of the infinite across her chest.

"Thank you." She surveyed the crowd. There were far too many wounds for her to heal. She was just one woman, even if she was the Hencha Queen. But maybe she could do this one small thing.

She moved to the next person in line, repeating the process and drawing out a little of the pain and exhaustion. Maura's line seemed as good as any. "Nor'Oss's blessings upon you." *Hencha give me strength.*

The middle-aged man — a farmer by the looks of his callused hands and sun-lined face — brightened. "And upon you."

Peace and love flowed into her through the bond for each person she touched.

The hencha were wounded too, a number of their gatherings wiped out by the invaders' threat. Still, they gave freely, and as she made her way through the crowd, the mood shifted from despair to the smallest, slightest bit of hope.

Raven was talking with some of the refugees too, mostly children. He let a little boy pet Breeze's snout, and the rest of the kids let out an *oooh* of appreciation. They stared at the beast in wonder.

She felt a spark of hope herself. *Surely such beasts can help us beat back these invaders.*

Aer'Lis returned with some others from the Station, carrying crates and some platters of food. An older man was with him, simply dressed in leather and homespun cloth, but with an air of authority that marked him as the station master.

"Mim, a moment?" He waited for her with his thumbs in his belt loops.

She nodded, squeezing the hands of one of the refugees, an elderly woman named Cir'Enea.

"Bless you, Mim." The woman kissed her cheek and put something into her hand. It was a little aur woven from trine grass, a toy she might have made for a child. Cir'Enea closed Silya's hand around it. "For luck."

"Bless you too." She let the woman go, wondering that someone who'd lost everything still found it in her heart to give a gift to the likes of her.

She tucked it into a pouch at her waist, silently thanking Dor and Keh'Sel, the Temple seamstress, for her new more practical clothing. Taking a deep breath, she turned her attention to the Station master. "Mas?"

He bobbed his head. "We're happy to help those in need, mim ..."

"But?"

"We barely manage with what we have with our regular ... guests. By the end of today, we'll be out of ... well, almost everything. And what then?"

She took a deep breath. She could almost feel the man's fear. He was as scared as the refugees. *We all are.* "Trouble is coming, Mas ... Lis? And war."

Raven materialized at her side.

He nodded. "Ahn'Lis. Ahner." He looked worriedly up the pass. "War? I thought this was some kind of natural disaster."

"It's a war, even if we don't yet understand the enemy fully. This —" She gestured to the refugees crowding the snow-trampled meadow. "I'm afraid this is just the beginning. This place is no longer safe. I need your help to get these people to safety, and yourself with them. The Temple stands ready to help, as does Gullton."

The man wiped his brow, sweating in the warm late-morning air. "Begging your pardon, Mim, but what can you do to help us? Croners won't get us more food. Not to mention chop wood, but I'd reckon food's the most urgent thing."

"I think we can help with that." Raven flashed her a grin.

Ever the cocky bastard. She suppressed a smile. "How? There are only a handful of verent riders."

The Station master raised an eyebrow, flicking a glance at Breeze. The beast was on its back, letting the children climb over him. "He ... she?"

"He."

"He's mighty and fearsome." He shuddered, taking an involuntary step backward. "But how will that help us?" Ahn'Lis couldn't take his eyes off Breeze.

The verent sneezed, knocking a couple of the kids into the grass of the meadow. They bounced back up, laughing.

"There are only a handful of riders, true. But there are hundreds of verent."

"There are?" A surge of hope filled her. "Of course there are. You told us at the meeting. Would they help us?"

Raven's eyes unfocused for a minute, and then he nodded. "Breeze says yes. Astrid will bring some of them here, and the rest to the Temple tonight."

She blinked. She'd forgotten he could speak with the other riders at a distance. *Wonders upon wonders.* Now she just had to convince the Council to part with some of their food stores and supplies.

She looked around for Dor. She found her talking to some of the refugees. "Wait here for a moment?"

The Station master nodded. "Of course, mim." Now that he had a promise of assistance, his feathers seemed much less ruffled.

She approached Dor from behind. The woman was nodding earnestly, speaking to a couple of Steaders.

"... a little young for a Hencha Queen. But she's *very* smart."

She smirked. "Glad to hear it."

Dor almost jumped out of her skin. "Mim'Aya!" She flushed red. "These are Mim and Mas Eydra, of Eydra Steading."

She nodded. "Good to meet you. I'm so sorry it had to be under such dire circumstances. Did your family make it out all right?" She could imagine the pain they were feeling. She'd felt it herself when she'd touched each of them earlier.

"Yes, Mim. Thankfully. One of the other Steaders warned us in time." Mim'Eydra was taller than her husband, and her dark hair would have been much more unusual in a crowd of Gulltonites.

"We'll have help for you soon, I promise." She tapped Dor's shoulder. "May I steal Sister Dor? The Station master will provide what he can while we round up supplies."

"How will they get here?" Mas Eydra frowned. "There are so many of us. Surely the Station doesn't have enough to feed us all, not for more than a day or two?"

She touched his shoulder. "Trust me. We will take care of you." She pulled a little of the worry from his mind.

His expression changed. He nodded and almost smiled. "You are a blessing, Mim'Aya."

Silya flashed him a smile. "Thank you, Mas. You're kind to say so." Tri'Aya always said a little honey went a long way. "Dor, a moment?"

"Yes, Mim." Dor followed her.

They stepped into a small copse of violet pines, and Dor pulled out the little long talker. "Let's see. Sister Tela said the little light would tell us if it was 'in range.'" She chuckled. "I'm still not sure what that means. I guess if it's working right now?" She stared at the black device with a frown. "Seems like magic to me."

"You and me both." So much seemed like magic these days, good and bad. When this was all over, she'd have to see about setting up a new guild to learn more about and catalogue the world around them.

"There. Green. That's good, I think." She seemed pleased with herself.

"May I?"

"Of course, Mim … Silya." She held out the long talker.

She growled under her breath. It was, apparently, a very hard habit to break. She pressed the talk button. "Coral, can you hear me?"

Nothing.

"Hello, Coral? Can you hear me?" If the cursed thing didn't work, they'd have to fly all the way back to Gullton to get things going.

The long talker crackled so loudly that she looked around wildly to make sure they weren't overheard.

"Yes, Mim. This is Coral."

Thank Ay'Oss. "Silya please. Coral, we're at the —"

"Things are going well here, although there was another shake —"

She shook her head. "We have to take turns."

She could hear the initiate's contrition over the connection. "Sorry, Mim. Silya …"

"That's all right. Let's say … hmmm … 'finished' when we're done talking? Finished."

"That makes sense. Fin."

Fin. I like that. She marveled at the ability to talk to someone on the far side of the great valley as if they were a meter apart. It truly was an age of wonders, if not also of extreme dangers.

"Silya? Fin."

"Sorry, Coral. Just thinking." She gathered her thoughts. "Things are worrisome here. There are hundreds of refugees, maybe a thousand, all of them scared and tired and hungry. I need you to step up today. As of this moment, you are no longer an initiate. You're a full sister now. Fin."

"But Mim ... Silya ... what about the tests? The ceremony?"

She could hear the excitement in the girl's voice. "We'll do the ceremony later, but you've already passed all the tests. Fin."

She could picture Coral blushing. "Thank you. That's ... unexpected. Thank you. Fin."

She wished she could have been there to give the girl a hug. "It's well deserved. When I get back, we'll see about raising the other initiates top. We need everyone we can find in this crisis. Fin."

There was silence on the other end of the line. Then finally Coral's voice replied. "Yes, Mim. Shall I tell the others?"

She thought about it. "Yes, go ahead. It will raise their spirits. But listen closely to this next part. I need you to prepare as much food as you can for transport. Dried goods are best, but fruit, cave cheese, whatever we can manage out of the Temple stores. Work with Verla. It will need to be placed in something that can be strapped to an urse or an aur—"

"We have a bunch of old saddle bags in storage. But won't the fresh goods spoil by the time they get to the Station?" There was a second of silence. "Um, fin?"

"Don't worry about that. You're about to have a bunch of flying visitors on your doorstep. Fin."

"Mim?"

She let that go. "The verent are coming. I should be back in time for their arrival." Oh what a sight that would be. "How goes the project? The hencha are building quite a map of Gullton and the caverns. Fin."

Coral was silent for a moment. "It looks like we're about a third of the way done. Sister Tela keeps bringing up new books from the archives. Fin."

"Good. Keep at it, around the clock, if needed. But don't kill yourselves." That was the last thing she needed.

"Yes, Mim Silya. On it. Fly safely! Fin."

She chuckled. She flipped the channel on the long talker to its second channel, the one she'd set for Kerrick's device. "Kerrick, can you hear me?"

Dor shook her head. "The light's red. He's out of range."

She sighed. She wasn't sure how these little miracles decided when they were "in" and "out" of range. Was it simple distance, or something else? So much she still didn't know.

She closed her eyes and reached out to the hencha. *Can you tell me if Angel and Jai are all right?* It was a long shot, but if the hencha really were connected to everything else ...

There was silence for a moment.

"You all right?" Dor's eyes shone with concern.

She blinked. She was so lost in other places she'd almost forgotten the woman right in front of her. "Yes. Just checking in on our friends."

"Ah."

Breeze says all is well. They're almost at the camp of the East Valley Clan.

Thank you.

The battle comes. They were worried. She could feel the weight of it in the back of her head.

I know. I just wish I knew how to fight it.

The hencha seemed helpless against this new threat.

She felt it too. *What would Triya do?* "Stop feeling sorry for yourself, for the gods' sake." She cracked a smile. Of course she'd say that. *I hope you're all right, Triya.*

"So what now?" Dor was staring at her, her brows knitted with concern.

"One thing at a time. Let's get these people moving. Raven can take me up to explore the caverns, while you get things organized here —"

The long talker crackled to life. "Hello?"

Kerrick? The voice sounded strange, though. Anxiously she pushed the button. "Hello, Kerrick? Is that you? Fin."

"This is Spin. Who is this?"

14

INTO THE EAST

KERRICK HELD ON to Elleck for dear life.

His sister was strong, as strong as he was, and even though this was only her second time verentback, she rode Angel as if she'd been born to it.

He was at home on the back of an urse, but this was a different thing altogether. You couldn't fall half a kilometer from urseback — not without the aid of a steep cliff.

Watching Jai become a part of the great beast had been strange enough, and what was with that strange lump on his neck? Elleck had never explained hers either.

When the verent had leapt into the air, his stomach had turned upside down and tried to exit his body from one end or the other.

He'd quelled his nausea by holding tight and closing his eyes, an unsuitable reaction for a man his age, and a Guard to boot. *It's like I'm five years old again.*

When he'd finally opened them, they were high above the Heartland, where the view was breathtaking. Literally breathtaking. Cold sweat covered his face, and his heart pounded, seeking the same exits his stomach had before.

Off to their right, the flitter and the other verent — Raven's Breeze — soared with them over the wide, fertile valley. How strange that he was now a verent rider. The thought distracted him for a precious moment before a bit of turbulence jerked him back to his present predicament.

To the north, the mountains of Heaven's Reach loomed like teeth, and for a brief instant, he wished they would swallow him whole and end his misery.

He closed his eyes again and tried counting to a hundred.

"You all right back there?" Elleck's voice was ripped away by the wind of their passage.

"I will be," he managed through chattering teeth. *Just the cold.* "How far is your clan?"

"A couple hours." She glanced at him over her shoulder. "It's fun, isn't it?" Some of their old sibling rivalry crept into her voice.

He forced his eyes open, not about to be outdone by his little sister. Strange as that still seemed to him. *I'll get used to it.*

If he didn't look down, it wasn't so bad.

"The Heartland's really beautiful, especially from up here. Look at the hencha fields!"

Easier said than done. He glanced at them, seeing mostly a rush of purple, and his stomach clenched again. He slammed his eyes closed and rested his head against the cool leather of Elleck's back.

"Afraid of heights?" The mockery was gone from Elleck's voice.

"Not usually," he grumbled. "Afraid of flying, maybe." He'd been in high places before, but there was always something concrete underfoot. The verent was solid enough, but she was buffeted by the winds and bobbed up and down in the air as she flew.

She squeezed his leg. "Remember that time we climbed to the top of Tucker's Rock?"

He flashed a weak grin and nodded, keeping his eyes closed. "You were so scared you almost shat your trousers."

She laughed. "*Almost* doesn't count." She was silent for a moment. "Do you remember what you told me?" she asked at last.

It had been such a long time ago, in the *before-time*, when Kerrick had been a normal boy with a normal family. Up early each morning to work the steading, done by sunset.

One of their rare days off in late fall, after the harvest. The sun had been particularly strong, warm on his face. He'd needed a challenge.

He'd planned to leave Enrick behind. Kerrick was almost ten, and Enrick was just two years younger, but he was annoying in the way that only younger siblings can be …

·   ·   ·

"Where you going, Ker?"

Kerrick rolled his eyes. "Nowhere. Don't you have an aur stall to muck out?"

Enrick grinned. "Nope, all done."

"Is the courtyard swept?" There had to be something to keep him busy.

"Done. Come on, let me go with you."

Kerrick frowned. "I don't know …"

"You *never* let me come. Mom's mad at Dad. She'll just take it out on me."

Kerrick nodded in sympathy. She'd been mad about something or other every day that week. "All right. I'm going to climb Tucker's Rock. You still want to go?"

Enrick's eyes widened. "Holy henchaballs, yes!" Enrick had been after Kerrick to take him *up the rock* for months.

"All right. Put on your thickest trousers and that shirt you wear when we cut back the trine grass."

"Got it." Enrick scampered off.

Half an hour later, his little brother had been clinging to the rock face, crying his eyes out, and Kerrick had been sorry he'd said yes. *You ruin everything.*

Still, he tried to be patient. "Come on. It's just a few more meters." He peered back at his brother, whose face was red from the effort. The rock was ten meters tall, made of dark black stone, and from the top had a view of the valley all the way to the ice shelf in the north and Lake Zeraya in the southeast.

"I … can't." Enrick's eyes were shut tight. "I'll just stay here."

"Until you starve or fall off?" He was starting to feel bad for Enrick. After all, he could have made his little brother stay at the steading.

Enrick's eyes flew open. "I don't wanna fall!"

He took a deep breath. Enrick was as scared as a cornered ix. *Maybe when you're almost ten, you'll be brave like me too.*

The first time he'd tried to go up the rock, he'd almost peed his pants. But that had been ages ago, when he was only nine. He heard his father's voice in his head. *You always look after your little brother. You hear?* "Close your eyes."

His brother stared up at him for a moment, and then nodded. "All right." He shut them, hard, like he was trying to imagine himself somewhere ... anywhere else.

"Don't let go!" Kerrick kept his own voice calm. "Now take a deep breath and hold it."

He breathed in, and some of the color left his face.

"Good. Now let it go."

He obeyed.

"Do it again. Air is magic. Feel it flowing through you, making you stronger. Braver."

"All right." Enrick breathed slowly in and out a few more times.

He grinned. "Are you ready?"

"I don't know ..."

Kerrick shook his head. "No doubts, or you'll ruin the magic. One more breath. And remember, the scary part is over. You just have to finish the job."

His brother obeyed, breathing in and holding it.

"Can you feel it?"

He nodded, breathing out again. He opened his eyes and met Kerrick's gaze. "I can!"

"Now slowly, climb up to me. One foot after the other, then one hand after the other. Do it while the magic's still in your lungs!"

Enrick grasped a handhold, then lifted his left foot. He was moving again — that was the most important thing.

He sighed, relieved.

In two minutes, Enrick navigated the rest of the climb, reaching the flat top of the rock and practically threw himself into Kerrick's arms. His momentum knocked his brother over into the patch of trine grass that grew atop the rock, cushioning their fall. "I did it!"

He grinned. "You did!" Enrick was a pain in the urse. But when he smiled, he lit up Kerrick's world. "When you're ready, we'll go down the easy way."

His little brother looked up at him. "Wait, there's an *easy* way? Why didn't we come up that way?"

Kerrick laughed. "Where's the fun in that?" He patted Enrick on the back. "Sit down a moment and look at the view."

They sat together at the edge, staring out over Aze Steading and the wide Highlands valley that spread out below them. Purple trine grass was interrupted by the ploughed fields of the steading — corn, cotton, and even a small hencha gathering.

He took a deep breath himself. For the moment, he was happy, content to enjoy one of those rare afternoons when he had nothing to do, and no responsibilities whatsoever. *Life is good.*

• • •

Kerrick snapped back to the present. "The magic."

Elleck laughed. "Yes, the magic. Take a deep breath and hold it." She paused as if for dramatic effect. "Air is magic."

He laughed but did as he was told. It was cool and calming, filling his lungs.

"Do you feel it?"

He breathed out. "A little." He took another deep breath, holding it for a few seconds before letting it go. "You know that wasn't real, right?"

"Maybe not. But you feel better, right?"

He opened his eyes. "I do."

"*That's* real."

Looking at the ground still made him feel queasy, but if he closed his eyes and took a few deep, long breaths, the feeling went away. Maybe air *was* magic. "I've missed you, Elleck. Gods, how I've missed you."

"I missed you too, Ker." She squeezed his leg again.

The sun was creeping past midday when they left the others behind at Gap Station. He watched the flitter descend toward the ragtag refugee tents in the wide clearing, followed by Raven on Breeze. *Stay safe, Sil.*

Elleck whistled at the sight of all the refugees gathered in the meadow around the station.

How bad are things in the Highlands? "I was there once. At Gap Station."

She glanced back at him. "After …?"

"Yeah. When they sent me to Gullton to live with Aunt Resalba." Mim Ina. Though she hadn't been his blood relative, she'd been strict but fair, raising him along with her wife Nes'Mora as if he were their own. "Was it hard for you?"

She didn't reply.

Maybe she hadn't heard him. The wind was growing stronger as they rode an updraft to the Highlands. "Was it hard for you, too?"

"I heard you the first time." Her voice was hard as rock.

He bit his lip. "Sorry."

Her shoulders slumped. "No. It's just … yes, it was difficult. I lost everything in an instant. I thought you were dead, too." She glanced over her shoulder at him, and her eyes were moist. "The ce'faine live a very different kind of life. No beds. No permanent home. Always on the move." He sighed. "Still, Alibeh took me in. She was kind to me, even when others treated me like an outsider."

"Your … eshem?"

"She wasn't then. She was chosen last year." There was an edge to her voice, which told Kerrick to let it go.

"I'm so sorry, Elleck. I wish I had known —"

"Me too." That seemed to be the end of it.

The verent flew on, passing from the Gap into the Highlands.

The landscape below shifted in an instant, from natural to … something else.

He gasped at the change, forgetting his flight sickness.

The grass at the edge of the valley quickly gave way to the strange white domes that dotted the former fields and meadows like diseased pustules. The very land itself looked ill, as if it had contracted some kind of monstrous disease. The air, even at this height, was far warmer than it should be.

Like a fever. He shook his head, awed by the devastation.

To the north, a massive cloud bank obscured the horizon, glowering and dark.

He found he was able to look at the ground below for longer now at a time without feeling nauseous. There really was magic in the air. *If there is, maybe it will help us find a way to beat this plague back, before it kills us all.*

He glanced over his shoulder at the rapidly retreating mountains of Heaven's Reach where they met the Red Flights. Somewhere back there, Silya was in the thick of things. *Be careful.*

The heat was almost oppressive, like holding his hands above a fire. At ground level it must have been stifling. It was usually cooler in the higher elevations, but as they passed over the ruined land, it practically radiated warmth. "You feel that?"

She nodded. "It's warmer than it should be."

The immensity of the challenge struck him suddenly and hard. *How are we going to fight this?*

Elleck seemed to be reading his thoughts. "I don't know, brother. I really don't know."

They fell into silence, each lost in thought as Angel carried them out over the cooler air above Lake Zeraya.

15

IN MOTION

"YOU MET HIM?" Raven had asked around the Station, looking for anyone who might remember Aik passing through a few days earlier.

"Yes." Aer'Lis, the station master's son, blushed. "He was here with a trading caravan, four days back, on Callasday."

"Did you talk to him?" Why was he so red?

The scarlet extended to the man's neck. "We … yes. A little."

Surely he didn't mean … "Did you two —"

"Mas Orn, Silya needs you." Sister Dor materialized at his side.

He growled under his breath. "I'll talk more with you later."

Aer'Lis nodded and turned away, almost running back toward the Station. It would have been comical, if Raven hadn't been so annoyed.

Did Aik sleep with him? He was handsome enough, and if Raven read him right, he would have been willing. The idea made his stomach twist. They'd never said they would only see each other. They'd had no time to talk about anything really. But after their night together at the Manor House, he'd just assumed … *Dammit, there was no time to figure anything out.* "Where is she?"

Dor's eyebrow raised, but she said nothing. She didn't miss much. "Follow me." She turned on a croner, much nimbler than her ample stature would suggest, and led him away. Not toward the Station, as he'd half expected, or even toward the flitter, but instead to a small copse of violet pines that hadn't yet been chopped down for firewood.

"What's going on, Mim Ala?"

Dor sputtered. "She's ... it's ... you'll see."

They entered the trees, their purple fronds providing welcome shade from the heat. Hard to believe it had been snowy here just a week before.

Silya was arguing with someone, bits and pieces of the conversation slipping through the trees. Blue flames flickered in and out of the staff, reflecting its holder's temper.

"... don't know what you mean. Your name is Spin? What kind of name is that? What's your surname?"

His pulse quickened. *Did she just say Spin?*

They found her speaking into one of the long talker boxes, frowning at it hard enough to break it, her brow so furrowed that he was surprised it wasn't squeezing out sweat.

She looked up and met his gaze, her grimace softening. "Oh good, you're here. Maybe you can help me make sense of this." She thrust the box at him. "Here, talk to Raven."

He took it and pushed the talk button, as he'd been taught, not sure what he was walking into. Or how he was going to explain Spin. "Hello?"

"Boss?"

He grinned. *I know that voice.* "Spin? Where in the seven green hells are you?"

"Where you should be." The familiar's voice sounded resentful.

I probably deserve that. He had forgotten all about his little familiar in the heat of the battle with the verent. Still, he was overjoyed to hear it.

"You know him?" The shocked look on Silya's face was worth having gotten out of bed that morning. "I thought maybe someone had stolen one of the other long talkers and was playing a prank."

"Nope, not a prank." He pressed the talk button. "Spin, how are you?"

"Just fine, boss. All systems in working order. How about you? Roger."

He laughed. "Also in working order. And who's Roger?"

"Just something we used to say at the end of a sentence when we used walkie talkies."

Another strange phrase. *He must mean long talkers.*

"We say 'fin.' Who is that?" Silya reached for the long talker, but Raven pulled it away, gesturing for her to be quiet.

She fumed, her face turning hencha berry red, but she nodded.

"Spin, where are you?" Silya was glaring at him. "Fin."

There was a short pause. "At 1.7786 N 4.5575 W."

He grinned. *Typical Spin.* Aik must have found him ... or Triya had. "In words I can understand, please? Fin."

"You're such a slacker, boss. We're at the south side of Anghar Mor. Fin."

He wasn't sure what *slacker* meant, but it sounded affectionate. He whistled. Someone had made it to the Mountain.

She tugged at his sleeve, impatient as a six-year-old. "Ask him who he's with."

"Way ahead of you," he said, his hand over the box. To Spin, he said "Who is we?"

"Aik'Erio and Des'Rya."

Aik's alive! His heart thumped like a galloping aur. "Can I talk with Aik?"

"Just a sec, boss."

Raven counted the seconds. *I'm going to talk to Aik!* Was it possible it had only been a week and a day since they'd been together?

"Raven?" The line crackled with static, but it was Aik's voice. He would have recognized it anywhere.

"I'm here, Aik!" His face flushed with warmth at his friend's voice. *More than friends.*

"How is this possible?" Aik sounded ... tired. Stretched thin.

What have you been through? He forgot to be angry — for the moment — for whatever Aik might have done with Aer'Lis. "Silya found these long talker things in the Temple caverns. I guess they can talk to Spin too. Fin."

"... amazing. Where are you? Gods, it's so hot here. Raven ... I miss you. You should be here."

He frowned. *What's he talking about?* Anghar Mor was cold —
it was right next to the ice shelf, for the godssakes. Raven *had* been
there, once. "We're at the Gap Station. Fin"

"...didn't hear that ... where ..." Aik's voice dissolved into static.

"Gap Station. Aik? Can you hear me?"

There was no reply.

He stared at the silent box in his hand. He'd sounded so close.
"What happened?"

Silya frowned. "Sister Tela said the long talkers work with ...
satellites?"

Dor nodded.

"Little ships that circle Tharassas. There may not be many
left. They were put up there when the original colonists landed,
more than four hundred years ago."

Raven looked up at the sky, though most of it was blocked by
the violet pine leaves. Spin had probably mentioned them once, but
he'd been too busy to pay attention. "When will one ... pass over
again?"

"I don't know. We're still testing things out." Silya put a hand
on his shoulder, her blue eyes searching his. "This is good news,
Raven. He's alive."

"I know." Impulsively, he pulled her into his arms, and the
emotions that he'd kept in check came flooding out. "Gods, Silya,
he's *alive*." He started to shake like a leaf in her embrace. He'd
hoped, but how could he be sure?

She squeezed him tightly, all animosity between them vanished.
Her emotions through the emp were fuzzy and imprecise compared
to Jai's or Elleck's, but they were still readily apparent. She cared for
him, and she still loved Aik, in a fashion.

He was glad they were alone, save for Dor. Their tears flowed
freely, and she seemed to understand how much this meant to him too.

"I didn't think I'd ever —"

"I know, Raven. I know." She held onto him, and he squeezed
her tightly as if she were all that was keeping him attached to the
ground.

"He and I ... we ..." He closed his eyes, remembering that last
night.

She laughed. "Everyone figured that out a long time ago."

He laughed too, and at last he let her go, sniffling and wiping his nose with the back of his hand. "I have to go after him."

She nodded. "I know." She wiped her own eyes, somehow managing to look much less clumsy and torn to pieces than he was sure he did. "But first you have to tell me about Spin. And … this." She touched the lump on his neck, and his emp shifted in its pouch.

He sighed. He was itching to go find Aik, but she was right. She deserved answers. *I can do this quickly.* "Spin was the brain for the *Spin Diver*."

Silya and Dor looked at him blankly.

"The ship from the Last Run?"

"Ah." Silya nodded. "More old Earth technology. Seems like we're haunted by it." She held out her hand for the long talker, and he gave it to her. She handed it back to Dor, who slipped it into the holster on her waist.

"I found him out in Landfield. I was playing in one of the empty fields and came upon this shiny little sphere. I cleaned it off and took it home, and that night … he talked to me." He smiled at the memory. He'd had it under his covers, and when it spoke to him, he'd been afraid of it at first, and then scared it would wake Jimey or Mim'Aza.

Spin had been his. He didn't want to share it with anyone else. "It — he?"

"He prefers to be called *him*." That had been a surprise too.

She pointed at Spin. "So this little …"

"I call him my familiar."

"Your … familiar." She rolled the word over her tongue. "He knew Jas?"

He nodded.

Silya glared at him. "I can't believe you didn't tell me about this before, Rav'Orn."

He winced at the use of his formal name. Silya's mood could flip in an instant. "We weren't on the best of terms, you know. And Spin was my friend. He was the only one who was always there for me." What he and Spin had — what they used to have — it was precious to him, and before Aik, he'd never shared it with anyone.

She bit her lip. "I understand that. But this is huge. Do you have any idea how much we could learn from … from him?" Silya looked angry still, but he could feel the curiosity and wonder just behind her anger.

"I didn't think about that." Truth be told, there was a lot he hadn't thought about. He was only just starting to realize how detached he'd been. From everything and everyone. Breeze had changed that.

She sighed. "You're not the only one." Regret flooded her, and he wondered what that was all about. "And this?" She touched the pouch again. "It's almost like there's something alive in there. Dor, look at this."

Dor stood on tiptoe to look at Raven's neck. "It's strange. Like some kind of growth." She poked at it.

"Hey! Don't do that." Raven took a step back.

Dor nodded. "It's sore. Are you sick?" She felt his forehead.

He fended her off with flailing hands. "Stop that. I'm not sick. It's an emp."

Again the blank stares, like they thought he'd gone daft.

Raven caressed the pouch and the emp settled down. "It's a little creature that helps me communicate with the verent. And other things." He was reluctant to tell Silya he could read her emotions. She might get angry again. In fact, he could feel her annoyance levels rising.

"Other things?" One eyebrow raised, a warning sign for sure.

"It's not something —"

Someone screamed in the distance.

"What in the green holy hell?" Silya looked over her shoulder, searching for the source of the noise. "We're not done with this, Rav'Orn." She turned to run toward the noise, leaving him relieved but worried.

He followed through the closely packed pines. *Breeze, what's going on?*

They're here.

He burst out of the trees with Dor a couple steps behind him and almost ran into Silya, who had stopped dead at the edge of the copse. She was staring at the sky.

It was as if the gates of hell had opened up and let loose their denizens. Except it was a red hell, not a green one. *And most decidedly not holy.*

Swarms of red lights descended on the pass, a murmuration that twisted and flowed like a living cloud, their buzzing loud enough to hurt his ears. "What in Heaven's Reach are they?"

Silya bit her lip. "Fireflies. The beginning of the end. I don't know." She turned back toward him, and there was fear in her eyes.

Of course, he didn't need to see it to know it was there, and he felt it too. "What do we do?"

"Come on. We'll figure it out." She ran toward the danger in the midst of the chaos.

Sister Dor trundled after her, faithful to the end.

Raven's first impulse was to run as far away and as fast as his two legs, or Breeze's wings, would carry him.

But the verent was in the thick of it as the host of fireflies started streaming down to the ground, and he wouldn't get far on foot alone. Not that he would ever abandon Breeze.

With a sigh, he plunged into the crowd after them.

•   •   •

A great flapping of wings drew Chala out of the Kitchen, where she'd been preparing something for lunch for herself and the other two riders who'd remained behind.

She stared in disbelief — all the verent were in the skies, disturbed like a nest of jexyn surprised by an eircat. They flitted about through the air, narrowly missing one another, making a great cacophony of roars and a flapping of wings.

Astrid appeared by her side. Her eyes unfocused, as if she were somewhere far away from Mountainhome.

Talking to Sleeker. Chala tried not to be jealous about that. She'd had her chance and failed. *Why do I stay?*

Surely Elrys would welcome her back to the clan. Or had she married the Masrin yet? She shoved the irrelevant thought aside. "What's got them all disturbed?"

"The Rise. It's begun." Astrid turned to her, eyes focusing as if she'd just noticed Chala was there. "Raven needs us."

"You ... can hear him too?" She shoved her jealousy down. Hard.

Astrid blinked. "I know. It's strange, but rather wonderful ..." Her voice trailed off as she seemed to realize who she was talking to. "There's still so much we don't know."

Chala looked away, not willing to show how much it hurt to be excluded from the circle. "You and Olly are going?"

"Yes. The Heartland needs our help. The Highlands ..." A shadow passed over Astrid's features. "The Highlands are lost."

Chala swallowed hard. "How is that possible? So soon?"

Astrid nodded, looking lost herself. She was holding something back.

Chala could feel it. She teased out a tiny strand of it — it was grief. *Zeraya. She had a brother there.* "I'm sorry." Chala took Astrid's hand. "Were there any survivors?"

"I don't know." Her eyes were wet, but she wiped them with the back on her hand.

"What about your little brother?" She had no siblings of her own, but family was family, even among the wetlanders.

Astrid nodded. "I can't think about it too much right now. I have to hope. But Raven says ... everything is gone."

She closed her eyes. "The gods willing —"

"Thank you for that." Astrid squeezed her hand. "I have to get my things. The fireflies are attacking the refugees at the Gap." She let go of Chala.

"Astrid ..."

Her friend 's face was lined with worry. "What?"

"What can I do to help?"

Astrid shook her head. "Nothing. I'll manage. Maybe he got away." She took a deep breath. "We were planning to leave soon anyhow to head to Gullton. This just speeds things up a bit. Stay here and keep a lid on things." She turned and disappeared into the darkness of the Kitchen's cavern.

Chala's gaze followed her. Astrid was in pain, but she was as stubborn about showing it as Chala was. *You would make a good suifaine.*

She rubbed the emp at her neck to calm it. *Peace, little one.* It had felt Astrid's suffering too.

Her options were limited. She could stay at Mountainhome and play the domestic, cleaning rooms, preparing, and storing food, and being "useful."

She could go out on the hunt, find that damned ix, and exorcise some of her frustrations.

Or she could do something unexpected.

She *liked* unexpected.

A verent shot up into the sky from a nearby ledge. Chala squinted. It was Astrid's Sleeker, by its markings. The egg-layer had a thin pale blue line along its side.

A host of other verent flew up from their own caverns and the lake below to join Astrid. They spun around in the sky together, finding and riding the updrafts, and then the whole flight turned like a flock of birds to wing its way westward, disappearing over the mountain walls.

Once they were gone, Chala retreated to the Kitchen, pulled out a leather sack from the stores, and stuffed it full of dried aur meat, fruits, nuts, and flatbread. She'd been on verentback before, with Olly, Astrid, and the others. She'd also ridden a cayah back home. *How hard can it be? If I can just get one of them to listen to me …*

Surely not all of them had left.

She hurried back to her room to gather her things. The caverns felt hollow with the verent riders gone. Things were happening out there, and she was stuck here, sweeping floors. *Burn me if I'm going to be left out of it.*

She packed lightly, retrieving her long knives, a change of clothing, and one of the full canteens she always kept on hand. You never knew when you'd have to run.

Not that she was running *away. Not this time.*

I could go home. The thought struck her like a bolt out of the green. She could take a verent and go back to the desert, to Elrys. Surely she still belonged there — the suifaine all had emps, and they would welcome her back with open arms.

Chala discarded the thought almost immediately. They needed her here, and if they lost the coming battle, there would be no home to go back to.

With her travel sack packed, she slipped out of her room, a bare cavern at the back end of Mountainhome furnished only with an oil lamp and a sleeping palette. She picked up a spare saddle from stores, hoping it was small enough for what she planned. Then she went in search of a verent to tame.

She chose the western caverns, where many of the younger verent had taken up residence. The adolescent verent were kept close by until the adults could teach them, especially the lakeborn. As Jai had explained it to her, the *lakeborn* ones were still a mix of their original creatures, and it took a while for everyone to "get it together" in there.

Chala had decided she had the best chance convincing one of these newer verent to help her out.

It was a bit of a walk, but the exercise was invigorating, even as it reminded her how alone she was there.

In one of the wider caves, filled with stalagmites and stalactites like melted candle wax, she found a younger female verent sunning herself, her white scales edged with a beautiful ruddy brown. She paused at the entrance, admiring the lovely creature for a moment.

The verent looked up at her, her big eyes meeting Chala's. She could feel the verent's curiosity through the emp. She pulled out a strip of dried aur meat. It was small enough, the barest taste for a beast as big as the verent, but she sniffed it, flicking out her white tongue.

Chala pulled it back, and the verent reached for it. Impulsively, Chala scratched the skin between the verent's forehead ridges, and was rewarded with a deep purring sound.

Chala pushed reassuring images and feelings through her emp, hoping the verent would interpret them the right way, and then she gave her the jerky.

The verent took it almost daintily, wrapping her purple tongue around it and chewing on it thoughtfully. She swallowed, and her mouth splitting into an eerie grin. She nosed at Chala's shirt looking for more.

She pulled out another piece and fed it to the verent, being careful not to lose a finger in the process.

That one went down the gullet much faster.

"You need a name." Chala looked her over, admiring the verent's powerful form. "Elrys. I'll call you Elrys."

Elrys huffed, and Chala took it as agreement.

Her lover wouldn't mind, though it might be awkward if she ever went home again. "*Hello Elrys ... This is* verent *Elrys ...*"

Elrys lifted her head, sniffing round the travel sack on Chala's back.

Chala laughed. "Yes, there's more. But I need you to do something for me first."

The verent's assent came through the emp, like being dipped in a warm bath. *It's working.* Chala grinned.

With the verent's permission, Chala strapped on the saddle and slipped onto her back, hoping she could figure out some way to get Elrys to go where she needed her to go.

This is going to work.

16

INTO ANGHAR MOR

THE PROGENITOR IS HERE.

The spore mother resisted the urge to send a flock of forerunners to him. Better to let him find his way to her himself. She didn't know how strong his control over his host was, and she didn't want to break the spell.

Still, hope washed through her. Hope for an end to her loneliness. For some intellectual companionship. Her children were beautiful and strong, but they were only extensions of herself.

Soon, though ...

Besides, only he could help her unlock them.

She allowed herself one watcher, floating on the hot breeze, far above him.

There was another of his kind with him. *Strange.* Why would it come with the progenitor?

No matter. She would deal with it when the time came. For now, its presence was just a distraction.

She focused on him.

Come to me, my little one. It's time.

•   •   •

"I think I found something." Aik was a few paces ahead of her, though he might as well have been a world away. His voice was dull and monotone.

Every now and then he'd glance up into the gray sky, as if expecting something — or someone — to materialize out of the mist.

Desla wiped sweat and warm rain from her brow. Her hand came away black, covered in wet soot. *Lucky me.*

"I'm coming." The sky was awash with angry clouds, and the crash and clamor of the ice sheet as it melted in the heat set up a terrible background chorus as the storm lashed the slopes of Anghar Mor.

The whole world has gone mad. She shivered despite the heat. She trudged across the rock-strewn skirts of the mountain. *What I wouldn't give for a real bath.*

Nothing grew here, not even the strange alien coryx that had filled the valley. They'd rounded the smooth edge of the mountain a half hour earlier, crossing into this rocky verge where Anghar Mor's side had collapsed an age before.

How did I get into this mess? Just a week before, more or less, she'd been enjoying three square meals a day in the Temple and a warm cot at night. *Silya, you owe me.*

"Is he all right, Spin?" She still carried the little familiar.

"Does he *seem* okay?" Spin sounded worried too.

Aik looked almost frantic now, his gaze darting back and forth as she caught up to him.

"No, I guess not."

He looked back at her, his eyes bloodshot.

Most definitely not all right. "What did you find?"

He pointed through the rain. "Wait for the flash."

She followed his gaze. They stood at the base of a craggy ravine that sliced the mountainside, funneling a flow of water around their feet. It was hard to make anything out in the maelstrom that swirled around them, but there was *something* up there. A patch of *darker* dark in the darkness.

Lightning struck nearby, the crackling sound nearly deafening her, but it was enough for her to see it. There was a cavern entrance up there, possible shelter from the storm.

Then again, did she really want to crawl into a dark hole in the heart of enemy territory? "What if that's a lava tube?" Anghar Mohr was a volcano, after all, right? *I should have knocked you unconscious and dragged you back to Gap Station when I had the chance.*

"It's not."

"How do you know?" She had to shout to make herself heard over the wind and rain.

His hair was plastered to his head, and he was covered in wet soot just like her. He raised his arm, a pained expression on his face. The gauntlet flickered in and out of existence.

Ah. Well, we're as likely to die out here as we are in there. After hours of horrid weather, she was ready for a break. "All right. Let's go."

She followed him up into the ravine. They picked their way over boulders and sharp outcrops of rock. The constant flow of water coming down the chute made footing treacherous, especially in the dim light. The pack weighed her down, but Aik seemed to be in no shape to carry it.

They needed illumination. She tapped him on the back.

"What?" His eyes narrowed.

"Spin. Light."

"Ah." He nodded.

She pulled him out of her pocket. "Spin, can you brighten things up a bit for us?"

"What am I? A flashlight?"

Flashlight? Like lightning? "This climb's too dangerous in this dim light. Please, Spin?"

The familiar's voice softened. "At your command, Cheese." He lit up, his golden glow filling the gap as he flowed into his spherical shape.

Aik's eyebrow raised at the pet name, but he said nothing.

She held on to the silver sphere tightly, and together they managed the rest of the climb step by careful step, only slipping a couple times.

They reached the top of the chute after a twenty-minute climb. Her muscles ached — every single one of them, from her forehead to the tips of her toes.

She sent a prayer to Ay'Oss that the cave would be safe and dry.

The entrance was bounded by twin waterfalls, pouring off the black rock of the mountainside and then down the narrow ravine they'd just climbed. The water here was cleaner — or maybe it just seemed that way in Spin's golden light.

They slipped past the cascade and into the tunnel on the other side, and the wind stalled. "Thank the gods." She set down her pack and looked around.

The cavern walls were mostly smooth, as if they had been carved out of the mountainside. Upon closer inspection, she could see that they were cracked and pitted in the dim orange light. Whoever had done the carvings — if they weren't natural — had done so a long time before.

The orange light —

She turned to look at him. "Your gauntlet."

It was back again, solid this time, complementing Spin's golden glow.

Aik looked down at his hand and grimaced. "So it is." He grunted. "Well, we're here. What now? Where's Raven?"

As if in response, Spin brightened in her hand. "Aik, Raven wants to speak with you."

His eyes widened. "What? How —"

"Yes, Spin. Let's hear him." *How* was important, but right now hearing a familiar voice was even more so.

"Raven?"

"I'm here, Aik!" His voice was punctuated by a crackling sound, but it was Raven.

"How is that possible?" Some of the color came back into Aik's face.

"Silya found these long talker things in the Temple caverns. I guess ... talk to Spin too."

"Thank the gods. That's amazing. Where are you? Gods, it's so hot here. Raven, you don't know how much I miss you. You should be here."

She wiped sweat off her brow, nodding in agreement.

"We're at ..." His voice dissolved into a series of clicks and crackles.

"Raven? We didn't hear that. Where are you?"

There was no reply, only static.

She frowned, torn between worry and wonder. "Spin, what happened? Where did Raven go?"

"We lost the signal. The satellite carrying it passed out of range." He paused — if he'd been human, she would have sworn he gulped. "Sorry, Chief."

Aik turned away. "Not your fault." Though he certainly sounded like he thought it was.

Desla glared at his back. It wasn't the little guy's fault. "Spin, can you tell us where he is?" If this was magic — or even technology — they might as well explore its limits.

Spin's lights flashed. "Maybe. Give me a sec."

She was intensely curious about how Spin had been able to talk with Raven. It was good to hear his voice, but what magic — or technology, which seemed to be just another word for it — made it possible? If Spin could reach Raven, who else could they talk to?

"According to the signal location information, he's near Gap Station."

Aik's shoulders slumped, and he stared at the familiar as if it had stolen his lunch. "He's not here. After all of this ... he's not here." The crystals on the gauntlet flared, and his face changed again, his broken expression draining away like wine out of a cask, leaving a blank mask.

A cold sweat broke out on Desla's forehead. *He wouldn't hurt me ... would he?* It was the first time she'd been afraid of him. "Aik, are you all right?" She set Spin on her pack and reached out to touch his arm.

He shrugged her off. Then his gauntleted arm jerked up into the air, and he lifted his left leg almost comically, as if he were a marionette and something were pulling his strings.

The thought made her shiver.

He lurched around toward the darkness of the tunnel.

She slipped past him and put herself in his way, determined to block him, to talk some sense into him. She'd done it before. She put a hand on his chest, stopping him in his tracks. "Aik, you have to wake up. I know you're in there."

He wouldn't meet her gaze. He looked directly ahead, pushing forward against her.

She bit her lip. Normally she didn't condone violence, but she had to do something. She slapped him, hard.

He blinked, and his eyes focused on her.

For a second she thought she'd gotten through to him.

Then he grunted and shoved her out of his way, using his considerable strength to slam her into the wall.

She hit the rock hard, the air rushing from her lungs. Unable to speak, she slumped to the ground, and then everything went black.

•   •   •

Come to me.

The world around Aik swirled and changed. His blood pumped through him like lava, boiling in his veins, and the tug that had pulled him to this place increased to a burning need that made him stumble forward into the cavern as something inside him replied. *I'm coming.*

Someone blocked his way.

He tried to make it out. It held him back, kept him from going to *her*.

Pain slammed through him, and for just a second, he saw the obstacle.

Desla.

Then she was gone, and the thought with her. He shoved the blur aside, and it made a satisfying crack as it hit the wall, clearing his path.

He started forward again, toward … *Mother.* He was home at last.

The heat felt good, energizing. He stripped off his shirt, letting it fall as he walked. Then he took off his boots and his pants, leaving a trail behind him. His small clothes were the last to go.

He continued on toward her, naked as the day he was born.

The cavern dove down into the guts of mountain. The walls here were covered in some kind of sticky goo, long silver ropy strands pulsing with sickly red light. With every step it got warmer, like a furnace.

It didn't bother him. He sucked it in like a sponge soaks up water. His pace quickened, and soon he was walking on a soft, yielding surface. It was comforting, familiar, like something he remembered from a long-ago childhood.

He came to a blockage, where the strands coalesced into a white barrier that stopped him cold. He paused, annoyed that his forward progress had been halted. Then he put out a hand to touch it.

The white surface shifted and flowed, at first up his arm, embracing the metal of the gauntlet. Then it receded like an ocean wave with a loud hiss. The barrier withdrew, letting him continue forward.

He passed through three more of the white walls, each one hiding a wonderland of strange and yet somehow familiar creatures, colorful things that clung to the walls around and above him, all reaching out toward him as if he were the sun. Names for them came back to him like old friends. *Acchea, eesiil, aoochhaa* ... and the *eeechiia*, the membranes that marked off one section of the tunnel from the next.

When he passed through the last one, he stopped, shocked out of his stupor for just a moment by the strange sight as he stepped into a much larger space.

The cavern was a riot of colors. Things in every conceivable shape and size and color clung to almost every surface — tiny blue caps, wide frilly red things, gold and orange spikes that hung down half a meter from the ceiling. One of the spikes exploded, scattering sparkling spores over its neighbors.

In the center, mysteriously clear of the strange growths, sat a strange silvery-white structure.

His eyes narrowed. It looked familiar. Like those coryx he'd seen on the surface. But different. Instead of a smooth dome, this one was segmented into eight parts, separated by thick beaded ridges. It was huge, easily five times as tall as he was. It moved up and down in slow succession. There were other parts of it too, partially hidden in the darkness at the back of the cavern.

It's breathing.

For a second, panic overtook him. *What am I doing here? Why am I naked? What happened to Desla?*

Then *she* spoke to him, her voice rich and warm. *Welcome home, Iihil.*

His fears fled, along with his old name. He held up his arms, staring at his naked flesh. *Who ... what am I?*

Mother purred in his ear. *You are my son, Iihil. You are the progenitor.*

As if that explained everything.

Except that it did. Memories filled him like an empty glass, imperfect recollections that reminded him of who he was, and why he was here. *Mother.*

He felt a surge of warmth. Of love. *Come to me. We have much work to do.*

Iihil. He nodded. It felt *right.* She was his mother, and she had brought him home at last. He was exactly where he was supposed to be. The skull he'd found — where was that again? — no longer haunted him. It was a part of him.

His human memories — of Desla, Raven and Silya and the rest — were forgotten as his mother opened herself to him to welcome him.

The spore mother's side split to let him inside. She radiated red light like a furnace, drawing him into her embrace.

He went to her willingly to be reforged. As her walls closed around him, he felt safe. Protected. Loved.

It's good to be home.

17

THE CAVALRY IS HERE

S PIN WATCHED IN HORROR as Aik knocked Desla — his little girl — into the wall.

She crumpled like one of her rag dolls.

She's not Sera. His old and new worlds were running together, the barriers of time slipping away in his mind.

Spin struggled to ground himself in the moment, to remember where he was. Where they were. Inside Anghar Mor, a stark volcanic peak on an alien world, twenty-five light years from Earth.

Aik disappeared into the darkness, and Spin let him go. Not that he could have stopped Aik, but there was something dark eating at his soul, something from the gauntlet.

He wished he had arms. He missed his old body acutely, the one he'd taken for granted in his previous life.

He could only sit and watch.

Or maybe not.

He shifted his shape, the way he did when Aik tucked him into a pocket. It gave him a crude ability of movement, like a snail.

Shifting from form to form, round and flat, he inched his way to the edge of the pack where Desla had laid him. Then he slipped over the edge, dropping half a meter to the hard stone ground.

He softened his shell, landing with a *plop.*

He stopped there for a moment, checking himself over. Nothing seemed broken. Thank the engineers back on Old Earth for his pliable metal form.

Satisfied, he slowly crawled over to where Desla had fallen. It was slow going, taking him the better part of ten minutes, but at last he reached her.

A quick scan indicated she was mostly undamaged. She had taken a blow to her head, but he judged it was not fatal. Her chest rose and fell in a mesmerizing rhythm.

Thank Jaz. Relief flooded him, then amusement at the colloquialism. *I'm going native.*

For a long time he just sat there, watching over her. Then he grew tired of it.

He worked his way up her arm, into the space between her arm and her side. Changing shape once again, he settled in next to her and let himself fall back into electronic dreams.

•   •   •

Triya wiped the rain from her eyes.

It was ungodly hot out for autumn in the Highlands. Not that she even recognized these lands anymore. The whole countryside was infected, covered by blisters and pustules that belched their sparkling spores at regular intervals. One of the things had shuddered and shot them into the air as they passed by, and she'd breathed a few. Hopefully they were doing her no harm on the inside. *Not that there's anything to do about it.*

Now they marched through a nightmare of loose shale, soaked by the incessant rains. She glanced up at the dark, pregnant sky. Visibility had shrunk to a matter of meters, and she hadn't caught site of their little red escort in at least an hour. "Think we lost it?"

Mes looked grim — more so than usual. "Not sure, Mim. Doesn't matter, does it?"

Another thing we have no control over. "I suppose not." All they could do now was to put their feet forward, one after another. She took another precious sip of water, keeping her throat moist. There was water everywhere, falling from the sky and running in rivulets around the husks of the coryx, warm and full of ash. None of it fit to drink. Or at least, she wasn't desperate enough yet to try it.

Damned fool boy. What was Aik thinking, pressing on through this hellscape? Then again, maybe he had as little choice as she did. The end of the world was here, and she couldn't just sit it out.

They'd found the safe house inside a rock outcropping, where Desla and Aik had likely spent the night. There were signs of recent inhabitation, including still-cooling embers of a fire, but the two were long gone. *Why did they need a fire?*

They'd also taken any food that might have been stored there.

Triya had considered staying and spending the night, but the longer they delayed, the farther ahead their quarry would be.

In the end, the three of them had decided to press on, hoping to catch the pair before they arrived at Anghar Mor. Now Triya was regretting that choice. *Where else will we find shelter to get out of this dirty rain?*

After another hour's march over the tortured ground, they reached the mountainside. The slopes of Anghar Mor loomed above them, invisible except when lightning struck, momentarily extending their range of sight. The mountain looked especially forbidding in the dim, rain-washed light, as if it might suddenly tumble and swallow them all in its collapse.

Triya shook her head. *No sense getting carried away by fear.* Besides, there were other, more immediate dangers to worry about. As warm as it was, a fair amount of ice must be melting up ahead, and the shin-deep flow of water could easily become a flood. It would be worse in the valley below, but nowhere outside was safe.

Where are you, Aik'Erio? She touched the slick side of the mountain, as if it might give up its secrets. But there was nothing but warm, wet rock. "Standing around here does us no good. You two fan out. See if you can find any sign of them. Come back here in thirty minutes."

"Yes, Mim," her two guards said in unison and dropped their packs. One went east, the other west.

It's good to be the boss. Triya slipped her own pack off her shoulders, grateful for a few moments without the heavy weight dragging her down. She stood at the base of the hulking mountain, considering. *If I were a lovesick Guard and a Temple initiate, where would I go?*

She had no idea what was driving Aik, other than a desire to find Raven. Still, the weather was abysmal, a hot, clinging dampness. The air stank, filled with a foul sulphury smell that made her nose itch.

He and Desla would seek some kind of shelter.

She looked around. The rain had let up for the moment, though rolling volcanic fog still tainted the air. It was clear for a couple hundred meters, though there wasn't much to see — rock, rock, and more rock. Even the coryx seemed to avoid this place.

At the edge of her vision, a vast pool of water flowed slowly downhill toward Lake Zeraya as the ice sheet melted in the oppressive heat.

She'd been right about that. *We're lucky we made it here alive.*

The ground shook, and a spray of hot rocks flew through the sky, landing in tepid pools of water and making them sizzle. She pressed her back to the warm mountain wall, hoping none of them landed on her.

Triya didn't believe in hell, green and holy or not, but if she did, it would look something like this. She longed for the safety and comfort of the Manor House. *Once this is over, I'm never leaving home again.*

Even as she thought it, she knew it was a lie. But a month or two behind the safety of those walls sounded like heaven.

Em returned, making her way carefully along the skirts of the mountain. "Nothing much to the west. Just more of this." She pointed at the wall.

"Any caverns, nooks, hidey holes?"

"None at all."

Triya nodded. "All right. We'll see what Mes finds —"

"I found her!" Mes materialized from the smoky darkness like a ghost.

"Desla?" Triya grinned. Some good fortune at last.

Mes nodded. "Not far from here. There's a ravine that cuts up into the mountainside. And a cavern near the top. She's alive, but unconscious."

"And Aik?"

Mes shook her head. "No sign of the gully rat." She spit, and Triya laughed despite herself. The brief truce between the two of them seemed to be over.

"All right. Take me to her. We'll see what we can do for her, and when she wakes, maybe she can tell us where Aik went." She pulled out one of her water flasks. Thank the Norja they'd filled up at the last clean stream. "Drink up. Can't have any of us falling over from heat exhaustion."

Mes and Em followed her lead and then stowed their own flasks. "Gods, I hate this weather."

The guards rarely complained. Then again, their current situation was abysmally bad.

Triya snorted. "You and me both. Where did you find her? Take us there."

Mes shouldered her pack. "This way."

Triya picked up her own reluctantly and followed.

The rain started up again, a heavy curtain that closed off the view and soaked her already damp clothes.

Triya sighed. It seemed to her like life had always been like this, an exhausting trudge through mud and heat and rain and ash. When she got home — if she got home — it was going to take an epic bath to make her feel clean once again.

If she'd been a believer in fate, she might have thought it had brought them this close to Desla on purpose. That there was a divine purpose to it all.

But she'd long known you made your own luck in this world, through experience, smart choices, and perseverance.

Still, she whispered a quick prayer of thanks for their good fortune to Jor'Oss. *Just in case.*

After a short jog along the mountain's edge, Mes led them up a narrow ravine. Water splashed down the rocks at their feet, making the climb treacherous. More than once, Triya fell on her backside when her foot slipped on the slick rocks, or they shifted underfoot. Each time, one of the others caught her, and her heavy pack helped cushion the fall.

Up ahead, past Mes's lean form and her bulky pack, Triya caught glimpses of a cavern opening, dark against the general gray of the late afternoon. Each time she saw it, it was closer, but the afternoon seemed to stretch out.

She was forced to focus on putting one foot carefully before the other, one step up at a time. The world narrowed to that simple action. Step, look, step. Even the dampness and heat seemed to fall away.

Until it actually did. The rain, at least.

Sensing its absence, she looked up to find they'd entered the cavern, through a pair of waterfalls that poured over a rocky outcropping. "Oh thank Jas." *And Jorja too.* She took a breath of air. It wasn't sweet, but it was less rank than the air outside, and a shade cooler.

She dropped her pack, looking around as her eyes adjusted to the dim light.

The cavern was simple — no stalactites or stalagmites — its smooth walls diving back into the heart of the mountain. "Where is she?"

"Back here." Mes was kneeling next to a crumpled form, highlighted by the dim light from the tunnel's entrance.

Triya knelt next to Desla. *Poor thing looks like a rag doll.* She turned the girl over gently, checking her limbs. Everything seemed in place, though there was wetness at the back of her head. "Get out some blankets for her to lay on." She went back to her own pack and pulled out her small lantern. It had enough fuel for a few hours of light. She would use it for a moment or two to assess the girl's injuries.

There was something tucked in next to her. Curious, Triya touched it.

Golden light filled the cavern. "Hello, Triya." Spin's voice knocked her back on her heels. "Is Desla okay?"

Mes and Em flattened themselves against the tunnel wall, looking wildly around for the source of the voice.

Triya grinned. "Hello, Spin." It was good to hear the familiar's voice, like greeting an old friend. "I think so."

She was delighted to find him here. It was curious how he'd ended up next to her, curled up against her side like a kitten.

Maybe he could explain a few things.

"It's all right. He won't hurt you." She picked up the AI gently and held him aloft as he shifted back to his normal spherical shape. "Spin, meet Mes and Em."

The two guards stared at the little ball of light, their eyes practically popping out of their skulls. Both had their knives out.

"Hello, Mes and Em."

Mes took a cautious step forward, keeping the sharp blade between herself and the silver sphere. "What under Freja's green sky is it?"

"*He*. What is *he*." Spin sounded aggrieved.

Triya cracked a smile. She'd forgotten how touchy Spin could be.

Mes looked at her, brows knitted, waiting for an explanation.

"Let's just call him a friend. He belonged to Raven. And now he belongs to Aik."

Spin's golden lights flashed angrily. "I don't *belong* to anyone, thank you. Aik and Desla are my friends."

"Magic," Em and Mes whispered together.

Triya chuckled. "Close enough. You can put away your knives. He won't hurt you."

Mes and Em exchanged a glance, and then as one sheathed their blades, eyes fixed on the little AI.

"Is he dangerous?" Mes's eyes narrowed.

Triya sighed. They'd come around. "Only in the way that knowledge is dangerous. By which I mean, very."

Spin's golden light ran over Desla's body. "She likely has a minor concussion, and she's dehydrated. But she should be all right with some rest and some water."

Triya wondered how he could tell. *Silya would have my hide if I let Desla die.* "Well, come on. You heard what the little guy said."

With a sideling glance at the glowing orb in her hand, Mes and Em got to work, laying a couple blankets on the hard cavern floor. They folded them to make a cushion, and together they lifted Des's unconscious body up onto them.

Triya checked her over more carefully, her hands probing the girl's arms, legs, chest and neck.

As Spin said, nothing seemed broken, and there were no apparent wounds other than the one on the back of the initiate's head. She'd probably been knocked against the cavern wall by someone — or something. Triya glanced warily into the darkness of the tunnel. "What happened here, Spin?"

The golden lights spun, agitated. "Aik's under the influence of something. He threw her out of the way and then followed the tunnel into the mountain."

Triya bit her lip. "The gauntlet."

"I think so." Spin's lights blinked in agitation, lighting the cavern like flashes of golden lightning. "Will we go after him?"

She rubbed her chin. "Not sure yet. I need more information first."

Mes and Em were setting up camp in the protected space. The air was cleaner than outside, almost as if something was filtering out the volcanic fog.

Triya nodded her approval. "I'll be back in a moment. Move her a little closer to the entrance?"

Mes nodded. "Yes, Mim." She stepped aside as Triya passed her with Spin, giving them both a wide berth.

Triya took Spin with her and went fifty paces down the cavern, using his light to search for Aik, or anything else that might give her a clue about what had happened here. There was nothing, only bare walls. "Was Aik acting strangely, before he left?"

"Yeah ... like someone was pulling his strings."

That's a weird description. "How's that?"

"Like this." The darkness around her lit up, and she was staring at a full-sized version of Aik, though she could see through him. He moved, his limbs jerking like a puppet's.

She watched the image. "How ...?"

"It's called a holographic projection."

Maybe you are *magic.* She'd read enough about old Earth to know he was a product of technology, but she wondered what else he was capable of, good or ill. Still, she watched raptly, wincing when Aik shoved Desla hard against the tunnel walls. "That's ... upsetting."

"Right? I didn't want to disturb him in his strange state."

Makes sense. Just as she was about to turn back toward their improvised campsite, she noticed something in the darkness ahead. Taking a few steps forward, she found a discarded shirt.

She picked it up and sniffed it. It was ripe with a man's body odor, along with the sulfur smell of the fog from outside.

A few paces later, she found the rest of Aik's clothes.

She peered into the darkness, considering. *So you went into the belly of the beast, naked?* Something was badly wrong. "What's going on here?"

Spin actually snorted. "Hell if I know. I just hope she wakes soon. She was … kind to me." He said it with such a melancholy tone that she looked at him in astonishment.

Do you have feelings? When she'd first found out about him, she'd wanted to have him for her own, thinking of all the things she could learn. And how she might use them for personal gain.

But what if you're just like us? It was a disturbing thought, another mystery in a day too full of them. She shook her head, pushing the thought away. A mystery for another time.

With a heavy sigh, she collected Aik's clothes. She trudged back toward the entrance, where Mes and Em had finished setting up camp.

She told them what she'd found, leaving out the bit about the strange images Spin had projected. There was strangeness enough already.

They nodded as they took it in. "We'll figure it out, Mim." Em put a hand on her knee.

"I suppose we'll have to." Triya required more information if she was to go after the boy. There were too many pieces to the puzzle, and they all seemed to contradict one another.

She needed Desla to wake up.

18

FIRE AND ICE

"**W**E'RE HERE."

Kerrick blinked, looking around. *Did I fall asleep a verentback?*

It had been a long week, and once he'd put his anxiety to rest, the exhaustion must have caught up with him. Still, he'd kept his arms wrapped around Elleck's waist the whole time.

They were descending into a snow-lined valley, beneath a row of peaks almost as sharp as Heaven's Reach. These had a reddish tinge that showed here and there beneath piles of snow and ice, creating beautiful cascading patterns across the mountainsides. Farther down, violet pines clung to the slopes and thickened into a forest that hugged the lower reaches, save for patches of snow-covered meadows.

It was much cooler here, and he went from sweating to shivering and wishing he'd brought his winter clothes.

One of the open heaths at the heart of the valley below was bustling with activity, its snow trampled into mud. A wide purple circle sat in the middle like a bullseye. A dozen people were gathered around it, dressed in loose purple clothing of various shades, with arm and shin guards of beautifully carved leather polished to an almost golden hue — not unlike Elleck's own garb.

They were all staring at the approaching verent.

"Are they expecting us?"

Elleck shrugged. "It looks like it. I can feel Alibeh. She's in the circle."

"How do you know?"

Elleck rubbed the lump on her neck with one hand. "I'll tell you later."

Somehow they'd never gotten around to talking about the whatever-it-was on the long flight.

He bit his lip. He was close to his limit with change — something he'd never been overly fond of to begin with. Verent, the earth shaking, long talkers, the return of his long-lost sibling ... any one of them would have been momentous on their own. *So many new things to deal with.*

Angel/Jai set down neatly in the middle of the circle and *rumbled* at the crowd.

Kerrick had expected shouts, cries, even outright fear from the *ce'faine*. He remembered his own first encounter with the fearsome beasts at the Manor House, and the short-lived pitched battle.

Instead, the ce'faine waited patiently for him and Elleck to dismount, looking at the verent with interest but with about as much fear as they would have shown for a large rock.

He climbed down after his sister onto the purple mat — woven from hencha leaves, Kerrick could see now.

"Ali!" She abandoned him to run across the circle to embrace a woman who somehow commanded her own space amongst the crowd.

The woman who embraced her was clearly a clan elder. Her hair was gray, as long as Elleck's, and pulled back in a neatly woven and tied braid that dangled over her sage-colored robes. Her dark purple tunic was embroidered with a stylized mountain on the chest. Her face was lined, but she still quite comely. She must have been stunning when she was younger.

The air of dignity she exuded was only partly spoiled by the wide grin that split her face when Elleck threw her arms around the eshem and half-squeezed the life out of her.

"Gentle, Elle. I have fragile bones, remember?" Her voice was high and lilting.

Elle?

Elleck's eyes widened. "Brittle as iron, maybe."

She laughed and touched Elleck's cheek — she was taller than the eshem by a head. "Welcome home." Her gaze met Kerrick's, and she nodded. "I see you have brought your brother to me."

How did you know? That thought was sidetracked as a collective gasp went up from the gathered crowd. He turned to see Jai's naked form emerging from the verent's back. He grinned. *The ce'faine aren't quite as jaded as they seem.*

"A little help here?" Jai sounded mildly annoyed that they'd forgotten to remove the saddle. Kerrick had promised to take it off as soon as they landed.

"Sorry." He rushed to unbuckle it, freeing the verent rider, who didn't seem at all embarrassed to be naked in front of another clan. "We were distracted."

Jai shook his head. "I gave you *one thing* to do." Still, he seemed more amused than angry as he slipped to the ground and rummaged through his saddle bag to pull out his clothes.

Alibeh stepped forward and held out her arms. "Welcome to the East Valley Clan. I have waited to meet you for a long time, Kek'Aze." Her eyes met Kerrick's, and she seemed to see right into his heart.

How does she know my full name? He was supposed to be angry at these people. Was, in fact. He'd nursed a thirst for vengeance for two decades, vowing that one day he'd get his revenge on those who had killed his family. Staring at the woman who was like a mother to Elleck, that promise felt suddenly hollow.

Still, the anger remained. "We have a lot to talk about." He tried to make it sound like a threat, but she simply nodded.

"Please, come with me." She turned to go, moving as smoothly as water across the woven mat at the heart of the encampment, the chill breeze playing with her hair. There was an air of serenity about her that Kerrick had rarely seen.

He looked at Jai, who shrugged.

"When the eshem calls ..."

He was in a strange place among a stranger people. He'd have to follow their rules. For now. They set off after Elleck and Alibeh, and the clan made way for them, lining their path through the camp.

The ce'faine were a varied lot, blond and dark-haired, tall and short, but every one of them carried a sharp knife at their waist, curved like a scythe. A few children peered through the legs of the adults, staring at him wide-eyed. There were a few hundred in evidence.

He wondered if there were more camps like it, or if this was the whole clan.

The encampment was a series of tents, each constructed of tanned hides neatly stitched together and staked up by a central pole. They looked like they could be taken down in a hurry if the clan had to move.

Alibeh led them to the largest of these, its hide walls stained in purple. The workmanship was beautiful, the colors overlapping in curled waves like clouds, from soft lilac to a deep mauve. White cord held the panels together, neatly threaded through punched holes in the leather.

He expected guards, but the tent was unattended. *Maybe she doesn't need them? Or maybe everyone's a guard.*

He felt as nervous as an inthym in an aur corral.

The eshem met his gaze and the corner of her lips quirked up, as if she'd sensed his surprise. "Not so uncivilized after all, are we?" She lifted the tent flap and gestured them inside.

Kerrick ducked under the short entrance and stopped, staring at what he found. He wasn't sure what he'd expected, but this certainly wasn't it.

The cheff as he'd known them were savages, lawless brutes who existed only to hunt and kill innocents like his own family. And yet these people seemed nothing like that.

Alibeh's quarters were simple. In one corner a small sleeping pallet covered by a very warm-looking embroidered blanket. In another, a few cushions surrounded a low desk or table, which looked to be made of polished flopwood by the golden grain and lazy lines that crossed it. A map was etched into the wood's surface. Several hand-woven rugs in reds and purples and golds provided a warm flooring underfoot. Everything was neat and in its place.

The space was lit by blue sparks that moved around the room like insects on a breeze. He'd seen them before, of course. Everyone had, especially in the spring, usually floating far above the ground and out of reach. But not like this. "Wisps?"

The eshem grabbed one out of the air. Its glow faded in her hand, and she held it out to him. "Do you not have them in Gullton?"

Kerrick took it, staring at it in wonder. It was a tiny thing, no bigger than the center of his palm. Its fuzzy shape tickled his skin. "I've seen them flying by. Are they … seeds?" Now that he thought about it, there'd been a lot more of them lately.

"They are. And more." She plucked it out of his hand and flung it into the air, where it settled and glowed once more. "Please, sit. I have prepared some hot akka for us to drink." She lifted a tray from another corner of the tent, using slow, deliberate motions. She set it down on the table and poured into a beautifully carved wooden mug as he sank down on one of the gold-embroidered cushions.

He took the offered drink and sipped at it, inhaling the rich smell. *Some things are universal.* Sitting cross-legged so close to the floor felt awkward, like when he'd been a child.

That thought brought back memories of Enrick, and home. He set the cup down angrily with a clatter.

Jai flashed him a warning look that said *Don't piss off the eshem.*

He was probably right, but his anger had smoldered too deep and long. It burst out of him before he could stop it. "Why did you kill my family?"

Alibeh paused in mid-pour and then finished off the cup and handed it to Jai before responding. Her hands were shaking, just a little. "That is a difficult tale to tell."

The aroma of fresh-brewed akka filled the tent. She poured another mug-full, taking her time, her brow knitted in concentration or concern. She handed it to Elleck, then poured one for herself and set the pot down.

She settled onto a cushion and took a long sip, her eyes meeting his over the rim of the cup. "Are you sure you want to hear it?"

He nodded. "I've waited twenty years for this." He dropped his hand to the hilt of the short sword at his side.

"As you wish." If she noticed, it didn't seem to bother her. She took another sip, as if considering where to begin. "As I am sure you are aware, the ce'faine have a long and difficult history with the Steaders. We came here first, fleeing your Heartland and its restrictive ways —"

"I don't find them all that restrictive."

She silenced him with a look. "You wouldn't. You look the part."

His eyes widened, but he held his tongue.

"Things have changed these last twenty years. Some for the better. Surely you have seen how our people are ... different." Her eyes met his.

He cocked his head. "Different?"

"Yes, we are ... much more varied than the Heartlanders. Different skin, different hair, eye color ..."

He frowned. "There are people with dark hair and brown eyes in Gullton."

"Yes. Now. But once it was not so. There were only a few of us — throwbacks, the sons and daughters of the angels. Those who did not fit neatly into Heartland society." She sighed, setting down her mug and putting her hands in her lap. "I am sorry. This is an old grievance for us."

He looked away and saw Elleck nod.

She was right, if he thought about it. Sure, there were people of all sizes and shapes in Gullton. But most of them were like him — blue eyes and blond hair. He'd never thought about it much, beyond noticing how exotic someone with dark hair looked. Or red hair, like Raven. "I get your point. But what does that have to do with my family —"

The tent flap opened, and a young girl entered carrying a tray filled with small rolls, dried meat of some type, and a strange creamy white substance in a bowl. She was dressed in undyed homespun clothing, with small purple and yellow flowers embroidered on the shoulders. She flashed him a shy smile as she set the tray down on the table and made a short bow.

Alibeh touched her arm. "Thank you, Misell. That will be all."

"Yes, Eshem." She curtseyed, and then scrambled out of the tent, leaving Kerrick to take in the bounty.

She gestured at the food. "Please, eat. You must be starving after your journey."

"Thank you." He *was* hungry. His stomach rumbled at the mere sight of the proffered meal. He took a roll and some of the dried jerky, but balked at whatever was in the white dish.

Jai and Elleck helped themselves, and the verent rider tore off a hunk of the bread and dipped it in the bowl. "The *auddah* is delicious, Eshem."

"*Auddah?*"

His sister nodded, licking her fingers. "Aur cheese."

Cautiously he dipped his own bread in the creamy white stuff and tasted it. It was as sour as Silya on a bad day. He shuddered, reaching for his cup of akka to wash it down. "No thank you. I'll stick to bread and meat."

Jai laughed. "Suit yourself. More for us!"

Alibeh cleared her throat. "As I was saying, when the Steaders came, we owned the Highlands. There were Clans scattered across both ends of the valley. We even traded with the Heartland from time to time." She scooped out a bit of *auddah* with her bread and swallowed it whole. "Delicious."

"Agree to disagree." He wished she had a bit of cave cheese. *That I would eat.*

"Your loss." She smiled as if to show that she didn't take offense. "The ce'faine are a nomadic people, taking only what we need and leaving a light touch on the world. When the Steaders arrived, they saw wide open land. So they took it for their own, fencing it off one steading at a time."

She took a sip of her akka, staring at him as if to see if what she said was sinking in.

He'd never thought of it that way. He'd grown up on the steading, on land that had always been theirs. The ce'faine — it was so hard to think of them that way after all these years of pain — were the invaders, the usurpers. Her version of events made him distinctly uneasy.

"We let them at first, thinking there was plenty of land. That the world as big enough for both our peoples. We retreated toward the lake, and for a time ce'faine and Steader lived in relative peace."

Kerrick took a sip of his own akka, wondering how she'd heated it. There was no fireplace or pit in the tent, no opening to allow the smoke to flee. "And what does this have to do with my family?"

A ghost of a smile crossed her face. "Patience, young man. I am coming to that. There was an ...incident. One of the Steaders raped a Highland woman." She clutched her cup tightly, veins standing out from her fingers. "Her clan retaliated, killing only her attacker, but the Steaders took it as an act of war. They banded together, and most of the *veifaine* — the valley clan — was slaughtered." A shadow fell across her face. "It was a dark time."

His brow knitted. He'd never heard it told this way. "When was this?"

"Almost a hundred years ago." The pain on her face made it seem like it had been just yesterday.

"Ah, the Cheff War."

She frowned. "Do *not* call it that. It wasn't a war. It was a wholesale massacre. Men, women, children … it took weeks for word to spread to the other clans, so thorough was the reprisal. Only a few survived to tell the tale. Now the four clans are only three." Her hand flared with blue flame, and the akka in her cup began to steam again.

Kerrick stared at it. *That answers one question.* "You really are like her."

She set her cup down on the tray. "Please forgive me. I shouldn't allow myself to lose my temper like that." She met his gaze. "The world is far bigger than you Heartlanders realize."

That was you losing your temper? He turned to Jai and Elleck. "You knew all of this?"

Jai nodded. "We're taught it growing up."

It was a terrible tale, one he'd only heard from the Heartlanders' perspective before, how the cheff — ce'faine had attacked and started the war. "Still, this is all old history. Very tragic, but —"

Alibeh's eyes met his. "Sometimes history repeats itself."

"What do you mean?"

She got up slowly, carefully. She slipped her embroidered shirt off her shoulders to reveal her bare torso.

Kerrick tried not to look at her naked breasts, but he couldn't help himself.

She was older than him, probably a good ten or fifteen years, but in surprisingly good form. His gaze fell to her stomach, and he inhaled sharply.

A nasty scar ran across her left one and down her side, disappearing there beneath folds of cloth.

"What happened to you?" But he as pretty sure he already knew.

She pulled the shirt back up, wrapping it around herself like a blanket. "His name was Annick."

"Sweet mother of Jas." He closed his eyes. He knew the name. Uncle Annick. A rough brute of a man who'd lived alone in a cabin on the edge of the steading. "It can't be —"

"He came upon me one afternoon. I was on my Aud'ling, all alone, refilling a canteen with water at a small stream." She closed her eyes, and pain flickered across her features. "This … man appeared on the far side of the meadow. He was watching me, like a hunter watches an ix. At first, I felt no fear. I was more … curious. I had never encountered a Steader before."

Her hand slipped down to touch her left breast, running down the hidden scar in an almost gentle caress. "He crossed the stream and sat next to me, introducing himself. He was charming. We talked for an hour, him telling me about his world and me sharing about mine. He wasn't handsome, exactly, but he was … exotic. Blond. Blue eyes like the sky." She stopped, her eyes focused somewhere far away. "I should have been afraid."

He was speechless, for once.

She pulled her shirt back on, settling it properly on her shoulders, and sank onto the cushion. "Even now, all these years later, I can still hear him whispering in my ear. 'You're so beautiful.'" The flames were back, running down both her arms.

He wondered if she was even aware of them. "What did he do?" He didn't remember much about his uncle, only that the man had always scared him. He'd been prone to anger, prickly as a blade of trine grass.

"You know what he did." She set her cup down on the tray, the tremor returned to her hand. "The sweet talk ended and the kissing began, and then the rough caresses." Alibeh closed her eyes. "I told him no, but he took my knife and threw it away, into the grass. I was … weaker then."

Elleck reached across the small table to touch her knee. "*Emma, you don't have to —*"

"It is all right, Elle. He deserves an explanation. He lost you that night, after all." She patted his hand, then lifted it off her knee and took a deep breath. "I closed my eyes and let him do what he wanted, thinking of mother sky and father earth, of home and friends, of anything other than what was happening to me."

"I'm so sorry." He was horrified. How had someone he had known, a part of his own family, been capable of that?

She took a deep breath, sitting up straight, and her hand trailed across her stomach. "After he was through with me, he gave me the scar 'to remember me by.' And then he left me for dead."

His anger had fled, dissolved in a flush of horror. *I didn't know. How could I have known?* "That's why they came that night."

She nodded. "It was a second wrong, to try to redress the first. We shouldn't have done what we did to the rest of your family. Justice should only have been served on the man who committed the crime."

She wiped a single tear from the corner of her eye with the edge of her shirt. "I survived his assault, tending my own wounds in the cavern I'd chosen for my *aud'ling*." She bit her lip. "When I was finally able to return home to my clan, my father flew into a fit of rage at what had been done to me. He gathered up his warriors, and they raided the steading at night, killing everyone they found." She leaned forward and cupped his cheek. "I begged them not to go. Violence only begets violence."

He tried to find words, but nothing came out.

"When they came back, they brought me Elleck." She flashed Elleck a warm smile, like a mother looks at her child. "Enrick then, but things change. They missed you, wherever you were hiding, or you would likely have been here with us too."

"Or killed with the rest."

She met his gaze. "Maybe that, too."

He appreciated her brutal honesty. He glanced at his sister. There was pain etched on her face too. "I'm so sorry. I didn't know ..."

"Don't apologize to me." The flames went out, and she let go of his chin. "You were no more responsible for it than I was, and you have suffered for it too."

Kerrick took a deep breath and then exhaled, a chill running down his spine. All those years of rage, of anger at the *ce'faine* for what they had done. *What am I supposed to do with that now?* "Is your father ...?"

"Dead, three years back." She picked up her mug and took a long sip.

He nodded. *Of course he is.* Too late to find the man responsible.

Elleck leaned over and put her arm around him, squeezing his shoulder tightly. "You're here now. We're together again. That's all that matters."

He hugged her back. He wasn't entirely sure if that were true. The pain had settled too deeply to be eradicated with something as simple as a good explanation. And yet, it was something.

At least I have you back. That had to be enough for now. He let go and eased back into his seat, turning his attention back to Alibeh. "Thank you for telling me."

"Of course. You deserved to know. And I have put it behind me, for the most part." She picked up her cup and took another sip, smiling. "Life offers us so many simple pleasures, if we know where to look. It was a terrible thing that happened, but we must live our lives for what comes next, and not let the past hold us hostage." That seemed directly aimed at him.

"Maybe so." He grimaced. *I have a lot to consider.* "Still, you didn't bring me here just for a family reunion."

Alibeh nodded. "Handsome *and* perceptive. You would have made a good ce'faine warrior."

Elleck grinned, and Jai laughed at his obvious discomfort.

He growled. "Enough with the flattery. What do you want from me? Tell me why I'm here."

"Of course." She rubbed the lump on her neck gently. All the ce'faine seemed to have them.

He'd asked Elleck about it, more than once, but she'd told him the time wasn't yet right. *Apparently the time has come.*

Something slipped out of it and into her palm.

Kerrick shuddered. "What ... is that?"

She held out her hand. It held a small gray-white creature covered in soft fur ... something like an inthym, but only about the size of his thumb. It snuggled in her palm like a kitten.

His revulsion fled. Something about just looking at it made him feel ... happy.

"This little creature is called an emp. It's a symbiont, a pathway between humans and Tharassas, if you will. They help us bring down walls."

"City walls?" *What in the holy green hell?*

She smiled, and it transformed her face, making her look a good decade younger. "No, young man. Walls between people." She rubbed it gently, and it squirmed in her palm, emitting a purring sound, just like a tiny kitten. The sound increased in volume, and a wave of contentment washed over him.

He closed his eyes, feeling like he had when his mum had tucked him in at night in the before-time, with his little brother at his side. As she was now.

The feeling intensified, and his eyes grew wet, his heart filled with nostalgia for that long-ago time when he'd felt safe and warm. he took Elleck's hand and squeezed it.

He opened his eyes, and the little creature was glowing blue like the wisps. It split into two, and then the glow was gone. "What happened? Is it ... all right?" The warmth faded, leaving him cold and alone once again.

"Yes. This is how they make new ones of themselves." She took one of them and returned it to the lump on her neck. It slipped back into its pouch, and Alibeh hummed in contentment.

He shivered, as much at the sudden loss of emotional warmth as at the strange sight.

For the other, Alibeh took a silver box from beneath the low table and opened it on silent hinges. She placed it gently inside on a bed of mur silk.

She closed the box and handed it to Kerrick. "Take this to Silya. I am sending it for her and her alone. Ask the verent riders — they will know what to do." With that she stood once more, shaking out her skirts.

He frowned. Apparently the visit was over. "So that's it?"

She nodded briskly. "War is coming, Kerrick son of Lauria. Time runs short. When the Heartlanders have need of us, we will be there."

He started at the mention of their mother's name. He glanced at Elleck, who nodded.

"We should go. Thank you, *emma*, for your time." She bowed, and Kerrick copied her awkwardly.

"You're not staying here?" That was welcome news. He'd hoped to have a bit more time with his sister — they'd only begun to reconnect.

Alibeh nodded. "Elleck will come with you, to act as a liaison between our two peoples."

"What do I tell Silya?" Kerrick held up the silver box uncertainly. How could he give it to her, not knowing what it would do?

"The emps help us connect to one another, but none so strongly as the one who bears its twin." Her hand returned absently to rub the emp pouch at her neck. "Once she passes the test, she will understand."

Understand what? "I'll take it to her. The rest is up to her. Silya is … she does what she wants."

"She will make you a good match." Alibeh cupped his cheek. "Good luck, Kek'Aze. I hope we will see each other once again, when all this is through. You seem to be a brave and upstanding man. For a Heartlander."

At least she didn't call me a wetlander. He bowed again. "Thank you … eshem." He wasn't sure of the terms of formal address for the *ce'faine.*

She ushered him and his companions outside the tent, under the late afternoon sky. "Fly true."

When he turned to ask her about the flames, about how she and the other eshem were connected to the hencha, she'd already closed up the flaps of her dwelling.

Kerrick sighed. "Shall we?"

Elleck met his gaze. "You all right, big brother?"

He grimaced. "I will be."

Elleck nodded and squeezed his shoulder. "I'm glad you came. That you know."

The eshem's words tumbled about in his mind, shaking up everything he thought he knew about that terrible night. "Let's go."

Silya was waiting for him.

Time to go home.

19

BATTLE IN THE GAP

S CREAMS FILLED THE NARROW CANYON of the Gap.
The red swarm was descending like the angry fist of a god, its low buzz filling the air, setting Silya's teeth on edge and making her ears hurt.

She grimaced. This was how Aik and Triya must have felt when they confronted these things the first time. She planted her feet and her staff on the ground in the midst of the burgeoning chaos and called upon the hencha. This time they came to her immediately, their immense power flowing into her, washing away her fear, pushing away the noise of the swarm.

As Steaders ran in panic all around her, she became an oasis of calm. Time slowed as she closed her eyes and gathered her power. Blue flames erupted along her arms and legs with such strength that they burned off her clothing, bathing her in a bright light that must have temporarily blinded anyone who was looking right at her.

She savored it for an instant, feeling full of life, surging with power and connected to the world in a way she'd never felt before. She could feel the blood of the world flowing beneath her, connecting everything around her in a web of glorious life.

She wasn't just Silya anymore. *I am the Hencha Queen. I will burn you out of the sky.*

No! The word came from the hencha themselves, deep and low in her mind, reverberating through her and shaking her to her core.

She hesitated. She had the power. Surely she was meant to use it. *What do you mean, no? I have to save them!*

Not like this.

She brushed the voice aside. *I am the Hencha Queen. Not you.* Her people were frightened, being attacked by something against which they had no defense. She would do whatever was necessary to save them. She was heady with power, stronger than anything that might oppose her. *I can save them.*

She pointed the tip of the black staff at a part of the swarm swirling in the air over the station, willing that power to flow from her and into the oncoming assault.

Raw blue flame poured out of it, out of her, exploding into the sky with a vengeance, billowing in the air and expanding like a fireball.

For a moment, everything stopped as the world held its breath.

Her flames slammed into the cloud, engulfing those cursed red fireflies in blue light. Power surged through her, shaking her to the core. She was a goddess astride the land among mere mortals.

An explosion shook the world, knocking her back a step. The air itself shivered, the station walls groaned, and the trees behind her all shuddered so hard they lost half of their needles in a whispering rush of sound.

Silya pulled back her flame, peering at the cloud of black smoke that had erupted where the fireflies had been. It expanded, rising into the air like a thundercloud.

Then the column exploded, shooting smoke in a hundred, no, a thousand directions.

She stared at them in disbelief. The red lights were back, and there seemed to be more of them than before. *What happened?*

The hencha's voice was heavy and sad. *Heat can't kill them. They were* made *for heat.*

How did you know? What else hadn't they told her?

The fireflies were descending again, and people were starting to panic.

The world has turned many times before this.

That was cryptic. *What can?*

Cold.

Despair overcame her as the fireflies filled the air, chasing down the Steaders, who had been shaken out of their stupor by the explosion. *I only have fire.*

A man ran past her, screaming and swatting at a swarm of the creatures as they chased him down.

She watched, helpless in the face of the overwhelming assault. Her flames sputtered and threatened to go out. She was naked before them all, stripped of not just her clothing but her stubborn belief in herself.

Where does your fire come from?

She frowned. She'd never given that much thought. *I don't know.* Something came to her, from Jas's writings, maybe. Or from the hencha? "Nothing new is under the sun. Everything has a source."

She must have been drawing the heat from somewhere. The gods knew she didn't have that kind of power inside her alone. She held up her hand and looked at the flames. She could feel their life force, their power. Closing her eyes, she traced the thread of it down her arm, through her body. It came from below, from somewhere in the earth itself. Somewhere deep.

The blood of the world, made flesh in her. She could sense it now, currents of it far underground, moving sluggishly past her, lending her their strength. She was a fountain for the world's blood.

I'm just one woman. She but her lip. She still didn't understand what they wanted of her. *I can't do this.*

Yes, you can. Suddenly the flames surged around her again, clothing her in warmth, love, and approval. *We chose you because we knew you were strong enough.*

She blinked. There it was, the validation she'd been waiting for all of her life, coming to her at last, unexpected in the middle of a battlefield. They believed in her. She had to believe in herself, too, or all was lost. *How?*

Reach out and feel their warmth.

All right. She closed her eyes, squeezing the staff, and sought the heat immediately around her. She could feel it, like smoke in the air. She tugged at it, directing it into the ground through the black wood like water into a well. The flames around her flickered and hardened, freezing around her like ice, and the temperature dropped precipitously. *I can do this.*

She opened frost-covered eyes and took in the chaos all around her. Each firefly was a prick of warmth in the air, a disturbance in the natural world that left a bright mark.

With the hencha's help, she increased the flow, sucking more heat out of the air around her and funneling it into the earth. She shivered at the cold. It penetrated her skin, turning her arms blue, but it still wasn't enough.

The red glow of the fireflies closest to her flickered and spun out as she pulled away their heat. They dropped into the half-melted snow, which quickly hardened into ice.

I need more. Knocking a few of the little creatures out of the air wouldn't win this battle. She had to go deeper.

There's a price.

She sighed, and it turned into a shiver. *There's always a price. I will pay it.* She couldn't let these people suffer.

We will pay it as well.

The cold surging through her increased threefold. More of the fireflies fizzled and dropped to the ground, pummeling it like black hail.

Silya wrapped herself around the hencha's comforting warm glow, keeping her core from freezing. Pride surged through her, and a cold joy at finally having surpassed her own limitations. *It's working. We can do this!*

She pushed farther, drawing the heat from the attackers, freezing them into hard pebbles that pelted the ground below with satisfying sharp *thuds*.

Something exploded, but she was too far into the flow to pay it any mind.

She rode the tide, exulting in her power, reaching further and further from herself into the sky, sucking the heat from it and channeling it into the blood of the world.

Ice covered her eyes, and she saw no more, but still she fought, with the hencha at her side.

20

THE ICE QUEEN

RAVEN STARED AT SILYA, stunned by what she was doing. She had taken up a place in the midst of the chaos and planted her staff. Flames licked up her legs and along her arms, blue flames that gave off so much heat he could feel them ten meters away, and yet they left her skin untouched.

Her clothing wasn't so lucky, flaring and burning away to ash in a matter of seconds. *I'm the wrong one to appreciate this sight.*

The wry thought came and went quickly. This was no time for humor. *Breeze, to me!*

His verent battled a swarm of the things, nipping at them and swallowing them in his great maw. He would have laughed at the sight if he weren't as frightened as a cornered ix. The verent snapped at one last bug and surged toward him, breaking free of the swarm.

No time to get naked. He'd love to figure out Silya's clothing immolation trick, though it would be hell on his wardrobe.

He jumped onto Breeze's back as the verent rumbled by, narrowly missing trampling a couple Steaders who crossed his path.

"Take me with you!" a woman screamed after him, but they were already past her.

The verent spread his wings, catching an updraft and lifting both of them up into the air just before they reached the tree line. They flew past the tips of the violet pines, missing them by an arm's length.

Silya exploded in blue flames, a fireball rushing up to meet the attackers. It surrounded the fireflies, and a concussion in the air nearly knocked him from his perch.

Something hit his neck, and he slapped it away with one hand, holding on to Breeze's neck with the other.

Breeze soared into the sky, rising quickly above the melee. Soon they were fifty, a hundred, a hundred and fifty meters above the ground.

He peered at the expanding cloud below. *Did she do it?*

Seconds later, the little red lights burst out of the black smoke, and there seemed to be even more than before.

And yet, none of the fireflies were up there. *Why not?*

His neck was sore — Raven touched it where the firefly had struck him.

There was something sticking out. He pulled it out with his free hand, wincing at the pain. It was a wrinkled black thing. A stinger.

He blinked. *What did you do to me?*

Are you all right, little man? Breeze radiated concern.

I think so. It ... stung me. He touched his neck again. The bump was gone.

It won't hurt you. It takes many more than that to fell a verent rider. Or a verent.

Well isn't that just swell? He grinned. *Can you reach the others?*

Help is coming. An image of Astrid and a flight of verent flashed through his mind.

Astrid, can you hear me?

He could feel her surprise through the emp. *You really can talk to all of us.*

I suppose I can. This whole verent rider thing was turning out to be the best thing that had ever happened to him, despite its inauspicious beginning. *Where are you?*

Passing over the edge of Lake Zeraya. The Highlands...."

I know. He could feel the ache in her voice. Didn't she have family there. *Get here as fast as you can. Those fireflies ... they're attacking.* Though what the verent could do, he wasn't sure.

Will do.

She had a brother in Zeraya. She'd mentioned him a few times. *I'm so sorry, Astrid. Maybe he's here, with the other refugees.*

There was no reply, but her gratitude reached him through the emp.

He peered down past Breeze's wing. Something was happening below. *What in the holy hencha?* "Take me closer. I want to see what's going on."

Will do. They descended, and it hit him that he was speaking aloud and the verent understood him.

I hear you inside too. Breeze looked back at him and winked.

No secrets from you. He would never be alone again, as long as he had Breeze and his verent family.

Never. That came with an affirmation of love that warmed his heart.

I'm the luckiest thief in all of Gullton.

That elicited only a mental snicker.

They swooped down toward the strange battle being waged below.

Silya looked … bigger. She towered over the others, but her fire was gone. Instead she was encircled by a strange blue mist.

He shivered. It was usually cooler up high, but there was a distinct chill in the air at odds with the midafternoon sunshine on his face. Goose bumps ran up his arms, and he shivered. "What's she doing?"

Then the red lights started to disappear. First the ones closest to Silya, flickering out like candle flames in the wind and dropping into the trampled mud and snow. *What is she doing?*

She is learning. The hencha are teaching her.

Then one of the violet pines exploded. Or maybe disintegrated? He started, almost falling from his perch on Breeze's back. "What in the green holy hell?"

Where the tree had been, a white cloud had erupted. No, not white exactly. More a whitish blue. It was cold, sure, but cold enough to make a tree explode?

Then the white cloud moved. It shifted and swirled, twisting into the air and bending … toward him. *What in Heaven's Reach is that?*

Friends.

He turned to look at Silya again. Even from a distance, he could see that her skin was tinged blue. She looked like an ice statue.

The ice queen. It suited her, somehow. But what was she up to?

Another tree erupted, and then another. The cloud expanded, extending a finger toward him and Breeze. As it drew closer, he realized what it was. What they were.

"Wisps!" *How are you friends with wisps?*

They're a part of us, and we're a part of them.

Well, that's as clear as mud.

There were hundreds of the things. No, thousands. They jostled one another like carts trying to get into Gullton on a busy market day, filling the air behind him and then around him. They danced and sparkled in the sun, and when he closed his eyes, an unearthly music filled the air.

They brought a wave of cold with them, enough to make Raven shiver. Since his change, extremes of temperature hadn't bothered him like before, but this ... *Sweet mother of Jas, that's cold.* His teeth chattered. *Will they follow us?*

Yes.

He grinned. *Then take us down.*

Breeze responded enthusiastically, and they dropped like a stone, trailing a cloud of wisps behind them. He held on for dear life as they plunged into a cloud of fireflies. The little things slammed into his chest and arms and into Breeze's tough hide, and he had to cover his face with the scale-covered back of his hand to protect his eyes.

There was a loud sizzling sound and a series of pops, and then they were out of the swarm and winging back up into the sky.

Raven looked over his shoulder. The wisps were still there, but only half as many as before.

The cloud of fireflies was gone.

"Woo hoo!" He raised his arms in excitement, forgetting he was a verentback, and almost lost his seat. As Breeze rose, he grabbed the verent's neck and held on for dear life.

Still, there were thousands — maybe hundreds of thousands — of the fireflies scattered across the gap, with more pouring in from the Highlands to the East.

Too many. Even with the wisps' help, they'd never get them all.

"Need a hand down there?"

He looked up to find a sky full of verent, and one in particular carrying a human rider, whose fist was held high. "Astrid!"

"In the flesh." She looked like an avenging angel on her verent. "Good to see you too."

He held his fist up, too. "And Olly?"

Right here. His voice came to Raven through the emp as he swooped by, trailing a line of wisps.

More trees were erupting below, filling the air with the little blue sparks.

His arms erupted in goosebumps. "We need to —"

"Save your breath, Gullton. Breeze already explained it to Sleeker. We'll talk after." Astrid shifted in her saddle, and Sleeker followed Olly's Flit into the fray.

He nodded, grateful for the help. *Thank the gods.*

Suddenly the skies were flooded with wisps, and the riderless verent launched themselves into the swarm with a collective roar that shook the canyon.

How they kept from flying into one another in the blue and red confusion, he'd never understand. But somehow they wove past the others without so much as clipping a wing.

At his signal, Breeze dove back into the madness, trailing a cloud of wisps, and fireflies flickered out and fell all around them.

One of the verent screamed, attacked by the swarm. It fell to earth, landing with a sickening crunch just a few meters in front of Silya. He looked away, feeling the sharp pain in Breeze's soul.

Trails of blueish white crisscrossed the Gap, and red lights winked out as the fireflies were destroyed or frozen, or both. The battle waged across the narrow canyon and beyond, the roars of the verent mixing with the angry buzz of the invaders.

"More coming in through the gap!" Astrid's voice sounded ragged. They'd never flown the verent this long or this hard before.

"Come on, Raven." Olly/Flit grinned as they slipped by to intercept the newcomers, trailing a comet's tail of wisps. Olly was merged with his verent.

Was he safer that way, or not? He wished he was safely ensconced inside his own verent. "On my way!" He sweated under his riding leathers despite the cold, holding on tightly to Breeze as he corkscrewed through a horde of red lights. "Woo hoo!" Another hundred flickered out and fell toward the ground below.

Then another verent was felled. The pain of its fall cut him to the bone, and a hundred verent howled their distress.

Raven and Olly led a small flight of riderless verent that met the new invaders head-on, decimating the red wave on the first pass. But a few got through.

He swatted one of them angrily away. "How many more are there?"

Too many.

They fought on, and violet pines continued to explode beneath them, their demise echoing through the Gap. The air was so thick with wisps now that he had a hard time seeing the canyon walls on either side. Breeze snapped some of the fireflies out of the air with his toothy jaw. *Tasty.*

They fought on, while Silya took out any of fireflies that made it too close to the ground.

And then, suddenly, it was over. In what seemed like both seconds and an eternity, an eerie silence settled over the land below.

It is done. There was a heavy sadness in Breeze's tone.

"We should be thrilled. We won!" *Didn't we?*

But then he understood. Both humans and verent had taken losses, and many of the wisps — whatever they were — were gone too.

We only won the battle.

War still loomed ahead, a great, dark unknown like the clouds that covered the northlands.

The ground was covered in new fallen snow, mingled with the small corpses of the enemy.

Breeze landed a few meters from Silya, and Astrid's Sleeker landed nearby. The other verent — a couple hundred of them — took their places on the bluff above the narrow pass, alighting there like a giant flock of birds.

There was a price. Breeze nosed at where the stand of trees had once stood, emitting a sad keening sound.

"They're just trees —"

Trees that have stood there for an eon. Everything they knew, all that they saw, is lost.

He looked at the blasted grove in confusion. How could trees *know* anything? They were just trees. *I don't understand.*

"What's wrong with her?" Astrid bounded off her verent and ran toward Silya.

Olly/Flit landed behind them.

He followed Astrid, staring at the frozen form of the Hencha Queen. His friend. *Yes, she is my friend.* It was strange how things had shifted between them in such a short time. "I think she took away all of their heat."

The fireflies littered the ground around her, piles of them, black dots on the ice and snow.

He stomped on the ones nearest to him, eliciting a satisfying squishing sound. "Just in case." It felt vindictive and satisfying.

He approached Silya cautiously. She was — quite literally — frozen in place, encased in blue ice. Her features were blurred, and she was absolutely still.

He touched her frozen cheek. "Sil, can you hear me?"

Nothing.

"We need to get her out of there." He looked around for something — anything to break the ice. A stick, or a rock, or —

"Will she be all right?"

Raven turned to see a crowd had gathered. There were hundreds of them, many with angry red bumps on their arms and faces.

The woman who had spoken took a step forward. She was young — maybe sixteen? Her face was marred by a scowl.

Mara?

Maura, Breeze supplied.

Thank you. "I hope so, Maura."

She looked startled that he had remembered her name. The young Steader radiated a sense of fear, but under that, he felt a sense of wonder. "She saved us. You saved us."

"She did." His respect for Silya went up another notch. If she kept this up, he'd have to quit insulting her, sooner or later.

"Raven, look." Astrid was staring at the Hencha Queen.

Where he had touched her, the ice was melting. A tiny blue flame flickered around the edges of his handprint on her cheek. It burned slowly outward, her skin turning from bluish white to pink underneath it as it crossed the left side of her face.

The fire crossed her nose and passed down her neck, exposing the rest of her face. Her eyes remained closed, as if she were fast asleep.

The line of flame slipped past her naked waist and down to

her legs, but still she didn't open her eyes. Instead she slumped toward the ground.

Maura leapt forward to catch her before she could pitch over into the frozen mud. "Got you."

Someone handed the young Steader a cloak, and she wrapped it around Silya's rapidly thawing form.

He looked around. "Where's Fen?" The flitter pilot had to be around somewhere. They needed to get her home to the Temple. Sister Tela would know what to do for her.

"Here!" Fen slipped out of the crowd. He nodded appreciatively at Maura. "Fen'Ost. Nice to meet you."

"Maur'Isa."

Was it his imagination, or was she blushing, just a bit? "Can you get her back to Gullton?" Silya needed time to recover. What she'd done here had to have cost her dearly. His respect for his former nemesis went up another notch.

"Of course. We're all ready to go." The pilot turned back to Maura. "Can you help me carry her to the flitter?"

"Flitter?" She raised an eyebrow.

"The flying machine over there."

She followed his gaze. "Ah. Never seen one before." She grinned. "What a strange world we live in."

"Strange indeed." Fen also grinned. "Come on." Together they lifted her and carried her across the field.

Raven hoped she would recover soon. They needed the Hencha Queen for the coming war, and besides ... he cared about her. It was a hard thing for him to admit, even to himself, but there it was. *Besides, the war's not coming anymore. It's here.*

He looked northward at the darkening sky. *Aik, where are you?* The urge to go after him was strong, but Silya had to come first. They would have to make sure things went ahead in her absence.

"I'll go back with her."

He turned to find Dor standing behind him. She was covered in mud, bits of snow in her graying hair, but otherwise she looked all right.

"How did she ...?" He didn't even know how to form the question.

Dor knelt to pick up Silya's discarded staff, grunting at the weight. "She's the Hencha Queen." As if that were explanation enough.

He supposed it was. "Let me help you with that."

She smiled gratefully. "She makes it look like it weighs nothing."

He took the staff, surprised at how heavy it was. "Has she taken up weightlifting?"

She laughed, transforming her face and smoothing away the worry lines. "Something like that."

They walked toward the flitter together, the dead fireflies and freshly fallen snow crunching underfoot. "Take good care of her. We're going to get things situated here, and then I'll see you back in Gullton."

At the flitter door, she surprised him, stepping up to kiss him on the cheek. "Be careful. She needs you. We *all* need you."

A thrill of unexpected pride filled him. People were counting on him. It was followed by a pang of doubt. *What if I can't live up to their expectations?* "I will. She needs you too."

Dor shook her head. "She doesn't need the likes of me." She climbed up into the flitter behind Silya's unconscious form.

He touched her shoulder. "You know that's not true. You're the Hencha Queen whisperer." He flashed her his trademarked grin and tucked the staff into the flitter at her feet.

Dor chuckled. "I suppose I am." She took a deep breath and then exhaled, but it seemed to fill her with new purpose. "Thank you for that, young thief."

"That's *verent rider* now." He gave her a short bow and backed away from the flying machine.

"Fair enough. Take care of yourself, young verent rider."

The flitter blades started to spin, and the *thump thump thump* seemed to release the crowd from the thrall it had been under.

Things would descend into chaos quickly if they didn't get a handle on them.

Raven sought out the Station master's son. The young man was in earnest conversation with a couple older Steaders. "Pardon me. Can I steal him for a moment?"

The woman, dressed in fine leathers that marked her as an urse rider, nodded. "Of course. We were just asking what accommodations might be made for our youngest." She patted the head of a dark-haired girl who couldn't have been more than five.

"We'll get everyone settled soon, Mim ..."

"Eyl. Enla'Eyl."

"Mim Eyl. I promise."

"Bless you."

He steered Aer'Lis away. "We have a lot of work to do, and we don't know if another attack might be coming."

The young man nodded. "Of course." He was handsome enough, but he seemed fairly intelligent too.

He tried to ignore the handsome man's charm. "First off, we need to get the wounded over to the station. Aer'Lis, can you organize that? Anyone who was stung ... we need to pull out the stingers." He rubbed his neck. The sore where the firefly had stung him was gone. *Must be a verent thing.*

Aer'Lis nodded. "We can put them in the dining hall."

"If you see one of those dead fireflies, stomp on it. We don't want any of them coming back." He scanned the crowd. "Where's Maura?"

The Steader woman came forward. "Right here."

"I need you to organize everyone who is healthy enough to travel. We're going to airlift you to the caverns up in the cliffs there." He hoped someone knew where they were. "Where you should be safest from attack." For now. It was a holding action, nothing more.

"Airlift? Are there more flitters?" She looked around, confused.

He grinned. "No. But we have a crap-ton of verent."

It felt good to help people, though his heart pulled him northward, toward Aik.

They need me here. Aik would have to wait.

21

CHALA

CHALA SNORTED. It had been rough going with her new charge at first. Adolescent verent were far more stubborn than she'd had counted on. Luckily, *she* was stubborn too.

Elrys wanted to go down to the lake to swim.

Chala needed the verent to take her west, to Zeraya, the largest — maybe the only? — town in the Highlands. Or what was left of it. She could do that much for Astrid, and it would get her out of the lonely valley and into the action with everyone else. She hated feeling useless.

She'd tried threatening the beast, but that hadn't worked. Elrys had no fear of a puny thing like a human being, though she probably should.

So Chala started thinking about how beautiful that other lake — Lake Zeraya — was, and how much bigger it was than the tiny one at Mountainhome. She pushed it all through her emp, hoping it would entice the young verent to carry her there.

Despite Chala's lack of a verent half, it must have worked. Maybe Elrys was picking up more than just emotions through the link, because she reversed her downward glide to catch an updraft that lifted them toward the green skies above.

Chala threw her arms around the verent's neck as they shot upward, afraid she'd be knocked off by the sudden rush of wind.

She caught a whiff of curiosity, followed by a distinct thought. *Where?* Elrys bent her neck to look back at Chala.

Now we're getting somewhere. She pointed toward the western wall of the valley, and Elrys turned that way, her powerful wings sweeping down to lift them toward the rim.

They burst through a cloud of wisps and crested the edge of the valley to a stunning view of white-capped peaks that receded into the distance like stubby teeth.

The scent of disappointment was sharp in Elrys's mind. *Where?*

Chala grinned wryly. So Elrys wasn't much of a conversationalist. She tried to project a sense of distance. *Farther.*

That seemed to satisfy the verent. She headed westward, following the sinking sun.

The air was cold up there, the wind blowing steadily from the north where the land was covered in perpetual ice. Chala was glad she'd wrapped up in layers before leaving Mountainhome by verentback. She didn't have the same cold tolerance as the others — a gift of their dual natures.

Chala had never been to the Highlands, but she'd studied the map Astrid had brought with her. The huge valley was due west of Mountainhome, and Lake Zeraya was big enough that it should be apparent when they passed the last peaks of the Red Flights.

Zeraya township was on the lake's southern edge, where the Elsp began, before running down through the Gap and to the Heartland and eventually to Gullton itself. How hard could it be to find?

To pass the time as they winged their way westward, she practiced communicating with the verent. She thought of herself, picturing her features as she'd seen them many times in Elrys's precious mirror back home, or reflected in the still waters of a pond or lake. *Chala. Chala.*

Verent Elrys responded with a plaintive rumble and the distinct taste of aur jerky in Chala's head.

How did you do that? Chala stared at the verent. Now she was getting hungry.

Soon, she promised, hoping the meaning would be clear. She let go of the verent's neck and stretched her arms, leaning to the right in the process.

To her surprise, Elrys veered to the right.

Chala leaned left, and the verent followed her lead, turning back toward their previous course. *Good!* She squeezed the verent's neck gently.

Warmth flowed back to her through their link.

The mountains and valleys flew by below, serrated peaks and long ridges topped by violet pines. Snow covered most of them, descending from the peaks into the higher vales, but some of the lower ones were covered in the purple of the pine trees, with scattered meadows between them.

It was a rugged but beautiful country, much different from the Great Southern Desert where Chala had lived before she'd been brought to Mountainhome. The desert was a brutal mistress, hot enough to kill you some days if you didn't have any water, but sweet and warm as a lover at night when the temperatures dropped and the orsia trees opened their fragrant blooms. And when the rains came —

The pungent smell of orsia blossoms exploded in her mind. Chala blinked. *Where did that come from?*

She lifted her heavy head up to the tree, nibbling at the sweet fruit inside the wide purple blossom. They were just right, sweet and tart, full of beautiful liquid hoarded from the last rain. She shuddered in pleasure as they slid down her long throat to the first of her three stomachs, filling her with happiness. Above, the smaller moon shone down on the desert, painting everything pink with her serene glow.

Chala blinked. *What in the burning sands was that?*

Elrys rumbled happily.

A memory. But not the verent's. Part of one of her former selves, maybe? Probably one of the cayah. She'd seen them sometimes, eating the fragrant blossoms. The whole idea of merging creatures was so bizarre, but she'd seen it herself, along with the other verent riders.

Other verent riders. She laughed ruefully at that. "I guess I am one now too." Some of the pain at her earlier loss of her own verent companion subsided.

Elrys glanced back at her, curious again.

It's nothing. She scratched the verent's neck.

It was true, though. Maybe she couldn't *become* a verent, like Raven, Astrid, Jai and Olly. But she could still ride one.

For the first time in weeks — in months — the sense of sadness that had filled her soul lifted.

They shot out past the last of the Red Flights in the late afternoon. The sun was descending toward the far edge of the Highlands, where the peaks of Heaven's Reach challenged the sky. The lake's water glittered ahead.

Chala was dumbfounded. It was more water in one place than she had ever seen, or even imagined.

Water was precious in the desert — more precious than gold. Yet here it was gathered in great quantity, just sitting there in the valley, ripe for the taking.

Chala rolled her eyes. *Lazy wetlanders.*

Elrys dove toward the lake, intent on bathing in those waters as she'd been promised. She'd been "born" there, after all.

Not yet! She squinted into the sunlight. *There's a better place, over there.* She wasn't sure if the verent understood all of that, but something must have gotten through. Elrys's flight path leveled out, and soon they were flying just five meters above the lake's glimmering surface.

Fear gripped her at the sight of all that water. It extended into the distance as far as she could see, ready to swallow her up in its damp embrace.

She wrapped her arms around Elrys's neck again. *What if I fall in?* She had no idea how to swim. She'd bathed in the lake at Mountainhome, but that was shallow and calm. This ... this was like an ocean. *How big is the real ocean?*

She slapped herself, hard. *Focus on Astrid.* She'd come to help her friend. To find out what was left of her old home, if anything. *Or anyone.*

The flight across the lake seemed to last forever, or at least long enough for her to recite the list of her matriarchal ancestors twenty-five times. *Zedya, Hemma, Dyella, Ecka ...*

But at last the far shore came into view.

Higher.

Elrys obliged, and soon she could see things more clearly. They were off-course — the river egress was off to the right. She leaned that way, and Elrys adjusted her direction.

There?

Chala nodded, then realized the verent couldn't read her body language. *Yes. There.*

As they approached the shore, the peaks of roofs appeared, though they were hard to make out against the glare of the lowering sun.

Strange hills. It was more a picture of hills than a word, but Chala understood what she meant.

We built it. Well, not her exactly, but that was too complicated a thought to try to get across to the verent with their rudimentary communications.

Zeraya. She knew little about the village beyond what Astrid had told her. It was the hub for the western Highlands, the place where Steaders came to trade food and wares. It had a small local population — maybe five hundred — and a governor and a magistrate who settled disputes. It had once been a steading on its own, and still had an agricultural base.

Astrid made it sound quaint and charming, which was why it was such a shock to see it as it was now.

The place had fallen apart. There were roofs still, but many were half collapsed and in disarray, along with most of the rest of the wooden structures. The lake was encroaching on the edges of town, flooding the lower-lying streets, with broken rooftops sticking out of the calm waters like skeletons.

She only got a brief glimpse as Elrys settled on the lake edge, landing between a couple damaged structures. Small wavelets washed up with a repetitive sound that was mesmerizing.

The verent waited impatiently for her to slide off and then almost plunged into the water with her saddle still on.

Wait!

Elrys stopped, her feet already in the water. *What?*

For her response, Chala pulled out another piece of aur jerky and fed it to the beast, and then proceeded to unbuckle it. It took a bit of work to loosen the straps — they'd been cinched tight, and the clasp had dug into them.

She admired the craftsmanship. Olly did good work.

At last it was off, and she slapped the verent on the haunches. *Go and play. Back soon.*

Pfffft.

Chala snorted. Their communication was short and to the point, just the way Chala liked it. With verent *and* with people.

She found a place to leave the saddle, away from the water on top of a still-standing hitching post, and then started up the hillside through what was left of Zeraya.

They'd landed near the heart of town, where a wide, cobblestone-paved road let into the tangle of broken buildings. Everything was wrecked. What had once been one and two-story buildings had mostly collapsed or been blown out from within, replaced by strange white domes.

She'd seen their like before, she was sure of it, but she couldn't remember where.

She picked her way between them, stepping over broken bits of debris to make her way through the center of town. "Hello?"

Her voice echoed back at her, but there was no response.

Chala touched the edge of one of the domes. It was warm, both firm and soft, like leather.

She pulled out one of her long knives, considering. She touched the tip to the white surface, and it parted as if repelled by the metal. When she pulled it away, little filaments jumped across the gap like fast-growing blades of grass, pulling it back together. In a minute the surface was as smooth as it had been before.

Interesting. She picked up a piece of wooden debris and a sharp rock and tried to cut the thing's skin.

Neither made more than a scratch.

Knife it is. She made a long incision, starting about half a meter above her head and ending at the ground, and the skin peeled back, making a narrow door. She peered inside — the interior was relatively bright. With a deep breath, she stepped inside before the rift could begin to heal itself.

Her eyes took a minute to adjust to the dim light inside. The shell was semi-transparent, letting in sunlight and filtering it into a pinkish glow. The air was warm and humid, filled with an alien smell, something like the fungus Astrid harvested from one of the caverns in Mountainhome.

The inside was as filled with debris as the ground outside. Apparently these things had just grown over the wreckage.

Then she noticed the skull.

It was turned sideways, its mouth opened in a silent scream, staring up at her. Half a meter away, the rest of the person's bones lay in a piled heap.

Taking a deep breath and suppressing the sick feeling that rose in her throat, she knelt to get a better look at it. She'd dressed animal carcasses before. This was no different.

Except of course it was. But she kept her emotions in check — this was no time to panic.

The skull had been picked clean of everything — flesh, sinew, skin — as bare as if it had been cooked in boiling water.

She looked up at the dome with suspicion. The door she'd cut for herself was sealing itself up again.

Then she remembered where she had seen its like.

•   •   •

Chala trembled. Her twelve-year-old legs refused to carry her any farther into the Oracle's domain. "I don't want to go."

She looked over her shoulder.

Her mother stood there, shoulders back, her braid draped over her muscled chest. A fierce pride shown in her eyes, which met Chala's across the moonlit expanse of white sand. Her mother nodded once.

That was enough for Chala. She would not shame Nidelle, the fiercest of suifaine warriors. Not before the Oracle.

She turned back to the strange scene before her and squared her shoulders.

Instead of the sparse desert scrub, the Oracle's home was surrounded by trees — tall things with red trunks and broad heart-shaped purple leaves that rustled in the darkness as if they had a life of their own. The well-trodden dirt path led under their branches into a darkness as black as a moonless night.

Chala took a deep breath and set one foot in front of another, crossing from the known into the unknown.

In an instant, the world behind her vanished and she was in a wonderland.

Her eyes adjusted. It wasn't as dark as she'd first supposed. The path wound under the wide boles of the trees, which were hung with what she first thought were some kind of strange decoration, but later realized were a spiky fruit.

Something perched in the branches above, staring down at her with bright yellow eyes. They blinked and then disappeared, accompanied by a frantic scurrying as whatever it was vanished into the foliage.

Ahead, a silver glow lit the tiny jungle, and a burbling sound filled the air. She knew what it was at once. Everyone did. The spring that gave life to the Oasis of the Oracle.

The glow came from a strange dome that sat in the clearing next to the bubbling pool. Chala stopped to stare at the water. So strange to see a pool of it, just sitting there for the drinking.

There were other watering holes scattered throughout the desert, but most were muddied things, trampled by the cayah as they stopped to sip from their bounty. This looked clean and pure.

A hand settled on her, old and gnarled. "Hello, Chala. I've been waiting for you."

•　　•　　•

Chala blinked.

That had been such a long time ago ... ten years now. And she could still feel the Oracle's hand on her shoulder.

She knelt and put her own hand on the skull, whispering a short prayer to Hel'Oss to guide the owner's soul to peace. Then she turned to the place she'd entered the dome. It was already half sealed.

Her knife made short work of that, opening it up again and letting her pass through. She was careful not to touch the edge of the gap, worried about what it might do to her. Once she reached the open air, she breathed a sigh of relief.

She could feel Elrys at the edge of her mind. The verent seemed agitated. *Coming back soon?*

Soon. I promise. She needed ... something before she left.

She was sure now that no one was left alive in Zeraya. They'd all fled or had been consumed like that poor soul inside the dome.

She threaded her way along the roadway through the strange growths. It was getting late, the rays of the sun slanting across the broken village. At last she arrived at the old town square.

What she saw there stopped her dead.

It was the Oasis. Or at least it could have been.

The square was filled with the same trees — bandy trees, Astrid called them. There were groves of them up in Mountainhome too. But the most shocking thing was how the white domes stopped right at the edge of the square, giving the trees wide berth.

Maybe it was a coincidence. Maybe they just hadn't taken over this part of the town yet. Chala growled. She didn't like coincidences.

The sight of the spiky fruit plunged her back into memory again.

•   •   •

The Oracle was the oldest woman Chala had ever seen.

Her face was more lines than skin, its color hard to determine in the dim golden light — almost translucent. There were a myriad of stories written there, a long life of pain and pleasure, joys felt and tragedies witnessed that Chala could only guess at.

"For me?"

The woman nodded. "Yes, dear. For you. Come with me." She led Chala to a wide, flat rock near the spring. "Sit, child."

Chala did as she was told, catching a whiff of the woman's scent. It was strong and clean, not like some of the old women in the Desert Clan's camp, who smelled of old sweat, spoiled meat and dust. The Oracle had a bright smell, like heartroot.

The woman touched a few of the spiky fruit hanging from the nearest tree, selected one, and cut it off with a short, sharp knife she kept hanging on the belt at her waist. She came to sit next to Chala and placed it on the rock between them. "This fruit is sacred. It will help you see what you need to see."

Chala's nervousness returned. "Will it hurt?"

The woman laughed, but it was a kind one. "No, my little one. Not now. It will show you things, but when you awaken, they will fade away like dew on the grass in the morning."

Chala nodded. She'd seen dew before, when her clan had camped close to the sea. It was a rare and special thing. She frowned. "But what good will it do if I can't remember?"

The Oracle cupped Chala's cheek in her gnarled hand. "You will remember when the time is right."

That sounded like adult doubletalk, but Chala kept her mouth shut and just nodded. You weren't supposed to doubt the Oracle.

"Are you ready?" Her gaze was kind, and Chala wanted nothing more than to please her.

Chala screwed up her courage. "I guess so."

The old woman cut the fruit, splitting it in half. Inside, there was a dark purple pulp filled with bright yellow seeds. She scooped out a gob of it with two fingers and smeared it across Chala's cheek, over the bridge of her nose, and down the other side.

The cool pulp was already beginning to dry on her face in the arid desert night. "Is that all?"

The Oracle's eyes narrowed. "No, my dear. That's just the beginning." She stood, extending out her hand. "Come with me." She led the girl to the white dome. With her knife, she cut a long gash in its side, making a doorway just big enough for her to pass through. She knelt next to Chala. "You are special, girl. Never forget that. You will do great things and bring honor to your people."

She looked up at the Oracle. "I am? I will?"

The Oracle nodded. "Now go inside. Your dreams await you."

She regarded the dome. "What is it?" It reminded her a little of her family tent that she shared with her parents.

"A resting place. Go on, lay down inside." She nodded encouragingly. "You will sleep, and when you awaken, your time here will be finished."

Chala reached up to touch the woman's wrinkled face. "How old are you?"

The Oracle harrumphed. "Old enough to know you *never* ask a woman that question." She tousled Chala's hair as if she were a baby. "Go, child. Sleep. Dream." She turned her around and gave her a gentle shove. "You have an important part to play in what is to come."

What does that mean? She turned back to protest, but the woman was gone.

Her earlier unease returned, doubled.

Chala considered running out of the strange grove, back to the safety of her mother's arms, but the thought of her mother's disappointment stopped her.

This was her rite of passage, her test. *I will not fail.*

She took a deep breath and stepped into the silver dome. The floor was covered in soft purple moss.

Feeling suddenly tired, she knelt to unlace her boots and set them aside. She lay on the yielding floor, as comfortable as her mother's lap, as the doorway sealed itself up behind her. In seconds she fell asleep.

She dreamed of a dance of lights, flickering like the wisps that sometimes floated through the suifaine camp. But not just blue — these flashed at her as if they were inviting her to play. Green-red-green-green-blue-yellow.

She tried to touch them, and they slipped out of her grasp, flying around her head.

The whole world shook beneath her, as if the ground were about to open up and swallow her whole. She fought her tears. *I will not be afraid.*

The lights hovered in the air above her head, following one another in a circle like cayah across a sand dune.

She grasped at them, and they collided with her palm, green-red-green-green-blue-yellow.

Then they were gone, and she was plunged back onto darkness.

•   •   •

Chala blinked. She hadn't thought about that day in years. She still didn't understand it, and the Oracle had been no help. *When the time is right, the meaning of your dream will become clear.*

Chala snorted. That was as likely to happen as her wearing a dress.

She picked one of the spiky fruits. It resisted, so she used her knife to sever it. She set it on the ground and cut it open, spilling out the pulp on the hard-packed road. With her two fingers, she smeared a bit of it over her cheeks and the bridge of her nose and closed her eyes.

Nothing happened.

Maybe it's not time. Or maybe everything the Oracle had said *was a steaming pile of cayah shit.*

Still, she was curious. *Why are the domes avoiding this place, these trees?*

She picked up half of the fruit and approached the nearest one, smaller than the others and about half her own height. Kneeling, she took a handful of the pulp and smeared it across the white surface.

The skin of the dome bubbled and boiled, opening a gap in the white dome that spread quickly across its surface. It turned a bruised purple, then black, and then the ragged edges dissolved into dust. The destruction spread across the dome, and in less than a minute the whole thing was gone, leaving only a patch of dirt and a tiny skeleton behind.

An inthym, if she guessed right.

She looked at the fruit with newfound respect. Whatever these alien invaders were, she now had a weapon against them. *I have to tell Raven and the others —*

Something rustled in the trees behind her.

Chala set down the fruit, becoming very still, listening to the wind, the lapping of the distant water, the rustling of the leaves.

There.

She spun around, knife out, and slipped into the grove. In three quick bounds was face to face with the creature who had been watching her.

It was a young boy. He was no older than she'd been when she'd visited the Oracle.

"Don't hurt me!" He cringed, as if he expected her to gut him with her knife.

Not an unreasonable thought, given how she must have looked to him.

He was a mess, his clothing dirty and torn, his face smeared with purple ... from the bandy fruit, no doubt.

"I won't." She sheathed her knife. "I'm Chala."

He looked up at her, tears squeezing out of the corner of his eyes. "Jerrr ... reck." He was still shaking.

"Stop that. I said I wouldn't hurt you." Children could be annoying.

He made a visible effort to calm himself, though his hands kept trembling. "Who are you?"

She shook her head. "I already told you. Chala. Not so smart then, either."

He frowned. "I mean, where did you come from? I've been all alone here since ..." He glared at the domes. "Since they came. Since everyone else left." He sniffed, looking like he was about to break into tears.

Chala knelt next to him, touching his cheek, at last feeling a smidgen of pity for him. He must have been through a lot, after all, first losing his family, and then bring trapped here all alone. She remembered how she had felt as a little girl, facing the Oracle. She could spare a little compassion. *I was scared once too.*

"I came to see what had happened here." She looked around. The afternoon was quickly passing into evening, and she had no intention of being here when darkness fell. "I had a friend who lived here once. Her name is Astrid."

Jereck's eyes were as wide as platters. "Astrid? Astrid's alive?"

Chala blinked. "You knew her?"

The boy nodded. "She's my sister."

It came to her all at once. "You're Jereck."

This time it was his turn to snort. "I already told you that." His tone turned defiant.

She sighed. This was why she hated children. Well, maybe *hate* was too strong. This was why she found children so annoying. "I know your sister. She ... was very worried about you."

"She's alive?"

"Yes. I just saw her this morning."

"Really?" He sniffed, wiping the snot from his nose on a dirty sleeve.

"Really." Chala shuddered at the disgusting display. "How about your family?" She looked around the grove. "Are they here too?"

He shook his head. "No, I was hiding from them when the ... red things came."

"Red things?"

"The lights. They started biting everyone, and people ran and left me all alone here."

In the bandy tree grove. "You were very brave."

Jereck shook his head. "I don't feel brave."

"A little warrior like you? Your sister will be so proud."

The barest start of a smile crossed his lips. "Is she ... is she all right?"

"Yes, she is. Would you like me to take you to her?"

"Yes please, Mim!" He threw his arms around her.

Chala hugged him back awkwardly, trying not to smell his unwashed little body. She normally had no use for children, but supposed she'd have to make an exception in this case. It was why she'd come, after all. "Can you carry some of these fruit, if I cut them down?"

He let go of her and nodded eagerly. "If you hold them by the stems, you can avoid the spiky parts."

She smiled approvingly, something that didn't come easily to her. *Especially* with children. "That's very good advice. Help me collect a few more."

They harvested as many as they could carry. She found a scrap of cloth in the wreckage to wrap around them, making a workable sack. "Come on, then."

He looked nervously at the domes that lined the roadway. "Is it ... safe?"

"I think so. They seem to be quiescent."

"Kwee ...?"

She frowned. "Asleep."

He shook his head. "Why didn't you just say that?"

Chala rolled her eyes. Children were too damned inquisitive, and had no manners whatsoever. "Come on, you little brat. We have a verent waiting for us."

"What's a verent?"

"You'll see." She turned away from him, determined not to let him get under her skin.

Jereck didn't seem to notice. He trailed after her, chattering away happily.

EPILOGUE

AIK LAY IN A WARM POOL, the purple sky spread above him, the giant moon staring down at him as if he were a thing of great curiosity.

He was melting, bits and pieces of himself falling away into the green waters. A finger here, a toe there, and something was eating into his gut with a vengeance.

He couldn't bring himself to care.

He felt safe. Loved. Wrapped in the warmth of Mother.

Though she wasn't his mother.

It was all very confusing, and he supposed he should worry about it more.

His hair fell out with a splash, and his dissolution accelerated.

"What's happening to me?" Something in him still cared, apparently.

Hush, little one. You are being made anew.

That sounded nice.

Maybe he'd just close his eyes, before they decided to roll out of his skull.

Nothing could hurt him, not here.

Not when he could just let his worries and cares melt away with the rest of him.

GLOSSARY

Adley Narrows: A narrowing of the Elsp between Vulture Spine and the North Shore, near the egress to the Harkness Sea

Aik'Erio aka Aiken (Mas): Guardsman in Gullton and loyal friend to Raven

Ais'Vellin aka Aisel (Mas): Trader and associate of Tri'Aya

Akin-yo: A martial art the sisters practice

Akka: A bitter drink made from the leaves of the Akka bush; the local equivalent of coffee

Auddah: Cheese made from aur milk

Alaya: The Tharassan native name for Tarsis, the bigger golden moon

Angels: What the Tharassans called Runners from Earth (LR)

Anghar Mor: One of the mountains in the Redflight range, with lots of volcanic activity

Anya'Enn aka Anyassa (Mim): A Temple initiate

Arsday: Fifth day of the week

Aryx (Cat): One of Breeze's kits, female

Ast'Una aka Aster (Mim): One of the Temple sisters, head of the Temple stores

Auley Tree: A spindly tree with strong fire-resistant sticks

Aur/Auracinth: Large beasts of burden that don't develop a gender until their third year

Ay'Oss aka Ayja: God of magic, technology, wisdom, and earth whose sign is the wisp, and who presents as a handsome young man

Ayvin/Aaveen: An alien race that arrived on Tharassas before humanity

Bacca Root: A minty local root that people chew on for flavor with anti-nausea properties

Bandy Fruit: Red fruit with purple spikes, sweet and juicy

Bandy Trees/Heart Trees/Evrit: Native trees with wide red trunks, broad, heart-shaped purple leaves, where heartroot and bandy fruit come from

Beast Guild: The Gullton guild in charge of domesticated beasts (aur, urse, etc)

Black Cheese: A variety of cheese from aur milk, grown in the caverns under Gullton

Breeze aka Kalix (Raven): male verent with a green tinge to his white skin

Builder's Guild: The contractors' guild in Gullton

Callasday: Sixth day of the week

Capton: Small oceanfront town north of Gullton

Car'Ost aka Carel (Mim): Junior cook in the Temple

Cayah: Desert dwellers with tan and brown dappled skin and spiral horns

Ce'Faine: Human clans that live in the far east and south, past the borders of the Highlands and the Heartland

Cekya: Temple cook

Cephlant: A grazing herd animal similar to an elephant

Cer'Ella aka Ceryl (Sister): The fourth Hencha Queen, only served for a year

Cheevah: A small flying creature

Cheff: Derogatory name for the Ce'faine

Cherry Fly: Thumb-sized insect with twelve legs

Clayton: Small town in the eastern part of the Heartland

Cleffer Bush: A red-leaved plant with yellow "brush" flowers

Cor'Lea aka Coral (Mim): An initiate at the hencha Temple

Corinth: The small village on the south slopes where Queen Jas came from (Last Run)

Crosston: A small town in the middle of the Heartland

Dalney: Small oceanfront town north of Gullton

Dam, The: A hydroelectric dam built just after landing to power the colony, recently refurbished

Day'Ima aka Daya (Sister): One of Silya's teachers, ace, wears violet pine perfume

Dem'Errol aka Demtrius (Mas, Ser): Aik's squad captain

Der'Iza aka Derik (Mas): Tri'Aya's husband and Silya's father

Des'Rya aka Desla (Mim): A Temple initiate originally from Devon

Destrayer's Song: An old battle song from the Heartlander-Ce'Faine conflict

Devon: Village in the southern part of the Heartland

Dor'Ala aka Doria (Sister): Sister appointed to be Silya's aide

Ecin: Fifth month of the year

Edgeton: A small town south of Gullton

Edie: Tenth month of the year

Edu: Second month of the year

Eeechiia: Living membranes used to separate spaces

Eemscaap: Digger creatures from Uurccheea

Eesiil: Red, glowing star-like fungus with seven points

Eev-uurccheea: Literally "New Uurccheea," the aaveen's second homeworld. Also the name given to Tharassas by the Spore Mother

Eircat: Cat analogues – Highland hunters

El'Oss/Elohim/The Old God: God of the past and love, sign is the cross, once the Christian god, now folded into the local religion

Electrical Guild: A new guild in Gullton responsible for the electric lights and the dam

Elsp River: River that runs from lake Zeraya to Gullton through the Highlands and the Heartland

Em'Asa (Mim): One of Tri'Aya's private guards, born in Dalney

Eneet: A squirrel equivalent

Eno: First month of the year

Eoto: Eighth month of the year

Equa: Fourth month of the year

Erphin: Dolphin equivalent

Esei: Sixth month of the year

Eset: Seventh month of the year

Eshem: The ce'faine equivalent of the Hencha Queen

Etré: Third month of the year

Evro: Ninth month of the year

Fellin Root: a yellow root that serves as an anti-dolorific, also a sleep aid in larger quantities

Fess'Ima aka Fessryn (Mim): One of the Temple initiates

Fexin: Deep purple Highlands herb, used as topical germicide

Flitter: Small helicopters used to transport people in the Heartland; sparkling "wings" (LR)

Flop Trees: Big-leaved trees used to provide islands of shade in the hencha plantations

Flyx (Grey): One of Breeze's kits, male

Foldovers: A sweet or savory pastry

Fre'Oss aka Freja: God of air, weather, and health, sign is the lightning bold, presents as a child, sometimes male, sometimes female

Fri'Oss aka Frija: God of fertility, birth, the harvest and sex, sign is the leaf, presents as a woman

Gap, the: Pass connecting the Highlands with the Heartland to the East

Gap Station: The way station in the middle of the Gap

Grayleaf: A seasoning often used in steak rubs, also used as an essential oil

Great Southern Desert: The huge desert south of the Heartland, beyond the Onyx Mountains, where the suifaine live

Guard's Honor: Used to swear something

Gullton/Gullytown: The main city on Tharassas, where the colony was founded

Gully Birds: Black seagull equivalents found in Gullton and the heartland

Gully Fowl: Three-legged chicken equivalents

Gully Rat: Derogatory term for citizens of Gullton

Gully Rats: Larger cousins to the inthym that live in and around Gullton

Gully Weasels: See gully rats, also used as a derogatory term for Gulltoners

Hacka Berries: Highland berries known for their sweet, salty taste

Haifaine: East Valley Clan - Elleck (Enrick)

Harkness Sea: The sea to the west of Gully Town

Heartland: The original colony lands, with Gullton as the capital

Heartlanders: People who live in the Heartland

Heartroot: Spicy highlands herb, similar to cinnamon

Heaven's Reach: The mountain range along the northern edge of the Heartland

Hel'Oss aka Helja: God of death, war, and problems, sign is the black staff, presents as intersex

Hencha: A food crop that's also semi sentient, human height with red stalks and purple leaves

Hencha Berries: Berries produced by the hencha plants that are edible by humans - red (sweet), orange, blue (sharp-sweet), and yellow (tart, citrus/vitamin c)

Hencha Leaf Scroll: Paper made from hencha leaves

Hencha Mind: The animating group consciousness of the hencha

Hencha Oil: Used for lanterns

Hencha Queen: The woman who can talk to the hencha; also the animating consciousness of the hencha en masse (see *Hencha Mind*)

Hencha Tea: A healing tea made from hencha leaves

Henchwine: Wine made from hencha berries

Hera River: The other major river in the Heartland

Hes'Enn aka Hestra (Mim): The Temple sword master

Heurcinth: Purple Highlands flowers that grow with pezzywinkles in matched pairs

Heyfa Weeds: Yellow semi-sentient weeds that strangle the hencha plants for food

Highlanders: People who live in the Highlands; can refer to Steaders or sometimes Ce'Faine

Highlands: Wide valley inland from the Heartland, accessed via the Gap

Highlands Treaty: Treaty signed between Gullton/the Heartland and the Ce'Faine

Iichili/Forerunners/Fireflies: Spies for the Spore Mother

Initiate: An acolytes of the hencha Temple

Inthym/rinkin: Little harmless white mouse-like creatures that hunt insects in packs

Jai (m, reifaine): One of the ce'faine, then a verent rider

Janusday: Fourth day of the week

Jas'Aya aka Jasinaya (Mim): Hencha berry farm worker, later the Hencha Queen; dark hair

Jel'Faya aka Jelin (Mas): Contemporary fantasy author

Jellybug: Small, brightly-colored beetles that inthyms eat

Jer'Est aka Jeryl (Mas): One of Aik's friends

Jexyn: Hive-minded birds in the Highlands; dangerous when they find fresh meat

Jim'Aza aka Jimey (Mas): Nel'Aza's son and Raven's first crush

Jor'Oss aka Jorja (wild nature/unpredictability/luck - dice): God of wild nature, unpredictability and luck, sign is the dice, presents as a scarily beautiful young woman

Jyn'Eln (Doctor): Medic for the Gullton Guard

Keh'Sel aka Kehla (Mas): Temple seamstress

Kek'Aze aka Kerrick (Ser): One of Aik's superiors in the guard

Kerint: Ocean fish-equivalents with a sweet, tangy meat

Lake Zeraya: The huge central lake that defines the highlands

Lamplighter's Guild: Gullton guild responsible for lighting the lamps and the natural gas lines

Landfield: The suburb that sprung up on the western side of the old landing field

Lo'Oss aka Loja: God of fire, change, strength and protection, sign is flames, presents as gender-fluid, and can appear in all of the forms

Local Population Contact Regulations (LPCs): Rules governing contact with a local population

Lowlander: Derogatory term the Highlanders use for the Heartlanders

Lyn'Rya (Mim): Des'Rya's mother, and a tanner in Devon

Machinists' Guild: Gullton guild responsible for fabricating anything needed by the other guilds

Mad Blade: Aik's mother's armory/book shop on Raven Spine

Manor House: Tri'Aya's home in Heaven's Reach

Mar'Orn aka Marea (Mim): Raven's mother

Martasday: Second day of the week

Mas: Title for adult men

Meer: Mayor

Menagerie: Bestiary of real and imagined beasts created from Sera's original works by Sol'Eria

Mes'Ena aka Meslyn (Mim): One of Tri'Aya's guards

Mif (Mas): One of Aik's friends

Mim: Title for adult women

Mir: Title for adult non-binary/fluid

Mir'Ust aka Mirrel (Mim): One of the Temple initiates

Mohr'Una *aka* Mohria (Mim): The Temple astrologer

Mountain Ix: Swift-footed mountain animals prized for their colorful green-gold hides

Mountainhome: What the humans call the valley where the verent live

Mudmole: A large rodent equivalent

Mur beatles: Silk-weaving beatles

Mur silk: Silk spun by mur beatles

Nel'Aza aka Nellie (Mim): Raven's neighbor who takes him in when his mother dies

Noninalya: One of the songs of the Sisters of the Hencha

Nor'Oss aka Norja: God of water, the sea, and prosperity, sign is a wave, presents as an old man

Northlander: A less derogatory term for the Heartlanders and Steaders

Norton: Small town in the middle of the Heartland

Onyx Mountains: The range just south of Gullton and the Heartland

Oosill: Finger-sized uurcheean worms that leave behind fertilizer mucus

Oracle, the: The eshem of the suifaine clan

Orinth Honey: A sweet sticky substance made by orinths in their nest

Orinth: Green and orange insects that nest in muddy columns, analogous to termites

Ost Farm: Vegetable farm outside of Gullton that sells produce to the Temple

Otherlings: What the verent call humans

Pellin: Tharassas's smaller, pink moon, Erreh in the native tongue

Peregrine Spine: The smallest spine, where many of the rich have mansions

Pes'Osa aka Peslyn (Mir): One of the sisters in the Temple

Pezzywinkles: Orange Highlands flowers that grow with Heurcinths in matched pairs

Puffer Hen: Domesticated fowl; also used to describe gossips

Raising, The: The coronation of a new Hencha Queen

Rav'Orn aka Raven (Mas): Thief from Gullton

Raven Spine: The central "spine" of Gullton where toe Temple and city hall are found

Redflight Mountains: The range that defines the southern edge of the Highlands

Redhawk Spine: The southernmost spine, and also the poorest, home of the Open Market

Reifaine: Red Flight clan of the ce'faine

Ring Tree: Spiral tree with purple fronds found in the foothills of Heaven's Reach

River Grass: Cattail equivalents that grow along river shores

Rock Ferns: Red ferns that grow along the spines of Gullton

Russet Mold (powdered): Used for fever

Sadie's Cove: Small oceanfront town north of Gullton

Sal'Moya aka Sallia (Mim): One of the Sisters, head of the initiates

Scill'Eya: A homeless woman in Gullton

Sea Guild: The main transportation guild in Gullton

Sera Collins (Ahsera): Pilot of the Spun Diver; black

Sil'Aya aka Silya (Mim): Aik's old flame and an initiate at the Hencha Temple

Sister: Title for the women who work in the Temple

Skeef: A tick equivalent

Skerit: A bat equivalent

Sol'Eria (Solene): A Sister in the Temple who had a talent for art, and who collected many of Sera's works into leather-bound volumes

Solsday: First day of the week

Southford: A small town in the southeastern corner of the Heartland

***Spin Diver*:** The last ship to make the run from Earth (LR)

Spin: AI of the *Spin Diver*

Spore Mother: Mysterious alien entity

Squint aka Sorix: Breeze's female mate, reddish brown

Steader: Someone from one of the steadings in the Highlands

Stones: A gambling game where flat, etched stones are thrown for points and sets

Suifaine: Desert clan of the ce'faine

Summer Meet: Gathering of the Highlander tribes along the southeastern side of Lake Zeraya

Tarsis: Tharassas's larger golden moon, dominated by a big heart-shaped crater

Tartan Hills: The hilly region bordering the southern edge of the Heartland

Tel'Esta aka Tela (Sister): One of Silya's teachers and the Temple archivist

Temple/Hencha Temple: The seat of the Hencha Queen in Gullton

Terasday: Third day of the week

Tess'Esra aka Tesslyn (Initiate): One of the Temple initiates

Tharassas: A human-colonized world

Theolin: A stringed instrument with strings made from aur hair

Thieves' Guild: Loose, unrecognized Gullton guild comprised of master thieves and apprentices

Tri'Aya *aka* Triya (Mim): Silyas' mother, a wealthy merchant with a mansion called the Manor House on the slopes of Heaven's Reach

Trine Grass: Tri-bladed purple grass that covers the Highlands valley

Tucker Narrows: A narrowing of the Elsp between Raven Spine and Eagle Spine

Umvit/Vrint: Small, fast, nimble three-winged flying creature used as messengers

Urse: A smaller version of an Auricinth, a horse equivalent

Uurccheea: The long-destroyed home world of the Aaveen

Vale: A small town at the eastern edge of the Highlands

Veifaine: the Highlands Valley clan of the ce'faine that no longer exists

Verent/Skirryn (s/pl)**:** Dragon-like native beasts that change gender periodically

Verla'Olk (Mim): Temple cook

Violet Pine: Native tree with spiky needles

Vulture Spine: The northernmost spine, also the location of most of Gullton's industry

Wil'Ock aka Willem (Mas): Tri'Aya's husband and Sil'Aya's father, an artist from Sadie's cove

Wisps/Esh: Mysterious glowing blue sparks that have suddenly become more common

Yen'Ela aka Yendra (Mim): The previous Hencha Queen

Zelaya: A bustling town on the southeastern shore of Lake Zelaya in the Highlands

Zev'Nek aka Zevrell (Mim, Sea Master): Sea Master of Gullton

ABOUT THE AUTHOR

J. Scott Coatsworth writes stories that subvert expectations, that seek to transform traditional science fiction, fantasy, and contemporary worlds into something new and unexpected. His writing, whether romance or genre fiction (or a little bit of both), brings a queer energy to his stories, infusing them with love, beauty and power and making them soar. He imagines a world that *could be* and, in the process, maybe changes the world *that is*, just a little.

A Rainbow Award-winning author, Scott's debut novel, *Skythane*, received two awards and an honorable mention. With his husband, Mark, he runs Queer Sci Fi, QueerRomance Ink, Liminal Fiction, and Other Worlds Ink. Scott is also the committee chair for the Indie Authors Committee at the Science Fiction and Fantasy Writers Association (SFWA).

ALSO IN THIS SERIES

THE DRAGON EATER
THE THARASSAS CYCLE: BOOK ONE

Raven's a thief who just swallowed a dragon.

A small one, sure, but now his arms are growing scales, the local wildlife is acting up, and his snarky AI familiar is no help whatsoever.

Things are about to get messy.

THE GAUNTLET RUNNER
THE THARASSAS CYCLE: BOOK TWO

A guard and a thief. What could go wrong?

Aik has fallen hopelessly in love with his best friend. But Raven's a thief, which makes things ... complicated. Oh, and Raven has just been kidnapped by a dragon.

Things were messy before ... but now they're much, much worse.

Available from Water Dragon Publishing in
hardcover, trade paperback, and digital editions
waterdragonpublishing.com

You Might Also Enjoy

Memory and Metaphor

by Andrea Monticue

Civilization fell. It rose. At some point, people built starships.

Smash the World's Shell

by Daniel Fliederbaum

A fractured world. An impossible friendship.

A Wreck of Dragons

by Elaine Isaak

Teens and their giant robots search for a new home for mankind, but the planet they discover belongs to the dragons.

Available from Water Dragon Publishing in
hardcover, trade paperback, and digital editions
waterdragonpublishing.com

www.ingramcontent.com/pod-product-compliance
Lightning Source LLC
Chambersburg PA
CBHW032015310726
48972CB00002B/408